BOAR ISLAND

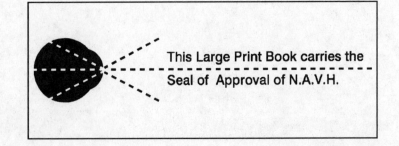

BOAR ISLAND

NEVADA BARR

WHEELER PUBLISHING
A part of Gale, Cengage Learning

GALE
CENGAGE Learning®

Farmington Hills, Mich • San Francisco • New York • Waterville, Maine
Meriden, Conn • Mason, Ohio • Chicago

Wheeler Publishing Large Print Hardcover.
The text of this Large Print edition is unabridged.
Other aspects of the book may vary from the original edition.
Set in 16 pt. Plantin.

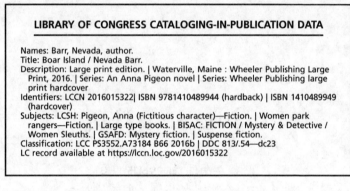

LIBRARY OF CONGRESS CATALOGING-IN-PUBLICATION DATA

Names: Barr, Nevada, author.
Title: Boar Island / Nevada Barr.
Description: Large print edition. | Waterville, Maine : Wheeler Publishing Large Print, 2016. | Series: An Anna Pigeon novel | Series: Wheeler Publishing large print hardcover
Identifiers: LCCN 2016015322| ISBN 9781410489944 (hardback) | ISBN 1410489949 (hardcover)
Subjects: LCSH: Pigeon, Anna (Fictitious character)—Fiction. | Women park rangers—Fiction. | Large type books. | BISAC: FICTION / Mystery & Detective / Women Sleuths. | GSAFD: Mystery fiction. | Suspense fiction.
Classification: LCC PS3552.A73184 B66 2016b | DDC 813/.54—dc23
LC record available at https://lccn.loc.gov/2016015322

Published in 2016 by arrangement with St. Martin's Press, LLC

Printed in the United States of America
1 2 3 4 5 6 7 20 19 18 17 16

*For Julie, a most
excellent friend*

ACKNOWLEDGMENTS

With special thanks to Linda Eddings, Stuart West, Bill "the Rock Nazi" Weidner, June Devisfruto, and all the fine folks at Acadia.

Apologies to the demolition crew that took down the derelict barracks on Schoodic. I rather liked the old heap, so I put it back.

ONE

Fists white-knuckled on the crutches, sweat running into her eyes, Heath grunted like a sumo wrestler. She was walking to the window of her front room. Walking, as in proceeding forward in an upright bipedal manner by putting one foot in front of the other. For some people, toddling around a fifteen-by-twenty-foot room would be as nothing. For Heath it was a miracle, and she was sweating buckets for it.

Eight years before, she had fallen while climbing rotten ice in Rocky Mountain National Park and broken her back: no movement, no sensation below the waist. For an eternity of hopelessness she'd wallowed in self-pity. Finding in Elizabeth a daughter, and in Anna Pigeon a friend, had convinced her to abandon her plan to drink herself to death. It was then she had begun to embrace every nerve's worth of life she could win, earn, fight for, or steal.

During all those years, eye level had been precisely forty-four inches above the floor. One of the first things she noticed when she stood up — stood up out of her wheelchair on her own two feet — was that nobody had dusted any surface more than forty-five inches above the floor in at least five years. Who knew?

She smiled and looked at her reflection standing — *standing* — in the plate-glass window. Dem Bones, Elizabeth called it. Iron Woman in Dem Bones, Heath thought.

Anchored to the outside of each thigh was a long silver-colored piece of contoured metal that linked to a round hinge at knee and hip. Below, another metal lozenge ran down the side of her calf to attach to a horizontal brace that went beneath her shoe. A wide strap, reminiscent of a weight-lifter's belt, circled her waist. A battery pack the size of a hardcover book rode on the belt at the small of her back. On the right hip of her harness was a small control panel with buttons that allowed her to use the electronic exoskeleton to sit down and stand up. The rest was done with body movement. If she leaned slightly forward, wonder of wonders, she *walked* forward. If she leaned back, the walking stopped. The entire assemblage weighed twenty-one pounds three ounces and could be folded into a case slightly smaller than a golf bag.

This was her second day with the skeleton. The first time she had stood up on her own — sort of on her own — she had suffered an attack of acrophobia so sudden and severe she'd nearly fallen. She, who had led precipitous climbs up sheer cliffs for fifteen years, looked down the five feet three inches from her eyeballs to her feet and felt as if she stood on the edge of a chasm a thousand feet deep, a vacuum sucking her into oblivion. She'd managed six steps before she hummed back into her wheelchair, exhausted from movement and terror.

Terror had quickly mellowed into excitement. Still, she felt fifty feet tall, a giantess looking down on a world of dwarves. A rush of power and awe fueled her every time she stood up.

Unfortunately, the machine wasn't hers. There was no way Heath could afford it. She was testing it for her friend Leah Hendricks, the research and development brain of Hendricks & Hendricks. Leah's device had three times the electronics of other models, was smaller and lighter, executed more minute movements, and was able to "learn." Heath had yet to tap into a fraction of what it could do. One of the drawbacks

11

was that Leah had yet to figure out how to get the thing's battery to hold a charge for more than twenty minutes.

In a couple of months Leah would take it back to the lab to tinker with its finer points.

Heath chose not to think about how she would feel, who she would be, when this miracle was taken from her.

For now, she would only think of now, walking now, standing now. Now was good.

Twice she had walked the length of the room. Forty feet. Hooray for the para brigade, she thought. Give us forty feet and we'll take a million miles.

Harsh, repetitive racket shattered her moment of triumph. Rap music, an oxymoron to Heath's way of thinking, rudely pounded down the long hallway from the direction of Elizabeth's room.

Until recently, Heath's adopted daughter had been an aficionado of the lightweight modern version of what Aunt Gwen called bubblegum rock. That and, because children never cease to amaze their elders, anything by James Taylor. Heath had been unaware Elizabeth ever listened to rap. Boulder, Colorado, wasn't much of a Mecca for rappers; too white, too rich, too much spandex. The stuff playing now was ugly and dark, "bitch" and "whore" making up a good percentage of the lyrics.

Why Elizabeth would want to listen to this brand of aural poison was beyond Heath. Why Elizabeth would think Heath would allow it to be broadcast throughout her house, smashing all good karma in its path, was an even greater domestic mystery.

Heath waited a couple of minutes, catching her breath and hoping Elizabeth would come to her senses. The first goal was met with satisfying rapidity. The second was not.

"Wily," she said to the dog laying on the hardwood, watching her workout with narrow, sleepy eyes, "go to Elizabeth's room, boy. Unplug her whatever. Good dog!"

Wily yawned hugely, his mouth wide and crooked like his spiritual guide Wile E. Coyote.

"You're a big help," Heath said.

Pivoting with painstaking slowness, she got herself turned around and centered facing the hallway, the crutch braces biting into her forearms. There was a gizmo built in that gave Dem Bones balance, but she'd not yet come to trust her mechanized lower body, hence the crutches. Leah had tried to explain the engineering to her, but Heath's brain had stalled at the gyroscope analogy.

Fear of falling was an acquired — and necessary — paranoia for paraplegics. Given

13

her fatigue level, it would have made more sense to use her wheelchair for the journey to the back of the house. Still and all, wheeling up, no taller than a hobbit, to lay down the law to a teenager didn't appeal to her.

From behind the crutches, extended like forelegs in front of her, the view down the carpeted hallway — to be replaced with hardwood the moment her bank account caught up with her special needs — looked impossibly long, the doors at the end appearing as distant as the pins in a bowling alley.

Heath sighed and began to hum "Who Were You Thinking Of" as she clasped her crutches through the sweat on her palms and began her robotic version of the Texas two-step. When it came to the two-step, nobody could beat the Texas Tornados.

By the time she'd made it across the living/workout/rehab room to the hall, Wily padding arthritically along behind, she was regretting her impulse to stand high and mighty over her daughter and wishing she'd dropped her rear end, exoskeleton and all, into Robo-butt — Elizabeth's name for the wheelchair.

Having reached the point of no return, equidistant from the rude noise in Elizabeth's room and the security of her wheels,

Heath rested a moment before pushing on. Elizabeth had more reasons than an over-crowded psych ward to be moody and rebellious. It was the miracle of the child that she was blessed with a naturally sunny disposition. One of those enviable souls whose brain seems to effortlessly create sufficient serotonin to power a lifetime of optimism in the grimmest of circumstances.

Until a week ago, when sullenness and darkness had replaced the sun.

Or was it two weeks? As much as a month? No. Even a Johnny-come-lately mom like Heath wouldn't fail to notice over that length of time.

Heath told herself what she always told herself when she worried that an unmarried, crippled, ex-rock-climber was not the mother a girl as fine as Elizabeth deserved; what she lacked in experience she made up for with love. Also, they had E's godmother — Anna — and Dr. Gwendolyn Littleton. With Anna and Aunt Gwen for backup, Heath figured she could pull off the mother thing.

Leaning against the wall for support, Heath reviewed the past couple of weeks with her daughter. There had been red flags: Elizabeth found in tears and insisting it was "nothing." That was eight or ten days ago.

Elizabeth switching screens on her computer, and snapping at Heath for sneaking up on her — as if Heath-cum-apparatus could sneak up on any hearing individual. Had that been a week back? Less. Five days.

The dark, hard rap music started day before yesterday. Elizabeth was listening to it on her iPod so loud Heath could hear the beat. She'd had no idea what the lyrics were, but Elizabeth had looked as if they were driving spikes into her brain.

Then today. The rancid, hate-filled, misogynist rant out in the air, poisoning the hearth fairies that protected the house. Aunt Gwen had made up the fairies when Heath was a little girl and afraid of the dark. This new dark was scarier.

Lots of red flags.

Heath had noticed. She'd mentioned Elizabeth's uncharacteristic behavior to Gwen. As they did with every step in the girl's development, the two of them hashed over Elizabeth's every move.

She was in the midst of the hormonal storms of puberty.

She had a fight with a girlfriend.

She had a secret boy-crush.

She had an embarrassing disappointment.

Heath and Gwen agreed not to interfere.

That was before the rap, Heath thought.

This crap was not a red flag, it was a cry for help.

With an effort, Heath pushed away from the wall. White-knuckled, muttering, "Dem bones, dem bones, dem dry bones," she began the final, interminable few yards of hallway, cursing the carpeting with every laborious shuffle of her feet.

Sweat dripping from her nose, breath coming in puffs and gasps, she bumped open her daughter's bedroom door without knocking. Elizabeth was not there.

The bathroom door was ajar, rap blasting out, steam augmenting its hellishness. Forgetting the pain in her shoulders, Heath muscled her way across the room. Using a crutch as a battering ram, she bashed the bathroom door open with so much force it struck the commode.

Tail down, Wily growled.

Steam obscured the mirror and made a wraith of the girl in the tub. Momentarily disoriented, Heath would have fallen if she hadn't been wedged between crutches and doorframe. Vision cleared. What remained was a child — a young woman really, sixteen — in a bath so hot her skin had reddened below the waterline. She was holding a razor blade to her wrist. Tears and sweat poured down her face to fall like rain into the bath.

A girl and a razor and an angry voice shouting "fuck that bitch" to the beat of a machine gun in the hands of a madman.

Heath reached over and pulled the iPod out of the speaker. Silence bloomed like a blessing, broken only by the drip, drip, drip of slow tears. Pressing a button on her wrist, she activated the metal bones. With a hum like that of an electric window in an older-model Cadillac, they eased her down onto the seat of the commode. She moved her crutches so they wouldn't be between her and her daughter.

"Honey . . . ," she said gently, and held out her hand. Elizabeth laid the razor carefully in her palm. Heath set it on the sink counter.

Elizabeth had been contemplating suicide with the layered blades of a Lady Schick. At best, she could have given herself what amounted to nasty paper cuts. Though she was in a hot bath, as the media always portrayed suicides for some reason, Elizabeth, being a modest girl by nature and upbringing, was wearing the iridescent blue one-piece bathing suit she wore for swim races.

Much to laugh at.

Nothing funny.

For a minute neither spoke. Elizabeth,

flushed with heat, eyes and mouth swollen from crying, long dark hair sleek as a seal's pelt on her shoulders, looked so small and young.

A lump hard and hot as a burning coal formed in Heath's throat. "What can I do?" she managed, her voice burned and choking. "What can I say? Who can I kill? For you, Elizabeth, I will do it. Whatever you need, I will do it."

Two

Denise sipped her Coke, flat and warm from neglect. Just like me, she thought sourly, then reminded herself not to let the sourness seep into her face. Pleasant expression neutralizing her muscles, she let her eyes casually wander past Peter Barnes and his entourage.

Park picnics had become exercises in self-control. Denise loathed them, but she was damned if she was going to let Peter keep her from attending. Tables were scattered on the grass behind park headquarters. Two, shoved together, were loaded down with hamburger buns and condiments in the oversized squeeze bottles that always struck her as mildly obscene given the flatulent sounds that sputtered out with the ketchup, mustard, and, especially, the pickle relish.

Peter was sitting with his new wife, Lily. *Lily.* Could it get any worse? He couldn't have married a Sheila or a Judy?

Or someone remotely his own age?

Like me, she thought again. Hatred burned like acid in the back of her throat. Peter was forty-six, four years older than she. Pretty little Lily had just turned thirty. Their baby, Olivia, was three months. Married fourteen months and a baby girl. Lucky, lucky Peter. Lucky Lily.

Three years had passed since Denise had been the one sitting next to Peter Barnes at the picnics. More. Thirty-eight months. Yet the wound had not healed. She still felt as if her skin had been peeled from her body, and her flesh, newly flayed, screamed silent and bloody for everyone to see.

For a time — months, maybe as long as a year — Denise had thought things were getting better. Then they started getting worse. Hate would roar like a lion, then tears would sting, but not fall. Thoughts of *them* flooded her mind in muddy rivers, bursting their banks. When the baby came, the flooding grew worse. Some days Denise could not escape endless tape-loops of images of that baby girl.

She hated Peter, hated Lily, though Lily hadn't been the Other Woman, just the next woman. How could she not hate Lily? Lily was young and pretty. Lily had Denise's life, Denise's man, and just to make sure the knife was twisted, the baby Denise could never have.

Could never have because of Peter.

She realized her eyes had been stuck on the happy little family too long, on the baby. Lily was holding the baby, feeding it from a bottle. Lily never nursed. The little cow had no milk.

Lily caught her, smiling, happy, welcoming.

Denise forced a smile that probably didn't work. Peter had undoubtedly told Lily about poor, old, pathetic Denise, the reject who had taken on the role of the ghost at the manor window, always present, never invited in.

Deciding she'd stayed long enough to prove she wasn't brokenhearted, Denise stood and carried her Coke to the nearest trash bin. In an impotent act of defiance, she didn't put the can in the recycle bin. Given that Peter had chosen to trash her life and recycle his own with the lovely, fertile Lily, she was damned if she would support his pet program.

Artie, the gung-ho new district ranger, sat at a table with one of the secretaries. Young and eager, he was trying to make being a park ranger more like being an Army Ranger, itching for black ops. Denise forced herself to smile at him.

After making it a point to saunter slowly from table to table saying her good-byes so it wouldn't look like she was slinking away with her tail between her legs, Denise made it to her Miata. The last few steps she staggered like a drunk. What the hell was that about?

Holding on to the low door to keep from falling, she took deep breaths. Tremors rattled her bones. Almost as if Peter — his eyes, all the eyes — the baby, Lily, everybody knowing, had brought on some kind of seizure, as if around Peter and his postcard-perfect life she could no longer fill her lungs. Bony fingers of a monster hand wrapped around her rib cage, squeezing and squeezing.

Paranoia rampaged through her veins.

No. No monster. No seizures. Hyperventilation is all. Lily doesn't know. They are fooled. I have them all fooled, Denise told herself. For the most part she knew she was right. Certain people had a knack for seeing the ghost behind the eyes. Those people Denise avoided. The rest, when they bothered to think about her at all, believed she had moved on, that she was just as thrilled as they were with the assistant superintendent's spiffy new family.

When she could do so without stumbling, Denise opened the car door and slid into the low bucket seat. A Mazda ragtop in northern Maine was a rich man's summer toy, but a foolish purchase for a woman who could afford only one car. Denise had bought it a week after Peter announced he "needed space," then promptly gave himself that space by throwing her out of the house they'd shared for eleven years.

Two months later he threw her out of his life.

At the time she bought the convertible she hoped it would make her feel free, sexy. For a brief moment it seemed to, then it didn't, and she'd come to hate it. The list of things she was coming to hate lengthened daily, each new loathing attaching to the anchor that was Peter Barnes. The chain of hate had grown so heavy that some days Denise felt she couldn't carry it another foot, that she would collapse under it and lie helpless until all vestiges of life were crushed from her body.

Before — as in before she was ruined and dumped — Denise used to enjoy the short drive on Route 233 to Bar Harbor. August, high summer, hot days and cool nights greened the park. The coast, with its islands like jeweled rock gardens scattering in a sea of whitecaps and blue water, took on a fairy-tale beauty.

Beauty was not yet on the list of things she hated, but she supposed it would come under the pall eventually.

Bar Harbor, draped in schmaltzy cuteness, was a place she'd used to avoid during tourist season. Alcohol, in its myriad forms, was another thing she'd once scorned. This evening, after suffering through another picnic with the royal family, she craved a place as fake as the promise of Happily Ever After, and a beer. Beers. One had ceased being enough long ago.

On the outskirts of town she pulled into the wide circular drive of the Acadian Lodge. In the 1940s and '50s — the heyday of lodges and camps — the almost-wealthy summered at the Acadian, basking in the shadow of the truly moneyed.

There were cottages then. Denise had seen pictures of them — trim, freshly painted, lawns and gardens in careful rustic disarray, and "campers," looking happy and coddled by armies of servants, mostly girls who'd come up from the cities by train to earn a little money and enjoy a summer by the sea.

No more.

The cabins had long since been torn down

and the property sold off in half-acre lots. The lodge had grown as sad and tacky as a drunken old woman. Touches of new paint, sporadically and inexpertly applied, soaked like cheap drugstore makeup into the wrinkles and cracks of wood that had weathered too many winters.

In its glory days, the bar had been a fashionable watering hole. Now it was the haunt of locals, lobstermen mostly. It was dark and smelled faintly of the sea and dead fish. Stale cigarette smoke had permeated the walls and carpets so deeply that all these years after indoor smoking had been legislated into a crime, the smell persisted.

Usually Denise drank at home and alone. For reasons she didn't understand — and didn't want to — she was drawn to the Acadian when things in her mind got too ugly. Slipping into a dark wooden booth in a dark corner, she took off her sunglasses. The room was dominated by a once-elegant long bar backed by a mirror easily six feet high and fifteen feet long. Black age spots pocked the silvering around the edges, contributing to the sense that the place was diseased or moldering back into the stone and lichen upon which it was built.

The bartender raised an eyebrow. "Draft, dark," Denise said, and then worked herself into the corner of the booth until the shadows closed around her. Other patrons had no business seeing memories ripping at her flesh, sharp-taloned and as vicious as harpies.

A couple of lobstermen on barstools were talking about the old guy who'd shot another old guy by the name of Will Whitman for robbing his traps and moving in on his territory. Yet another skirmish in the lobster wars that had been waged along these waters for generations and showed no sign of letting up. Law enforcement was worthless for the most part. Whose traps were where, and who ran which lines, was a mystery to everybody but the men who harvested lobsters for a living. They knew the bottom of the ocean around Maine as well as landlubbers knew the streets of their own neighborhoods.

Denise had heard that the dead man's son, Walter, had been excommunicated from the fishing community because everybody figured his dad was guilty of robbing traps — sins of the father, acorns falling near trees, chips off the old block. She smiled to herself. The bozos knew nothing.

Lobsters disappeared, lobsters were never there in the first place, lobsters were poached. These jokers in their little boats on top of the water could only guess who or what happened right underneath them.

A young couple — tourists, lost or slumming — slid into a booth on the end wall. Both on the same side. The old Denise would have thought it romantic. This new Denise wanted to bite their heads off and spit them into their imported beers.

At the near end of the bar, where the wood curved gracefully toward the mirrored wall, a lone woman sat hunched over a glass. Bleached-blond hair formed a curtain between her and the lobstermen. Denise's booth was on the opposite side of the ersatz veil, so she could see the blonde's face. She was sporting a black eye and a split lip.

Revulsion swept through Denise in a sick-making wave. She couldn't stand that the woman's outside was a public image of her own insides: battered, abused, ashamed, and drinking alone.

Despite that, every few minutes, Denise's gaze found its way back to the blonde on the barstool. Denise had been in law enforcement all of her adult life. A national park ranger, she'd seldom dealt with city-cop stuff. Parks were peaceful places for the most part, even in Acadia, where park and town and resort and sea came together in a patchwork of populations, each with its own agenda. Not once had she pulled her gun, used her baton or her pepper spray. What minimal compliance and self-defense training she'd gotten at the Federal Law Enforcement Training Center in Georgia had long since been forgotten.

Black eyes and split lips, though, were a form of violence she was familiar with. Family troubles don't go away on vacation; they get worse. The damaged face wasn't enough of a novelty to hold Denise's interest, but something was. As she sneaked peeks over the rim of her first beer glass, her second, and then her third, she tried to figure out what was so fascinating.

It became evident that the battered blonde was known to the bartender. Maybe a regular. Denise hadn't seen her here before, but then she never came to the Acadian this early in the evening. The lobstermen came here a lot. Usually, by the time Denise slunk in, they were three sheets to the wind. They might know the woman. Either the acquaintance was slight or they didn't like her. Both pointedly refused to look in her direction. This suited Denise. If they didn't look at the blond barfly, they couldn't look at her.

There was something bizarrely familiar about the woman. Had she arrested her? No. That process was long and, in many ways, intimate. Denise would have remembered.

Acadia, for all it had a large and fluid population in the summer months, was a small town for year-round inhabitants. Had she seen the blonde in a grocery store or, given the face, a hospital emergency room? In her capacity as an EMT she had been to the ER at Mount Desert Island Hospital enough times with injured people.

The woman looked to be in her late thirties or early forties. The barstool made guessing her height tricky, but Denise figured she was about the same height as she was — five foot six — and probably weighed about the same, one hundred thirty pounds. Her face — without the obvious damage — was the kind that can be dressed up or down. Makeup and a good haircut and she'd be pretty. Without it, she was fairly ordinary. Still, there was something . . .

After a while the blonde began looking back. Their eyes met, and Denise stopped her furtive surveillance. The last thing she wanted was to get into a "what're you lookin' at?" bitchfest with a stranger.

Another beer, a trip to the ladies' room.

The lobstermen got up and left. As they passed the blonde, working on her third

30

drink since Denise arrived, one ducked his head and said, "Miz Duffy." The other nodded politely.

Miz Duffy. No lobsterman Denise had run across would call a woman "Miss" unless she was their kid's schoolteacher. Miz Duffy must be Mrs. Duffy. As Denise made her way unsteadily back to her booth, she wondered if they'd made a point of ignoring Mrs. Duffy because they didn't think a married woman should be alone in a bar, or because they were acquainted with Mr. Duffy, and the fact that he'd beaten on his wife made social intercourse awkward.

Mrs. Duffy watched them go, a tired look on her face, and something more energetic in the curl of her upper lip, disgust possibly.

The blonde shifted on the stool. Again their eyes met, this time in the long mirror backing the bar. Realization hit Denise with the force of near-sobriety. Not disgust. Hatred was what burned in the blonde's eyes. She knew. Denise had seen it. It greeted her in the bathroom mirror every morning. For a long time they sat, eyes locked, watching a slurry of emotions, memories and shocks flickering across the faces in the glass at dizzying speed. Never breaking eye contact, the blonde stood, picked up her drink, and carried it over to

Denise's booth. She slid into the shadows on the opposite side.

"I was beginning to think I'd made you up out of whole cloth," she said, and laughed.

The laugh made the hairs on the back of Denise's neck prickle.

THREE

Elizabeth wouldn't tell Heath why she'd been contemplating slitting her wrists. When pressed, she cried and looked so desperate it scared Heath into silence.

Dem Bones hung like a Space Age suit of armor on its stand in the corner; Heath, collapsed in the familiar embrace of Robobutt, was putting water on for tea. While the water heated, she rolled onto the back porch to call Gwen in her persona of doctor and great-aunt. She also called Anna Pigeon in her persona of law enforcement ranger at Rocky Mountain National Park and Elizabeth's godmother. Surely, between medicine, the law, and Heath's blind determination, they could find out what had driven Elizabeth to despair and put the child back together again.

Curled up on the oversized leather sofa, and in her pajamas though it was not yet sundown, Elizabeth accepted the tea without comment. Elizabeth couldn't care less about tea, but it was all Heath could think to offer, and she was grateful her daughter took it.

Heath had not seen E this hopelessly totaled since, at nine years old, she had wandered out of the night woods weeping and nearly naked.

A year earlier, during a nightmare canoe trip on Minnesota's Fox River, Elizabeth had been as strong and canny as any battle veteran. Heath had almost forgotten she wasn't Rambo; she was a sixteen-year-old girl. Evidently, whatever this evil was, it was of a variety that struck at the heart of where that wonderful, vulnerable girl lived.

Anna arrived first. Soundless in moccasins without socks, she appeared in the doorway between the kitchen and living room. She must have dropped everything and left work as soon as Heath called. Heath probably sounded as panicked on the phone as she was. She refused to feel guilty. They were talking about Elizabeth's life.

Anna had changed out of her uniform. She was wearing Levi's so worn the knees were white and stringy with age, not artifice, and an oversized, man's white shirt, probably her husband Paul's, rolled up to the elbows.

A while back Anna had turned fifty. More gray twined through her braid now than when Heath had first met her. Decades in the sun had freckled and creased her skin in a way that suited her skull and her soul. Anna had grown to look like a person you would want to tell your darkest secrets, all the while harboring an uneasy sense she already knew what they were.

"Hey," Heath greeted her. She didn't expect a hug. Anna was not a touchy-feely kind of woman. Both in greeting and departing, Anna nodded. A modified bow of respect, Heath guessed. Or dismissal.

Perhaps because Elizabeth was so young and damaged when she'd met Anna, she had crept through those boundaries. Leaping off the sofa, the girl threw herself into the ranger's arms. As tall as Anna, and a few pounds heavier, Heath expected Elizabeth's onslaught to knock Anna back into the kitchen, but Ranger Pigeon stood staunch as an oak and wrapped her arms around the clinging girl.

Relief only slightly tainted with jealousy washed over Heath. Chest muscles loosened. She drew her first deep breath since she'd found Elizabeth in the bath. It saddened her that, physically, she could not be Elizabeth's rock. Without bitterness, Heath knew she'd gotten the harder job, to anchor and support her emotionally.

Anna folded down onto the floor, her back against the sofa, legs crossed Indian fashion. Elizabeth curled up on the seat behind her and played with Anna's pigtail the way she'd done when she was a little wreck of a girl, still in shock from the multiple ordeals that brought her into Heath's life. Holding on to the braid, Elizabeth whisked the tail over her eyes and cheekbones as if sweeping away cobwebs.

"I wish you hadn't changed out of uniform," Heath said to Anna. "I was kind of looking forward to having a gun close to hand."

Before Anna could respond, Gwen blew in through the outside door. Gwen was in her late seventies, small-boned, fragile-looking, with wildly curly hair that she ignored with the exception of taking time every three weeks to keep it as resolutely red as it had always been. Dr. Gwen Littleton was the antithesis of a little old lady. Heath thought of her aunt as a whirlwind, a dust devil, a genie in a tiny bottle, a force that, though small in size, was most definitely to be reckoned with.

She gusted into the living room, dropping the black leather doctor's bag she'd been given when she graduated from medical school — and still carried every day — on the floor. The air that came in with her was the kind that can only be found during dry high-mountain summers, a draft so light and crisp, so warm and full of optimism, you feel that if only you could spread your wings wide enough you could fly.

"I left the door open," Gwen announced. "Fresh air. My unbottled, unpatented, priceless, free cure-all." Dumping her purse, Heath's mail, and a long turquoise-and-gold scarf she'd been carrying for some reason, she put her hands on her hips, surveyed the three of them, and said, "Okay, now, what's this all about?"

Elizabeth started to cry again, mopping at the tears with the tail of Anna's braid. Though it had to be absorbing a bit of snot on the side, Anna didn't look like she had any intention of rescuing it.

Gwen swooped down onto the sofa and folded her great-niece in her thin arms. Anna took one of Elizabeth's narrrow feet between her roughened hands and began to massage it gently. Heath rolled nearer, closing Elizabeth into a circle of love. An impenetrable circle? Probably not. Love did not conquer all, but sometimes it made it bearable.

"Baby, what is it? You have to tell us," Gwen crooned.

"Or we'll never go away," Anna added.

"Not even to go to the bathroom," Heath said. "How disgusting would that be?"

"I am so ashamed," Elizabeth mumbled through her tears and the soggy end of Anna's braid. "I swear I'm going to die of embarrassment. Just die! I want to die," she said with bone-chilling sincerity. "I'm so ashamed." Tears clogged her throat then, and she sobbed into Gwen's bony bird-shoulder.

"I accidentally fell on a friend of mine and killed her," Anna said. "That was pretty embarrassing."

Heath almost blurted out, "What the fuck?" Leading technical climbs for much of her adult life, Heath was fluent in the modern vernacular, and "fuck" was such a jolly good bad word. But when Elizabeth came into her world, Heath had determined to clean up her language. Saying the F-word was one thing; hearing it on the lips of a fairylike little girl was obscene. Worse, it was tacky, low rent.

Anyway, it had been ruined. On the Fox River one of the thugs had, quite simply, used it up. He had used all possible, probable, and improbable applications of the word, finally rendering it absurd. Now, when E and Anna and Heath heard someone say "fuck," they'd lift an eyebrow, exchange a smile.

Left without it, Heath fell back on the classics. Twelve apostles and forty thousand cowboys couldn't be wrong. God damn it to hell, bastard, SOB. All were workable.

"The hell you say," she amended. From the corner of her eye she noted Elizabeth was listening. The sobbing had quieted.

"No kidding," Anna said somberly. "Squashed her throat. Now that's something to be ashamed of."

"I once told a woman her fetus was going to be stillborn," Gwen admitted. "She mourned and wailed through seventeen hours of labor. The baby never moved, its heart never beat, I swear it! The moment she was born, that baby girl was wiggling and giggling. The wretched little thing had been lying doggo, or hiding behind Mom's liver or some darn thing. I thought I was going to die of humiliation before the mother killed me for scaring her to death. Thank God that was back before mothers sued for every little birthmark. I was so ashamed I didn't show my face at the hospital for nearly a week. When I did, doctors, and even some nurses, started calling me Dr. Lazarus."

"I never killed anybody or scared anybody half to death," Heath said. "But in college I got drunk and made a bet with this guy that I could free-climb the front of the administration building, no lines, no belays, no shoes, no gloves, no nothing. Bet him a hundred bucks. He upped it to a hundred and fifty if I did it totally naked. I was halfway up and doing great when the cops showed up with the spotlights. I was charged with drunk and disorderly, disturbing the peace, and — this hurt worst — defacing university property, apparently by plastering my bare-naked ass on it."

"You did not!" Gwen exclaimed.

"Spent the night and half the next day in jail. I was too ashamed to call you. The only reason I wasn't expelled was that the boy who made the bet with me was the president of the university's son. Cross my heart and hope to die."

Elizabeth stared at her wide-eyed, completely engaged now. "Oh gosh, Mom, how did you stand it?" she cried.

Absurdly pleased that her tale had trumped accidental death by falling on, and nearly terrifying to death by misdiagnosis, Heath said, "This was before everybody had iPhones. I was only totally humiliated in front of twenty or thirty people, not millions on the Web."

Elizabeth's face went deathly pale. Heath had read the phrase "deathly pale" many times, but this was the first time she'd ever witnessed the phenomenon. It was as if she watched the blood drain from beneath her daughter's skin, leaving a gray pallor in its wake. For a moment she thought E was going to faint or scream or vomit. What she did was far more frightening. She began striking herself in the face with her balled fists.

Heath ached to hold her. She knew that the best she could manage was to lurch upon the pile like Frankenstein's monster. Cursing the ice that had bested her, she turned her wheelchair sharply and sped from the room, left the hardwood and hit the carpet without slowing down. Robo-butt had never moved so fast. In an instant she was down the hall and in Elizabeth's room. The pink iPhone, a gift from Gwen, was on the bedside table. Elizabeth's laptop was on her desk, holding pride of place in the midst of a landfill's worth of cosmetics, tissues, magazines, earrings, and whatever else had been dropped there over the past two years.

Heath took both electronic gadgets and dropped them into the saddlebags on her

41

chair. Another twenty seconds and she was back in the living room parked beside the couch. "Elizabeth," she said in a tone that cut through the soft fuzzy outpourings of Gwen and the somber attentions of Anna. Elizabeth looked up, eyes and cheeks wet, lips red and swollen.

Heath held up the pink cell phone.

"Noooooo," Elizabeth begged. She covered her ears and squeezed her eyes shut as if waiting for the fuse to burn down to the dynamite.

"Yes," Heath said. "Rotten ice." Rotten ice was their code for *This will try to kill you. Face it or run away fast.*

Gwen glared at Heath. Anna nodded slightly. In the minute or less Heath had been gone, Anna must have figured it out. Heath pushed the message button. Seventeen new messages in the in-box. "I've never had seventeen messages in my entire life," Heath said. A small whimper from Elizabeth. Not funny. Heath opened the first message and read it. Then she read it aloud in a flat voice. " 'Have you been on the page? Dweeb said you did the basketball team. TNT?' "

"Kimmy?" Heath asked as she noted who it was from.

"She's in my geometry class," E said miserably.

"TNT? Explosive?" Anna asked.

"Totally Not True," Elizabeth said. "How could she have to ask?" Tears started. She knocked them from her eyes with the backs of her hands.

E was going to be brave. Heath hoped she was. She opened the second. " 'Check The Page.' Tiffany sent this one," Heath noted. "The Page?" She raised an interrogative eyebrow.

"It's a blog the kids all read." E hid her eyes with the tail of Anna's braid. "Somebody posted that I did things I didn't do."

"Like the basketball team?" Anna said dryly.

"Like that," E said.

Heath opened the third message: " 'Who hasn't screwed you yet?' My God, this stuff is insane. Somebody is going to get their skull bashed in if I have any say in the matter."

The fifth had a picture attached, an image of a woman being mounted by a Great Dane. Heath didn't read it aloud. She passed the phone to Gwen.

" 'I guess you like being done to by dogs.' "

"Holy Mary Mother of God," Gwen whispered.

Anna had taken the laptop from the saddlebag and had it open on her thighs. "What's the address of the blog?"

E told her. Anna typed it in.

Heath rolled her chair over to read it. " 'EJ pulled a train — you hear that? After the game.' "

" 'True. I was the caboose.' That one's signed Spike," Anna said.

"It's this creep everybody calls Dweeb. He signs himself Spike," Elizabeth said. "God, the *Dweeb*!" E cried. "Nobody could think I'd have anything to do with the Dweeb!"

" 'No sloppy seconds for me.' This one is signed IceBlow."

"A slime bag Dweeb hangs with. You should have let me kill myself," E whispered.

" 'Sloppy twenty-seconds more like,' " Anna read on relentlessly. Heath considered stopping her, saving Elizabeth the pain, but she believed Anna was right in what she was doing. Elizabeth already knew what they said. Aloud, in Anna's flat, almost bored tone, they lost some of their snickers-in-the-dark malice and sounded as stupid as they were. Almost.

" 'Not in all orifices.' " Anna looked

around. "Orifices?" she asked no one in particular. "Big word for this moron." She returned her attention to the computer and read the last two quickly, as if the whole thing were too foolish for words.

" 'No shit?' asks bozo," Anna said.

" 'Meat sandwich with a blow job topper.' This from thug number two. Who started this ball rolling?" she asked Elizabeth in cold even tones.

"I don't know," E sobbed. "The only names I recognize are Dweeby Spike and his creep pal, IceBrain. If cooties weren't extinct, they'd have them big-time."

Of course, Heath thought. Once the story was out, the dweebs and the creeps wanted to be part of the action. If a girl was having sex with the other boys, why not them? "This is good," Heath said. "Nobody cares what they say. They're creeps." That sounded good and might even be true.

"Your Facebook password?" Anna asked.

"WilyCoyote2015," Elizabeth said softly. "Capital W, capital C." At the sound of his name, Wily thumped his tail on the floor. Pushing to his feet, the old dog ambled over and stuck his head under Heath's hand. It was as comforting as it always had been.

Anna looked up from the laptop. "More of the same," she said. "Where else?"

"Everywhere," Elizabeth said hollowly. "There's a website the kids go to, like a Mean Girls thing. That blog. I've found three others. Things are forwarded to my whole class sometimes."

Cyberbullying: vicious, anonymous, all-pervasive. Heath forced her voice to calmness, then asked, "Who started sending these first?"

"I don't know," Elizabeth whispered. "Honest, I don't know. Don't tell anyone," she begged. "Anna, promise me, no cops. No cops, Heath, nobody. Gwen, no doctors, and please, please, please don't talk to any of my friends' parents. Pleeeeease!"

For a second, Heath suspected Elizabeth knew, not only why she was being targeted, but by whom, and her sixteen-year-old mind was telling her that if she ratted out the culprit, it would dump her into a hell worse than the one she was already in. The one that could only be escaped by razors to the wrist.

Heath changed the subject. "When did" — and she waved the cell phone rather than speak the evil words — "this stuff begin?"

"I don't know," Elizabeth said automatically. Then, "About a week after school let out for the summer." Elizabeth was a rising senior at Boulder High. Not in with the in crowd or the jocks, but at the moderately comfortable level of acceptable anonymity that allows a majority of kids to survive high school without permanent scarring.

"Who?" Anna demanded.

Shocked into honesty by Anna's tone, Elizabeth said uncertainly, "Tiffany?"

"Tiffany? Tiffany's your best friend," Heath said. Not a friend of Heath's choosing. The girl's parents were Christian fundamentalists, or at least her mother was. Heath figured Elizabeth had suffered enough at the hands of religious fanatics for several lifetimes, but Tiffany seemed like a nice girl.

In Heath's opinion the friendship was more one of opportunity than genuine attraction. Tiffany, her folks, and her two-year-old brother, Brady, moved into the house next door; she and Elizabeth were the same age and starting their freshman year together; both settled at the same level in the high school pecking order. Admittedly, Elizabeth seemed to enjoy Tiffany's company. Most days either she was at Tiffany's or Tiff was over here. It suddenly occurred to Heath she'd not seen the girls together for a while, a week or more.

Rotten mother, she scolded herself. Blind as a bat.

"I don't think we're friends anymore,"

Elizabeth said.

"Did you guys get in a fight?" Heath asked. She should have asked this a week ago. She should have been paying better attention.

"Not exactly. Momma, could I have some more tea? It really helps." When Elizabeth called Heath "Momma," either they were having a moment or Heath was being conned. Obviously Elizabeth really, really did not want to talk about this. All three adults homed in on the vibe like hounds on a scent.

The only thing missing was the baying.

Four

Bad idea to be doing this drunk, Denise thought, but continued dragging the straps of her scuba tank up over her wetsuit. Cold water would sober her up quick enough, she rationalized. If it didn't, and she drowned, that was all right, too. Since all of her children had been murdered, and Peter had thrown her away like so much damaged goods, death didn't seem like such a bad option.

Except that Peter would be glad she was dead.

Except that the son of a bitch would go right on living his spiffy little life. With his precious Lily and the baby. They would watch the baby that should have been hers grow up without caring that Denise was fish food.

Mouthpiece adjusted, gear hooked to her harness, she made a final check of the gauges with her flashlight. How drunk could

49

she be if she remembered to check gauges? It wasn't as if she was planning on going deep or staying down long, half an hour max. Hell, I dive drunk better than I do sober, she thought. *Drunk diver.* The phrase amused her, and as she went over backwards into the ocean, she forgot to hold on to her mask. Cursing and sputtering, she managed to catch it before it sank and get it back on. So much for the "better drunk" theory of diving.

Mask adjusted, she got her bearings. The night was perfect. Warm, overcast, and as dark as the inside of Jonah's whale. Her navy blue runabout on a midnight sea in a great big ocean was as close to invisible as a corporeal body was likely to get.

She upended.

Following the anchor line toward the bottom, she thought about Will Whitman, the lobsterman who got shot for robbing that old guy's traps. Whitman might have been rustling lobsters, but the traps he got shot over were in her territory. The murder had renewed hostilities in the long-running feud.

Not that she cared. People shot people. People did a lot of awful things to other people. Nobody gave a damn. Her own mother had dumped her. She'd been adopted by borderline assholes. Cry me a river; nobody cares about anybody other than themselves.

Enough! she told herself and quieted her mind. Stopping thoughts from spinning was hard. It was like her mind had developed a mind of its own, and maybe neither one was her friend.

No! she shouted silently. The dueling minds couldn't have this place. Clenching her jaw, she forced herself to look outward.

She loved that only the circle of her lamp and the anchor line existed. Under the Atlantic at night was the only time she felt anywhere near free or whole anymore. Contained in apparatus and silence, held in weightlessness and peace, she savored the balm to her soul. Above, in the light, in the world of men, she devoured herself, ripped the flesh from her bones with her teeth, like a coyote chewing off its own leg to free itself from the jaws of the trap.

Watching the line play through her gloved hand as she descended, she let herself think about the woman she'd just met in the bar of the old Acadian Lodge.

Neither one of them had said anything for the longest time after the blonde slid into the booth and made her cryptic announcement. "I'd begun to think I'd made you up."

They sat and stared at each other in the

dim light of the bar. Denise was struck dumb. She'd never quite known what was meant when people said that. She did now. There were no more words in her head at that moment. Had there been, she wouldn't have been able to move her tongue or push out the breath to say them. Words had become futile pathetic little things, not fit to bring into the immensity of the idea that had slipped in with the blonde.

"Takes some getting used to, doesn't it? I've been thinking on it for months now, so I'll talk while you get your mind around it, how's that?" the woman said. Her voice sounded creepy, the way Denise's always did when she heard herself on a tape recorder, familiar but alien. Not right.

"My name is Paulette Duffy. I'm forty-one." She smiled. Denise drank down the last of her beer, then waved at the bartender for another. Paulette's teeth weren't the same. Denise had gotten her front incisors busted in a schoolyard fight and had neat straight caps. Paulette's leaned in as if they needed each other for support.

"I think I'm forty-two," Denise managed. "But that could be off a year either way."

"Forty-two on March sixth of next year," Paulette Duffy said. Her hand shot out for no reason Denise could see and banged the metal napkin holder. "Sorry," she laughed. "I guess I'm turning into a klutz in my old age."

"Nerves," Denise said to be saying something. "Happens to me more and more." Her head was swimming. Too much beer. Too much everything. Sitting back, she let her head fall against the cracked leather of the booth. "Forty-one," she whispered. "Forty-two on the sixth of March. That kind of makes a person real, doesn't it? Knowing when you were born, knowing somebody cared enough to write it down."

"You never knew?" Paulette asked softly. Denise hated being pitied for her rotten childhood, hated talking about it, wouldn't talk about it. Peter was the only one to whom she'd told all the grit and grime, and now, every time he looked at her through the scrim of his new clean wife and spotless baby, she could see every bit of shit she'd ever been through clinging to her in his eyes.

Now she wanted to spew it all out like vomited beer here in this booth for Paulette Duffy. "Never knew," she said. "I'm not ready for any of this." She pulled the man's wallet she favored out of the hip pocket of her pants, then dumped the contents on the table. It was probably enough to pay for her drinks three times over. She didn't care. "I'll never be ready for any of this." Standing unsteadily, she waited a second for the room to stop spinning.

"Here," Paulette said. She scribbled on a bar napkin. When Denise didn't hold out her hand to take it, Paulette shoved it in Denise's pants pocket. "This is my address and the number of my cell phone. I got one of those prepaid ones at Walmart. I have lots of minutes left. Call me. Promise. Promise you'll call me."

Denise didn't promise. She made it to the Miata. Then to the runabout. Then to the sanctity of lobster rustling under the sea.

The ocean floor coalesced out of the gray-green circle of gloom at the farthest reach of Denise's light. Turning herself so her feet pointed earthward, she came to a gentle landing on the sand. Froglike, iridescent green in the glow of the lamp, her swim fins squeezed small swirls of liquid dust puffed from beneath her.

The depth gauge read twenty-six feet. Habit was all that made her check it. This stretch of Davy Jones's locker was, meta-phorically speaking, the back of her hand.

Moving with the slow grace of a hip-popotamus on the bed of the Nile she turned, letting her light drift in a circle until she saw the yellow line snaking down from the buoy she'd anchored near, the marker of a line of lobster traps. With a lazy kick she rotated to the horizontal and swam toward it.

Traps were on the end of lines connected to Styrofoam buoys on the surface. Lobstermen checked their traps every day, putting fresh bait in if they needed it. The buoys were marked with the license number of whichever fisherman owned the trap.

The traps on the ocean floor out from Somes were the old variety, wooden crates covered in rope mesh, with a circular opening just big enough for a lobster to crawl in. Occasionally, Denise mused, surely a lobster, smarter than her fellows, after having consumed the bait, would crawl back out to live and reproduce. Maybe man had created the ultimate evolution facility, and one day the giant spiders would take over Silicon Valley.

The first trap had two lobsters in it, but they were small. She passed them by. The next had one enormous old fellow. Lobsters could live a hundred years, though most didn't make it more than ten or fifteen. This guy looked to weigh close to two pounds. He had been around a while.

Careful to avoid the claws, Denise reached in and dragged him out. Her hand twitched as if she'd been hit by an electric shock, much the way Paulette Duffy's had. Her knuckles rapped on the side of the trap, and her fingers opened. With a flick of his tail, the lobster shot into the darkness.

Nerves.

Over forty and falling apart, Denise thought. The big spider would have been a good addition to the canvas sack trailing from a tether attached to her dive harness, but, in a way, she was glad it had escaped. Sad to end one's life in a tourist's stomach.

When she had ten good-sized lobsters, she switched off her light. Her bag could easily hold as many as fifteen, but she made it a rule never to take every one she found. If a trap had a couple of lobsters in it, she'd take only one. Those she emptied, if there was any bait left inside, might lure in another crustacean before the licensee came to check his catch. This way she figured the lobsterman would be pretty sure his traps had been poached, but not a hundred percent sure.

Denise rotated her lobster rustling through four different patches. All they had in common was that they were shallow and easily accessible from Somes Sound, where she moored her little boat. Other than running into somebody night diving — and probably up to no good either — while she was in the act of robbing the traps, there was no way she could get caught.

Denise liked that the lobstermen knew they'd been had, liked that she was thumbing her nose at the holier-than-thous in the park service, the Peter Barneses. Liked the feeling that, at least in this, she was the one in control. It was she, Denise Castle, who was making fools of them all. That was as important as the money she got for her catch with the less than honest owner of the Big Fat Lobster Trap, a seafood restaurant on the outskirts of Bar Harbor.

Lobster rustling was petty payback for what had been done to her since she was old enough to remember. Pathetic, if she thought about it, but it was the best she could do.

Until now.

Paulette Duffy.

There were possibilities opening to her that hadn't existed before.

Kicking off the bottom, she let herself rise gently to the surface. She had not been deep enough, nor down long enough, to make any decompression stops necessary. At the surface, she bobbed, a black sea creature in a black sea. Finding her boat was the most challenging aspect of her midnight forays into the seafood aisle of the Atlantic.

Under the gunwale, on either side of the bow, she had mounted three small LED lights. They were green. She'd been careful not to put them in a line or evenly spaced — the telltale marks of a work of man, not nature. Glimpsed by anyone, they'd be taken for a reflection, a bit of phosphorescent sea vegetation, or a trick of the light. For her they were homing beacons.

After a minute or two she saw them winking as the boat rose and fell on a gentle swell. She swam toward it. Having tied her sack of squirming arachnids to the starboard cleat, Denise heaved herself over the gunwale. As always, her first action was to remove and stow her dive gear, then pull on Levi's, a sweatshirt, and a ball cap to cover her wet hair. She'd established her reputation as a woman who enjoyed night diving. Still, diving at night, alone, was considered dangerous enough to raise questions she'd rather not answer on the off chance she ran into anyone. The lobsters she could always cut loose back into the ocean if need be.

An innocent, if nocturnal, ranger once again, enjoying the resource and preserving it for blah, blah, blah, she started her motor and headed back toward Somes Sound. Bear Island loomed to her port side, dark and forbidding, its mysterious, reclusive owners seldom in evidence, then Boar Island, smaller and virtually treeless. Boar had a jagged silhouette that reminded Denise of a ruined castle, the turrets half crumbling. The lady who owned it had a bad heart and was currently in a convalescent home in Bangor.

That's what happens to women who have no children to care for them, Denise thought. In old age they become orphans and are thrown on the state for their keep. Denise did not want to end her life the way it had begun, an unwanted orphan beholden to the state of Maine for a meal and a roof over her head.

That brought her back to the battered blonde, Paulette Duffy.

And all the new possibilities.

FIVE

Elizabeth knew she'd stepped in it, Heath could tell. As three adult stares bored into her, she groaned and rolled her eyes toward the ceiling. This show of sass did more to cheer up Heath than a thousand clowns in a barrel full of monkeys. "You said you 'didn't exactly' have a fight. What is 'not exactly' having a fight?" Heath asked.

Regardless of the incidents that should have aged Elizabeth before her time, she retained that magnificent innocence of face one seldom sees in anyone over the age of ten. When she was with people she trusted, or too tired to keep her guard up, her emotions could be as easily read as those of a two-year-old. Heath watched in loving fascination as Elizabeth decided to lie, thought better of it, decided to cry, changed her mind, and, finally, began.

"You know Mr. and Mrs. Edleson, Tiff's mom and dad?" Elizabeth asked. The question was meant for Gwen and Anna. Of course Heath knew them. Sam was around forty, thick sandy hair, nice build. If he hadn't been cursed with a seriously weak chin he would have been a handsome man. A chin implant probably would have changed his life. As it was, Heath noticed, Sam vacillated between arrogance and obsequiousness. Terry, his wife, said he worked as an apartment and condo manager for a company that rented real estate to vacationers by the week or month. Ostensibly this job was what brought the family from Coeur d'Alene, Idaho, to Boulder, Colorado. Terry was a part-time bookkeeper for an auto-body company. In her mid-to-late thirties, she ran to fat, twenty pounds or so overweight, no longer particularly obese by American standards. Her hair was the same color as Sam's, but hers was from a bottle. Overall she seemed pleasant: pleasant face, pleasant voice. Heath couldn't think of any serious drawbacks to her as a neighbor — or even as the mother of Elizabeth's best friend — except that Terry talked too much in general, and too much about her God and her husband in particular.

The moment she'd spot Heath outside, words would begin to flow, a river with no end in sight. Heath wasn't as quick at escaping as she'd been in her salad days. There was a long trek from the mailbox to the ramp beside the kitchen steps with nothing but a low hedge between her property and the Edlesons'. During these rolling social events, Heath had been informed in far more detail than she cared for that Sam was cut out for bigger things, Sam was unhappy in his job, Sam had always thought . . . God had a plan for Sam, but . . .

"I vaguely remember the Edlesons," Anna said, cutting into Heath's thoughts. "You had Paul and me over as backup when you invited them for dinner last summer."

Last summer. Heath was surprised. She'd thought she'd made it a point to socialize with her neighbors, and especially the parents of her daughter's best friend, at least two or three times in the past year. Evidently not. There'd always been an excuse not to set herself up for an evening of Sam's seesaw personality and Terry's mouth.

"I say hi whenever I see them," Gwen said. "Though if it's Mrs. Edleson, 'hi' can take a chunk out of one's day."

Elizabeth laughed. If the sound had been a dead fish, both Heath and Wily would have rolled in it. A child's laughter, particularly after tears, wasn't something Heath had ever fancied getting dewy-eyed over, but she was, and not for the first time, either.

"Well, me and Tiff —"

"Tiff and I," Gwen corrected, then looked abashed that she'd interrupted at such a time.

"You and Tiff," Heath said to get Elizabeth going again. She didn't want to give her time to reconsider that lie she'd seen sneaking across her face earlier.

"We were supposed to be looking after Brady, Tiff's little brother," she explained to Anna and Gwen, in case they'd forgotten about him. "He's a monster. A real monster — he bites and spits; he just never lets his mom see him doing it, so she thinks he's like this little angel and Tiff and I are the evil stepsisters or something. Anyway, we were supposed to be watching him because it was Wednesday night — remember, Mom? I wanted to go over even though we'd be babysitting so Tiff and I could decide what to wear on the last day of school? Not like it matters, but there's always stuff on the last day and, well, you know."

Heath nodded, though she didn't know, and didn't remember that particular Wednesday.

"Wednesday nights are big church nights. Usually Tiff and her brother both go, and sometimes her dad, but Brady had been pretending to have the flu all day, so Mrs. Edleson let him stay home if Tiff would watch him. Mr. Edleson stayed home, too, though I got the feeling Mrs. Edleson wasn't happy about that. Then, around eight or so, Brady disappeared to pull the wings off of flies or whatever —"

"Does the kid torture animals?" Anna asked darkly.

Elizabeth was untouched by the ice in her voice. "No," she said. "He's not like a little Hannibal Lecter in the making or anything. At least not that I've seen. He's mostly into torturing high school girls, as in Tiff and me.

"So Tiff went out to the backyard — you know what a big yard they have, part of it borders on the creek — because that's where the little monster likes to hide out in the dark and leap out and scare the bejesus out of us. I didn't want to deal, so I stayed in the living room, where we'd been watching boring kid movies to keep Brady happy.

"Turns out Tiff wasn't in the yard looking for Brady." Elizabeth faltered to a stop.

Heath, Anna, and Gwen waited in respectful silence. Heath wondered if they worked as hard as she did not to demand answers.

Elizabeth sighed deeply and resumed.

"Her dad had intercepted her coming in and sent her and Brady out for something at the drugstore. So, anyway, I was sitting on this big couch they have in the living room playing solitaire on my phone, and Mr. Edleson comes down from upstairs and sits on the couch and starts asking me the usual lame questions. How do I like school and what do I want to be when I grow up. Then he asks if I have a boyfriend, and I say don't I wish, and he starts in this long thing about some tribe in darkest wherever, and how fabulous it is that the old guys, uncles even — gross — introduce the virgins into womanhood. Way gross."

She looked up from where her hands were picking at the edge of a fray on the hem of her pajama top, swept an inclusive glance over Heath and the others, then returned to her hands. "It reminded me of something Father Sheppard would say."

Father Sheppard — Dwayne Sheppard — was the leader of the pseudo-Mormon cult Heath and Anna had rescued Elizabeth from when she was nine years old. Sheppard believed in multiple wives, the younger the better. Heath could feel her blood pressure rising. Anna and Gwen were as stone.

"Then what happened?" Gwen asked softly.

"He like put his hand on my thigh and leaned in and kissed me. A wet sloppy kiss that Wily would be disgusted by. I was, you know, so totally freaked, for a second I didn't do anything. I mean, I didn't kiss him back, but I just froze. I guess he thought I was saying what he was doing was okay." Elizabeth's eyes filled again, and her hands came up to hide her face.

Gwen took hold of Elizabeth's wrists, prying her hands from her cheeks. "You didn't do anything wrong. Nothing. Nada. Zip," she said firmly.

"And he didn't think what he was doing was okay," Anna said. "He's nearly forty, he is your best friend's father, and he's married. He knew it was not okay. You did not bring this on yourself. Mr. Edleson is a scumbag."

Anna rose to her feet. Heath, tuned in to the finer details of human locomotion, noticed she didn't move with the effortless grace she once had; still, she rose fluidly. Only the faintest of grunts and the crack of a knee or ankle attested to the effort.

"What are you doing, Anna?" Heath asked warily.

"I'm going to pay a call on the neighbors," she replied.

"Noooo," Elizabeth wailed.

"I'll take care of that end of things," Heath said, a hint of territorial challenge in her tone.

For a moment Anna swayed like grass in a gentle breeze. Heath waited to see if she would respect the role of mother or if she would go tear Sam Edleson's house down. Heath wasn't sure which outcome she was hoping for. Anna settled, folded down, and took up her position on the floor beside the sofa.

"Was that the whole of it?" Heath asked, sensing it wasn't and dreading the rest of the story.

"No," Elizabeth admitted. "While he was slobbering on me, and grabbing, Tiff came in. She hadn't gotten all the way to the drugstore. He'd given her the keys and told her to take Brady with her in the car! Tiff has a learner's permit, but it's not a good idea for her to be driving at night, even if it's only to the Walgreens. And not with Brady screaming and bouncing around."

Maybe because of what she'd been through in Sheppard's house of wives, Elizabeth seemed to censure Sam Edleson more for endangering his children than for making a sexual assault on her. At that moment, Heath loved her daughter so fiercely she thought she might explode.

"How long was she gone?" Anna asked. Heath moved rapidly from angry and proud of Elizabeth to shaking inside and terribly cold. Had the cretin stopped at a slimy kiss and a grope?

"If she'd've gone to the store, it would have been maybe half an hour. I don't know exactly. We've kind of quit speaking to each other. I guess she came back for something, and she came into the room while her dad was grabbing at me. I'd got over myself and was shoving and hitting to get him off me, and he was sort of flopping around. I don't know if he was trying to stay on me or get off me without getting kneed in the balls, because that was what I was trying to do.

"Tiff started screaming, and Mr. Edleson fell onto the floor. Right then Mrs. Edleson walked in, back way early from her church thing. It usually goes till nine."

"My guess is both Tiff and Terry felt there was something fishy going on," Anna said. "It probably wasn't the first time good old Sam had tried to get time alone with the girl next door. He may have been run out of Idaho for all we know. I'll check it out."

Elizabeth went on, "I managed to get up. Mr. Edleson had torn my blouse — not torn it, really, three of the buttons just popped off — and I was holding it shut, not knowing what else to do. Mrs. Edleson starts yelling, and Tiff stops screaming and starts yelling. Mr. Edleson is a creep, but I didn't want to hang around to watch him get chewed out. TMI big-time." Elizabeth stopped again and fell into what looked almost like a trance.

Staring at her hands, she turned them back and forth as if she'd never seen them before. After a few seconds Heath saw a tear fall like a raindrop on her left palm.

"Momma, they weren't yelling at *him*," she whispered. "They were yelling at *me*."

Six

It was late when Denise parked her Miata a few houses down from the address Paulette had given her when they were at the Acadian. Several days had passed, full days for Denise. Acadia was at the peak of its busy season. That wasn't the reason she'd put off visiting, however. Twice Paulette Duffy had called her cell. Denise hadn't picked up.

There was a lot to think about before she could distill even part of it into words. Paulette Duffy — Paulette — had had years to grow used to the idea. Until they'd met in the old lodge, Paulette had no proof, but she'd long had suspicions. Not Denise, not the trained law enforcement officer, taught to seek out disparities and make sense of them. Denise hadn't had a clue.

She had always been at pains to give as little thought as possible to her so-called family. Home wasn't "the place where, when you have to go there, they have to take you in," as Frost had written. Home was where, if you had to go there, you might as well put a gun in your mouth and blow your brains out. You'd be doing yourself a favor. The Denise who had suspicions was a deep-secret Denise, a Denise that Ranger Denise Castle had thought long dead.

Three days and two phone calls passed, and finally, at quarter past ten in the evening, Denise was parked on the outskirts of the small village of Otter Creek on a two-lane road that cut through a dollop of public land still extant in the midst of Acadia National Park.

When she'd first bought the Miata, the only concession to good sense she'd made was disabling the interior light, a practice customary in police vehicles. No sense in lighting oneself up for whatever miscreant might be waiting in the dark to take a potshot at the local constabulary.

Denise was grateful for that moment of sanity. Tonight she didn't want to be seen entering or leaving Paulette's place, wasn't sure she wanted the two of them to be associated with one another. Not sure she wanted any of it to be real. Not that she loved the devil she knew, but she was used to him. Paulette would change everything.

Moving quietly and casually, she sauntered

71

the hundred yards between her car and Paulette's cottage. Should one of the scattered residents happen to look out a window, she would appear to be an innocent out on a stroll enjoying the sweet-smelling night.

Paulette's home was what Denise's high school art teacher used to call a two-bit picture in a thousand-dollar frame. Because of its location, the smallish plot of land had to be worth a fortune. The tiny but picturesque shack squatting on it was hardly worth the match it would take to burn it down. It had to be family land. Paulette's husband's, Denise guessed. Had it belonged to Paulette, surely she would have sold it and run away on the proceeds.

Paulette's husband, Kurt Duffy, wasn't home. Paulette had said that in the text that finally brought Denise to Otter Creek.

She stepped into the deeper shadow of the dilapidated porch. Through the four frosted panes in the front door shone the bluish wavering light from a television. Either the volume was off or the old house had better soundproofing than its gaping weathered siding suggested.

Denise rapped lightly on the frame of the screen door.

The door opened so suddenly it startled

her. Paulette must have been waiting and watching for her. "Come in," she whispered, as if she shared Denise's desire for secrecy.

The house's interior was as sorry as its exterior. A battered, stained sofa, cigarette burns on the arms and one of the cushions, slumped against the left-hand wall, facing off with a huge television. The TV was the old-fashioned kind with a rounded glass front and three feet of tubes forming an ugly black hump on its back.

A scarred coffee table filled the space between, cup rings overlapping on the ruined finish, the surface littered with orange crumbs from a single-serving bag of Doritos. Blinds with broken slats, dents in the plaster walls, dirty finger marks on the woodwork, and the cracking linoleum floor attested to the misery Denise had sensed in the battered blonde on the barstool.

Nausea tinged with panic rose quivering and cold in Denise's midsection. Like Paulette's bruised face, the room was an outward manifestation of the ruin Denise carried inside herself. Scrupulous attention to her outsides kept it hidden. She hoped. Her apartment was spotless, neither cluttered nor Spartan; the art was tasteful, the dishes carefully selected. The same could be said for Denise — sharply pressed clothes, well-cut hair, clean unbitten nails, painstakingly maintained so no one would suspect that her life was no better than if she were living it out in this sad room.

Anger at the tawdriness of Paulette's house flared up, hot and bitter. This place was a slap in the face, insulting.

Paulette read her expression, or maybe her mind.

"It's not me," Paulette said hurriedly. "This room, it's not mine. What I mean is . . ." Shoving the ruin of bleached hair back from an eye now haloed in the faint yellows and greens of a fading bruise, she let her eyes wander over the desolate interior landscape. A sigh of such exhaustion Denise's anger was blown away on it emptied Paulette Duffy's lungs. "I made it nice, not rich, but orderly and clean, and, believe it or not, it had charm. I'm good with my hands."

Denise was good with her hands. For Peter's house she'd sewn curtains and created flower beds, stenciled bathrooms, and carved tiny animals on each kitchen drawer pull. For Peter's house. For Lily's house. For the baby's house.

"Kurt liked it once. Then, I guess, he knew how much it meant to me . . . I don't know. Things changed. Things got broken,"

Paulette finished with a resigned smile.

For Denise, too, things had changed. Things had gotten broken.

"Please, please, come," Paulette begged, and to Denise's surprise, Paulette took her hand and tugged her farther into the house. More to Denise's surprise, she didn't jerk her hand free. It was okay. It was good. It was right that her hand was in Paulette's hand. Nothing had ever been so right before. It was like she and Paulette were alone, alone together.

Paulette led her to the pathetic couch, where they sat side by side, knees almost touching. Paulette began to talk of the little girl she'd been. The joy she'd found in the tide pools, each a tiny universe of beings so incredible it was hard to believe they were real and alive.

Denise had felt the same.

Paulette spoke of a puppy she'd had in fourth grade. Rex, she'd called him. Rex was a mixed breed with dark mottled fur and a depth of intelligence in his canny brown eyes.

Denise, who hadn't been allowed pets — or much else in the way of comfort — had found solace in a stuffed dog, his fur mottled beige and brown. She'd named him Rex.

Paulette remembered winning the fifty-

and hundred-yard dash in track meets all through grade school.

Speed was one of Denise's strengths. Every morning until the snow got too deep, she ran five miles before breakfast. In a strange intoxicating way, Paulette was telling the story of Denise's life, not factually, of course, but perhaps the life another Denise Castle had lived in a parallel universe. Which, in a way, was the case.

At some point they moved to the kitchen, and Paulette made tea — not coffee, tea; not fancy, Lipton. Both women drank it unsweetened with a dash of lemon juice.

Seamlessly the conversation shifted to Denise, and she found herself telling not of the wretchedness of her bouncing around the foster system but of a pair of sunglasses, the lenses shaped like hearts, the plastic frames canary yellow, that she'd had in the second grade, her prize possession, then basking in the warmth of Paulette's throaty laugh of understanding.

Paulette's had been shaped like the eyes of a cat, the frames fire-engine red.

Paulette had grown up on Isle au Haut, the only child of a lobsterman and his wife. Her mother "did" for the summer people who kept houses there. Much of Isle au Haut was part of Acadia National Park, the southernmost patch in the patchwork quilt of federal lands.

In her work as a ranger, Denise had been by the tiny one-room school where the island kids went dozens of times. She'd been by Paulette's house. There had to have been times she had missed Paulette by hours, or even minutes.

At sixteen Paulette married Kurt Duffy, the son of a lobsterman who ran lines out of Frenchman Bay, and moved to the mainland, then to a tiny house on Otter Creek Road — a thin slice of public land cutting through the main bulk of the park on Mount Desert.

At sixteen Denise had planned to elope with a boy named Chuck Miles. He had been killed when a logging truck hit his Honda as he was coming to pick her up.

Paulette worked at Mount Desert Hospital.

Emergency medical work was Denise's favorite thing about being a ranger.

Paulette worked mostly nights. She loved the night.

Denise loved the night; she volunteered for the latest shifts.

Twice Paulette had gotten pregnant, and twice Kurt Duffy had beaten her so bad she lost the baby. After the second time she could never get pregnant again; there were complications.

Denise had gotten pregnant with Peter's child. He'd slaughtered it. Slaughtered all her children.

Kurt told Paulette that if she ever left him he would track her down and kill her.

Peter had made a family that Denise was not part of. A family with a baby.

Sometime after midnight they found themselves in the cramped bedroom Paulette shared with her husband when he chose to come home. Shoulder to shoulder, hip to hip, they sat on the edge of the queen-sized bed and stared at their reflections in the wide mirror over what had once been a fine dressing table. Denise's dark hair was pulled back from her face into a low-maintenance ponytail at the nape of her neck.

Paulette pulled her desiccated blond mop back and secured it with a scrunchie. Then they stared. Smoking had roughened the skin around Paulette's mouth, and the blow to her face had discolored the flesh around her left eye. Other than this, they were the same. The ears were identical; their noses were the same, a little long with a squared tip and thin nostrils. Their eyes were the same shade of blue. Each had a brown fleck in the iris of her left eye, dead center below the pupil. Paulette's eyebrows had been plucked, but the arch and the long winged taper matched Denise's.

"I always felt you out there," Paulette said, her voice soft with wonder. "When I was little, you were my playmate. Mom said you were my imaginary playmate. I knew better."

Denise said nothing. She was afraid if she spoke she would cry or, worse, the woman beside her would vanish.

"Did you sense that I was here?" Paulette asked timidly.

Denise shook her head, fascinated at watching her sister's — her identical twin sister's — lips move on precisely the same mouth as her own. "I felt you as not here." Denise tapped her chest over her heart. "Like I wasn't all here. I felt part of me had gone missing. I thought maybe the doctors had accidentally cut off some part of me when I was born. It confused me because I couldn't see any part the other kids had that I didn't. No extra toes or arms or anything. When I got a little older, maybe eight or nine, I lived with a fairly decent family that attended a Presbyterian church. For the eight months I was with them, I went to Sunday school every week along with their

79

kids. The teacher taught us that people had souls. After that, I assumed that I had accidentally been born without a soul. That that was the part that was missing.

"After that I put it out of my mind."

For another few minutes they sat in silence marveling at the faces in the mirror. Denise realized she must have known from the beginning that the battered blonde on the barstool was the part of her that had gone missing.

She had recovered her lost soul.

SEVEN

The specter of Sam Edleson filled the room with the stench of sulfur. Heath caught herself grinding her teeth and made herself stop.

"I'm going to make a few calls," Anna said, and slipped from the room as soft-footed as the apocryphal Indian.

Elizabeth excused herself to go to the bathroom.

Heath and Gwen waited in terror, neither saying anything, both afraid Elizabeth had gone to harm herself, both afraid they would never again feel safe when the girl was out of their sight.

"Should I go check on her?" Heath asked.

"No," Gwen said. Then, after a minute, "Do you think I should?"

"No."

Gwen began feverishly tidying the room. Heath pored over her daughter's cell phone, rereading the sordid texts, wanting to delete them but knowing she shouldn't. They were evidence. Elizabeth was adamant; she didn't want the police involved. Elizabeth was also sixteen. Heath wasn't sure police could do anything about the cyberattacks anyway. To ease the pressure, she finally allowed herself to delete one message. It was from herself to Elizabeth reminding her to put the wash in the dryer.

After what seemed a cruelly long time, Elizabeth returned. Relief flooded Heath when she saw she'd washed her face and combed her hair, signs of hope.

Then the three of them waited, Heath spinning her mental wheels. Gwen, having straightened every cushion, and aligned every book and magazine, sat on the sofa watching her great-niece with such intensity Elizabeth finally pelted her with a pillow.

Irritation, another sign the girl was beginning to engage in the world outside her misery.

Anna returned. "Edleson left his job in Idaho for making improper advances to a seventeen-year-old high school intern. In Idaho it's only a felony if the girl is sixteen or under. Nobody wanted to press charges, for all the usual reasons. The company didn't want to fire Edleson because of the adverse publicity and/or unemployment compensation. He was told to quit, and did. Shortly thereafter the family moved to Boulder." Having delivered the message in as few words as possible, Anna waited, her weight on the balls of her feet. Heath guessed she was hoping to be shot toward Sam Edleson as an arrow is shot from a bow.

"You called the cops!" Elizabeth cried.

"I did," Anna said. "The Coeur d'Alene, Idaho, police. They have no jurisdiction over you."

Reassured, Elizabeth's attention jumped to the next awful conclusion. "He's done it before?" she demanded, sounding shocked.

"Probably more than once," Anna said. "That's how these guys are."

"Then why were they yelling at *me*?" The indignation in her voice went far to soothe Heath. Because she was female, it was inevitable Elizabeth would be thinking she had done something wrong, brought this upon herself.

"Elizabeth, would you get my boots, please?" Heath asked.

"Which boots?" Elizabeth asked warily. "Your old climbing boots?" This last was asked with a small note of hope.

"Nope," replied Heath, dashing it. "The turquoise and silver." Elizabeth groaned. Almost said something, thought better of it, and levered herself up off the sofa cushions to vanish down the hall.

"What's with that?" Anna asked.

"Now we're going to pay that nice neighborly call," Heath said. Her voice came out flat and dark. Even if his wife and daughter lied to themselves and the world about Sam, Heath wanted him to know in no uncertain terms that she knew what he had done.

"No time like the present," Anna said.

"Good cop, bad cop?" Heath asked. She felt silly saying it, but it worked on television, and was the only plan that came to mind.

"Only if I can be the bad cop," Anna said without a trace of humor. "Are you going to wear your carapace?"

Heath thought she detected a note of excitement in Anna's voice. The electronic exoskeleton fascinated the ranger. Leah, whom Anna had gotten to know on their ill-fated trip down the Fox River, had strapped Anna into the prototype. Though she'd fought the machine as if it were trying to take over her body, she'd come to respect and admire it. Whenever Heath used it, Anna would whistle through her teeth or shake her head and mutter, "I'll be damned."

"Not tonight," Heath said. "I've used up

my quota of energy on that scale. Robo-butt will have to do the heavy lifting."

"Let me get my —" Gwen began.

Heath cut her off. It was best not to let the juggernaut pick up any speed. Gwen lacked self-control around people who harmed children. Though Heath wanted to rend the Edlesons limb from limb, burn their house down, and sow the land with salt so nothing would grow there for a thousand years, she suspected she would gather a lot more workable leverage and information by using subtle threats and blackmail.

"I don't think this is a good time to leave Elizabeth home alone," Heath said.

"Of course not," Gwen agreed immediately. "I'll make a fresh pot of tea." She smiled wearily. "It's good to have something to hate that can easily be dumped down the drain."

As if he understood every word that passed, Wily heaved himself to his paws with a sigh and made ready to follow them. "Protect the children and old people," Heath said fondly as she rubbed his head. There was a time she would have taken him. He was courageous and as wily as his namesake, but the years were creeping up on him.

Elizabeth returned carrying a pair of worn but beautiful turquoise cowboy boots with silver threading. "What's wrong with your sneakers?" Elizabeth asked forlornly. "Or even your hiking boots?"

"Tonight I intend to kick some ass," Heath replied. Elizabeth flopped down, her body awkward, her resentment obviously at war with what Heath suspected was the joy of having a champion, regardless of whether she rides out on a white horse or in a gray wheelchair.

Gentle, as she always was when touching her adoptive mother, Elizabeth waved away Heath's hands and put the boots on her feet for her.

"Aren't those a bit dressy for an unannounced call?" Gwen remarked, coming in from the kitchen with the threatened pot of tea.

"Power suit," Elizabeth said.

Anna said nothing, following as Heath rolled toward the front door.

The sun was behind the mountains, and though it wasn't dark, shadows pooled and the sky had grown soft and infinite. The day's warmth was drifting away from the skin of the mountains on a gentle down-canyon breeze carrying the scent of pine.

Lights were beginning to come on in the

neighborhood, people home from work and cooking supper. Sam's truck was in the drive, an outsized Dodge Ram that one should not keep if one doesn't own a ranch where it can run and play. Expertly, Heath wheeled around it. Fortunately, the Edlesons' house had a wide brick walk and a front door without a step, a rarity Heath hadn't noticed before her disability. Given this was to be a confrontation, she was glad she didn't have to be dragged up a front stoop, then wait while Robo was hauled clanking up behind like an albatross.

When they arrived at the door, Anna reached over Heath's head and banged the frame of the screen door. There was a doorbell, but Heath was happier with the "Open up. Police!" sound of Anna's knuckles and left it alone. Disquiet murmured from inside, muttering, then silence, as if a television set had been switched off.

More silence.

"Curtains twitched at two o'clock," Anna murmured. Heath had caught the tiny movement from the corner of her eye — Sam or Terry or Tiffany peeking out the front-room windows to see who was at the door. The phrase "at two o'clock" threatened to make her giggle hysterically, and she wondered when her anger had turned to fear. Heath had no fear that Sam would do them physical damage. Bizarrely enough, given she would probably come out on the wrong end of a physical encounter with a well-muscled man, she would have welcomed that. A compulsion to feel his flesh under her fists — or between her teeth — coursed through her so fiercely that, for a second, she felt she could rise from her chair and kick the door down. Her fear was that something she or Anna might say or do would make it worse for Elizabeth.

Anna banged again, louder and longer this time. Heath didn't allow herself to wince.

She was beginning to think the Edlesons weren't going to answer the door when she heard the bolt thunk back. The door opened halfway. No lights were on in the front room. The one in the kitchen, a light Heath had noticed when they crossed the drive, had been turned off. Dim behind the screen door, Terry stared out at them, her eyes like black holes in a dead-gray face.

"Hi, Terry," Heath said pleasantly. "This is Anna Pigeon, a friend of the family and, for the moment, chief chair wrangler." She smiled crookedly. Poor little paraplegic couldn't hurt a fly. It wasn't one of Heath's favorite strategies, but she wasn't above using it now and then if she thought it would give her the upper hand. Maybe she heard a faint snort from Anna; she wasn't sure. "Could we come in for a minute?"

Terry didn't want to let them in. She was breathing hard through pinched nostrils. Heath could hear each sniff. Terry's lips, usually full and soft-looking, were pressed into a tight little frown.

"I'm afraid I don't handle the chill of evening as well as I did before . . ." Smiling again, Heath waved a hand over her lap to indicate just how very sad and debilitated she was. Terry still didn't want to let them in, but, like a lot of people, she was intimidated by the wheelchair. How could she say no? Heath was a *cripple,* for Christ's sake. The door opened a bit more, and Heath got a wheel in, then, with a push from Anna, she was over the sill and into the house. All Terry could do was get out of the way so Heath wouldn't run over her feet.

Before the fall from Keystone, Heath had been brash and ballsy. After, she had been angry and self-destructive. When she finally realized that, though she couldn't walk, she was still a whole person, she found she'd changed. From the bastion of Robo-butt, the world was different, more layered and complex. Heath learned patience. She learned to watch people, to really listen, to genuinely *see* them. Something she'd not done much of when she was superwoman climbing tall mountains. Another skill she'd picked up was canniness, an ability to manipulate situations to her advantage, to manipulate people when she had to. Cunning wasn't a strength much lauded in literature or the media, but it was a strength all the same, and Heath respected it.

Once they had breached the walls, as it were, Terry's mood didn't warm. She did, however, assume the role of hostess, offering them coffee. Anna didn't accept. Heath did. Hard to toss somebody out before they've finished their drink. She parked herself advantageously, blocking the big, leather, man-of-the-house chair so the only remaining seating was on a couch that was too soft or a straight-backed chair that was too hard. She didn't want Goldilocks getting too comfortable.

Anna leaned against a dark wood highboy, her ankles crossed, her arms crossed, looking deceptively relaxed.

In the minute it took for this arrangement, Terry was back with two cups of coffee on a tray along with a bowl of powdered creamer and half a dozen packets of Sweet'N Low. "Sure you won't have anything?" she asked Anna politely. Being the hostess, probably

90

along with the fact that neither Heath nor Anna had lit into her, seemed to have dialed her hostility down a notch. Coffee served, Terry perched on the edge of the couch, her mug hands as plump and white as the Pillsbury Doughboy's. Where there should have been knuckles there were babyish dimples. The rest of her was as amorphous; her bland oval face just missed being pretty due to a lack of definition in her features.

"The girls haven't been seeing much of one another lately," Heath opened conversationally.

"That's so," Terry said, then took a careful sip of her coffee. "I think it will be good for them to have a little time just with family." She was recovering her equilibrium. Heath wanted none of that.

"So do I," she said flatly.

Terry looked up, annoyed or startled. Sam appeared behind her, backlit in the kitchen doorway, shoulder against one side of the frame. His hair was tousled, that nice gold-shot Robert Redford hair, and he wore a plaid shirt half unbuttoned. Heath suspected he'd been in the bathroom primping until this entrance.

"I know you sexually assaulted Elizabeth," Heath said to Sam. "Elizabeth's sixteen. In Colorado that makes your behavior child

91

molestation. A felony."

Sam stopped leaning. He, at least, was scared. Not so Mrs. Edleson. Clacking her mug down on the tray, she tried to nail Heath to the wall with a malevolent glare. "Now see here, Heath, Sam didn't do anything! Do you hear me? Your daughter, your *adopted* daughter, is no better than she should be, and you don't know the half of it."

Heath looked over Terry's head. "Sam, I know you arranged to be alone with Elizabeth, then assaulted her. I'm thinking the only reason it wasn't rape was that your wife and daughter got wind of it and came home before they were supposed to."

Terry was on her feet. "Your daughter made advances to my husband!" she shrieked, looking like she might fly at Heath and claw her eyes out.

Anna's voice cut cold from where she still leaned against the sideboard, ankles crossed. "Elizabeth's sixteen. Sam's forty —"

"Thirty-eight," he interrupted, his first words since entering the fray.

"She's a minor. He touched her. Either way it's a felony. Either way Sam goes to jail," Anna finished.

Terry quivered, fumed, sat, took up her coffee cup, breathed, sipped. "There's no need for that kind of talk," she said softly. "There's no need to embarrass yourself — or your daughter — by calling the police. I don't blame Elizabeth. Girls like Sam. He's a very handsome man."

A snort from the sideboard, and a murmured "Chinless wonder."

Heath suppressed a smile. Terry pretended not to hear. Sam's hand flew to hide the lower half of his face.

"Elizabeth made a pass at Sam," Terry said. The threat of jail hadn't silenced her, but it had toned her down.

"Just like the girl in Idaho made a pass at Sam?" Anna asked. She pushed out from the table she'd been tucked against and stepped into the light from the kitchen. Menace radiated from her. Heath could never figure out how she did it. It was just there, palpable, a sense of imminent threat that could be felt against the skin of the mind.

"That girl . . . that girl was . . . she . . ." Terry, her righteous anger temporarily damped, was flailing for words to fan it back to life. Heath took this moment of vulnerability to unlock Elizabeth's cell phone and open a text. Wheeling close enough that she bumped Terry's knees, she thrust the cell phone into the other woman's hands, where she couldn't miss the photo of a woman and a dog fornicating.

"Is that why you sent this to my daughter?" Heath demanded. Terry dropped the pink cell phone as if it were a used tissue.

"This is sick," Terry hissed at Heath. "Your daughter is disgusting and sick. This proves it."

Sam pushed his wife aside, then reached down to retrieve the phone. Heath watched him narrowly as he turned the phone right side up on his palm and pushed the button to unlock it. "Shit!" he said in what sounded like genuine shock. Terry tried to slap it from her husband's hand, but he dodged her blow. Anna moved from the shadows to stand behind Heath's chair. Making plans for a quick retreat, no doubt.

Before the Edlesons could stop their squabble to launch a counterattack, Heath broke into their concentration.

"Sorry to introduce that into your world so suddenly," she said acidly. "Someone has been using the Internet and cell phones — Twitter, texting, you name it — to cyberstalk Elizabeth. I need to find out who is behind it. Since the girls were at odds, I thought Tiff might be able to help me."

"Tiff had nothing to do with that!" Terry snarled. "Nothing. I kept her away from your . . . *daughter.*" She made the word sound like an epithet. "Because Tiff is a good girl." Terry's doughy round face hardened and took on a sly look. "Since there is no problem, but you are trouble-makers, what about I help you, and you promise not to try and get my Sam in trouble with the police?" she asked shrewdly.

"I promise," Heath said solemnly.

"What about you?" Terry glared at Anna.

"Elizabeth doesn't want the police in-volved," Anna said.

"We don't know anything about these . . . these filthy things," Terry said. "We don't know people who even know where to get filth like that. Nobody we know would ever *get* anything like on your daughter's phone. There. Now we're out of it. That's all the help I can give you."

The bitch was throwing it back on Eliza-beth. Heath said nothing, and that nothing burned in her throat like fire on gasoline.

Sam, still staring at the phone, as if loath to take his eyes from the image of the woman and the dog for fear it would van-ish, sat down on the sofa with a thump. "I've never seen anything like this stuff." He was thumbing forward on the touch screen, no doubt hoping for more.

Terry snatched the phone from her husband's hands. Heath was willing to bet she knew what Sam was, knew the lies she told herself so she could stay in the marriage.

"Is Tiff home?"

"You are not going to show this to Tiffany!" Terry exclaimed in horror. Marching over, she dropped the phone in Heath's lap with an exaggerated moue of distaste.

"The girls are estranged," Heath said. "Maybe Tiffany is doing this because she's angry, because you told her Elizabeth tried to seduce her dad."

"Tiff wouldn't do this," Sam said. "Tiff wouldn't even know what this is."

Heath could feel Anna hovering behind her like a brewing storm cloud. She shot her a warning glance; they needed to talk to Tiff. "I don't need to show her the photograph," Heath said with as much patience as she could muster. "But I would like to talk to her. The girls are close; Tiffany might know who wants to hurt Elizabeth."

Terry's eyes narrowed. "We're done here," she said. "Take your daughter's filth and get out."

"We need to talk to Tiffany," Heath insisted. "If you want to be around when we do, go and get her."

Sam stood, trying to pull his manhood up around him despite the missing chin. "You

heard my wife," he said, and took a threatening step toward Heath.

Anna moved from the shadows behind
Robo-butt. Her right arm shot out, stiff and
sudden, the heel of her hand catching him
in the solar plexus. With an *oof* he sat again,
his moment of macho a thing of the past.

"The girls are not close," Terry hissed. She
stomped past Anna and jerked open the
front door. "Elizabeth brought this on
herself. She probably gets stuff like that all
the time. She probably likes it."

Anna had turned the wheelchair so Heath
was facing the harridan at the door.
Throughout this adventure in futility Heath
had remained relatively calm. Terry's smugness and accusations blasted her self-
control. The old Heath rose from the ashes
of the one born of the ice fall. Heath never
moved, but she saw, actually saw, an image
of herself rise from her chair like a zombie
from the grave, arms outstretched, fingers
curled into claws the better to tear out and
devour the flesh of Terry Edleson's throat.
Maybe Terry saw the projection. Heath
didn't know. All she knew was that a look of
abject, pants-wetting terror deformed the
other woman's face.

Heath bared her teeth and braced her
hands on the arms of her chair. Murder

could be done in a state such as this. Had her legs been viable, she would have probably left the Edlesons in a squad car, never to see the outside of a prison cell again. As it was, blind rage could not be sustained more than a moment. Anna swept up behind her. Heath leaned back into the loving embrace of Robo-butt to be rolled unceremoniously over the sill and onto the brick walk. "You assaulted Sam," Terry shouted. "I helped you! So you can't call the police. They won't believe you. You promised!" She glared at Heath.

"I did," Heath said.

"You are a witness," she yelled at Anna.

"I am," Anna said.

The door slammed. The dead bolt thudded into place.

For a moment Heath and Anna stared at the door.

"Now we call the police?" Anna asked.

"Now we call the police," Heath agreed.

Empty and exhausted, she slumped back in the seat and said nothing more, letting Anna push her down the walk. The long summer dusk had settled into true night. A streetlight made shadows stark and colorless on the concrete sidewalk beside the asphalt. Black and white, Heath thought, and missed a time when she saw right and wrong that clearly delineated.

"Ms. Jarrod?" came a whisper.

Anna stopped pushing. Heath came out of her slump into full alert.

"Ms. Jarrod, it's me, Tiffany." The girl, her blond hair gray in the cold light, separated herself from the side of her dad's truck and crouched down by Robo-butt. At first, Heath thought it a sign of unusual sensitivity in a teenager, but realized it wasn't. Tiffany didn't want her parents to see her consorting with the enemy.

"I gotta get back," Tiff said. "Tell Elizabeth it's not me; my folks won't let me call. They took my phone and my laptop and I'm like in a black hole. I can't call anybody or get on Facebook or anything! I hope she's okay. Tell her I'll write her and put the note under the hedge where we used to crawl through when we were little kids. Nobody'd ever think of that."

"Elizabeth's being cyberstalked," Anna said curtly. "Do you know who's behind it?"

"I know about the stalking — everybody at school does. I don't know —"

"Tiffany!"

"Gotta go. I know what Dad . . . I . . . gotta go." She stood and ran, probably hoping to get back inside the house before Mom and Dad figured out she'd defected.

Anna pushed. Robo-butt rolled. Heath rode. Only the crunch of the chair's rubber tires on bits of escaped gravel accompanied them back to the kitchen door. Gwen, Elizabeth, and Wily were waiting for them on the couch, tense and wide-eyed.

Anna parked the chair, then sank down in her former place. Heath set the brakes.

"Well, open the envelope, for heaven's sake!" Gwen exclaimed.

"No winner," Heath said wearily. "It probably isn't Tiff, which is good news. She couldn't, her folks confiscated her cell phone and her laptop."

"Gosh," Elizabeth breathed, evidently shocked at the draconian nature of the punishment. "What did she do?"

"She saw," Anna said.

"Tiff said she would write you about it and leave the note under the hedge where you kids used to crawl back and forth to each other's yards," Heath said.

"On paper?" Elizabeth asked.

"No. She's going to scratch it on a piece of slate with a stylus," Heath retorted.

"That Tiffany wasn't doing it, that's good, isn't it?" Gwen asked.

"Not really," Heath said.

"We haven't a clue as to who is behind it," Anna said. "So we have no way to make it stop. Nobody to come down on. We don't have a motive. We don't, do we, Elizabeth?" The adults again stared at the teenager in her pj's like hawks at a baby duckling.

"No," Elizabeth said sadly. "At school everybody likes me, or I don't even know them. You know how it is. There's a bunch of boys who make a game of getting girls to have sex with them, and they keep score. They're creeps, and they've done some creepy things — you know, posting about the girls who put out, and even meaner posts about the ones that didn't. Both Tiff and I got asked sort of out by one of their bottom feeders — not like a date or anything, just stupid stuff by a guy who wants to be in on the game but is a total loser. Maybe the creep boys could be doing it. I don't think so, though. I mean, at school, I'm not all that *important*. Why take the trouble to stalk me? I'd probably be worth, like, half a point."

"Half a point?" Anna asked.

"You know, a cheerleader's worth five points, a girl on the student council two points. Like that."

"Time to cull the gene pool," Anna murmured.

"God, I'm glad you're here, Anna," Heath burst out as a boil of anxiety burst inside her. "For all we know this could turn to physical stalking."

Anna said after a moment: "Starting next week, I've got a twenty-one-day detail in Acadia National Park. Acting chief ranger. Their chief is fighting that big fire in Southern California."

This last was said without affect, but Heath knew it rankled with her friend. Like many rangers, Anna neighed and fretted like an old war horse when fire season came around. Heath couldn't understand this love of fighting wildfire. For some it was about overtime and hazard pay.

For others it was an addiction. Anna belonged to the latter group. She'd taken a bullet during the Fox River adventure, and her left arm never fully recovered. Though Anna'd never admit it, she probably hadn't the strength to swing a Pulaski for long.

To be acting chief in a park as important as Acadia would be welcomed by most rangers, a nice step up the ladder to being permanent chief somewhere else. Anna had dithered about the promotion to district ranger. Money meant little to her. Being out of doors and away from human beings meant a lot.

"You're leaving?" Elizabeth wailed.

Heath flinched, not because her daughter

cried out like an abandoned five-year-old but because, for an instant, she thought she'd done it herself and was mortified.

"They don't need you!" Heath said, then stooped to threats. "They're liable to give you a promotion."

"I'll be sure and offend the higher-ups," Anna said with a dry smile.

"Send someone else," Heath said, hating the whine in her words.

"Wildfires in California. Everybody is short-handed," Anna said.

Heath said no more. She'd already said too much.

Gwen, whose usual upbeat enthusiasm seemed to have been squelched by the points game and creeps and stalkers, perked up. "Acadia National Park? In Maine? Of course in Maine! For heaven's sake, I'm getting dotty. My first job out of med school was near there. I have to make some calls. Heath, Elizabeth, pack. We are going to Maine with Anna!"

Gwen kissed the air around everybody's cheeks, snatched up her black medical bag, and blew out on the wind the way she had blown in.

"Mary Poppins," Heath laughed.

"Who does Aunt Gwen know in Maine?" Elizabeth asked.

"Dez Hammond and Chris Zuckerberg. A couple of old hippies from the day," Heath said. Heath had met them on two occasions when they'd visited Boulder. She remembered liking them. "Chris comes from money. She inherited an island off Acadia. They spend most of their time rehabbing an old mansion and hosting artists."

"Where's Arcadia?" E asked.

"Acadia," Anna corrected. "Northern Maine, lobsters and nor'easters."

"I'm going to be marooned on an island with four old ladies," Elizabeth cried.

"In a crumbling old mansion," Heath said.

"You'll be there, won't you?" Elizabeth begged Anna.

Heath was annoyed that, though she had more years under her belt than Heath, Anna was not among the designated Old Ladies.

"Not me," Anna said. "A desert isle in the vast Atlantic? Too boring for this child."

Elizabeth groaned.

EIGHT

"Do you want to see where I really live?" Paulette asked. The question should have seemed sudden or peculiar, but it wasn't. In her core — her soul if the metaphor held — Denise knew her twin, her other self, could not truly live in this tragic wreck of a place with paper peeling from the walls and ancient linoleum curling at the corners and buckling along the seams.

They stood at the same instant, laughing at themselves and one another simultaneously. Denise felt as if scales, dirt, fragments of rotting lumber, cracking mortar, and broken roof slates were sliding off her. In the dim light of the bedroom's single shaded lamp, Denise imagined she could see dust rising from the cascade of debris as her old, worn-out, worthless, piece-of-shit life crumbled. When the dust settled, a new, clean, sun-filled life would be built around her and her sister. Denise communicated none of this. Paulette, she was positive, was feeling the same sense of sloughing off a diseased and decrepit skin.

Wordlessly, Paulette led the way through a dilapidated kitchen — appliances right out of Sears circa 1970 — and through the back door of the cottage. As they crossed the small weedy yard, a children's swing set, one chain broken, a rotted seat dangling like a broken limb, formed the yard's epitaph.

Paulette reached out. Hesitantly, Denise took her hand and was led into the black night forest.

"I don't go home much, and I always go a different way," Paulette whispered as they made their way through the darkness beneath the trees. "If Kurt found out, he'd spoil it just to be mean; just because he likes to hurt me by ruining my things. He thinks it's funny. Hitting isn't enough. He can't hurt me bad enough with his fists short of putting me in the hospital, which costs a lot, or killing me."

Holding tightly to Paulette's hand, Denise followed blindly, her story — her sister's story, their story — surging through her veins and arteries, down the capillaries until each and every cell in her body was caught up. Waves of fury crashed over deep valleys of sorrow; seas of compassion rose and receded. It had been a while since Denise had felt anything for anyone but herself. The hatred she harbored for Peter had hardened into bitterness. Wormwood and gall had been all she could taste, smell, see, touch.

Dead; she'd been dead to herself in every way that counted. Coming alive in this womb of pine-scented darkness, her hand warm and safe in her twin's, was so overwhelming she staggered like a drunk and fell to her knees, dragging Paulette with her.

Denise felt her sister patting her hand. "Shh, shh," Paulette murmured softly. "It's okay. We're together." Those words were the first and only lullaby Denise had ever heard. She began to cry.

Usually sick helplessness came on the heels of Denise's crying jags. This time, when the tears finally stopped, she felt renewed, as if the tears were poisons her body had expelled.

"We're almost there." Paulette's voice came from the darkness. Denise allowed the gentle tugging to bring her to her feet. "This land belonged to Kurt's mom," Paulette whispered as they crept along. "His grandma lived here. When she died we moved in. It's not like a city lot. It's only about forty feet wide where the house is, but it runs way way back, getting skinnier and skinnier like the tail of a comet. Kurt doesn't care anything about it except that it's his. I wanted him to sell at least part of it because he could get a lot of money for it and we wouldn't have to live in a shack. 'Shack's good enough for the likes of you' was his big-deal answer. If he ever found this, he'd kill me.

"We're here." Paulette let go of Denise's hand. The connection broken, for a second Denise felt as though she were falling, falling and freezing. It was only a dream: the twin, her soul, the Acadian blond barfly. All of it. A dream. A wail rose in her throat, as lonely as the howl of the last wolf on earth. The sound of fumbling, the scratch of a match being lit, then a flame that, born into such a lightless universe, hit Denise's eyes with the force of a supernova, aborted the cry.

Her sister was there. No dream. Tears began to flow again. No paroxysms of grief or wrenching sobs, only warmth and joy in liquid form. Fleetingly, Denise remembered a self that was not given to emotion, a self made stoic by life. No more. In the past months emotions came in sudden overwhelming waves. These were the first that

108

didn't threaten to tear her apart.

Paulette lit an old kerosene lamp she took from beneath a rusted overturned bucket, adjusted the wick, then handed the lamp to Denise to hold. They were standing at the door of a small shed. The eaves cleared Paulette's head by less than six inches. They would have to stoop to pass through the door without banging their skulls.

By the light of the lamp, Paulette found a short piece of dirty frayed string caught in a crack between two pieces of weathered siding. She pulled it out to reveal the key tied to the end.

"There are so many park visitors, folks would be wandering in all the time," she explained as she turned the key in the padlock that secured the door. "Visitors don't seem to know what's public land and what's private."

"Or care," Denise said.

Paulette pushed open the door, stepped inside, took the lamp, and held it up so Denise could see the room. Bitterness vanished. Delight took its place. The room — the entire house — wasn't more than a hundred and fifty square feet, roughly twelve by twelve, and the ceiling closer to seven feet than eight. On each of the four walls was a large many-paned window, the mullions, frames, and sills clean and painted white, the glass old, from back when glass had ripples and imperfections in it. The walls were painted soft gray, the color of a dove's breast, and hung with pieced fabric stretched over wooden frames, the bright bits of cloth making flowers and mountains, trees and ponds.

On the worn planks of the floor was a simple rag rug. A white crib with a small stuffed bear looking through the bars, a three-drawer chest painted China red, a round table with a lamp of the same color, and a rocking chair completed the nursery. Nothing fussy, nothing out of place, everything clean and necessary and beautiful.

As Paulette closed the door behind them, Denise walked around the room. The windows weren't windows at all. Frames with glass, sills, and half-pulled shades had been mounted on the wall. Behind them were paintings of a forest, much as it might look were the windows real and she was looking through them in the early morning. Shafts of sunlight slanted through dark trunks. The shadows of leaves dappled a small green clearing. Wildflowers surrounded a granite boulder. A bunny grazed fearlessly on new grass.

"I didn't dare make any changes to the

outside," Paulette said. "Kurt doesn't come back here, but when people can look in, they can break in, and will. And if Kurt did come this way for some reason, I didn't want to call attention to this old shed."

"He'd ruin it," Denise said. It wasn't a question. She knew he would as if she'd been with Paulette each time he'd made a wreck of what little beauty she'd managed.

Denise reached over the bars of the crib and laid a finger between the stuffed bear's ears. Though she'd never had much in the way of toys — at least not new ones — this one felt familiar to her.

"Kurt's a monster. A big fucking monster," Paulette blurted out.

At the outburst of obscenity, Denise turned to her sister.

Paulette laughed and covered her mouth the way Denise had done until Peter told her it made her look childish. Child*like,* she thought as she watched her twin. Childlike and charming. Another thing Peter had taken from her.

"I've never said that out loud before. Awful as it is, it felt good to say it. Isn't that weird?"

Denise didn't know what to say. It wasn't weird. Not at all. None of this was weird. All of it was exactly how it should be. That was what was weird.

Paulette sat in the rocking chair and let Denise explore the small ornamental boxes, the few books, the fabric art. "When I got pregnant the first time, I bought all these wonderful things for the baby's room. Then, you know, I lost the baby. Kurt said I had to take them back if I'd bought them, or sell them on eBay or whatever if they'd been gifts from my mom and dad — they were still alive then. But I couldn't. I just couldn't. I dragged them all back to this shed and told Kurt I'd given them to Goodwill. He half beat me to death for not getting any money for them. The second time I got pregnant, we got a few more things. Not as many. Mom and Daddy had passed. They were pretty old when they adopted me and died within three months of each other.

"I did the same thing with the new stuff; told Kurt I'd given it away. After that, I used to come out here and kind of fix things up, thinking it would be a nice place for the new baby. I got my nursing degree and started working at Mount Desert Hospital with newborns and infants."

"A nurse!" Denise was pleased. Another thing they had in common: nurse/ranger. Both were jobs helping people.

"When I found out there weren't going to be any more babies," Denise said with a shrug, "I just sort of kept on coming out here to get out of Kurt's sty for a while and remember who I am."

It was easy to forget who you were, Denise thought. She'd forgotten. No, she and Paulette had not forgotten who they were; who they were had been taken from them and thrown into the garbage. Forever, Denise had thought. Now here it was, her true *self,* with her sister's *self,* in an empty nursery in the woods.

"Peter's baby's name is Olivia," she said without thinking. "Olivia Barnes. The name I got was Castle. Now you're Duffy. What was your name before that?"

"Mallory, Paulette Mallory. The Mallorys adopted me. They were good people."

"Then when we're together, I won't be Denise Castle. I will be Denise Mallory," Denise said, and they both smiled.

Paulette stood, the chair still rocking as if her ghost remained behind, and walked over to a small painted table between windows half open on an imaginary forest. "I had time to get used to the idea of us, remember me saying that?" She didn't wait for Denise to answer, as if knowing that, of course, Denise remembered. Miracles tend to stick in

113

memory, and everything about finding a twin sister was miraculous. "I felt you, but then these started appearing in the newspapers in the personal ads. I've only found three. They could be in papers in Bangor and Portland and other places. We only get the local stuff. I've never bothered to try and do a search. I wouldn't know where to begin. Here." She handed Denise a clipping from a newspaper. It wasn't much bigger than the slip of paper found in a fortune cookie. "That one I came across four years ago and for some reason just cut it out and kept it."

Denise turned the bit of newsprint toward the lamp and made out the blurred message. *Seeking identical twins, female, born on the sixth of March and separated at birth. They would now be thirty-seven years of age. Urgent they contact me. Family legacy. If you believe you may be such a person send a postcard to P.O. Box 1597, Post Office, Bar Harbor, ME.*

"March sixth, our birthday," Paulette said.

"No name or zip code," Denise said.

"This one was from year before last." Paulette handed her another scrap. The message was the same but, this time, included a zip code. Still no name. "And this is from January this year."

114

"The legacy," Denise said. Her brain, unable to absorb so much so quickly, had slowed to a crawl for the moment. "It would be money, wouldn't it?"

"Or maybe a house or land, like that," Paulette said.

"Our birth parents, do you think?" Denise asked, not sure whether she would be overjoyed or furious if she were ever to lay her eyes on her birth mother or biological father.

"Maybe," Paulette said. "Or another relative."

"A lawyer," Denise said, unwilling to have any more relatives at the moment, wanting to be just sisters alone in a magical cabin in the woods. "We're the right age, aren't we?"

"And female and twins and separated at birth. How many can there be?"

"You'd be surprised," Denise said, remembering all the studies done on identical twins separated at birth.

"Born on the sixth of March? Girls who would be forty-one years old now, thirty-seven when I found the ad," Paulette said. "The babies must have been from around here, or who would run the ad in a tiny town like Bar Harbor?"

Before Denise could think of another reason the ad wasn't for them, the sound of sleigh bells or wind chimes leaked into the room, tinny and cheap.

Paulette pulled a cell phone out of her pocket and looked at the face of it, then up at Denise.

"It's him!" she whispered with all the terror of a trapped bird. Denise could hear her sister's frantically beating wings inside her own skull.

"I have to answer," Paulette said pleadingly.

Denise nodded. Of course she had to answer. If she didn't, Kurt would kill her.

Denise sat on a tiny chair with a rattan seat and a cavalry trumpet carved into the top slat on the back, a perfect, plain, lovely chair for a child, and listened as her sister made excuses for not being in the house when her husband called the home phone; listened to her lie about where she was and who she was with; watched tears roll over Paulette's cheeks, and the way her lips curved down as she rocked herself, begging him not to be mad, promising to be at the house next time.

When she was finally able to hang up, she let the hand with the phone in it fall as if lifeless beside the rocking chair.

"Kurt really is going to kill you," Denise realized suddenly.

Paulette nodded. "I've felt it for a while. He hasn't said anything, and hasn't hit me much, and not real hard. But I know he's planning on killing me and burying my body under the house. When he looks at me I can see it in his eyes as clear as anything. I can see him thinking about how he's going to get the shovel and hide it under the house so it will be ready."

Denise had spent her life in law enforcement. There was no evidence Kurt was plotting murder. He hadn't said he was. He'd laid no concrete plan. Yet Paulette felt it, saw it in his eyes, and believed her husband was planning to murder her.

Denise did, too. She, too, could see it.

This seeing of things hidden wasn't new. It had been growing for months. Change had crept into Denise around the time the park was informed Lily was pregnant with Peter's child. Though subtle, creeping, the change was in both mind and body. Her body responded with small betrayals of the kind that had let the lobster escape. Her mind responded by focusing ever more sharply, by knowing — sometimes — what was in the minds of those around her, just as she now knew her sister believed Kurt would kill her, and knew that Kurt, her *brother-in-law,* did, in fact, plan to murder

117

his wife.

Paulette was her identical twin. Denise knew without asking that she, too, had come to see things that others had hidden in their hearts.

"Kill him first," Denise said, and was mildly surprised that the idea was not shocking. Killing Kurt Duffy was no more than a simple act of self-defense.

"They'd know it was me. Everybody knows he beats me. Not that they care. They'd know it was me. I'd go to jail forever."

"Not if you had a solid alibi," Denise said.

NINE

"Everything is so green and blue," Aunt Gwen said for perhaps the third time. Her red curls as wild as Medusa's snakes in the wind, she was yelling over her shoulder to Heath. Robo-butt, with Heath in it, and Wily grinning on her lap, was firmly lashed in the aft of a small outboard motorboat piloted by a gruff cliché of a New Englander. At least seventy, maybe older, he smelled strongly of tobacco and bay rum, had a couple of days' worth of beard, squinted from a leathery face, and clenched an unlit pipe in his teeth. Central Casting couldn't have done it better, Heath thought.

Aunt Gwen sat in the seat next to him, no doubt charming the pants off Matthew. Luke? Something biblical and manly. Elizabeth, her back toward the rest of them, perched on a gunwale to Heath's right, her mouth set in a rigid line that added years to her face. The rest of the boat's limited deck space was piled with the women's luggage.

Anna had been sent to Acadia several days earlier. Left in Boulder, Heath felt childishly helpless and exposed without her friend. It was embarrassing. A big chunk of the eleven days since Heath found E in the bath with the Lady Schick had been spent getting ready for this trip. The other chunks had been spent watching Elizabeth turn from the compassionate, resilient girl she'd watched grow up to an angry, whining teenager, whom she felt like she didn't know.

Who she sometimes felt hated her.

The change depressed and confounded Heath. E wanted to escape the bullying, yet seemed angry and afraid to leave it behind, as if, unattended, it would metastasize until the cancer destroyed her life. The promised solitude had gone from a reprieve to a prison sentence in the girl's mind. In Heath's as well, on bad days. Like this one. Only Gwen had maintained her optimism. It had been temporarily damped by the news of her old friend Chris's heart attacks, and finally a stroke. The sadness was touched, Heath guessed, by a fear of her own mortality; Chris was sixteen years Gwen's junior.

No one was equipped to fight invisible

monsters, Heath realized. Monsters of the Id or the Internet. The kind that worked in the dark, unknowable, motives as twisted and murky as eddies in a polluted river. Creeping poisonous fog that insinuated itself through the cracks of the mind.

The kind Anna couldn't shoot and E couldn't run from.

"That be Boar," the pilot said. He lifted an arm and pointed with a hand that looked to be carved from an old oak tree. Arthritis bent his little finger at the second joint, poking it out to the side at an odd angle.

"You've got to be kidding," Elizabeth said.

"It'll be fun," Heath insisted with more determination than faith. The island was right out of *The Count of Monte Cristo,* or some other nineteenth-century romance. It looked like a broken molar thrust a hundred feet up from the ocean's surface. In the cavity of the jagged tooth, protected by a rugged cliff to the northeast, was the house they would be staying in for the foreseeable future. As luck — bad for Gwen's friend, the island's owner — would have it, it was unoccupied for the present. Chris was recuperating — or dying — in a medical facility in Bangor.

Heath hoped the house would prove less forbidding than the land it rested atop, and their sojourn there more salubrious than that of the former occupant.

The boat pulled neatly up to a stone jetty. The pilot turned off the engine, then, line in hand, jumped nimbly onto the jetty to tie the boat off. Wind keened around the granite base of the island. None of them spoke; Heath, Gwen, and E were staring up a fifty-foot cliff, steps carved into the stone.

"John, are you sure this is the right island?" Gwen asked the pilot. John Whitman, Heath remembered.

"Yup."

"This is not happening," E said.

"Why didn't you tell us?" Heath asked.

"Didn't ask," John said.

"Anybody mind if I shoot your pal Chris?" Heath asked.

"Ms. Zuckerberg is ailing." John said with mild rebuke. He tied a second line to secure the stern of the boat. Wily hopped from the boat to the jetty. Not hopped — his hopping days were behind him; scrambled was more like it.

John scratched Wily behind the ears.

"I think I might be able to do the stairs on my butt," Heath said. "Might" was the operative word. Leah had grudgingly given her permission to bring Dem Bones, but she was not to use it anywhere there was salt or damp. Not all that useful under the circumstances.

"Slippery as eel snot if there's any wind. And there's always wind," John said around the stem of his pipe, which he was lighting.

"That's insane," Elizabeth said. "This whole thing is insane."

"You could lose your balance and be killed," Gwen said.

"That would take the fun out of it," Heath admitted. She didn't have the kind of money it would take to stay in a hotel. The airfare had just about cleaned her out.

"Does this mean we get to go back to Boulder?" Elizabeth asked.

"Can you spell 'stalker'?" Heath wasn't going to let E anywhere near anywhere until she found out who was stalking her. The police didn't much care about cyberstalking — or, more probably, hadn't a clue what to do about it. Private detectives charged a fortune, and Heath doubted they could do anything she couldn't do if she put her mind — and Gwen's and Anna's — to it.

All she needed was three things: to know E was safe, a Wi-Fi connection, and time.

"This place has everything we need. I'll just carry my butt up those stairs, and we'll be moving in," she said firmly.

John puffed on his pipe and said nothing.

Wily watched with the somber attention of a fan at a tennis match.

"It's too dangerous, Heath," Aunt Gwen said.

"Could we just not do this?" Elizabeth whined.

"Can't be as hard as it looks," Heath said with the desperate good cheer she'd taken to injecting into the platitudes she seemed incapable of avoiding.

Elizabeth snorted. She sounded like Anna, Heath realized, and was careful not to smile, not to notice at all.

A metal ramp borrowed for the occasion was laid from the boat to the jetty. Heath and Robo-butt debarked in a maneuver as complex and intricate as the landing on Omaha Beach. Gritting her teeth against what she knew was going to be an event fit for the Special Olympics, she rolled to the first of the stone steps soaring in zigzags up the face of the cliff.

That she wouldn't make it, that she would slip off and tumble into the Atlantic, or worse, the rocks, that she'd get halfway and give out, and there'd be the huge humiliation of a ranger rescue: These thoughts she shoved deep into the well of hopeless thoughts in the back of her brain.

She wasn't taking Elizabeth back to Boulder. She was taking Boar Island. The temptation to yell, "Charge!" was tempered by the fact she'd be advancing butt first.

"I'm not climbing that," Elizabeth said. "No wonder Ms. Zuckerberg had heart failure."

"Elizabeth!" Gwen admonished, then said to Heath, "Let's wait and call Anna."

"For what?" Heath responded irritably. "Her to carry me up on her scrawny back?"

"Maybe she could drag you like a sack of laundry," E suggested. "That I'd like to see," John said. "Still and all, if it was me, I'd take the lift."

Heath and Gwen glared at him. He squinted into the wind and puffed his pipe complacently.

Heath's hope of a Batcave-like super-elevator bored into the living rock was quickly dashed. The lift was a wooden platform with rails made of old pipes. Steel cables were attached to the four corners, then tied off ten feet up on a ring at the end of another cable that snaked to the top of the cliff, where it disappeared into a rusted iron wheel.

"Electric winch," John said as he led them to where the conveyance sat, graying wood and dull pewter-colored metal rendering it almost invisible against the granite. "When

Ms. Zuckerberg had her first heart attack, and Mrs. Hammond came to look after her, she got this put in. Steps too hard for carrying groceries and what-all."

"First heart attack?" Aunt Gwen asked.

"This was the third."

"She didn't tell me that. Neither did Dez," Gwen said, her voice sharp with concern.

The boatman swung open a hinged section of the welded railing. "Who's first?"

"Don't look at me," Elizabeth said.

"I'll do it," Gwen said tentatively.

"No," Heath decided. "It has to be me."

"Right," Elizabeth said scornfully. "Who's going to hold it while you roll off? Could we please go back to the real world now?"

"The real world sucks at the moment," Heath said.

"Will it haul us all at the same time?" Gwen asked.

"Might could," John said.

"Forget it. I'm not getting on that thing," Elizabeth said, and got back into the boat.

Gwen and Heath would go first, leaving John to unload and get the luggage on the lift. Heath harbored no expectations that this new Elizabeth would help him. Wily whined and yipped and showed no inclination whatsoever to get on the thing, with or without people.

126

"Come here, Wily," E said. She lifted the dog back into the boat with her.

Once Heath, with chair, was rolled onto the lift, she locked her wheels. John handed her a small metal box hooked to a cable. The box had two buttons on it, one red, one green.

"After you're off, just push the button. That'll send the lift back down," John said.

"I take it green is up," Heath said with a look at John.

"We'll see," he said.

"Tally ho," Heath said idiotically, and punched the green button. Had she not been half blind with terror, the trip up would have been stunning. Through the waves of panic that crested each time the lift lurched, or Aunt Gwen squeaked, she barely managed to register the glittering expanse of unbelievably blue sea and sky, the dense green of the hardwood forest above the cliffs, breaking waves painting white lace around their feet. These were the good things. Heath kept her eyes resolutely on them. The one time she looked down, her daughter, her dog, and John were growing ever tinier, looking more and more like specks of chewed food caught in the sharp teeth of the rocks.

She wished controlling what she heard

was as simple. Fear honed her ears to bat-like sensitivity. Each creak of the winch wheel or groan of the platform signaled failed machinery and a splatty death before the eyes of her only child. In the end, she gave up, stared skyward at the wheel reeling in the cable, and prayed that God would not let a nice lady in a wheelchair die on such a sunny day.

"We're here," Aunt Gwen said as the last terrifying clank announced the end of the line. Heath was pleased to hear the quaver in her aunt's voice. It was not good to be the lone coward in a group. Moving from platform to clifftop wasn't as formidable as Heath had feared. The lift rose through a square hole in a larger platform, where it could be secured in place by four sliding metal plates about the size of a magazine. Ms. Zuckerberg had clearly envisioned a day when she might be commuting by wheelchair.

When the plates were set, the lift was as stable as the platform. Heath wheeled easily out onto solid ground. High, certainly, but solid, and worthy of a quick word of gratitude to the almighty.

The luggage followed, with John to unload it. He sent the lift back down. Heath refused to roll near the edge and holler at E to come up. Not yet.

"Used to be only a lighthouse here until city folk began piddling around in 1922," John said. "Waste of a good rock, if you ask me." He left them to get a cart for the luggage.

High on an island in the ocean, Heath could feel the elements in a way she usually didn't. The sun was a force against her skin, the wind a living thing twining in her hair; the light refractions from the sea were as sharp as the salt smell. Suddenly she felt very alive. Leaning her head back, she looked up a hundred and fifty feet to the top of the old lighthouse. The base had to be at least forty feet in diameter, and the walls fourteen feet thick, at least at the bottom.

The lighthouse was the single bit of architectural grace. The rest reminded Heath of the Winchester House in California, as if each owner had been driven to keep on building regardless of how haphazard the design. Forming an awkward V, with the lighthouse at the point, two wings — one of them two stories, the other three — blew back from the original tower, then petered out in drunken angles to finally die in piles of stone and timber. A century of winds had piled the debris along the skirt of the high granite wall on the northeast side of the island.

"If this place isn't haunted, I want my money back," Gwen said.

"I'm afraid we'll turn out to be the evil spirits," Heath said, thinking of the sudden — and to her, inexplicable — changes in her daughter. "Elizabeth has gone from Junior Jekyll to Rising Senior Hyde. It's like she's turned into a different person in a matter of days. Did I ever act like that?"

"For a year or two. You went through a bad patch when your dad remarried."

"Everything I do is wrong." Tears of self-pity and frustration flooded Heath's eyes. "Wind," she said, wiping them away. "I haven't a clue how to respond to her this way."

"Do what she asked you to do about a million times," Gwen said.

Her aunt's sharp tone offended Heath. It was as if Gwen thought she was a fool, or worse. "And what is that?" Heath snapped.

"Give her electronics back," Gwen said.

"You're joking," Heath said, aghast. The night of Lady Schick and the tub, Heath had taken everything of E's that needed a charge to run.

"That's what she wants. I think she's made that clear enough," Gwen said.

E had complained bitterly for a few days, then quit speaking of it. Why? Heath asked herself. Because she accepted that Mom was right? Decided her cyberlife sucked and she was glad to be out of it?

"Give her back her iPad, iPod, iPhone — whatever-all teens carry these days. Life as she perceives it is in the toilet, and now you're forcing her to go through withdrawal. Electronic media is an addiction of E's generation," Gwen said with exasperating patience.

"Addiction my ass!" Heath grumbled. Cocaine was an addiction. Heroin was an addiction. A telephone was not an addiction. It was an affectation.

"You saw the crap she's getting on her phone and laptop," Heath said.

"So did she. She knows what is there; is it any worse imagining what's there? Not being able to communicate with friends because *it* is there? Because we don't understand being addicted to social media doesn't mean it doesn't exist. Addicted isn't even the right word. It is the new normal. She feels like you're punishing her for something she has no control over," Gwen said.

Heath resented the intrusion into her maternal bailiwick as much as she wanted her aunt's advice. Lose-lose situation. "The last time I checked, there was one of a three-some with her face Photoshopped over the woman's. I can't bear the thought of her looking at that stuff," Heath said.

"How do you think she feels having you see it? Or me? Though I've delivered hundreds of babies, she sees me as a little old lady who doesn't know where babies come from."

"She doesn't see you that way, you know," Heath said.

"Elizabeth is drowning in shame."

"She's been through worse, real threats, and she was so strong," Heath almost wailed, and cursed herself for being a weakling. For respectable mothers, children are Achilles' heels.

"But she can't fight this one. You can't fight this one. The enemy has no face. The enemy might be her friends. Her friends might be sniggering at the pictures and talking behind her back. It's anonymous, horribly personal, and public all at the same time."

"We should have stayed in Boulder. I should have gotten her a psychiatrist," Heath said. A second mortgage on the house and it would have been feasible. Cheap if it helped E.

"Maybe. Since you didn't, you have to let

her be an adult with you. She survived the Fox fiasco because she fought back. This is her fight, and you've confiscated the field of battle. You two have to come to terms about how you're going to deal with this as a team."

"So sayeth the goddess of youth," Heath said with a wry smile.

"So sayeth the goddess," Gwen affirmed.

The winch groaned to life and began spinning up steel cable.

"Give her back her electronics," Gwen said. "I'm going to help John."

TEN

Anna sat across the kitchen table from Lily, sipping extremely good coffee and watching Peter Barnes make goofy faces at Olivia.

"Nice being your boss," he said. "We don't have much crime here, so I may order you to babysit." He grinned.

"Sure," Anna said. "I met a baby once."

"This may be Gris's last fire. He's been muttering about retiring for ten years. I wouldn't be surprised if he up and does it. Your duty station here might end up being for more than three weeks. Maybe for years."

"That's a lot of babysitting," Anna said somberly.

Anna had known Peter nearly twenty years, since law enforcement training at FLETC, the Federal Law Enforcement Training Center in Brunswick, Georgia. In the day, he'd been the epitome of "tall, dark, and handsome": black hair, brown eyes, a

134

few inches over six feet, with thick thighs and upper arms. In a test of endurance, Anna could best him. When it came to sheer physical power, she was as a spider monkey to a bull ape.

In his forties, Pete was still tall and handsome, but the dark at his temples had been painted gray — enough to suggest he was experienced, not enough to suggest he was getting old. Fatherhood was the big change. The Pete Anna knew always referred to children as ankle-biters and rug rats, harped on overpopulation, and eschewed the institution of marriage as nothing but a piece of paper.

Yet here he was, married and dangling a wee daughter on his knee, familial bliss oozing from every pore.

"They're pretty doggone cute, aren't they?" his wife, Lily, said with a smile and a wink at Anna. "I think Peter wanted progeny because a big man with a tiny baby is a megawatt chick magnet."

Anna laughed because it was true. Even she, happily married to the finest man on earth, was finding Peter positively adorable.

"I told Anna she could be chief babysitter as well as chief ranger," Peter said, never taking his eyes off baby Olivia's face.

"I could keep her alive," Anna said seriously. She was mildly offended when they laughed. "In Texas, I kept a younger baby alive under seriously adverse circumstances."

"They don't all make it," Peter said, gooey-eyed over Olivia.

"Culling the gene pool," Anna said.

"You don't mean that!" Lily said in the warm tones of a good person.

Actually, Anna did mean it, but had learned not to flaunt her darker side. Much as she liked Peter, her personal jury was still out on his new wife. So far she'd seen nothing not to like about Lily. Still, it was good to wait a few years before rushing into these sorts of decisions.

"I'd best go make myself presentable," Lily said. Having stopped to kiss first Olivia, then Peter on the head, Lily escaped upstairs.

"Sorry about the quarters. The fancy digs are getting repainted. Are you settled in on Schoodic?" Peter asked.

"I am," Anna replied. She liked the Schoodic Peninsula. Situated across Frenchman Bay from Bar Harbor, an hour by car, less than half that by boat, it was part of the patchwork of public lands that made up Acadia. The forested peninsula was mostly owned by an absentee landlord. The NPS had only the stony tip where it thrust into the sea.

With fewer tourist amenities, the peninsula received only a fraction of the park's visitors. On Schoodic, Anna could occasionally feel a hint of how it must have been when it was wilderness.

Peter was humming "Twinkle, Twinkle, Little Star" as he fed the child from a bottle.

He looked up and saw Anna watching. "Formula's not the best, I know, but sometimes, well, the magic doesn't work. Lily has no milk," he said as if Anna had asked, as if she cared, which she hadn't and didn't.

"You're the most beautiful girl in the world, yes you are, yes you are," Pete crooned, bobbing his big square head back and forth.

"You do know you look like an idiot," Anna said kindly.

"I *feel* like an idiot! I'm a prisoner of love," he said with an exaggerated sigh and a hand to his heart. "Who knew? Your own kid is different."

Anna would have to take his word on that. She'd never wanted kids, never had kids, and never regretted the choice. Kids were great; watching them was fun, talking to them edifying, and working with them occasionally revelatory. Anna liked kids. Then, too, she liked Irish wolf hounds. She just never much wanted one in the house.

The first few notes of Alice Cooper's "School's Out" sounded from the other room. Peter groaned. "Here, you hold her."

"I can," Anna said defensively as she took Olivia into her arms. Peter went to answer his phone.

"Hello, little citizen," Anna said. Round blue-gray eyes stared unblinkingly into hers. The infant interrogation technique. Anna always felt she was being asked, "Are you worthy? Can you keep me safe?"

"No," she said, and, "I'll give it my best shot."

Olivia stared at her in the unfathomable way of infants. Then her eyes squeezed shut. Her pretty little mouth formed an ugly square. She started to cry. Anna sighed. Babies almost always cried when she held them. It hurt her feelings. Was it that she smelled funny? Or was it that she was so paranoid about dropping the squirmy little beggars that her muscles tensed up until the creatures felt more as if they'd been nailed into a peach crate than enfolded in loving arms?

Peter appeared in the kitchen doorway, cell phone in hand. "That was Artie, the district ranger for Mount Desert. Courtesy call. They got an e-mail tip that your pal on Boar is receiving contraband." The look he gave her reminded Anna of how long it had been since they'd spent any time together, as if he was thinking that if he could turn into Father of the Year, maybe she could have turned into a person who consorted with underworld types.

"I told him we'd meet them at the jetty on Boar," Peter said. "Lily!" he roared, sounding like the old Peter. "We've got to go."

Anna's cell phone buzzed. She pulled it from its case. A text from Heath: *Weird shit getting weirder. Come when you can.*

"Ready when you are," she said to Peter. He led the way to the white Crown Vic, an older model. The NPS was a frugal organization. Anna slid into the passenger side, buckled her seat belt, and prepared to enjoy the view.

Visitors often asked her which park was her favorite. She'd never come up with a satisfactory answer. Today, a body of water encompassing a universe of light and life, a thousand blues in waves that rose and broke in sun-silver celebrations, the surf whispering secrets just out of hearing, it was Acadia.

The fancy houses infesting the multitude

of islands scattered in the ocean should have made the coast feel cozier, more inviting of human habitation. Instead, on the rugged coast of the Atlantic, the grandest homes man could devise seemed mere shacks. They hugged the rocky shore as if afraid to venture from sight of land. Those on the tiny islands were like orphans lost at sea.

Anna loved it when nature made humanity seemed trivial. It was a comfort to pretend that she was of a relatively harmless race; she felt safer when she could delude herself that in the battle of Man against Nature, Nature had a chance. For the short duration of the boat ride out of Somes Sound to Boar Island, she could almost believe Internet bullies and weird shit getting weirder did not matter.

The ride up the lift, accompanied by the towering form of Peter Barnes and the hulky muscle-bound district ranger, Artie Lange, was a tad more exhilarating than Anna liked. Not for the first time, she wished more of her compadres were small-boned women, less inclined to strain machinery. Still, she appreciated the view.

The bedrooms in the lighthouse, accessed one through the other by the original circular iron stairs, and the rooms around the lighthouse's base had been renovated.

The rest of the place, two wings, blew northeast and west like a tattered cape in a gale. Damp, winds, and harsh winters had had their way. The remains were more ruin than mansion.

"That was quick," Heath said as the lift creaked the last few inches to its mooring fifty feet above the rocks. "And with reinforcements," she said, not sounding particularly pleased. Heath, in Robo-butt, was sitting in the shade, an iPad on her lap. Wily lounged beside her, his chin on his paws. With a deep groan he forced himself to his feet and ambled over to greet Anna. Anna and Wily were old friends; they were pack. She was glad of the sun on his old bones, and the new interesting scents for his nose.

Scratching behind Wily's ears, Anna introduced Heath to Peter and Artie. The young district ranger was looking at Heath keenly, undoubtedly hungering for a perp worth his ambitions. Anna had never worked with Artie, never met him before coming to Acadia, but she suspected he would have been happier on a SWAT team than a bucolic island getaway. She also suspected he thought — hoped — Heath might be a major drug dealer and Anna a co-conspirator.

Suppressing a sigh, she asked, "Where are

Elizabeth and Gwen?"

If Artie was going to get all Long Strong Arm of the Law, she didn't want Heath accused of drug crimes — or, gods forbid, arrested — in front of her daughter.

"John took E and Gwen into Bar Harbor for mail and groceries," Heath said.

Peter shot Anna a look. Clearly he knew his district ranger and wanted Anna to take the lead. Anna folded down with her legs crossed Indian-style, the better to commune with Wily. Peter and Artie remained standing.

"You're looming," Anna said.

Peter sat down on the waist-high stone wall separating the patio from the drop to the sea.

Artie, continuing to loom, said, "I've never been on Boar. I'm not classy enough for Ms. Hammond and Ms. Zuckerberg. Mind if I poke around a bit?"

"Poke to your heart's content," Heath said easily.

Anna wished she hadn't. It was always a bad idea to let law enforcement — especially guys like Artie — "poke around." But then, Heath thought they were here to help her with weird shit, not investigate an anonymous tip. Before Artie could go more than a step or two, Anna said, "Artie got a tip.

142

An e-mail that said you were receiving contraband goods. Drugs. That you and Elizabeth were dealing to the kids in Boulder."

"You're kidding," Heath said, obviously — at least to Anna — stunned. Heath laughed. "You are kidding?"

"Nope," Anna said.

"You've stolen my thunder for weird shit today. This is what I got." Seeming completely unconcerned with the accusation, Heath rolled over to where Anna and Wily sat shoulder to shoulder and handed her the iPad. "Hit REFRESH," she said.

Anna did as she was told. Reading the screen was almost impossible in the direct light of the sun. Shielding it as best as she could, she squinted at the line of comments scrolling down the right-hand side.

"That's usually where the comments of people Elizabeth follows on Twitter show up," Heath said. "This guy — or girl — has been tweeting like a damned canary since last night."

The expected obscenities were in evidence, but the thrust of the argument had changed. Anna read aloud, " 'Kill yourself. The world will be better off when you're dead. Slit your wrists. Your Mother tried to abort you. When that didn't work, she

143

dumped you. Put a bullet in your brain. You alive will make Heath kill herself. Die, bitch, die.' "

Peter rose to his feet. Artie decided this was more interesting than poking around.

"I kind of like that last one," Heath said. "It has a certain simplicity the others lack."

"Has E seen these?" Anna asked.

"All but the last few. They came in after John took them in the boat. She may have seen them by now. She has her phone with her."

"I thought you were keeping her away from electronics," Anna said, her voice flat to keep the censure from leaking through. Anna had not rushed headlong into the twenty-first century. People scarcely noticed as life was remade by cell phones, GPS, Amazon, YouTube, Google, and Facebook. Big Brother was a mere piker compared to Amazon and its fellows. Clicking "accept, accept, accept" to unread contracts, whole countries and their children became citizens of this sudden and stunning world of bread and fabulous circuses without a thought or a backward look.

Anna knew there would be a reckoning. Even in the twenty-first century she doubted there was anything like a free lunch.

"Aunt Gwen made a good argument

against it," Heath replied a bit defensively.

"Like E needs to see this stuff?" Anna growled.

"Like E needs to have a sense of control. That and addiction," Heath said with the exaggerated patience Anna knew she'd inherited from her aunt.

"Addiction?" Artie asked. Had he been a dog, his ears would have been pricked.

"Evidently," Heath said. "Aunt Gwen said it's common, almost epidemic."

"Gwen Littleton is a pediatrician," Anna explained to Artie and Peter. To Heath, she said, "Elizabeth is not an addict," and then, "Addicted to what?"

"Electronic media," Heath said.

Anna snorted. Peter wore a neutral ranger mask, the kind put on when taking reports of flying saucers and sightings of Kokopelli.

"Be that way," Heath said to no one in particular. Shaking a cigarette from a pack kept in Robo-butt's saddlebag, she went on. "For all the reasons we had talked about, I did take E's iPhone, iPad, laptop, everything but her Kindle." Cigarette in her teeth, Heath cupped her hands to protect the lighter's flame from the onshore wind and lit it. "E grew sullen, irritable, had trouble sleeping, had little appetite, trouble focusing, exhibited obsessive behaviors, paranoia, hypersensitivity — all the things she would have if she'd been a cocaine addict and I'd cut her off cold turkey."

"Or heroin," Artie said.

Heath glanced at him, mild confusion in her eyes, then went on. "The only thing missing was hallucinations." Taking a deep drag of the smoke, she glared around at the three of them.

Wily, Anna noted, was not included in the malevolence.

"She's been under a lot of stress," Anna said.

"That, too. But after Gwen convinced me, I Googled it."

"That's asking the dealer about the junkie," Anna said.

"As Ripley said, believe it or not," Heath retorted.

"So you just handed her back everything? Fornicating threesomes, goats, pederasts, and donkeys — the whole filthy business?" Anna asked.

"We talked. I told her she had to show me everything. If it was so shaming she just couldn't bring herself to let me see it, she had to forward it to you."

"Thanks a heap," Anna said, but was honored.

"I gave her electronics back and the

symptoms cleared up almost immediately," Heath said.

"Freaky," Anna said, shaking her head. To her, social media was about as entertaining as mosquitoes whining around her ears.

"Yup. Strange but true," Heath said, the wind whipping the cigarette smoke from her lips.

The bell on the pole by the lift clanged; then, with a piteous groan, the machinery began paying out steel cable.

"That will be my little addict now," Heath said.

The love in her voice made Anna smile.

Minutes later the platform appeared filled with bags, Gwen, Elizabeth, and John. When the retired lobsterman saw the field of green and gray, his eyes narrowed and his teeth clamped harder on his pipestem. Acadia was one of many parks that had frequent interface with previous residents, inholdings, shared or debated boundaries, and clashing cultures. Locals often eyed park rangers askance, figuring they were only around to make up rules about things that were traditionally none of their damn business. Conserving resources for the next generation was of little interest to those of the present generation who were just trying to get by.

Anna didn't blame them, but it was of

greater importance that the native plants and animals survive and thrive. Humans had much in common with kudzu, Russian thistle, and other invasive species. They needn't be wiped out entirely, only uprooted where they threatened the natural balance.

Gwen, her hair made wild with salt wind, looked fifteen years younger than she had in Boulder. The sea air? The change of scenery? No, Anna decided; it was John. Gwen was enamored. The boat pilot had the same sort of sex appeal as Spencer Tracy, Humphrey Bogart, and Robert Mitchum. The kind that doesn't depend on youth or good looks.

Even E appeared happy enough. When she saw Anna studying Gwen, she rolled her eyes and made a face. At sixteen, geriatric romance was grossing her out. A wonderful problem, given the other things that had been grossing all of them out for the last weeks.

"John, get the cart so we can get the perishables in the fridge," Gwen bossed him happily. From the look on the man's face, he was teetering between enchanted and terrified.

"Got a present," Gwen said as she dumped envelopes and a shoe-box-sized package on Heath's lap.

"Do you want me to come help put groceries away?" E asked, batting her eyes innocently.

"That won't be necessary," Gwen said.

E flopped down beside Wily and Anna. "I just offered to annoy her. For a while there in Bar Harbor I thought she was going to ask him to carry her books or give her a ride home on his bicycle. That or get a motel room. Yuck."

"Amore," Anna said, and sighed deeply.

"Somebody to sit next to at the old age home more like," Elizabeth said. Then, "Sorry, Mom. I know she'll want to park her wheelchair next to yours."

"Not if I take my medicine," Heath said, waving her unfiltered Camel. "The cure for old age."

E was not amused.

Nor was Anna.

"What's in the box, Ms. Jarrod?" Artie, the district ranger, cut in. Anna had totally forgotten why they'd been called to Boar, the anonymous tip that Heath and E were drug dealers come to the East Coast to corrupt the youth.

Now a box appears right on cue.

"Haven't a clue," Heath said and began ripping at the paper.

"Don't open it," Anna said suddenly.

"Think it's a bomb?" Heath asked, laughing as she smashed the paper beneath the box so the wind wouldn't snatch it away. She was as gleeful as a child on her birthday. Relief from stress, Anna guessed.

"It's not ticking," Heath said as torn paper revealed a shoe box.

"Bombs don't tick anymore," Anna said as she leapt to her feet.

Heath lifted the lid off. "What in the hell . . . ," she said.

The District Danger Ranger was beside Heath's chair in an instant. "I'll need that box, ma'am." Before Anna could snatch the box or slap Heath upside the head, Artie had it in his big, long-fingered hands.

Wide-eyed, curious, Heath waited like a sitting duck.

"Looks like heroin to me," Artie said with barely suppressed glee. He bounced the box in his hand as if weighing it. "An eight-ball or thereabouts."

"Like *heroin* heroin?" Elizabeth asked.

"This could be serious," Heath said. Now that it was too late, she was finally catching on, Anna thought, but Heath wasn't paying any attention to the drugs in the ranger's hand; she was staring at the wrapping paper spread across her knees.

"This wasn't forwarded from Boulder,"

she said. "This was sent to the PO box we rented in Bar Harbor."

"The e-mail was sent to Acadia," Anna said.

Unconsciously, Elizabeth raised her hands to her throat. "Whoever it is knows where we are," she said softly.

ELEVEN

Denise and her sister had neither seen nor spoken to one another since they'd decided something had to be done to keep Kurt Duffy from beating — or killing — Paulette. Not that Denise wanted to be alone; she never wanted to be alone again. Space to think was what she needed. After three days of thinking, of no contact with Paulette, she went to her sister's house during the day when she knew Kurt would be at sea. She moored her runabout in Otter Cove, a tiny inlet with little to lure visitors. From there she hiked overland to Otter Creek and her sister's back door. This way no one would see her car parked anywhere near Paulette's. The car was one of the things she had thought of while she was in her lonely thinking space.

Not phoning Paulette was another thing. Cell phones were wired to record every call, every text, and, with GPS, where the phone was at any given time. Denise didn't know how many of these invasive pieces of technology dwelt in her phone — it was four years old — but if they were going to do something serious about Kurt, she didn't dare take chances.

The previous night she had taken her phone apart, cooked the SIM card in the microwave for a few minutes, then cut the nuked card into pieces with tin snips. That done, she smashed all the parts of the phone that could be smashed with a three-pound sledge hammer. Over the remaining rubble, she poured lighter fluid and burned what would burn, melted what would melt. The resulting black mess she tossed overboard where the channel was deepest.

It never made sense to her that criminals couldn't destroy evidence properly. She had to suppose they never really put their minds to it. Paulette's prepaid cell from Walmart would have to be destroyed as well.

The way her sister's face lit up when she saw who was tapping on her kitchen door made Denise's heart fill her throat. Along with her soul, she'd thought unconditional love went missing when she was born. The open trust and joy she saw in her twin's eyes she'd only ever expected to see in the eyes of her newborn child.

Paulette came out onto the porch. She was wearing a calf-length skirt in lime green and pink. The pink was in geometric patterns and the green in paisley swirls. The waistband and the bottom third of the skirt were green, the rest bold pink. On her feet were mules of tan-colored canvas with green ankle ribbons and wedge heels. Over the skirt she wore a white tunic, belted with a narrow lime green ribbon.

Denise wore trousers. Always: for work, for home, for fancy dress. The palette of her wardrobe ran the gamut from dull Park Service green and gray to totally grim. Seeing "herself" in a bright skirt, she was startled at how pretty she was, they were.

Without any need for discussion, Paulette headed toward the trees. Again she led Denise in a circuitous path to the nursery so there would be no obvious trail worn in the duff. Neither spoke until they were closed behind the wooden door, lamp lit against the artificial night inside the windowless shed. This time Denise sat in the rocking chair and Paulette on the child-sized chair with the trumpet carved on the back.

"That's a nursing rocker," Paulette said of the chair Denise had taken. "That's why the arms are so low and curved; so you can hold the baby and rest your forearm on the wood."

Unconsciously rounding her arms as if she held an infant, Denise rocked gently. "It feels right, good," she marveled. For a long moment, both she and her sister gazed out at the never-changing forest painted behind the window frames, a world no one but they could inhabit, no one but they could alter.

Paulette began as if telling a story that would be important to Denise, one that Denise had been asking for in her head. "I first brought the baby things out here fourteen years, two months, and nine days ago; you don't forget the day you lose a child. I was just storing them, you know, for the next baby. Hiding them from Kurt so he wouldn't sell them or break them. He wasn't too bad back then."

"He beat you so hard you miscarried," Denise said.

"I guess. Yes, I mean, I know he did," said Paulette with a wan smile, her head shaking slowly from side to side. She looked as if she were fighting clear of a fog she'd been lost in for a long time. "I guess what I was thinking was that back then, when he hurt me, he didn't mean it like he does now. He'd get stirred up over money, or he'd get jealous of the way I supposedly looked at

155

some guy, or he'd get mad because I wanted to go visit Mom and Dad or whatever. He'd get mad for some reason, lose his temper, and take it out on me.

"At the hospital we've got this old man who comes in every few months. He's got this awful abscess on the side of his calf that fills up with yuck and bursts. We clean it up, the doctors prescribe salves and antibiotics, and it seems to heal. Then, in a month or two, he's back in. Kurt used to be like that, this abscess that filled with yuck. Then he'd get drunk and beat up on me, and he'd be okay for a while. Even sorry in the beginning. Shoot, by the time I was twenty-six we'd been married nearly ten years. What else did I know? I guess I figured most men slapped their wives around. I didn't have much in the way of girlfriends to compare lives with." She smiled at Denise. "I didn't have a sister."

Denise smiled back without thinking, and realized she had been so strung out, weirded out, on guard, and paranoid for the last few months that she'd reacted in the same way Paulette had to Kurt's abuse. It had become the norm, the real, the way life was. This sudden relaxing of vigilance was a revelation. Abuse was not the way life was. It was the way men made it. Women could subject it to change without notice.

"After I lost the first baby, I never forgave Kurt. Him beating me, I could forgive that. But not beating the baby to death inside me."

That was why Denise couldn't forgive Peter. Dumping her? Sure. Marrying a younger woman? That, too. The loss of her baby? Never. Maybe Peter was another person who needed to be dead. He hadn't beaten her, but he had certainly browbeaten her into getting an abortion. Murder twice removed was still murder. Even in a species gorging on death every day, killing babies was genuinely despised. Nobody cheered baby killers. They didn't get medals. People paid more than lip service to wanting to stamp them out.

"Then, three years, three months, three weeks, and five days later, I lost a little girl, my daughter. She was fairly well along. Tiny hands and fingers, a nub of a nose, ears, all perfect. I saw her in the bathroom overhead light. That's where I miscarried. Kurt looked sick seeing us there on the floor. I thought he was going to pick us up, but he sort of shook all over like a goose walked on his grave and said, 'Clean up the mess.' He didn't come back for a couple of days, and when he did it was like nothing happened.

Nothing. He comes through the door, turns on the TV, and says, 'What do you have for supper?' That was it. After that he didn't hit me for a long time. A year or more.

"That's when I fell into a kind of sleep, I think. I gave up on the house, except for keeping it clean enough to be sanitary, and I'd come back here and tidy up. Bit by bit, this room became what it is. While I was walking in my sleep all those years, this was the dream I was dreaming. Does that sound crazy?"

"No," Denise answered. "It's a beautiful dream. A wise dream. I must have fallen asleep, too. I dreamed of dark places and rotten people. Walking around this park we so loved when we were little, I would see nothing but my pain. Finally, my world was made of pain, and that world got smaller every day."

Denise knew she hadn't been a child in Acadia National Park. While her twin was being raised by kindly old folks on Isle au Haut, Denise was being kicked around trailer parks in Brewer and Bangor and Winterport. Still, she wasn't lying; she knew that their childhood playing in tide pools was more real than hers playing on train tracks and around warehouses. Paulette would

158

know this, too.

For an instant she was outside herself, looking at the two of them sitting in the painted room. Panic surged up her throat; she was going crazy, had gone crazy, Paulette did sound crazy.

Then she was back in her body. The terror abated. She looked around the space her sister had created, calming herself with the fabric art pieces, the windows that showed the world as it should be rather than as it was, the crib with the stuffed bear, bright-eyed, head tilted inquisitively. The true insanity was not what she and her sister dreamed. It was the actions of those who had made their lives so miserable they needed to dream it.

"Then I woke up," Paulette said simply, cutting into Denise's thoughts. Still on the little chair, her skirt flowing to the floor in a bright blossom, she spread her hands with a shrug. "About a year ago . . . six months . . . I don't know. Around that time I started feeling again, then I started feeling everything was odd, off somehow. At first Kurt didn't notice I'd woken up. When he did, he didn't like it. He knocked me around some — not a lot, but I could feel he meant it this time. Meant to kill me."

"*The Burning Bed*," Denise said.

"I loved that movie."

"Self-defense. There's no way around it."

They were quiet for a moment, the only sound the soft beat as the rocker rocked back and forth on the wooden floor.

"Do you know how to kill people?" Paulette asked. "Rangers have guns and all. Do they teach you that?"

"Not in so many words," Denise said. "They use the word 'stop.' A gun has to have 'stopping' power. We shoot at targets shaped like people, and we learn to aim for center body mass — bigger and easier to hit than the pinhead of the usual criminal. We learn to hit people with batons in places that will disable them."

Paulette thought that over for a couple of minutes. Denise rocked and thought about killing. Death was standard operating procedure: Cows died for hamburgers, grass died for cows. Little lambkins were slaughtered for Easter dinners. Turkeys died by the millions for Christmas and Thanksgiving. Animals were different, the people who ate them always insisted. People pretended that killing people wasn't the same as killing animals, that killing people was horrific. Then they voted to fight in Iran, Iraq, Afghanistan, Vietnam, Korea, Libya — always somewhere, and mostly not because anybody wanted or needed soldiers marching around their backyards shooting. Humans liked killing humans. They were good at it. They celebrated it with medals and movies and songs. Then they pretended to themselves that a woman killing a violent bastard like Kurt Duffy was so horrible she had to go to prison forever. It made no sense. Either it was okay to kill people deemed bad or it wasn't. It was pretty obvious to Denise that in America, as well as the rest of the world, the consensus was in: Killing was fine and dandy, good even. Admirable.

The only thing bad about killing was *saying* it was okay. Like the "family values" politicians: They could fornicate, whoremonger, go with same-sex hookers, commit adultery, and still get reelected by the Evangelicals as long as they *said* those things were wrong.

So nobody was going to care that Kurt Duffy was killed. Not a bit. They only paid lip service to the idea that killing a Kurt Duffy was wrong. Really, most people didn't care at all; they just wanted to curl up on the sofa and watch *Saw III* or *Dexter*. What she and Paulette needed to do was find a story that would help people explain the murder of Kurt Duffy to themselves so they could stop thinking about it, stop pretending it was bad, and get back to their own rat killing, as one of her old high school teachers was fond of saying.

"I don't want to disable Kurt," Paulette said. "I think he needs to be dead for a long, long time."

"For the rest of his life," Denise said, and they both laughed at the absurdity.

"My gosh!" Paulette gasped, covering her mouth. "Are we awful? I mean, we're laughing about killing people. Killing *Kurt*! I don't feel awful, but I know I should."

"Don't feel awful," Denise said when they'd stopped giggling. "He does need to be dead."

"Poison?" Paulette ventured.

"Do you know anything about poison? I don't," Denise replied.

"We'd have to buy it somewhere. That would make a trail," Paulette said. "I could burn him in bed, like Farrah Fawcett did in the movie. She got off on a self-defense plea."

"It wouldn't work a second time. Too obvious," Denise decided. "Besides, you can't be anywhere around when it happens. You have to have an iron-clad alibi. We could screw with the brakes on his truck. I know how to do that."

Paulette shook her head. "He only drives from here to Bar Harbor and back. Nothing bad would happen, not bad enough anyway."

"Yeah. Bad idea. Even if it worked, we wouldn't know the exact time it would happen, so maybe no alibi. How about the lobster boat?" Denise asked.

"I don't know how to sink one even if we could get near it, and his crew would go down, too. Probably they'd all drown and Kurt would swim to shore and come kill us both. If he knew there was a both. Me for sure."

"Push him off a high place?" Denise mused.

"No. He's too big and too lazy. When he's not on the boat he doesn't exert himself at all. If you managed to get him to go up on some rock, somebody could see. You can't be seen to be with us, with me."

Denise sighed. "Okay. We shoot him."

"We shoot him three times," Paulette said firmly.

TWELVE

Heath lay in the ground-floor bedroom of the tower, exhausted from the sheer effort it took to go to bed. Before she'd been hospitalized, this had been Gwen's friend Chris Zuckerberg's bedroom. Other than a few pieces of truly stunning artwork, the decor was not what Heath had expected from a woman who owned an entire island. Though the mattress and the bedding — down comforter over fine cotton sheets — were excellent, the bed was narrow, an old-fashioned kid's bed. The armoire, obviously made for this lighthouse or another round dwelling, was an antique but in bad condition. The single wooden chair and writing desk were scuffed with use.

Gwen said Chris was land- and house-poor. The place was a money pit on a grand scale. Probably most of it went to fixing leaks in roofs and buying better mousetraps. There had to be mice. The decaying wings of the house looked like prime rodent habitat.

The room still held Ms. Zuckerberg's scent, faintly spicy; her clothes still hung in the armoire, and papers were strewn across the desk as if she'd expected to return. Something Gwen thought was unlikely. In the days since they'd arrived, and Dez Hammond had phoned to welcome them to the abandoned house, Ms. Zuckerberg had suffered several more transient ischemic attacks.

Heath found the Spartan utility of Chris's room pleasing. Simplicity had always suited her. The world presented enough treats and turns for her eyeballs that she didn't feel the need to spread too many of them around indoors.

The room above Heath had been used by Dez Hammond. Dez was a childhood friend of Ms. Zuckerberg's. Aunt Gwen said Ms. Hammond moved in pretty much full-time after her husband died and Chris's health began to fail.

This second-story room was claimed by Elizabeth of the young strong legs. It boasted two wide windows. The view, so Elizabeth said, was spectacular.

The topmost room, where the lighthouse's lantern had been housed, had a three-hundred-sixty-degree view. It had been Chris's before the first heart attack had driven her to ground level. The penthouse suite was where Gwen had chosen to bunk.

Heath's ground-floor room had only two windows, slits that medieval bowmen would have found claustrophobic. Despite the lack of a view, she liked the space. There were times when only a fortress on a crag surrounded by a cold, deep moat could make one feel safe.

Pulling the comforter up under her chin, she stared at the electronic suit Leah had so generously allowed her to bring. In this historic environment it looked at home on its hanger, more like a suit of armor than an exoskeleton. Though she had yet to try it on Boar, Heath liked having it in sight.

Hah! And they said she'd never walk again.

Through the hole cut in the thick plank flooring for the stairs, Elizabeth's music — real music, thank God — trickled, punctuated by the occasional thumping footfall. Light and lithe as a gymnast, yet the girl had a habit of walking on her heels. She made more noise coming and going than a troupe of clog dancers.

The noise, like the fortress of a house, was comforting. Elizabeth was safe. Anyone who wanted to harm her would have to cross half the continent, swim icy seas, scale cliffs, and pass through Heath's bedroom.

Lord knew, tonight, if they/he/it ran the gauntlet she wouldn't be asleep when they reached her room. Annoying, vaguely electrical twitches in her legs were driving her nuts. Horrid buggers felt nothing, were useless for anything but making laps for cats; still they leapt and kicked and jerked. Obviously they could move. They just wouldn't take orders. Most irritating.

Since sleep was off the menu, Heath sifted through the poisons someone was dripping into her daughter's world. After Tiffany Edleson fell through as the favored suspect, Heath, Anna, and Gwen had assumed the cyberstalker was one — or more — of Elizabeth's fellow students at Boulder High School.

Heath had spoken with E's high school principal and her English and geometry teachers. They'd been kind but useless. As it was when Heath was in high school, the phys ed teacher was the one to whom the kids opened up. Ms. Willis knew about the points game E had mentioned. The clique of boys who played the game boasted they wouldn't date any girl who couldn't be counted on for a friendly blow job.

"They're considered the cool boys, the BMOC, go figure," Heath told Gwen.

"They are nasty pieces of work," Gwen said succinctly. "Is oral sex de rigueur?"

They'd both looked at Elizabeth, who, by choice, was in on what they'd come to call the Cybercreep Councils. Heath and Gwen were reassured by the spontaneous "Gross, like way gross!

"The girls they get? You know, who hang with them and do the blow jobs and whatever? You'd think they'd be the school skanks, but they're not," Elizabeth told them. "They're real hotties. I think it's that Stockholm thing, where the hostages fall in love with the terrorists."

Heath hadn't thought of it that way, but she wouldn't be surprised if Elizabeth was on to something.

Gwen said, "The boys are the skanks, Elizabeth."

A sigh and an eye roll were her reward.

Could the jerk boys, the high school rotters who made a game of degrading girls have smelled Elizabeth's virgin soul, and set on the trail like hounds on the scent of a rabbit? Heath wondered as she listened to the tattoo of her daughter's feet on the planks overhead.

Bullies tended to pick on the strays, the

oddballs. Though she'd never say so to Elizabeth, the child's peculiar upbringing didn't make it easy for her to blend in, be one of the crowd — an essential survival skill for a teenager.

From age four until she was nine E had lived in a polygamist compound that called itself Mormon, though the Mormon Church would have vehemently denied the relationship. Before kids in the cult reached puberty — the age when girl children were "married" off to the chosen elders, and boy children were run out of the community lest they become sexual rivals — they lived like the children of an enormous and amiable family circa 1898.

No Internet, no TV, no video games, newspapers, or magazines; they were seldom taken into the nearby town of Loveland. Their clothes were mostly homemade. All were homeschooled. They grew up knowing of the outside world only in a shadowy way. Though such an upbringing left them woefully unprepared for the challenges of the modern world, it did allow them an innocence denied children exposed from infancy to an overcommercialized, oversexualized, violent society careening into the future on laugh tracks and Big Macs.

Miraculously, Elizabeth still retained that

aura of innocence. Once, Heath had attributed it to her early cloistering. Now she believed Elizabeth would have been the same had she been raised in London during World War II, Berkeley in the sixties, or New York City in the new millennium. Nature winning over nurture.

Innocence was an almost irresistible target for kids who have lost theirs.

When Heath was in school, bullying had a bricks-and-mortar aspect: hallway taunts, locker vandalism, heads stuck in toilets. Bullies were a hands-on bunch; they liked to see the results of their work, enjoy the public humiliation, soak up the fear.

Since the Internet, things that used to be spray-painted under bridges were published for the world to see. Besides her personal electronic pages, a lot had been posted to a blog popular with Boulder kids, *whosewho andwhocares.net.* The site was known for unflattering pictures with "funny" captions, outing romances, derogatory remarks about fashion, belittling football players who screwed up, and naming cheerleaders who — so said the blog — didn't wear panties.

Whoever was bullying Elizabeth was too cruel for a bulletin board invented for petty cruelty. The kids who ran the blog deleted the graphic attacks on Elizabeth the moment they saw them, then blocked the source. The bully got multiple URLs and reposted after every block.

Messages, fielded by the Boulder police while Elizabeth's phone was quarantined, leaned toward the threatening. Nothing overt; crawling, spiritual cockroaches afraid of the light. The wording got darker, the pictures more sadistic. Though sympathetic, the police considered cyber malice out of their jurisdiction.

Sam Edleson was in their jurisdiction, but without witnesses or evidence, there was little they could do. A couple of female cops went to the Edlesons' home and scared the stuffing out of Terry. Two of their male counterparts "had a talk" with Sam that left him the worse for wear. Or so said the kid who raked Heath's leaves.

The detective assigned to Elizabeth's case wasn't so user-friendly. He murmured about kids being kids, modern moms being oversensitive, letting 'em duke it out — a song that he should have known went out of fashion in the eighties.

Snug behind her castle walls on Boar Island, Heath pondered the metaphorical roaches. She was not being a hysterical overprotective mom. Heath had never been given to the vapors, not even during the

171

dark days when she was newly disabled and Gwendolyn feared she'd off herself. Easier said than done when one can no longer access high places from which to leap.

At present Elizabeth was living on a rock made of nothing but high places and deadly falls. Heath thought of the messages urging her to kill herself. How many would it take to turn E's mind back to suicide? Ten? A hundred? After all that had happened, had the vicious words lost their ability to influence her? Heath hoped so. Hope and vigilance: Those were the only weapons she had.

Her thoughts left that miserable abyss and turned to the package of heroin and the anonymous tip, a tip given before the heroin had arrived. Obviously whoever tipped off the rangers sent the heroin. This attempt at a frame job was ludicrously amateurish. That fact would have been more reassuring had the excitement the district ranger evinced made her think he'd never smelled a three-day-old red herring before.

He'd scrutinized the contents of the box. It was filled with small rectangular packets wrapped in tinfoil. There had to be a hundred of the things. Heath had thought it was a box of toothpicks, two to a pack, the way they offer them in cheaper restaurants. With a look first at her, then at Anna, suggesting they might be in cahoots, Artie bundled the box into a paper bag, which he sealed and marked with a black Sharpie.

"Evidence," he said darkly.

Heath laughed remembering his barely concealed glee. The drug bust of the century, and he was on it! She doubted it would be as amusing if he got anyone else to take it seriously. In the justice system, things did go horribly awry now and again.

As soon as the rangers left, Heath jumped on the Internet. The tiny packages — if they even contained heroin and not baby powder or whatever — were probably one-twentieth of a gram and cost ten dollars on the street. Nicely set up for resale. An eight-ball was supposedly three grams. Eight-ball. Behind the eight ball? Was that the legal limit or something?

It was so absurd, so obviously part of the harassment of E, it had not crossed Heath's mind that the district ranger would consider her guilty. But he did. He might even have arrested her had Anna not laughed when he mentioned it. In the end he said, "Well, it shouldn't be hard to catch you."

Heath smiled to herself remembering Anna's muttered "That's what you think."

The package had no return address. The postmark was Walla Walla, Washington. A dead end, undoubtedly. Whoever was after E had spent God knew how much money to frame Heath for drug dealing. That was a lot of malice, a lot of planning — even if it was bad planning.

What they'd considered high school bullying was taking on a whole new level of threat.

Surely nothing would come of the drug charge. Surely Artie wasn't that stupid. Surely.

Idly, she wondered if jails were handicap accessible. In the movies they all had miles and miles of metal stairs.

Heath readjusted her pillow. Her shadow flashed on the tower's curving whitewashed walls. For a few minutes she amused herself making shadow puppets on the old plaster. A bunny, a duck, a wolf with its tongue lolling. At that, Wily groaned. Coincidence or not, Heath laughed. Taking that as an invitation, the dog jumped up onto the foot of her bed — not in one try, but he made it.

Doctor's orders were no lying down with dogs for Heath. Without sensation in her legs, the possibility of accidental damage was too great. Still, she didn't order Wily off. He'd worked too hard to get up, and she'd loved him too long to insist.

Scratching him between the ears, she felt

the bed shake as he echoed the pleasure with a scratching hind leg. A year or more before, that leg had been broken, leaving Wily with a limp, but it still worked well enough. At least as well as Anna's left arm.

"If not Tiffany, then who?" Heath whispered the question to Wily. "Who would set me up — us, me and E — for a drug charge? Why? Ruin our reputations? Make us less believable to the powers that be? Make me look like an unfit mother?" That seemed most likely. If Heath was a drug dealer and her daughter a whore, then . . . Then what? No one would care when one or both of them disappeared? Or died?

A sudden and desperate need to see E flooded Heath. She sat up abruptly. Rather, her mind told her body to sit up abruptly. Not a great deal actually happened. She twitched like a landed fish, then pushed herself up on her elbows.

Having thrown off the covers, she shoved her legs over the edge of the bed, then laboriously worked her slippers onto her feet. Gone were the days when she could unthinkingly run around barefoot. How would she know if she injured herself? Caring for her legs often felt like caring for ungrateful children.

Wily whined from his place on the foot of

the bed. "It's okay, pal. Nothing you've got to catch or kill," Heath reassured him. He thumped his tail on the coverlet.

Her electronic suit, with its gyroscope-that-wasn't-a-gyroscope thingy Leah was testing, was designed to be ultrastable. Even though there was a good sturdy handrail running up the curving wall, Heath had no desire to try the suit on the narrow stairway that corkscrewed up the tower. The wheel-chair, of course, was useless. There was no way she could climb the stairs in a dignified *Homo erectus* sort of way.

In the 1860s paraplegics were SOL.

Lowering herself to the cold stone floor, Heath scootched backward using her upper-body strength — a mode of travel at which she'd become quite proficient. If she could ever figure out how to do it without drag-ging her pants off, she would petition the Special Olympics to add the Backward Butt Traverse to their sports roster.

Wily was accustomed to Heath's unusual modes of locomotion. He eased off the bed, stretched, sketching a deep bow, and then padded over to collapse with a gusty sigh near the foot of the spiral stairway.

"Easy for you, my four-legged friend," Heath grunted.

At the bottom step she stopped, pulled up

her pajama bottoms, positioned herself with her back to the step, legs out in front of her, and caught her breath. The Backward Butt Traverse might be the best way to move without mechanical aids, but it wasn't easy. Heartbeat returned to near normal, she began the long circuitous ascent. Elbows back, palms on the step behind her, push up, swing her fanny back, settle, palms on the step behind her: twenty-three steps, twenty-three ten-inch lifts.

I shall have the triceps of a god, she promised herself.

She could have simply hollered for Elizabeth to come down, or blown the whistle that E insisted she wear around her neck, but where was the challenge in that?

When she was about three-quarters of the way up — eighteen of the twenty-three steps, and sweating like a pig — the query "Mom?" came from above.

"Coming," Heath gasped back. The tower, with its coil of stairs, didn't allow for doors. As Heath looked up at the rectangle of golden light where the steps passed through the plank floor of Elizabeth's room, her daughter's face appeared, long, straight brown hair falling down around it like the tentacles of a particularly relaxed jellyfish. Whenever she caught a different angle of

Elizabeth's face, Heath was struck all over again by the girl's beauty. Part of it, she suspected, was a lack of objectivity on her part. Regardless, Elizabeth was lovely, tall for her age, willowy, with flawless skin, eyes that seemed too big for her face and were the brown of expensive chocolate.

Pride in her child went cold with the realization that images of that sweet face were being defiled in the public forum. Facebook, MySpace, Google: Elizabeth's junior varsity girls soccer team made the state championships. Even though they didn't win, a team photo could have made its way into cyberspace. Elizabeth was in an online yearbook. Any pictures taken of her by her friends and posted on public media were out there. Every pervert in the world had access to her daughter's face.

"Privacy is dead," Heath said to the face floating above her.

"Yesterday's news. Can't a girl go a whole evening without her mom bum-thumping up her stairs? Why didn't you call? I'd've come down."

The mixture of irritation and concern gave Heath the strength to make the last five steps, and even hide some of the strain as she did so.

"Did you have a reason for this, or is it

just your version of jogging?" E asked as Heath levered herself onto Elizabeth's floor, her feet dangling over the dark stairs.

Heath hadn't much of a reason. *I had to see you with my own eyes, know you were real and alive* was too much emo to dump on one's child in the night. "I had a question," Heath said, hoping she'd think of one.

"Um . . . you lost one slipper and couldn't wait to ask me where it went?"

Heath looked down. During her ascent she'd lost a shoe. Damn. "I'm still better off than those with no slippers at all," she said unctuously, then admitted, "I just came up to see how you're doing."

"Okay, I guess." Elizabeth stared down between their dangling feet. "You don't have to come up, Wily." Wily laid his chin on the bottom step and made a whuffing noise.

"Any more interesting slurs on your character?" Heath asked carefully.

"I asked Tiff to keep an eye out, and I've been to all the regular places. The porn gets cleared out by the websites after a while. The 'die bitch die' stuff isn't showing up too many places. I guess it's the personal touch. My phone only."

Heath was pleased E could still make jokes, and scared that she was using humor to cover uglier truths.

"Will you get arrested?" Elizabeth asked suddenly. "You know, as a drug dealer?"

"You'd think even a blind carpenter could see this was a frame job," Heath replied.

"Ha, ha," E said, then automatically corrected Heath. "Visually challenged."

Surprised, Heath asked, "Isn't 'blind' still okay?"

"I don't know what's okay anymore," Elizabeth said miserably. Heath knew she was talking about more than politically correct language.

"If I go to jail, would you bake me a cake with a file in it?" Heath asked to cheer her daughter up.

"So not funny."

"Anna doesn't think it will amount to anything," Heath said seriously. "We don't even know for sure if it is heroin until they test it. That ranger guy, Artie, and Peter Barnes were here when it came; they could see I wasn't expecting it. There was no return address. Juries like nice middle-aged ladies in wheelchairs. They'd never get a conviction. Besides, I don't even know where you could buy heroin."

"I do," Elizabeth said.

Heath cocked an eyebrow.

"I don't know it like been-there-done-that," her daughter amended, "but I've heard there used to be a place called the Silk Road on the Internet where you could get anything except hit men. There were codes and secret e-mails and special wallets — the whole bitcoin thing — all untraceable."

"I remember," Heath said. "Then they captured the Dread Pirate Roberts and it was shut down."

"Tiff says there's another Dread Pirate Roberts," Elizabeth said. "There's always another Dread Pirate Roberts."

The Princess Bride was one of Heath's favorite books. She'd read it to E when she was ten.

"Maybe there's another one up now where you could buy something and have it mailed to anybody you wanted," E said. "Maybe somebody did that with the package you got."

"What would be the point?"

"Maybe to get you out of the way. If you went to jail, who'd get me?" Elizabeth asked.

"Anna," Heath said. "That's what godmothers do."

"That's okay then," Elizabeth said.

Heath laughed. "Thanks a million."

"You know what I mean," E said. Heath did.

For a while they sat, each lost in her own

thoughts. Then E asked, "Do you think the heroin sender guy was my stalker guy?"

Heath wanted to lie, say no, she didn't think it was in any way related, so she could save Elizabeth the angst of thinking herself a danger to her family. Parents lied to children all the time to calm their fears — or to increase them.

"You'll put your eye out with that."

"If you hold the knife that way, you'll cut your fingers off."

"If you make that face again it will stick forever."

"Girls who whistle come to some bad ends."

"Boys seldom make passes at girls who wear glasses."

Heath had been careful never to lie to Elizabeth. The girl had been brought up in a multilayered matrix of lies, half-truths, myths, and monsters. Their first two years together, Heath spent a lot of time sorting carefully through Elizabeth's tangled belief system trying to ascertain which lies the child needed to hang on to in order to feel secure, and which were increasingly damaging the longer they took root. Even the dangerous lies could not be snatched away. They had to be replaced by a truth that would fill the resulting hole, or heal the wound the old belief engendered.

Rescued children didn't come with baggage; they came with unexploded ordnance from former wars.

For a while neither of them spoke. Elizabeth, her long lovely legs hanging down the trap across from Heath's, was swinging her feet idly, a trick Heath would have given ten years of her life to be able to do again.

"I expect it's part of the same deal," Heath said finally. "Stalker/heroin guy is trying to make you feel responsible for the damage he's doing. It ties in with the kill yourself, kill yourself messages. He hurts me, you blame yourself, you get depressed, etcetera and so forth."

"In a way it is my fault," E said.

"If you go there, you're basically stalking yourself. We'll have to check with Anna on the legality of that," Heath said.

For a while Elizabeth said nothing. Heath couldn't tell if she was processing or sinking into the depression that had followed her around like a black dog waiting to be fed since the bullying began.

To Heath's immense relief, the girl screwed her face up, closed one eye, and looked at the ceiling with the other.

"Well, when you put it *that* way . . ." she said. Then they were both allowed to laugh. Laughter, even when forced, is a good thing.

"Aunt Gwen thinks this place might be haunted," Elizabeth said, clearly needing a change of subject. Heath wasn't sure ghosts were the best direction the conversation could take.

"She said it *ought* to be haunted," Heath corrected.

"It is," Elizabeth said sincerely. "I saw a light sort of flickering around in one of the dead wings."

E meant one of the two crumbling arms that swept back toward the northeastern crag.

"Are you making this up to scare me?" Heath asked.

"Nope."

"Broken glass, trick of the light, squatters, enterprising tourists, could be anything," Heath said.

"Or it could be a ghost," Elizabeth said.

"I think a few ghosts would be groovy," Heath said. "Maybe we could catch one."

E gave her an annoyed look. Elizabeth believed in ghosts. Sometimes Heath believed in ghosts. She'd read somewhere that forty-five percent of Americans believed in ghosts, spirits of the dead walking the earth. Ninety percent said they believed in God, which was more or less the same thing, but on an impersonal, galactic scale. Dead saints answering prayers, angels averting car accidents, the Virgin Mother healing a child: all were just ghosts costumed in robes and feathers. The cult E had been raised in was a bizarre mixture of rogue Mormonism, Christianity, spiritualism, and carnival act. The compound was funded by the myriad wives working what used to be called welfare scams: money for unwed mothers, orphans, food stamps, single-parent households; Medicaid, Medicare, any social service that could be conned, was.

The children were taught to hate the United States government, love their spiritual leader in the person of the prophet Father Dwayne Sheppard, and believe every single thing he told them. He told them if they left the compound, ghosts of late Latter-day Saints would get them. If they didn't say their prayers, Satan would reach right up through the floorboards and snatch them into a fiery pit. He told them God wanted them to serve Him by serving him — Dwayne Sheppard. He told them that the Mormon Church had the power to bring the dead into the Mormon faith, and that all their ancestors back to Adam and Eve stood by their beds at night watching them from the beyond.

Elizabeth had shaken a lot of that spiritual

olio from her proverbial sandals, but, like most Americans, she'd never quite given up the feeling that Something Was Out There.

"Should we buy it some chains to clank, or have they evolved, like vampires, into cute boys with dietary issues?" Heath asked.

"Don't, Mom. Ghosts hate to be laughed at," Elizabeth said, superstitious fear lowering her voice so phantom ears wouldn't overhear.

At that, the lights went out.

No flickering, no browning down: a sudden plunge into darkness.

"Holy shit!" Heath squawked.

Elizabeth squeaked, then laughed nervously. Power on Boar Island was capricious.

"Gosh, I hate that!" Elizabeth whispered, as if an entity in the dark might be listening.

"It takes some getting used to," Heath admitted. Ghost stories around the campfire always put the fear of God into her. She could remember when she was a Girl Scout kneeling beside her sleeping bag in a tent praying as hard as she could to keep the guy with a hook for a hand, who escaped from the insane asylum, from getting her. Forcing herself to speak in a normal tone, she said, "Time for bed anyway."

"Right," E said. "You talk about ghosts, then, bang! The lights go out for no reason, in the middle of the night, in a haunted house, on a deserted island, and you think I'm going to go to my little bed? I at least get Wily."

"I get Wily," Heath insisted.

"You can't get downstairs without a light," Elizabeth retorted. "I won't help. Don't help her, Wily," she called down into the inky darkness.

Wily whined.

Down was harder than up. Moving up, Heath used her arms and towed her legs along. Since she really couldn't push noodles, the only way to go down was on her belly like a reptile, the legs bumping along behind in more or less a controlled fall. In the dark it could be dangerous.

"Loan me a blanket and pillow," Heath said. "I'll bunk up here until the lights come back on."

"You can have my bed," Elizabeth said with a sigh. "I'll sleep on the cold hard floor with the rats."

Heath laughed. "Such a gracious invitation is hard to resist. I don't mind the floor. I'm used to hard beds. Better for my back."

A sniff in the darkness, then, "Yeah, right, and Aunt Gwen comes home from her big date and sees me all snuggled in a nice comfy bed and my poor old crippled mother in a heap of rags on the floor. Like I'd ever hear the end of that!"

Heath smiled as she listened to Elizabeth creep across the room toward her bed. Eyes recovered from the sudden onslaught of night, she could see stars through the two windows and yellow gleams from houses on shore. They had power. They always had power. Boar seemed to suffer from an intermittent short somewhere in the system between it and Mount Desert, the main island. A match was struck, the sharp smell of sulfur, then the steady warm glow of the kerosene lamp.

"I like the lamplight," Elizabeth said. Heath heard wistfulness in her daughter's voice. Had they had kerosene lamps at the compound where she'd spent her childhood? Did she ever feel homesick? Heath knew the compound had electricity. That Dwayne might have kept the electricity for the "elders" and the computer cons, and made the women and children use oil lamps, wasn't beyond the pale.

From downstairs came the sound of the door to the front room opening. Then a faint susurration, like the shush of waves against the cliffs, maybe footsteps. Elizabeth

188

heard it as well. Before she could say anything, Heath put a finger to her lips. Boar was a private island. Still and all, Heath had been a fool not to check the doors. She didn't even know if they had locks on them.

"Blow out the lamp," she hissed.

Eyes, wide and frightened, shone above the glass chimney, and then Elizabeth and the world disappeared in a puff of breath.

Heath listened with all the intensity a dark house and surreptitious sounds can put into human ears. The lighthouse was thick-walled and nearly as solid as the granite upon which it was built. The windows, a modern addition, rattled gently in the onshore breeze. Through the open casement came the sound of the sea. Elizabeth's bare feet whispered over planks worn smooth by more than a century of use.

Kneeling beside Heath, she called down, "Aunt Gwen? Is that you?"

"The lift bell didn't ring," Heath breathed.

Nothing but darkness rose from the tower rooms below.

"Anybody there?" Heath called, since the sanctity of the silence had been broken.

A creak? A tiny scrape of leather on wood? The hushed thump of a door closing? Nothing?

"A trick of the wind," Heath said firmly. "Light the lamp before we scare ourselves silly."

Before Elizabeth could find the matches, the radio blared, lights snapped on, and both women screamed.

E had been right.

Ghosts didn't like being laughed at.

THIRTEEN

Statistically speaking, getting away with murder wasn't all that hard to do. The key was to murder someone who had no connection with your life. A stranger. The thing was, nobody but a psychopath would do that. Denise found it ironic that you could only kill with impunity people whom you had no reason to kill. Cops — even rangers — tended to be rational individuals. They liked there to be a reason for a crime. If they scented a reason, a motive, they sniffed and dug and pestered until they had enough for an arrest.

The drive-by shooters, freeway snipers, the people who put poison in Advil bottles at the drugstore — those with universal malice were almost impossible to catch. Even serial killers who kept on keeping on with their personal death marches were hard to get. Lots of evidence, lots of proof of crime, but no rhyme or reason behind it. At least not that a sane person could understand. When they did get caught it was because they wanted to. A younger, nicer, Denise had thought they wanted to get caught because they wanted to be stopped, felt a need to be punished. Now she guessed it was because they wanted credit for their work.

Because she was in law enforcement, and because America was a nation in love with serial killers, Denise had read interviews with those who had finally been captured and prosecuted. Never, not once, did one of them give a satisfactory answer to why they did what they did. Son of Sam's "The dog made me do it" was one of the clearer explanations.

That was why Patricia Highsmith's *Strangers on a Train* was such a brilliant concept. Had both men been true killers, they never would have gotten caught.

Was she a true killer? Denise had never thought about it. She'd thought about killing: thought about killing Peter, Lily, and for a brief — very brief — time, she'd even thought about killing Olivia, to hurt them as she had been hurt, to take from Peter what he had taken from her.

Thinking about killing was not the same as being a killer. Thinking was not doing.

The Catholics were wrong; sinning in the heart didn't count.

As she sat in the hot airless dark of the nursery in the old shed, she went again through the plan she and her sister had come up with. Paulette would go to the old Acadian bar and stay there drinking from before Kurt's boat came in until after his body was discovered. Tuesday night was bowling night for him and his buddies, bowling and getting sloppy drunk on beer. Either Kurt would get a ride to the bowling alley with a guy named Lou, who lived a couple of houses away in the tiny town, or Kurt would pick Lou up. The pattern seldom varied.

That meant Kurt would come off the lobster boat about seven in the evening. He and his pals would hoist a few and eat burgers at a joint near the docks. Then home by nine thirty to shower, put on clean clothes, and be ready to fetch or be fetched by ten o'clock. Either way there was a half-hour window when he'd be home by himself.

Then the body would be discovered.

Lou would come to pick him up and find it, or Lou would come over to find out why Kurt hadn't picked him up and find it.

Paulette would stay in the Acadian, making sure the bartender noticed her, until eleven forty-five to be on the safe side. Then she'd come home and be surprised to find police cars all over the place. Not ranger cars — or maybe just a polite presence of green and gray in the background. The national park's law enforcement didn't have jurisdiction in Otter Creek. Who did have jurisdiction was complicated. On paper, the state of Maine and the national park (aka federal government) had concurrent jurisdiction. With Bar Harbor and other small-town police and fire departments figured in, it wasn't as straightforward as it might seem. That, too, would help. For a while state and local law enforcement might not be sure who had to do what.

It also helped that the chief ranger was out of the park. Artie was a joke. Gris was the real thing. Before he'd joined the Park Service he'd been a detective in D.C. Little Miss Bird Breath from out west would be gone in three weeks. She'd probably be only too happy to let the state do its job.

Nearly five hours in the bar at the Acadian for Paulette to establish an unbreakable alibi so she would be free and could inherit Kurt's property, thirty minutes for Denise to murder her brother-in-law.

Having greater expertise in the area of

violent crime, Denise had worked out the details. After choosing the day and time, she and Paulette hadn't talked about it. Maybe identical twins didn't need to verbalize as much as other people. Certainly Denise's thoughts and her sister's seemed to run down identical channels. The killing was necessary, Denise assured herself for the umpteenth time. One, Kurt would eventually beat Paulette to death, and two, he would track her down if he wasn't dead, pursue them into their new lives for the sole purpose of ruining everything for his wife.

After the dust from the killing settled and Paulette inherited, she'd sell the property; then she and Denise would leave. Law enforcement rangers could retire after twenty years of service, just like real cops. Denise could have retired six months ago. She only stayed on because she didn't want to move her hatred from Peter's field of vision. Being a thorn in his side, a shadow on his wall, a fly in his ointment, was better than having nothing. Hurting someone was something. You were there. Alive. Noticed. If she'd retired and quietly disappeared into the woodwork, what would have been left for her?

Now that was all changed. There was Paulette. There was Kurt's land to sell and, maybe, the "family legacy," if they were the twins referred to in the ads Paulette had saved. They would finish with the park. They would have the money from the land and Denise's pension.

Money was important. Denise had never been rich, but she had been dirt poor, and intended never to be that helpless and hopeless again. Besides, they would need new things; the family would need things. They would move somewhere nobody knew them and they would be able to be out in the open, two sisters, a family.

Unused to hope, Denise felt nervous entertaining the feathered thing. The picture was so pretty she wanted to stay in it, yet was afraid that would jinx it. The gods liked to snatch away hope. Accepting the risk, she allowed the movie to continue playing in her mind. They would both cut their hair short and style it the same way. Paulette could dye hers back to their natural brown — or Denise could go blond. Hard to picture that. Better brunette and short. Paulette's hair was in bad shape from all the bleach jobs. A cut would be good for it.

They wouldn't dress alike, not in public — too corny. In private they might. Denise would order her sister a pair of pajamas identical to the ones she always wore. No.

She would order new pajamas for the both of them. A new start. Together. They'd settle in a small town, maybe in the hills of North Carolina or Georgia. Someplace warm; they had already suffered enough winters in their lives. Eighty-two years of winters between them; nearly a century of cold. A house in an old neighborhood full of mature trees; a neighborhood where no one would know who they had been. What they had done. A small house, maybe three bedrooms, one for each of them and one for . . .

Hoping.

Damn.

Denise knew better.

The dream winked out with the suddenness of a match dunked in water.

Pushing the tiny button on the side of her watch, she read the time by the faint green glow. Nine fifteen. Paulette would be nursing a beer at the Acadian by now. In half an hour she'd be sipping the next and Denise would be murdering Kurt.

Would she respect herself in the morning? Yes, Denise decided, she would. Being a victim shamed her. Taking charge, killing the man who beat her sister, so that she and Paulette might have a new life together almost made her proud. It did make her proud. It made her a hero.

She rose from the rocking chair, then crossed the hand-hooked throw rug to open the shed door. With ancient trees blocking a quarter moon and stars, the dark of the woods was as complete as the darkness inside the windowless room. In black jeans, black running shoes, and a black T-shirt, Denise scarcely disturbed the void. Wearing all black was kind of theatrical but practical, and these days everybody wore black a lot. If someone were to see her, it wouldn't be remarkable. Should Kurt see her, it wouldn't ring any alarm bells in her brother-in-law's booze-raddled head.

Stretching, readying herself to be quick and calm and deadly, she listened to the sounds of the island. Mosquitoes whined; car engines hummed faintly on the road; there was a distant whispering that sounded like the ocean but probably wasn't. A faint breeze in the treetops was more likely. With the quiet and the open door, she would be able to hear Kurt's car pull onto the gravel in front of the house. She and Paulette had tried it. It wasn't loud, but it was enough.

As soon as she heard the car on the gravel, she would walk softly toward the house, using Kurt's car and entry noises to cover what sounds she might make. The back porch light was already on. As long as she walked directly toward it there would be no obstacles. When she reached the back porch, she would stand with her back to the wall between the door into the kitchen and the window where the bathroom was. Though she would be in the light, the rear porch could not be seen by neighbors or from the road. After Kurt stepped into the shower, she would let herself in through the kitchen — the door was unlocked — slip through the bedroom, open the bathroom door, and shoot him. A shower scene, like in *Psycho*. Life mirrors art.

She would leave the same way she'd come, returning to the nursery. There she would collect the flashlight. Using it, she would walk cross-country the quarter mile to Otter Cove. Her blue runabout was moored in the reeds, invisible in the dark. In the runabout, she would row out about a hundred yards, start the engine, drop the pistol over the side, and be back at the dock in Somes Sound before eleven. No one would be there at that hour, and if they were, she was known for going out alone at night in her boat. They wouldn't give it a second thought.

From there she would drive home. For good measure she would burn her gloves and clothes in her tiny fireplace. No muss, no fuss, no motive, and the prime suspect in full view at the Acadian Lounge. A job well done, Denise would pour herself a double vodka, no ice, and order two pairs of pajamas from Victoria's Secret online. Not sleazy sexy ones; flannel would be better, cute and comfy.

An engine purred in the dark, got louder; tires crunched on the gravel.

Killing time, Denise thought.

FOURTEEN

Before she got under her own covers, Elizabeth helped Heath down the stairs to her bed. They had a system. Elizabeth sat with her back to Heath and one step below. She then folded Heath's legs — which weighed less than one would think — across her lap. This way they could descend step by step on a three count. "One, two, three, push up with the arms and the butts bump down."

Goofy as it was, Heath knew Elizabeth enjoyed working out new strange ways of locomotion with her. She would, of course, die of shame if anybody but Anna or Aunt Gwen saw them doing it. As long as there were no witnesses, E had fun. So did Heath. It was like being little kids, crawling around and wriggling. Better than being a kid, because what Elizabeth did really mattered; it mattered because compassion mattered. Compassion and courage.

As far as Heath was concerned, cowards

were more dangerous than evil people. An evil person did an evil thing to get his evil way. It was focused, rational. If you didn't have what the bad guy wanted, you were safe.

Cowards were like broken safety rails or frayed climbing ropes. You counted on them, and one day, they gave way and down you went.

When she was a child of nine, Elizabeth had been slated to be married off to Father Dwayne Sheppard because E's mother was a coward. What happened to the biological father was a bit vague. Heath guessed the responsibility of a family scared him. He took off when E was an infant. At any rate, Elizabeth had no memory of him. Rather than to make it on her own, E's mom became Sheppard's fifth wife.

Though she'd been nine when she'd last seen her mother, E said she didn't remember her clearly. Heath did. Hard to forget a woman who had abandoned her child twice, once to Sheppard's demands and, finally, to Heath.

Even the all-powerful Prophet Sheppard had a yellow streak down his back. Why else work so hard to dominate weak people and children?

Cowards were dangerous.

Elizabeth was one of the bravest people Heath had ever known. Until this. This onslaught of threats and secrets and lies, and something E wasn't telling her or Gwen or Anna, was disabling her.

Heath knew herself to be a coward. Being disabled scared her. Being a mom terrified her. That she couldn't keep E safe made her blood run cold. As far as she was concerned her only saving grace was that she'd learned to hide what a big fat scaredy-cat she was. According to Aunt Gwen, that was courage, to be afraid and not let it stop you from doing what was right.

After what had happened to Elizabeth and the other girls when she was nine — what they had done, what had been done to them — it didn't surprise Heath that E's courage had holes in it. Being frightened was like getting a soft-tissue injury. Once, and you recovered. If injured again in the same place, it could cripple you. This web of mystery and unknown horrors was the third strike at the core of who Elizabeth was, how she fundamentally viewed herself.

The razor and the bath had been a call for help. It had also been an indicator of how deeply E had suffered — was suffering.

Elizabeth never spoke of the bad old days, not unless she talked about it with her therapist. As far as Heath knew, she'd never spoken to the other two victims about their experience, never contacted anyone from the old compound, never reached out to her mother, never even asked what became of them when the compound was shut down and the families scattered.

Once she'd admitted that sometimes she missed the compound. There were always lots of kids around. They played simple games like tag and Mother-may-I. All the girls played with dolls, handmade of rags and buttons. A lot of the dolls were pretty. The sister-wives took pride in their sewing. As an adult Heath understood that the simplicity and safety Father Sheppard promised were false, but to a little girl, they would have felt real.

For a little kid, it would all have been real: Sheppard's brand of religion, angels, plural wives, demons, pedophilia, ghosts.

For a long time after she'd moved in with Heath, E was afraid to sleep alone in her room at night for fear demons would get inside of her. Mormons — real Mormons — weren't big on ghosts or demons. Mormons were a practical people. Heath and Aunt Gwen explained over and over that Sheppard invented the evil spirits to use as another tool of control. Mostly she believed them.

Most wasn't all.

Then there were those damn ethereal footsteps. Given the situation, even Heath's skin had gone prickly and cold. Heath guessed that E, who still slept with every part of her under the covers because exposed bits were irresistible to monsters living beneath beds, had been more freaked out than she'd let on.

Elizabeth was hiding her emotions. Heath suspected it was a result of too much unconditional love. Gwen and Heath loved E way too much. Even Anna showed glimmers of it. None of them could hide the fact that they were bleeding to death behind their eyes, could diguise the great howling need to do something. If Elizabeth had said, "Hey, if you guys chop your hands off, I'll feel better," Heath would be rolling up her sleeves while Gwen ran for the surgical saw.

That kind of love had to be a burden. Like having a Dodge Ram parked on one's shoulders. Dealing with that, and the fact that she was being called a whore — with the pictures to prove it — to everybody she knew, and about a zillion people she didn't, that her social life was deader than roadkill, that there was no way she could go back to school in the fall without wearing a paper bag over her head so nobody would recognize her, and that some creep might actually be slithering out of his hole to lay his creepy hands on her to . . .

Take her, Heath thought suddenly. For a minute she thought she would vomit. Grabbing the bar over her bed, she dragged herself into a sitting position.

Take her.

The psycho who had taken her and the other little girls so long ago was dead, Heath reassured herself. Not imprisoned, not appealing his death sentence, not getting out for good behavior: dead. Good and dead.

Copycat.

She was definitely going to vomit.

Was E's stalker planning to re-create the Rocky Mountain horror?

Heath knew lightning did strike twice in the same place.

"Don't go there," Heath said out loud, but not so loudly E might hear and come down. "Not at night when there are ghosts whisking around." "There" was a place to be avoided. "There" was supposed to be where the bad things were. Tonight, "there" was here.

"Wily," she whispered. He was already awake and watching her, his eyebrows cocked. "Come up on the bed."

FIFTEEN

Using the noise of Kurt's tires crunching on gravel for cover, Denise moved through the dark as fast as she dared, heading toward the porch light. She cursed herself for not having gotten closer earlier. There were plenty of woods, plenty of darkness. It would have been safe enough to have halved the distance. More than that; she should have lain under the back porch or squatted behind the trash cans at the side of the house.

Paulette had timed the walk during the day, over country that was as familiar to her as the floor plan of her house. Denise should have timed it for herself, in the dark, with her lack of familiarity. There had been time to pace it off half a dozen times. Instead, she'd sat in the hot darkness of the nursery and toyed with the wicked imp called Hope.

The crunching stopped before she'd traveled thirty feet. Kurt's truck door screeched open, then slammed shut. One hand on a tree, a foot not yet fallen, Denise froze. The truck engine ticked as it cooled. A night bird called. She had no idea which one. She was law enforcement, not interpretation. An image of the Indians in old Westerns imitating birds to signal an attack struck her as horrifically funny. Hysterical. She held the laughter in with an effort, her chest twitching and her throat clenching.

No more sounds from the soon-to-be dead man. Was Kurt lighting a cigarette or checking his cell phone? Did he stand by the truck listening, sensing danger? Had Paulette accidentally tipped him off, and he was waiting for Denise with a knife or a pistol? Laughter dried up in her lungs, tickling like ashes when she breathed too deeply.

Denise really had to pee.

Crunch, crunch, crunch: gravel tread under heavy boots. He was coming for her. Fear paralyzed her mind, and Denise could not run. She could not even lower her raised foot, or draw in breath. Clomp, clomp, clomp: ascending the three wooden steps to the front door.

All was well.

Home, to the shower, to his death, just

like it was supposed to be. As Kurt banged the screen and front doors, Denise sucked in a lungful of air, then ran lightly toward the lamp on the porch, her light in the darkness, her star of Bethlehem. The flame the moth incinerated itself in.

Panting as if she'd sprinted a hundred yards rather than crept thirty, she stopped short of the circle of light leaching into the dirt-bare yard.

Kurt was inside the house.

Maybe Kurt was inside. Denise had heard the front door slam. Was it possible he'd quietly opened it again, gone back to the truck for something? No, he wasn't the quiet type; she would have heard him. Maybe he'd only pretended to go inside. Maybe he'd heard her and slammed the doors to make her think he was inside when, all the while, he was sneaking around the side of the shack with an axe raised over his head.

Don't even think that, Denise commanded herself silently. They'd been careful. He suspected nothing.

He was in the house. That was the end of it.

The end of Kurt the baby killer.

Denise breathed in slowly to settle her nerves. Everything was as it was supposed to be. No muss, no fuss, like clockwork. That was the plan. So the trek from nursery to house had cost Denise a few minutes they hadn't counted on. There were plenty of minutes left to blow Kurt Duffy into the next world. Bullets were fast, just short of Superman-fast. Three seconds. Bang. Bang. Bang. Kurt is dead. Denise is headed for Otter Cove. Paulette is making eyes at the bartender miles away. Everyone lives happily ever after.

Stiffly, she started across the dusty yard. The scratch of her sneakered feet on the sand was as the grinding of boulders in the surf, an internal cacophony more sensation than sound. Step and step and step and no matter how many steps she took, the light didn't get any closer, the kitchen door looked tiny, wrong-end-of-a-telescope tiny, Alice in Wonderland tiny. Denise noticed her hands had balled into fists. Her vision was blurring, and sweat ran from her forehead in rivulets.

Suck it up, she ordered herself. It wasn't like Duffy didn't need killing. It wasn't like anybody would miss him. Killing him would be no worse than dropping a rock on a black widow or stomping a brown recluse. A spider, that's all Duffy was, spinning a web that caught her sister and held her paralyzed while it fed off her soul. It needed to be removed from the world. It needed to be crushed.

The porch, a couple of rickety steps up from the bare dirt of the backyard, cracked into her shins. Shocked, she blinked twice, confused by how she had closed the distance from not possible to bruising her legs. It was as if she'd gone to sleep for a while, her brain in Zombie Land while her body traversed the ground. How long had it taken her? How much racket had she made? Was Kurt in the shower yet? Paulette hadn't timed his showers. She'd just said he'd come home around nine, take a shower, and go out around ten.

Had he showered already and left to go bowling?

Denise dropped to her knees, hiding in the shadow of the raised porch. She rubbed her palms against the dirt, drying the sweat and working feeling back into her fingers. Forcing her lungs to obey, she began breathing slowly in and out through her nose. Sweat wiped from her brow with dirt-smeared hands, she put her brain back in its skull case and sat back on her heels. Nerve returned — or at least motivation. She pushed the tiny button on her watch.

Nine eleven. A good number for terrorists. A bad number for innocents. Was she both? Neither? It didn't matter. Nothing mattered but that she focused, stay on point. Back in the days when the government dared to let its officers shoot for scores, she'd been one of the best. Now there were no scores. Too many juries would want to know why an officer with a perfect score on the range didn't just shoot the gun out of the bad guy's hand since she was such an Annie Oakley.

With an act of will, Denise got to her feet. She unzipped the black nylon pack on her belt where she carried car keys and water when she went running. With two fingers she lifted out her .22 caliber Smith and Wesson revolver. The gun was untraceable. It had belonged to a foster mother's boyfriend. Denise had stolen it when she was thirteen. Ever since she'd had a nightstand that wouldn't be searched by some interfering do-gooder or rotten foster "family" member, she'd kept it in her bedside drawer.

As she eased the .22 from the rip-stop nylon, her wrist jerked as if hit by an electrical shock. Her fingers flew open, and the gun thudded into the weeds beside the steps. For a moment she stared at the offending hand.

Nerves.

After she'd killed Kurt, when she and her sister were free of the spider, her nerves would heal. When they were free of the park and the state of Maine and settled in their cottage far away somewhere warm, the spastic nervous movements would stop.

She picked up the revolver, then checked the barrel to make sure it hadn't become jammed with detritus. Having squeegeed muddy sweat from her forehead with the side of her palm, she dried her hand on her jeans. Mentally she began singing "Itsy Bitsy Spider." On each syllable she took a small silent step. By the time the spider was up the waterspout, Denise was between the kitchen door and the bathroom window, her back pressed against the wood. Kurt was in the house, and was in the shower; she could see the water running through the clouded glass, and hear it through the thin walls of the shack.

Back on track. Back on point. Nerves back in alignment.

Once more she dried the palm of her gun hand on her trousers, then crept to the kitchen door and turned the knob. Bless Paulette! Not only was it unlocked, it was ajar. Not enough anyone could see, just enough the closing mechanism wouldn't catch. A gentle push and she was inside.

The kitchen was small, the linoleum old — real linoleum, not vinyl. Paulette had moved the scarred table — no bigger than most TV trays — and the two wooden ladder-backed chairs against the wall between stove and refrigerator.

Clearing the way for the exterminator coming to kill the spider.

Denise loved having a sister, a twin. Nobody, but nobody, had ever looked out for her the way Paulette did. Peter had pretended for a long time. Denise had been fooled for a long time. No more. Blood was the only thing you could count on. Family.

The door to the bedroom was open, the bedroom light off. Holding the gun at her side, Denise walked in. She didn't crouch, come in low or high, sweep the room, or step back against the wall. This wasn't like that. This was straightforward. A simple task: You walk in, you dispose of the spider, you walk out. She would touch nothing. When she'd been here before, she'd touched things. At the time she hadn't known fingerprints would matter.

Today Paulette had cleaned the house, scrubbed every surface, then touched them. No fingerprints was fishy. The wife's fingerprints were expected. Did twins have identical fingerprints? Denise would have to

Google that.

The bathroom door stood half open. Light spilled onto the double bed, drawing up the one bit of color in the dim room, peach blossoms on a white background, branches cutting across in slashes of black. Denise moved to the foot of the bed, shoved the door to the bathroom open with the toe of her shoe, stepped over the sill, and, holding it with both hands, raised the .22.

The shower curtain wasn't the kind you could see through. Colorful fishes swam on a dark blue sea. The spider was big, though, and Denise could see his bulk where he elbowed and shouldered the curtain as he scrubbed himself.

Nerves were quiet. No ringing or crashing in her ears; she could hear the water striking the spider's skin. Her hands did not shake, and the sweat had dried on her face. Mind still and blank and clean, she aimed for center mass and squeezed off two neat rounds. The bullets cut so cleanly through the plastic they didn't even disturb the curtain.

The spider grunted.

Denise had expected a scream of pain, or death. She hadn't ever been shot. Probably what you'd feel first was the bullets punching you, like fists or a ball bat. It might be a while before the pain set in.

There was a loud wet thud. The spider falling down or back against the wall. The curtain pushed out as if he grasped at it for support. Denise pulled the trigger again. A hole appeared in the middle of a bright yellow fish.

Silence, roaring after the gunshots, filled the small space.

It was done. Denise lowered the gun.

The curtain exploded out. Kurt Duffy crashed into her with the force of a freight train. Air was knocked from her lungs. Plastic covered her face. Her spine cracked against the footboard of the bed. Kurt's weight threatened to snap her in two. Plastic, and a naked wet man, trapped her legs. Her arms were forced up over her head, her face smashed against his chest.

The only thought she could muster was that she should have brought the .357, something with stopping power. In the movies a .22 was the gun of choice for executions. The long bullets could spin, maximize brain damage. This was supposed to be an execution. She'd overlooked the fact that the man she was going to shoot wouldn't be on his knees with his back to her, the muzzle of her pistol pressed up against his skull.

Air rushed back into her lungs. The Smith

216

and Wesson was still in her hand. She couldn't fire down at such a sharp angle without danger of losing the gun. She brought the grip down hard, not knowing what part of him she hit, only that the shock felt good up her arm.

He was grunting and pushing into her like a hog in rut. Disgust lent her strength. Bringing her right knee up into his groin with all the force she could muster, she simultaneously chopped down hard on his head with both elbows.

A beefy thigh took the brunt of the knee, but the pain of the elbows distracted him. Like a snake from under a boot, she coiled from beneath him, slid the rest of the way off the bed to land on hands and knees. Water and blood slicked the floor.

Blood was good. It had to be his. The more the merrier.

He should be dead. "You should be dead," she hissed.

Rearing up from the mess of the curtain, naked, hair on his chest and back and arms, streaming water, blood seeping from his shoulder, chest, and side, he growled.

Like a bear or a mad dog.

Like a monster in a horror movie.

Like a hog bent on eating long pig for lunch.

Like a bull ready to gore, his head swaying from side to side, he pushed himself up until he was kneeling. More hair blackened his groin and legs, his penis a pale worm in the matted nest. He was huge. On his knees he reached nearly to Denise's shoulder. His arms and legs were corded and muscled from a lifetime of working against the sea.

Three holes decorated his body: shoulder, left side of his belly, and, the last, nearly invisible in the hair on the right side of his chest. All were seeping blood. Seeping, for Christ's sake! They should be gushing. Great gouts of blood should be pouring out. Blood frothed on his lips. One had hit a lung. The big bastard could live to be ninety with those three bullets in him.

"Die, God damn you," Denise gasped. A paw the size of an oven mitt came up from the monster's side. "Die," she cried as she skittered sideways out of his reach. The corner of the bedpost banged her shoulder. The .22 flew from her hand and slid under the dressing table in front of which she and Paulette had so recently sat marveling at their twin features.

This was wrong; things weren't supposed to be this way. Spiders weren't supposed to be this hard to kill. "God damn it!" Denise threw herself flat and groped under the dresser after the pistol. Her fingers touched the barrel. A beefy paw curled around her ankle. A bellow of rage; spittle and blood spattered the floor. In the faint glow of the bathroom light the blood was startlingly beautiful, rubies cast upon the ground. Another bestial roar, and Denise was yanked backward like a rag doll in the hands of a psychotic toddler.

Hunching her shoulders and ducking her head, Denise rolled onto her side, stared into the bloodshot eyes of the spider, and kicked out with the force of thighs and butt. One foot connected with his hairy gut above the navel. She was rewarded with a woof! as the air was knocked out of him. Again she kicked, aiming higher, aiming for the bullet that had collapsed his right lung. Again she made a solid hit. He fell back on butt and heels, clutching at his chest as if he could force the lung to take in air. The next kick landed on the wound in his side. Screaming, he tried to sidle backward, escape her blows. The plastic shower curtain tangled between his feet and knees, and he fell back onto the plank flooring.

Quicker than she'd thought possible, Denise was on her feet. She caught up the bottom end of the plastic curtain and fell with it on top of the struggling man. He bucked, trying to throw her. Digging a thumb into the bullet hole in his shoulder, Denise rode him until pain and blood loss slowed his thrashing. Straddling him, knees on his upper arms, she shoved the plastic over his face, cramming what she could into his mouth as he screamed and fought for breath. Hands spread like starfish, pressing down on the plastic, Denise growled, "Die. Die, God damn you. Die. For God's sake, fucking die!"

Finally he grew still. Denise did not let up. Three minutes. She thought she remembered that from emergency medical training. Three minutes without air was enough. No. Couldn't be. She knew divers who could hold their breath three minutes.

Lights slashed across the room. Headlights from a car.

"Shit." Heart and lungs fought for ascendance, both in her throat.

A horn honked.

Denise rolled off Duffy, then stood, her legs shaking, knees wanting to fold. No time for feeling around. With one great heave she toppled the dressing table. Seven years of bad luck shattered around her feet. The Smith and Wesson was against the wall. She grabbed it up.

"Duff! Hey, Duff!" Pounding at the front

door loud as a battering ram.

As the front door banged open, Denise was running through the kitchen.

She kept running into the black woods.

SIXTEEN

"This is Anna Pigeon, district ranger from Rocky. We go back a long time," Peter said, introducing Anna.

"Yes, I know. The acting chief." Denise's voice had the flat amiability of old enmity. Was it a not-so-subtle reminder that she and Peter shared old stories, old times, old friends? Anna wondered. Peter used to live with a woman named Denise. This had to be her.

"Denise Castle," the ranger introduced herself before Peter could.

Anna nodded. Gray-green circles, eerily matched to the Park Service uniform, puffed beneath Castle's eyes, and her skin had the desiccated look of someone who's just come off a three-day bender.

"There was a murder in Otter Creek last night," Peter went on. "The state has this one — not on federal land — but we should go to show the colors, see if we can lend a hand. Anna will go with you. Anna is an aficionado of bullet-riddled bodies."

Anna was not amused. The people she'd killed west of the Fox River had needed killing.

"Not exactly," she replied dryly. "Although they do seem rather fond of me."

"She's only acting chief," Denise said, ignoring the exchange. "I doubt she wants to look at a corpse."

"Beats paperwork," Anna said.

To Peter, Denise said, "I don't need help on this."

"Anna's your boss," Peter reminded her coolly. "Anna?"

Despite herself, Anna was interested. When someone else saw to the dirty work, a murder could be quite entertaining. Rather like turning over stones or poking around tide pools, digging around a murder turned up all sorts of interesting flora and fauna.

"Who knows," Anna said to Denise. "I've never been the chief ranger before. I might turn out to be helpful."

Denise's smile was on the watery side, as if she'd had to dredge it up from secret depths to meet the social norm. Then she said, "I'm retiring."

"Today?" Peter sounded confused.

The statement appeared to be as great a

223

surprise to Denise as it was to Peter. She gasped a tiny gasp, then gusted it out on a laugh. "Soon," she said. The wavering smile firmed with what looked like smugness.

"Hop in," she said to Anna as she opened the door to her Crown Vic. "We might as well get this dog-and-pony show over with."

Anna slid into the passenger side of the patrol car, then buckled her seat belt. There was a reassuring sameness to Park Service vehicles, equipment, housing, even war stories. Six degrees of separation did not apply in the NPS. After a certain number of years, often there was scarcely one degree left. Everyone knew — or knew of — everyone, and had an opinion about them. Park people were like a hugely extended cantankerous family, complete with black sheep and heirs apparent. Some rangers felt claustrophobic in such an intrinsically small world. Anna felt at home.

Seldom did she get to ride shotgun. Rangers didn't work in pairs. She leaned back in the seat as Denise pulled out of the headquarters parking lot. It was a treat to relax and look at the scenery, enjoy the park tourist-style. A park existed for every mood, and Anna was a woman of many moods.

"What did Pete tell you about the murder?" Denise asked.

"Lobsterman shot sometime last night. Possibly a domestic. State and local police notified last night. The park, this morning. Concurrent jurisdiction. That's about it. No particulars."

"Ever heard of the lobster wars?" Denise asked.

"Sounds like a bad science fiction movie," Anna replied.

"It's serious business in these parts. Kind of like range wars in the Old West. Lobstermen are rough customers."

Anna had never known a lobsterman, but she'd worked with shrimpers out in the Dry Tortugas. Very rough customers.

"Do you think another lobsterman killed him? For lobster rustling?"

"Probably. Who cares? Otter Creek isn't on park land. The state guys, or the sheriff, whoever caught this one, probably cleared it last night. Duffy's — the lobsterman's name was Kurt Duffy — bowling pal found the body. May have been some bad blood there." Denise spoke in a bored monotone, her face a mask of indifference.

Anna watched her in the sideview mirror. Law enforcement rangers were never indifferent to murder. Parks were inconvenient places to deal drugs, host gang wars, or run prostitution rings. They were bucolic places filled with potato salad–eating people whose greatest crime was feeding the chipmunks. Most rangers never worked a single murder in an entire career. Wicked as it was — or sounded to outsiders — when a nice juicy murder did come along, the dilemma wasn't getting rangers to work the case but keeping them from trampling each other to get in on it.

"My guess is it's a lobster-war thing," Denise said as she conned the big Crown Vic along the narrow road. She was a skilled driver. She worked the mirrors with her eyes, and her hands loved the steering wheel. The only other person Anna had noticed driving with that kind of innate concentration was an ex-NASCAR racer who'd taught her defensive driving. Really good drivers tended to drive fast. Yet Denise was poking along ten miles under the speed limit. Apparently she was not only bored by the prospect of a murder investigation but didn't want to reach the scene any time in the foreseeable future.

"We had a guy shot for robbing his neighbor's traps — Will Whitman," Denise went on with a bit more enthusiasm, warming to her subject. "Whitman's son was implicated along with his dad for poaching lobsters, but he's gone AWOL. It's probably what saved his life. These guys are the Hatfields and McCoys, Earps and Clantons — you name it, feuds go back four or five generations. There's a range war going on under the waters around here that makes Texas in the ranchers-and-farmers phase look tame."

"Did they catch the man who shot this Will Whitman?" Anna asked to be asking something.

"Sure. No problem. They threw him in jail, but he's out now. Shooting a man for robbing your traps in Maine is akin to the 'stand your ground' law in Florida."

"Whitman. Any relation to John Whitman?" John Whitman was the taxi man ferrying Heath and company around.

"John is — was — Will's father. When John retired, Will got his patch. Then there was the shooting. Since John's grandson ran off, the lobstermen have been haggling over who should get his territory."

"Any relation to Duffy?"

Denise started as if Anna had poked her with a pin, then settled. "Kurt Duffy? Probably. Everybody is somebody's cousin around here." On that she closed her mouth into a firm line that suggested the conversation was finished.

Anna let the subject drop. "Any news on

the package sent to Heath Jarrod?" she asked.

"That's a strange story," Denise answered, seemingly more comfortable talking of drugs than of murder. "We field-tested a couple of the foil packs. Black tar from Mexico, the cheapest, nastiest sort. The rest we sent to the lab. If they all contain heroin there should be about three grams total. Dime bags, cut with something. I doubt the whole amount is worth more than a few hundred dollars."

Anna didn't know a lot about heroin. In the parks, other than visitors taking a tab of acid, munching a mushroom for the visuals, or smoking a little dope, drugs were urban problems. "Doesn't the stuff come in bulk?" she asked. "Then the dealer makes it up into packages?"

"I'd think so," Denise said. "I suppose there's people for that if you're willing to pay. Here we are."

As soon as they crested the gentle rise in the road, it became obvious where in Otter Creek the murder had taken place. Four cars — two police and one sheriff's and Artie's Crown Vic — were parked around a shiny blue pickup in front of a small cottage, little more than a square of weathered wood bisected by a door with a tiny pointed roof over the porch to keep the snow off the step. Two windows flanked the front door, both blinded by pull-down shades brown and curling with age. Yellow police tape crisscrossed the door. The front was not graveled, per se. It was simply stony soil that had suffered the sudden stops of too many tires.

It didn't strike Anna as the sort of home one would build on real estate that had to be worth more money than she'd ever see. Old, then, a homesteader from way back.

"Lobster fisherman and his wife," Denise said, as if reading Anna's mind. She parked the Crown Vic fifty yards from the house and made no move to get out. "Wouldn't you know it? Artie, on his day off. What a twerp."

Anna followed Denise's sour words to the district ranger, out of uniform but with a pistol in a holster at his belt.

"Not in the mood for a clusterfuck today," Denise said, switching off the ignition.

"Beats sitting in a hot car," Anna suggested.

"Not today it doesn't."

Anna didn't know what to say to that. Miss out on murder? Ridiculous. "Mind if I go?"

"Knock yourself out. Wait," Denise said

suddenly. "I would like a look inside, at the murder scene."

That was more like the rangers Anna had known.

"Let's do it," Anna said.

A civilian around sixty, arms and hands scarred, face weather-beaten, sat smoking a cigarette on the downed tailgate of the pickup truck. A short distance away, not part of the group but near it, her back turned to the men, was a woman with too much bleached-blond hair. Oversized sunglasses hid her face. She was holding one elbow, her free hand keeping a long white cigarette close to her lips between drags.

Anna walked with Denise toward where the men were standing around the pickup's tailgate. Under concurrent, or shared, jurisdiction, if the incident was not actually on park land it was customary for the NPS to give way to the state. If it was on NPS soil, the state would usually take a secondary position. Since this wasn't exactly Acadia's jurisdiction — and Acadia wasn't even Anna's park — she didn't want to ruffle any feathers. "Just a tourist," she said as she glided up next to the district ranger.

"Anna Pigeon," Denise said.

"Right." Artie looked down at her from his considerable height. All Anna could see of his eyes was her own reflection in his mirrored sunglasses. The set of his mouth was not welcoming. Anna reminded herself to corner him about the heroin and Heath. Make sure he thought it stank to high heaven as he ought to.

"Hello, Ms. Pigeon," he said coolly. "This is Sheriff Cotter."

Anna gazed at Artie expectantly, a neutral smile on her lips, until he caved in and added, "Ranger Pigeon is acting chief while Gris is out west fighting fire."

Anna nodded to Sheriff Cotter, a red-faced man in a dun-colored uniform. His skin was the type that probably burned and peeled three months of the year. Blond stubble glittered on his jowls, and his eyebrows were nearly white.

"We got this one," he said.

"Peter told me," Anna replied. Cotter nodded. No territorial fights over this murder.

"And Deputy —"

"Dremmel, Jack Dremmel," the sheriff's exceedingly young companion answered, sticking out a bony hand for Anna to shake. Anna wondered if it was just her or if law enforcement personnel were getting younger. Jack appeared to be about fourteen. Acne still clustered on one side of his

231

chin. She couldn't imagine him shaving.

"Bar Harbor police," Artie said.

Two middle-aged men in blue nodded at Anna. No names were exchanged. They were just being nosy.

"I'd like a look inside," Denise said. If the set of her jaw was any indication, the disinterest she'd shown in the car had transformed into a grim avidity.

"Crime techs are all done," Cotter said. "We're just waiting for the coroner to come claim the body. How about you?" he said to Anna. "You want to take a look around, too?"

"Might as well," Anna said.

Cotter removed the tape. He held the door open. Denise and Anna walked into one of the most depressing rooms she'd seen in a while, and it wasn't the one where the murder had taken place.

"The bedroom," the sheriff said, pointing to a door.

There was only one door off the cramped sitting room. The house was a shotgun: sitting room, then bedroom, then kitchen at the back, no halls. Anna crossed to the bedroom door but didn't go in. Denise pushed past her, eyes searching everything from walls to floors to under the bed and dresser.

"Guy was shot three times, then wound up in the shower curtain. Cause of death might be suffocation. The shower curtain was shoved halfway down his throat. The autopsy will let us know," Cotter told her.

"Find anything else?" Denise asked. "Murder weapon?"

"No such luck," Cotter said.

"Sounds like you got another victim in the wars," Denise said, then abruptly left the room. Anna heard the front door close seconds later.

She looked over the detritus of the bedroom: a dead man, naked, blood mixing with a thick pelt of hair on his chest, face in a rictus of death, overturned furniture, plastic curtain with bright fishes. Shards of mirror reflected shards of what had been, to all appearances, a miserable life ending in a miserable death.

Murder was so often pointless and pitiful. Anna lost her fascination with who murdered whom or why.

"I've seen enough," she said, and she had. All she wanted was to get back out into the sunlight with the living things of the park around her.

Cotter followed her out the front door. As he was replacing the crime scene tape, Artie asked, "Where did Denise go? She's the one on duty today."

Anna glanced around. Denise was already back in the Crown Vic, seated behind the wheel. Her enthusiasm had been short-lived. Obviously there were undercurrents Anna was not privy to: Peter, a surprise retirement, mood swings. She felt as if she'd walked in on the end of a family fight.

"In the car," Anna replied.

Artie's lips curled into a sneer, but he said nothing.

"I'm Lou," the guy on the tailgate volunteered. "I found the body. Me and Kurt were buddies."

Close up, Anna could tell she'd misguessed the man's age by at least fifteen years. Lou was closer to forty-five than sixty. His face reminded her of the men she'd met who worked shrimp boats all their lives, or rode with a motorcycle gang back before the gangs were comprised of lawyers and doctors on pastel Harleys. Hard lives made hard faces. Lou's was carved by exposure and, most likely, alcohol. Only his hair retained the softness of youth; brown and thick, it swept over his forehead, as jarring against his creased skin as the tresses of a bad wig.

Lou was obviously proud of having found the body. Lots of people were like that. Being part of a murder investigation was their fifteen minutes of fame. Though, given the speed the Internet churned out fame, the average dose was probably closer to sixty seconds.

Whether or not he was broken up over his pal's death, Anna couldn't tell. His face was not the kind to share warm fuzzy emotions with strangers.

"I'm sorry," Anna said. "That had to be a blow."

"Yeah," Lou said. He dropped his cigarette and shifted his butt closer to the edge of the tailgate so he could grind it out with the toe of his boot. The cigarette was only half smoked. Lou moved stiffly, his head ducked as if to hide his face. Manly grief?

"Sheriff here'll be looking for a big man, and strong," Lou said as he straightened up. "Kurt put up a hell of a fight. Tore the whole bedroom up. I'm surprised I didn't find two bodies. Kurt was tough, I'll say that for him. Tough as they come."

He lit another cigarette, sucked in a lungful of smoke, then spat between his knees, the smoke trickling out his nose. "Anyway," he said on the last wisps of smoke, "glad it was me as found him. Polly isn't much good at the hard stuff."

The woman with too much hair and the

wraparound blue plastic sunglasses, standing with her back to the men, said over her shoulder, "Paulette. My name is Paulette." Peeking from beneath the dark glasses was a patch of makeup, slightly off color and applied too thickly. Bruises were a bitch to cover.

Lou's lips pursed in annoyance. Paulette turned her head away quickly as if her boldness in correcting him frightened her.

"Polly," Lou said, hitting the word hard, "was Kurt's wife."

The spouse, always the number one suspect. A battered spouse, better yet.

"Hi, Paulette," Anna said, moseying over. "I'm Anna Pigeon." She smiled. Sensing the woman would be less forthcoming at a show of force, Anna downplayed her authority. "Don't be fooled by the uniform. I'm just passing through. The park brought me to cover for the chief ranger for a few weeks." She stuck out her hand. Shaking hands wasn't her favorite thing, and the modern penchant for hugging made her blood run cold, but it was a nonthreatening way to take somebody's temperature.

Paulette's hand was cold and clammy, limp as a three-day-old fish.

Before Anna loosed her grip, the fish came alive and jerked away.

"I haven't had much sleep," Paulette apologized. She took another drag on her cigarette. The hand holding the cigarette was shaking so badly she could hardly get the butt to her mouth. She didn't look Anna in the eye.

"I bet not," Anna said sympathetically.

"I was down at the Acadian Lodge from six until nearly midnight. I didn't know what had happened until I came home and the cops were here."

Getting her alibi out right up front; not a guilty reaction exactly. Battered spouse, she had to know the sheriff was thinking she was a suspect. Lou seemed fairly hostile toward his good buddy's wife. Regardless of his talk of searching for a big burly murderer, Anna wondered if he thought she'd killed Kurt.

The insistent *Polly* chimed in her head, and she doubted it. Lou would have more respect for a murderess.

Paulette dropped her cigarette on the dirt, then ground the filter into the gravel with the toe of her wedge sandal. Her legs were pretty. Shapely and slim. The mass of fried hair and bruised cheekbone had blinded Anna to the fact that Paulette was attractive and not much past forty. Fishing a pale blue crumpled pack of menthols from the pocket of her skirt, Paulette shook out another cigarette.

"Would you like one?" she asked politely.

"No thanks," Anna said. "I'm trying to cut down."

Paulette nodded, as if to say every smoker she knew was always trying to cut down.

"How are you holding up?" Anna asked. Just because her husband knocked her around — if it was the husband who blacked her eye — didn't mean the woman wouldn't be heartbroken at his demise. Women were funny like that.

Paulette Duffy shot her a sidelong glance from beneath the temple of the glasses. She seemed to think it was a trick question. Anna smiled back with bland concern.

"I'm okay," Paulette said. She lit the fresh cigarette and took in a deep lungful. "The house is going to be creepy for a while."

"Do you have anyone you can stay with? A brother? A sister?" Anna asked.

Paulette twitched as if Anna had poked her with a hot iron. The hand holding the cigarette flicked out. The newly lit cigarette went flying. Paulette dropped the lighter she held in her other hand. Moaning, she fell to her knees to gather her belongings up.

"I'm an only child," she said as she scrabbled in the dirt.

Anna hadn't meant to push any buttons. "I have a sister," she said as a peace offering.

"Would you mind asking Sheriff Cotter if I can have my house now?" Paulette begged without raising her eyes from the ground. Her fingers closed around the bright yellow Bic lighter, but she made no effort to rise.

With a creeping crunch, a white fender brushed Anna's thigh. Willing herself not to squeak and leap, she glanced back over the long gleaming hood. Denise. The car crept forward. If Denise hadn't braked when she did, Anna would have had to leap back to avoid being eviscerated by the sideview mirror.

The passenger-side window smoothed down with an electric hum. "Get in," Denise said shortly. "We're done here."

Paulette crawled — actually crawled on hands and knees, the tops of her canvas sandals and the front of her skirt gathering dirt as she went — several feet before rising. Without a backward look at Anna, she scurried toward the knot of men, brushing at her skirts as she walked. The lighter and the unsmoked cigarette were still on the ground.

Anna leaned down to retrieve the lighter and return it to her.

"Leave it," Denise snapped.

Straightening, Anna gave her a level stare. She considered reminding her who was the acting chief, and who was the badly behaved subordinate.

"Sorry," Denise said with a crooked smile. "Got a call. Gets my nerves crackling."

Anna decided to let whatever Denise was playing at play out. She climbed into the Crown Vic. "What's up?" she asked, and began buckling belt and harness.

"What do you mean?" Denise asked.

"The call," Anna said. "What is it?"

Denise laughed nervously. "If these guys don't need us anymore, maybe we could get a bite of lunch."

Anna gazed at her. Denise wasn't being a smartass. From what Anna could read on her face she had forgotten — more than forgotten — she'd said she had a call. Her eyes were a total blank, as if the moments before had been taken from her brain and destroyed.

Everyone reacted to violent death differently. Most people were inured to it by years of seeing it on television, on the news, in the movies. If it didn't happen to a personal friend, most people just clucked, "Oh my, how awful," and went about their business. Except in politics and football, people cared very little about anything that didn't apply to them directly.

But for the crime scene, Denise had evinced little interest in the incident. Anna realized she been braced for the usual discussion. How much blood? How many bullet holes? Denise didn't start the conversation.

Anna sighed. She had lost interest as well. The instinct for the hunt had vanished with the sight of the pathetic dead man in his pathetic bedroom. Maybe she was mellowing with age. Maybe she was just getting old.

"Lunch is good," she said.

SEVENTEEN

Heath wasn't sure whether she was making any headway or not. There was no end to sites, articles, and blogs about cyberstalking on the Internet. As often happened, there was not a lot of content in any of them. Most simply described the phenomenon: stalking via electronic media, the cell phone the most common method. As in the schoolyard, the incidents could be anything from a snide remark to a death threat. Sex and shame were favored tools, and, though she'd thought it unique to Elizabeth, children telling other children to kill themselves wasn't all that rare. School and government sites had tabs marked "Prevent Cyberbullying," but they were little more than advice columns on how to police your own children and teach them what to post and what not to.

Several sites were informative as to how to report the incidents and get them removed from personal media. She learned there were things called "bashboards," sites where visitors could vote on who was the fattest or ugliest or meanest kid in class. There was one for Elizabeth. Someone else had already reported it. It still existed, but Heath couldn't open it.

On the subject of how to track down a cyberbully — or stalker, as she thought of the individual tormenting E — was vague and spotty. There was no clear path through the ether if the sender was even halfway clever.

A scream snatched Heath out of cyberspace.

Shoving the laptop off her legs, she yelled, "Elizabeth, are you all right?" Then, "Aunt Gwen!" Moving as quickly as long practice allowed, she levered herself off her bed, where she'd been sitting working, and into Robo-butt parked next to it. "Gwen!" she yelled again as she rolled across the old painted concrete floor of the lighthouse and toward the archway leading to the newer part of the house.

In reality the archway was a tunnel cutting through walls thirteen feet thick. Ms. Zuckerberg had painted the sides and curved ceiling with Peach Dawn at floor level and Midnight Blue with stars overhead.

Heath shot through it like a mechanized comet.

"Elizabeth!" she shouted.

Wily began barking frantically.

"I'm coming," she heard her aunt call from the top of the lighthouse.

A wide living room formed an arc around the base of the lighthouse. Curved windows gave views east and west. Large overstuffed chairs and sofas, backed by heavy dark wood tables, lent the peaceful air of an old library or a high-end lodge from the turn of the century.

Heath rolled through the charming room, seeing nothing except that her daughter was not in it.

The barking escalated.

Another scream cut across Wily's shrill cries.

"I'm coming!" Aunt Gwen again. Heath could hear her footsteps rattling down the circular stairs.

The nightmare sensation of moving in slow motion through an atmosphere as thick and unyielding as bread pudding caught Heath. She felt as if her hands could not spin the wheels of the chair, as if she couldn't see properly, her vision dusky at the edges. Had she not been able to hear rubber squeaking loudly on the tile floor as she took the corner from the living room into the kitchen, she would have thought herself trapped like a fly in invisible amber.

Ms. Zuckerberg's kitchen was spacious and modern, with antique touches tying it to the island's past. The floors were of wide planks, aged and scarred, either salvaged from old ships or made to look old by an artisan. A kitchen island stood in the middle of the space. The sides were of dull beaten tin, the top of dark marble. Beyond was the sink, and more counter space beneath cupboards built of dark wood with perforated tin where glass might have been in another home.

Elizabeth was on her hands and knees atop the utility island. Wily was on the floor, hind end up in the air, forelegs on the planks, barking like crazy at something Heath could not see between the island and the sink. Heath jerked her wheels to a stop, and her chair slid another couple of feet. The floor was covered in water.

"What in the hell is going on?" she roared, panic making her voice big and angry.

Elizabeth snatched her eyes from whatever Wily had cornered and, to Heath's relief and fury, began to laugh. She was laughing so hard she was holding her sides and gasping, feet dangling over the edge, rear end on the cutting board, when Gwen came running into the room. Before Heath could shout a warning, Gwen hit the water-slick and careened across the floor in a comic-book slide, arms windmilling, to fetch up against the island.

This sent E into another round of hysterical giggles.

"She could have fallen and broken a hip!" Heath shouted at her daughter. "We both could have been killed."

For reasons that Heath had no interest in, this struck not only E as funny, but Gwen as well.

"Damn it, Wily, shut up!" Heath roared. To her surprise he did. He grinned at her foolishly, then trotted over to her chair. Grabbing his collar, though he was the only one who appeared to be paying any attention to her, she waited with grim patience until Elizabeth and Gwen saw fit to stop snickering.

"Are you done?" she asked acidly when they'd quieted. Careful not to look at one another lest they burst out all over again, they both nodded.

"What the hell is going on?" Heath demanded.

"Elizabeth was playing with her food," Gwen said. That set them off again. Heath sat and fumed. She'd have lit a cigarette if she'd been anywhere but inside a house. There was nothing she could do when Gwen was encouraging E. Aunt Gwen was in her seventies, but when the two of them got going Heath could easily see what her aunt had been like when she was thirteen. Finally they wound down to intermittent giggles.

Wily whined.

A skritching of hard, sharp objects clawing at the floor emanated from behind the island, where now both E and her great-aunt sat swinging their legs, heels banging lightly against the tin sides. Gwen was in lime green capri pants and aqua tennis shoes, E in sweats, T-shirt, and purple flip-flops.

Brownish green and curved, a claw protruded from behind the island, then another, smaller, then the rest of the lobster.

"There are two," Gwen managed, fighting to keep her face straight. "John dropped them by for dinner tonight."

Gwen had come home at two in the morning. Heath had checked the time when the lift bell awakened her. Then she'd heard her aunt and John giggling in the kitchen. By the time Gwen had tiptoed through her bedroom and up to her tower room, Heath had been asleep. Now Gwen's paramour had come by to drop off gifts. Things were certainly moving along in that quarter, Heath thought sourly — the sourness of the proverbial grapes, she suspected.

"I took the lid off that bucket." E pointed to an overturned metal pail by the refrigerator. "And they just came out."

Again she and Gwen went into gales of giggles. Regardless of the shock of thinking her only child was being slaughtered by barbarian hordes, Heath could see the humor and allowed herself a smile.

Gwen hopped off the island. Expertly, she grabbed the first lobster behind its claws. After a lifetime of dealing with squirming children, lobsters evidently were no challenge. While E squealed, "Eeew!" Gwen dropped it in the bucket and then caught the second one.

"I've got to go down the lift and get a bucket of seawater. Our friends here will die if they stay out much longer."

"Aren't they supposed to die?" E asked. "They're food. Shouldn't they be in the refrigerator or somewhere? Not running around the kitchen frightening the children?"

"You cook them live," Gwen said.

Elizabeth's face went stiff with shock, her

mouth open. "You do not!" she exclaimed.

"You do. It doesn't hurt them," Gwen said matter-of-factly. In her soggy sneakers, her pail of lobsters at her side, Gwen marched out of the kitchen toward the lift.

"It doesn't *hurt* them?" E asked incredulously. "How can being boiled alive not *hurt* them?"

Before Heath could think of an answer, Elizabeth had run out of the kitchen. Heath rolled to the doorway, but E was not standing at the lift waiting for her aunt to return. She was nowhere in sight,

Unexploded ordnance, Heath thought miserably. Gwen should have known. She didn't know who to pity most, Elizabeth for her memories, or Gwen when she realized what she had done.

EIGHTEEN

Elizabeth couldn't run far. There was no "far" on Boar. Besides, Maine wasn't flip-flop country; it was all rocky ups and downs. She wouldn't dare be gone for long. Because of her depression and suicidal impulse, she knew if she was out of Heath's sight for too long, Heath would call in the marines.

Worse. She'd call Anna.

Heath had tried to make E know she understood thinking one wanted to die, thinking what a relief it would be to let all the pain and ugly drain away while she went to sleep. She also tried to bring home to her daughter the fact that that sleep was forever. A permanent solution to a temporary problem. What life had taught Heath, and what she clung to, was that if you didn't die, things got better.

Then, of course, you did die, Heath thought as she tried to decide whether it would be better to shout for Elizabeth to come back or let her have a little time by herself. But that wasn't the point.

Heath wanted desperately to talk to E about the lobster thing, though she knew Elizabeth was drowning in talk, advice, reassurances, and platitudes. "Love claustrophobia," E had self-diagnosed, suffering from too much love in too small a space. Occasionally, Heath wondered if E couldn't take love at the level she and Gwen were dishing it out because she had gotten too little love as a child. At other times, she assumed she and Gwen were a tad overbearing, both having been childless until Elizabeth.

Parental EMO. Elizabeth insisted it was enough to shrivel a person into a Cheeto.

Heath smiled at that, then yelled, "Elizabeth! Come back! We need to talk!" despite her better judgment.

When E was nine, a psycho had captured her and two other girls. Jena, E's therapist, had helped her work through it. Fervently, Heath wished Jena were on Boar Island. Without giving advice or passing judgment, Jena had the gift of herding a patient's thoughts the way a dog would herd sheep until they were all going in the right direction, then keep the patient company until she reached the place she needed to be.

Heath knew she and Gwen committed the sin of listening too hard. They couldn't help themselves. Sometimes Heath listened so hard she could almost hear her eardrums cracking. Aunt Gwen's face looked like Wily's when somebody had a piece of cheese he really, really wanted but was too well behaved to beg for.

Because of conferences with Jena, Heath knew what the kidnapper had tried to do to Elizabeth and the other girls. Making them kill mice was only the half of it. What the kidnapper had tried to do — had done — was rob them of themselves, then implant a version of his horrific psycho self in their brains.

The cyberstalker was trying to do the same thing, Heath realized. Using filth and threats and shame to take away E's sense of who she was and replace it with horribleness. No wonder she wanted to kill herself.

"E! Come back! Let's talk!" Heath shouted.

Wily trotted across the natural stone patio in the direction of the landward wing of ruins behind the lighthouse.

"Thank God," Heath breathed. There was no hiding from the nose. Elizabeth would never jump off a cliff in front of Wily, and

Wily wasn't fool enough to jump off a cliff just because the other kids did, Heath consoled herself.

Elizabeth might not want a fairy god-dog along. She might try to evade him. E thought she knew all Wily's tricks. She didn't. Nobody knew all Wily's tricks.

Heath rolled herself across the flat apron until she could see a sliver of what existed behind the imposing buttress of granite that backed the house. Huge blocks with deep fissured shelves tumbled down toward the ocean. Beyond was a light fog, breaking like liquid in pure white waves against the shore of Mount Desert Island, poking feathery fingers into low places and humping up over rocks.

The lift bell rang. Machinery clanked. Gwen returning with her freshly seawatered lobsters. The platform clanked into place, and silence fell.

"Elizabeth!" Heath cried again.

There was no sound but for the ocean murmuring its secrets to the rock.

Gwen, slopping water from the bucket, crossed to Heath. "Why are you shouting?" she demanded.

Heath told her.

"Maybe it won't be so bad." Gwen's optimism sounded strained. "Lobsters are just big brownish green spiders, after all."

"It was the alive part. Boiling them *alive*," Heath said dully. "I don't know if she still does, but back when she said her prayers aloud she prayed to mice — prayed to rodents — begging them to forgive her. I don't want to hear her praying to arachnids."

"And me fetching a bucket of saltwater, toting living sacrifices to toss in the pot like cannibals toss missionaries in old cartoons! How could I have been so stupid!" Gwen moaned.

On the tail of the moan rode silence, the kind that sets like concrete in the ear.

NINETEEN

Anna stood at the edge of Thunder Hole, a favorite tourist spot. A keyhole-shaped inlet in the granite cliffs forced waves into a narrow aperture, creating wondrous booming thunder and geysers of silver spray, some a hundred feet high. A walkway with metal handrails descended partway into the hole for those who wished to be misted — or drenched, as the sea saw fit.

Lunch with Denise — Subway sandwiches gobbled in the car — had been uphill work. Denise said little, showed no interest in talking of the park or the park personnel, yet the silences were not comfortable. Anna had the same feeling around Ranger Castle as she had around a kid with a balloon and a pin. Any minute there was liable to be a big bang that would scare her half to death.

As acting chief, there wasn't a whole lot to do in reality. An ambitious "acting" on a short-term assignment could louse up a lot of paperwork. Anna had stepped in for other district rangers often enough to know that unless something momentous occurred — and the state of Maine had snatched the only good murder on the books — general housekeeping was the rule.

With nothing important to do in the office, Anna opted for foot patrol, asking Denise to swing back around the Mount Desert Island loop to pick her up in a couple of hours.

Being free of the Crown Vic and Ranger Castle was more of a relief than it should have been. Castle put Anna on edge in some indefinable way. The woman wasn't right. She was out of sync. Anna was a great believer in vibes. The eye and the subconscious mind were often better at reading the small print, and making sense of it, than the conscious mind.

Leaves swirling on waters suggested deep and troubling currents. Denise had enough swirling leaves to make Anna's scalp prickle. It lent her a greater appreciation of having escaped to blue sea, golden sun, salt breezes, tourists to annoy, and cigarette butts to pick up.

She was happily ensconced with a trio of visitors, holding forth in excellent ranger style, adroitly avoiding admitting she knew zip about the flora and fauna on the coast of Maine, when her cell phone vibrated.

"Excuse me," she said as she took it from its wallet and glanced at the face. "It's a call I need to take," she apologized.

As she turned away, she heard the woman say, "Isn't that nice! She apologized!" The teenaged son said, "For what?"

"The stalker is here," Heath said without preamble.

Caller ID had done away with the need for most of the old rotary niceties, an advance Anna appreciated.

"In Maine. In the park. Or says he is," Heath said.

Phone to ear, Anna walked across the loop road and into the trees. Talking to a ranger in uniform was too great a temptation for visitors to resist, regardless of what the ranger was in the middle of. She switched the phone from her left to her right hand. Since she'd taken a bullet in her left bicep a year or so before, the arm had been opposed to remaining in static tension for any length of time. Unless she kept it moving, it stiffened and ached.

Oddly, that the stalker was in the park jolted Anna. With Heath sequestered on Boar, she'd fallen into the trap of feeling Elizabeth was safe, as if she were vacationing in a secure resort, and being stalked was no more real than a death at a Mystery Dinner.

Cybercreep was here.

"This is good news," she decided, settling cross-legged on the pine straw, careful not to lean against the tree. Sap was impossible to get out of polyester.

"You're kidding, right?" Heath asked.

"No. In cyberspace we had the chance of a snowball in hell of finding him. In a national park, it may be doable."

"Good point." Heath sounded relieved. "Except that he intends on doing more than slinging porn at E. He wants to meet with her."

Cybercreep had escalated. Anonymous bullies usually stayed anonymous. If this one was calling for a face-to-face, it was because he wanted to do something more than shame and frighten. He wanted a hands-on experience.

"Start at the beginning," Anna said.

"I got two texts — in reality, Elizabeth got the texts. Her phone buzzed. I grabbed it. I've saved them," Heath said unnecessarily. She, Anna, Gwen, and E had already had that talk. "The first says, 'I know where you are.' Not very original; we knew that from the heroin. The second says, 'Come to Cecelia's Coffee Shop today at six. Come by yourself if you want your real life back.' Cecelia's is in Bar Harbor on the town square. I Google-Mapped it."

"Better and better," Anna said. "A time and place." Silence followed that. Heath was no dummy. She would know the "better and better" could involve using E as bait at some point. Without knowing who the stalker was, or what he wanted — other than the obvious: rape, white slavery, psycho amusements of all sorts — there was danger in letting him within shooting distance of E. Then again, if they did use E as bait, at least they would be there when whatever trap he had planned began to unfold.

"This is not usual for a cyberbully, is it?" Heath asked. "More like a blackmailer, but so far nobody has asked us for anything."

"You're right," Anna said. "Poison pens and cyberstalkers thrive on being hidden, anonymous, watching the havoc they create from the safety of their webs — spider or otherwise. They wouldn't want to meet for coffee in public. Has E seen the texts?"

"Not yet. She and Wily are off somewhere licking their wounds."

"Wounds?"

"John gave Gwen two lobsters. She mentioned to E that they were boiled while alive."

"The mice," Anna said, remembering the little corpses nailed to the side of the outhouse at the cabin in Rocky. Nailed while they still lived. Not an image a young girl should have burned into her brain. Or a ranger of a certain age, for that matter.

"Get your real life back," she said, changing the subject. "What do you figure that means? If they're talking reputation, that ship has sailed."

Heath groaned. "God, don't say that."

"When I was in high school there was a girl all the boys called Rosie Rotten-crotch," Anna said, remembering. "Supposedly she was the school hump. At that age, I never thought to question it. Now I wonder if Rosie said yes, or maybe no, to the wrong boy. Or if a jealous girl started it. Rosie was an American Indian girl from the local Paiute tribe. Scapegoat. Nobody cared to dig any deeper." Anna felt a stab of guilt. She hadn't cared either. "Rosie was ruined. There's no way to rehabilitate this sort of reputation wreck."

"Yes there is," Heath insisted firmly.

Anna let that stand. If Heath said it, they'd figure out a way to make it true. Later. She glanced at her watch. "It's four

260

thirty. Our stalker might know you're in Acadia, but I bet he doesn't know you're on Boar, or he'd have given E more lead time to make the meeting. I think I can make it."

"So can I," Heath said. "I'll call a water taxi and meet you in Bar Harbor."

"No," Anna said. " 'Come alone if you want your life back.' Elizabeth was to come alone. We should assume this person knows something about you. We don't want to scare him off."

There was a long silence, then a gust of air that Anna suspected was tainted with tobacco smoke. "Right," Heath said finally. "A woman in a wheelchair is noticed. Then ignored."

"It's the first part that would wreck the surveillance."

TWENTY

Denise picked Anna up ten minutes after she called. Denise's unsettling aura, the one that made Anna's spine tingle, evaporated as Anna told her what she wanted. The abrupt loss of Denise's erratic hypervigilance made Anna wonder what she'd been expecting. What she'd been fearing. Given Ranger Castle's behavior, Anna didn't think "fear" was too strong a word. Maybe whatever had inspired her sudden retirement was still haunting her.

"So," Anna finished, "Elizabeth's stalker is here in Maine. Wants a meet-and-greet. E's off somewhere communing with the spirits, but we don't want to let the opportunity slip past."

Denise leaned forward until her chin was almost resting on the steering wheel. "Are all men such bastards?" she demanded. "Serial killing, child molesting, rape, bestiality — you name it, men do it."

"Women, too," Anna said because she was in the mood to poke a hornets' nest.

Denise sucked an audible breath through her nose, then puffed the air out of lips loose with scorn. "Sure. One, two maybe. Not enough for a decent statistic. Get real. Women do shitty things, no doubt about it, but the twisted male victimization of women is front page every day. Got a cult leader? What's the first thing he does? Makes all the women sleep with him. Got a God? First thing the guy says — and the gods are all guys nowadays — is 'Obey your husband. Put yourself in a black bag so nobody can see you.' Root of all evil, Eve and the god-damned apple my ass! More like Adam and his snake."

Anna laughed. "I like that. I have to remember to tell my husband. He's a priest."

Denise looked at her, her eyebrows in a shocked V. "Like defrocked?"

Anna laughed again. "Episcopal."

"Sorry I shot off my mouth," Denise said. She sounded more sulky than sorry. Rather like a child who got caught doing something she wasn't supposed to.

"Don't be," Anna said easily. "In this case, you're preaching to the choir. This victim is a particular friend of mine." She didn't mention that E was her goddaughter. Being married to a priest was condemnation enough to a cynical ear.

Having cleared the change in routine with Peter, Anna and Denise would swap out cars so they weren't in a marked NPS vehicle. Denise would accompany Anna to the coffee shop. It was unlikely, but whoever was behind the bullying might recognize Anna on sight. Denise had the advantage of being an unknown.

"Do you know anything about stalking via the Internet?" Anna asked as Denise pulled the patrol vehicle into the parking garage beneath her apartment building in Bar Harbor.

Denise's head jerked back as if Anna had flopped a nasty fish in her face.

"What are you implying?" she asked, an edge to her voice.

Maybe Denise had done a bit of cyber-spying after the split with Peter. Before the Internet, dumped girlfriends had to drive by "his" house to see whose car was parked there. Now, armed with personal information, they could read credit reports, check Facebook. All manner of interesting new methods of self-torture were available.

"I'm pretty ignorant when it comes to this stuff," Anna replied mildly. "I hoped you might know more."

"Oh," Denise said. "No. I'm not into that. I don't even have a cell phone."

For a law enforcement officer not to have a cell phone was tantamount to dereliction of duty. More was the pity; a cell phone saw to it that no one was ever truly off duty, or home from work. Anna tossed this lack of modern technology onto the pile of Weird Denise Castle Things growing in the back of her mind.

With the nervous reluctance of a jeweler ushering in a cat burglar, Denise let Anna into her apartment. To Anna's eyes there was nothing to be ashamed of. The place was neat to a fault — no books, no magazines, no cats or dogs or dirty underpants on the floor. White walls were decorated with framed photographs in black and white of the park both above and below the surface of the Atlantic. The carpet was white, no off-color spots where beasties vomited or booted feet left dirt. The couch was white, black-and-white zebra-print pillows standing sentinel at either end. A glass coffee table and a flat-screen TV finished the decor.

With the air of a wary damsel inviting a vampire over the threshold, Denise said, "This way," and ushered Anna into the apartment's single bedroom. It was as monochromatic as the living room. Both rooms had the impersonal feel of having been "dressed" by a Realtor looking to sell.

"These should fit well enough," Denise said, pulling a pair of gray linen slacks and a white pleated-front blouse from the closet. A narrow black belt was hooked over the hanger by the buckle. The clothes in the closet were all arranged in outfits. She laid the clothes on the bed, then took a shoe box from a neat arrangement of shoe boxes on the closet floor. "Size seven and a half," she said.

"That will work," Anna replied.

Denise looked around the sparsely furnished room, then left reluctantly as if she thought Anna might pocket any valuables left lying around.

Having put on Denise's outfit, Anna studied herself in the mirror on the sliding closet door. In any mall in America she would have gone unremarked. Salespeople would trust her. PTAs would welcome her as a member. Anna felt deep, deep undercover. Still, it was good to be free of the Kevlar vest. Anna missed the days when they were an option, not a requirement, for law enforcement rangers.

In the mirror's reflection she noted the

single personal item in this impersonal lair. A photograph stood on the black wooden nightstand. Drawn to it, Anna picked it up. A narrow rectangle, matted to fit the standard frame, showed a much younger Denise in her Park Service uniform. Three fingers wrapped around her right arm. It must have been taken when she was with Peter. He'd been cut out and the mat redone to cover the excision. Symbolic, this hiding of the past with a black mask. In the photo Denise was smiling, an expression Anna had seldom seen on her face. It had been taken before Denise had gotten her teeth capped. Her old incisors, the way they neatly overlapped, struck Anna as familiar.

"Are you done?" Denise demanded. She had entered without knocking and stood in the bedroom door radiating disapproval.

"Yes," Anna said. "Is this you?" she asked, holding up the photograph.

"It was," Denise said.

"You remind me of somebody," Anna said, turning the picture to study the image.

Denise laughed, a cartoon laugh, "Heh, heh, heh." In two steps, she'd crossed the small room and taken the picture from Anna's hands. "I have that kind of face. I always remind somebody of somebody else." Opening the drawer on the nightstand, she dropped it in facedown, then snapped the drawer closed again. "Let me get dressed."

Summarily dismissed, Anna slunk back into the living room. She'd thought the woman had been warming to her. Evidently that phase of their relationship was abruptly at an end. Why? Was Denise hiding something? Shame at having cut Peter from a picture? Embarrassment at having her crooked teeth on display? Her sudden iciness seemed overkill for such minor humiliations.

Unless Anna had stumbled on a sore spot, pushed an old button. Perhaps Denise had been teased about the teeth. One never knew which closets harbored a stranger's skeletons.

In moments Denise emerged from the bedroom in black slacks and a white sleeveless mock turtleneck. "Let's get on with it," she said as she walked to the door. Opening it, she held it, whisking Anna out with a sweep of her hand.

Door closed and locked, Denise relaxed marginally. By the time they'd traveled down the stairs to the garage, she seemed nearly her usual slightly weird self.

She opened the door of a forest green Mazda Miata. The top was down. "Cool,"

Anna said as she slid in.

"Not very practical," Denise said as if she quoted a stern and humorless mother.

Cecelia's Coffee Shop was on the town square in the heart of Bar Harbor's tourist district. Had the Miata not been so small, parking would have been a bitch; as it was, Denise slipped into a slot between two SUVs less than a block from the square.

She and Anna were intentionally early. They bought ice cream in small foam cups from a vendor in a pseudo-nineteenth-century cart complete with horse, then wandered to a bench in the square where they could watch the coffee shop.

"Your stalker can't have too sinister an intent on his mind," Denise said as she carved out a neat bite of ice cream with her tiny plastic spork.

"Not here," Anna agreed. This wasn't the haunted house at midnight. There would be no kidnapping, raping, or pillaging. Café tables sat beneath a striped awning, mothers and students and tourists perching on the ironwork chairs. People in shorts and T-shirts carrying plastic bags emblazoned with the names of local shops entered. A few minutes later they exited, iced coffee or mochaccino in hand. Nothing fishy, nothing shady.

On such a sunny afternoon, in the middle of a town set above the glittering blue of the Atlantic, and Disneyesque in its adorability, kidnapping, raping, and pillaging seemed an alien concept. Surely a species that invented ice cream, kites, and flip-flops would be incapable of harming a hair on a puppy's head.

The mystery of humanity wasn't that people were starkly evil or magnificently good but that they were both all the time. Sanity and insanity dwelt side by side in the human brain. Only when one grew so big it overshadowed and starved the other was it noticed.

People tended to either keep their crazy to themselves or gather with others sharing the same delusion. Churches, synagogues, temples, covens, mosques: If enough people believed a thing, it was declared sane. One person speaking to invisible beings was a nutcase. A thousand was a cult. Ten thousand, a religion.

Fortunately, most human madness was harmless, creative even; it made life rich and memorable and annoyingly real.

"Any clue as to what we're looking for?" Denise asked, cutting into Anna's thoughts.

"Nope." Anna took a small bite of pistachio ice cream and let it melt on her tongue for a moment. "Early on I would have said teenage boys or girls, but they aren't the sort who track victims across land for a couple thousand miles. That takes money and autonomy."

"Any Dirty Uncle Ernies on the radar?" Denise asked.

"Not since she was nine."

"Goddamn sons of bitches," Denise said.

Two white high-school-aged girls and a woman who could have been their mother sat at one of the tables. Both girls were on iPhones. Mom, evidently old school, read a paperback novel. An older white male with a fat dachshund on a pink leash sat at another table and read a newspaper. Two boys came, opened their laptops on the third table, and ignored each other.

The older man finished his coffee. He and his hound ambled off. A barista cleared away his paper cup. Two middle-aged black women, both in capri pants and high-heeled sandals, took his place, sipping iced coffee. Obeying some psychic — or cyber — signal, the boys simultaneously folded up their laptops and left, still not speaking.

Time for the rendezvous came and went.

As afternoon on the square melted into evening on the square, Anna told Denise the details of the bullying. "At first we

271

figured it must be a kid — or kids — in her school. As it turns out, if the victim doesn't know the bullies or the bullies don't ID themselves, or friends rat them out, there is virtually — and in this sense I mean virtually literally — no way to track them."

"There's got to be," Denise said, settling on a bench near an old cannon on a concrete slab. "They can hack into your computer and record every keystroke you make, redirect your browser to ad sites, turn on the volume when they want to sing you a slogan, pinpoint your position anywhere on the face of the earth, find out what color panties you're wearing, then try and sell you Viagra. How can they not track some pricks bullying a girl?"

"I guess we're talking different theys," Anna said as she spooned up a bit of the green dessert and laid it neatly on the end of her tongue, where it would melt over as many taste buds as possible on its journey to her esophagus.

"The capitalist theys are more motivated and tech-savvy than the don't-bully-children theys," Anna finished.

"And you can bet not one of them gives a flying fig about lost girls. Not one," Denise said as she savagely attacked the chocolate chunk with her spork. "What makes you think it isn't scumbag kids?" she asked around a mouthful of ice cream. "It stinks of scumbag kid fun to me."

"Asking for a face-to-face," Anna replied as she watched the people coming and going at the coffee shop. "To make a trip cross-country suggests an adult with the independence and money to travel."

"What does the girl . . . Elizabeth?"

Anna nodded.

"What does Elizabeth think of the new development?" Denise asked.

"She doesn't know yet. Her mother said she needed some time by herself. The combined concern of her mother, her great-aunt Gwen, and probably me can't be all that easy to deal with. Poor kid."

"Yeah, poor kid," Denise echoed dully.

Anna was thinking of her husband, Paul. Never had anyone loved her like he did. More than she deserved. More than she could accept sometimes. There were moments it was as if she dared not feel pain because he would feel it as well, when she could not choose to spend herself as she would like because of what it would cost him.

"Unconditional love, in large doses, can be a burden," she mused.

"I wouldn't know," Denise said.

Her tone snapped Anna out of her reverie. "There's an odd one," she said to deflect the feeling of guilt Denise's sudden exposure had awakened. Using her spork, she gestured toward a woman nearing the coffee shop. She was plump, tall in platform sandals. Screaming red hair was styled in a short curly cap and set off by oversized glasses framed in turquoise. An enormous straw bag flapped at her legs as she walked, gripped by a hand as round and dimpled as that of a child, though the woman was probably in her mid-to-late thirties.

"What's that in her bag?" Denise asked.

"Damn," Anna said, then laughed. "It looks like a welding glove."

"I think we've lost our window of opportunity," Denise said finally.

"Maybe a no-show," Anna said.

"Maybe," Denise replied.

"Got cold feet?" Anna wondered.

"Made us?" Denise suggested.

"More likely, we didn't make him." Two college boys online, one old guy with a dog, one fat guy with badly behaved offspring. Woman with a Bozo hairdo. Nothing screamed stalker.

"We're nowhere," Anna admitted. Her cell phone buzzed. "Excuse me," she said as she looked at the screen. "It's our victim's mother, probably wanting to know how we're doing." Anna poked the green phone icon and put the cell phone to her ear. "Heath," she said.

"Elizabeth has gone missing."

"You said she needed time alone," Anna said, surprised at the terror in Heath's voice.

"Hours ago, damn it! Hours ago. This island is the size of a postage stamp. She hasn't come back," Heath said.

Her fear awoke Anna's. This wasn't like E, to worry people she loved.

"Is Wily with her?" Anna demanded.

"I guess," Heath said distractedly.

Anna smothered the urge to say, "That's okay then." Absurd as it was, the fact that the old dog was with E reassured her. Anna and Wily had forged an odd connection in the North Woods of Minnesota. It wasn't something Anna chose to talk about. She doubted Wily did either.

"Anna, I'm pretty sure she's not on the island," Heath almost wailed. "I've looked everywhere I can, and called until I'm hoarse."

While Anna had been neatly occupied eating ice cream in Bar Harbor, E had disappeared. Were the two connected? Had Anna been made a patsy? "Is Gwen with you?"

"No, Gwen and John went to Bangor for the evening. Dinner and a visit with Chris Zuckerberg."

"I'm on my way. Give me half an hour," Anna said. It would take her that long to talk somebody out of a boat and get to the island. Elizabeth's body — Anna shuddered as she thought the word — would be found only by boat if she had fallen.

Or jumped.

TWENTY-ONE

Heath half crouched near the wall of boulders ringing the area that had been leveled to build the tower and house. She had on Dem Bones, her high-tech robotic walking suit, legs and belly strapped in, bright silver lozenge-shaped pieces of machinery on the outside of her thighs and calves, hinges at hip and knee. The armbrace crutches lay fifteen feet away where she'd flung them in a rage when they got in the way of her attempts to get this so-called wonder of modern technology to complete the simple task of moving her bony ass up and over the chunks of stone calved off the granite wall.

"Goddamn useless piece of shit," she cried. Her hands clawed at the slick rock as the weight of her lower limbs, and the titanium skeleton, dragged her down. Using the motions available to her, she could only manage to kick uselessly at the rock with feet like senseless clubs, and knees not worth the effort it took technology to bend them.

As she slid back for the third time, leaving long white scratches on the glossy silver finish of the thigh and calf pieces, she screamed like a wounded panther.

Frustration consumed energy that, left alone, would turn to thoughts. There was nothing Heath could think that wasn't insupportable, that wouldn't sear the marrow in her bones. Someone was stalking her daughter; now her daughter was missing. Heath had been a fool to think cyberfilth would be the sum total of it. She was a fool not to have taken E to London, put her into witness protection, hired bodyguards. Such was her arrogant stupidity, she had thought a cripple, an old dog, and a septuagenarian pediatrician could keep her child safe.

E hasn't been missing all that long, she told herself.

"Damned she hasn't," she said aloud. Only a few hours, but Boar Island wasn't a few hours' worth of adventure. Heath automatically reached down her right hand. No wheelchair, no saddlebags, no cigarettes. "Piece of shit," she muttered.

Never would E intentionally scare her or Gwen by staying away so long. Wily would have come back if he could have, if for no other reason than his dinner was served at five every day. If E was hurt, Wily would have howled when he heard Heath calling his name. There was no girl and no dog, and the only way that could happen was if they'd been taken.

Not jumped or fallen, Heath thought. E wouldn't take Wily with her into the grave, and Wily wasn't the type to leap off a fifty-foot cliff even if E did. Besides, Elizabeth was past suicide. She was.

The lift bell rang. Frankenstein-like, Heath turned, then lurched toward where the elevator would release its passenger. "It better be you, Anna," she shouted as she monstered across the level rock. Anna didn't deserve that. Scarcely thirty-five minutes had passed since Heath called. The super-woman suit didn't deserve to be called a piece of shit either, for that matter. Heath didn't care. Choices were limited: She could rage or she could fall apart.

The lift clattered into its dock with a groan that, no matter how often Heath heard it, seemed to presage immediate disaster. Anna stepped off. "It's me," she said unnecessarily. She was in her full ranger costume, gun and all. Heath was so glad to see her, she could have burst into tears.

"About time," she said.

Anna paid no attention to the snarling dog that had possessed Heath. Undoubtedly she'd seen that fear hound more times than she'd care to remember. Heath was grateful.

"Where have you looked?" Anna asked.

"Goddamn nowhere," Heath admitted. "I got back into the ruins a ways and called. There is so much crap on the ground and the floors are so rotten, I couldn't do much inside. The rest of this godforsaken rock might as well be Mars. I can't get out of this bear pit. I went up and down the lift a few times and saw what I could from the dock. I butted myself up the whole piece-of-shit tower, one hundred and seventy feet of metal stairs, and couldn't see a damn thing from the windows. Couldn't hold myself up to look over the sills for more than a second. That's it. That's it."

"How long has she been gone, and how did she go?" Anna asked.

Heath sputtered out the tale of the lobsters and Wily. "John picked Gwen up a few minutes later. It never occurred to us that E wouldn't be right back. I am an idiot," she finished.

Anna nodded as if Heath had given her a measured professional report of the search to date. She looked around the open space at the rocks and rubble, then up at the sky.

"Light's going," Anna said. "We'd better figure out where she headed and then get moving. You want to come?"

Heath wanted to. She wanted it so much she could feel her fingers curling around Anna's from where she stood.

"No," she said through stiff lips. "You'll move faster alone."

TWENTY-TWO

Denise sat behind the wheel of her car shaking. Not shaking. Twitching like a doll with its legs stuck in a garbage disposal. Tears — a luxury she seldom enjoyed — poured down her face. Before Paulette came and gave her permission to feel, one of the few times she'd cried was the day she heard Peter was engaged. Those tears had been turned to steam by white-hot anger before they'd reached the air. She'd almost missed the days when her tear ducts had been welded shut. Now great fat drops ran down the side of her nose to drip on the black linen of her trousers.

Ranger Pigeon was finally gone. She'd been in Denise's bedroom — again — changing out of Denise's clothes, then used Denise's bathroom, no doubt rummaging through the medicine cabinet, and the towel cupboard, and under the sink, looking for anything that would trigger the memory of who Denise's photo reminded her of. Her ferreting brain ticking like a bomb.

Denise had screwed up royally at the scene. She'd acted guilty as hell, searching the murder room for traces she might have left while the pigeon watched from the doorway, running back to the car and hiding, practically running the woman over to get her away from Paulette, going part postal over the old picture. Anna Pigeon was one of those people who saw, who looked and saw the person behind the eyes. Denise had run up about a dozen red flags.

"God damn me!" Denise cried and struck a fist against the steering wheel. "I didn't think. I didn't fucking think!" When she'd offered Anna a change of clothes, and the use of her car for the undercover stint, she hadn't thought of Paulette, of the plan. She had a family now. She had to think of them first, before the job, before cyberstalkers, before endangered citizens, before herself. Family came before everything. Family was everything.

"Don't screw this up," she muttered fiercely, then turned the key in the ignition, bringing the Miata to life. She had to see Paulette. They needed to talk this through. Denise was still in her civvies, still in the Miata, her radio on the passenger seat monitoring the traffic. It would be a risk, but the sense of urgency driving her made it imperative. She looked at her watch. Seven fifteen. Paulette was a nurse. Three days a week she worked the two-to-midnight shift in the infants ward at Mount Desert Hospital. This was one of her nights. Pulling out of the NPS headquarters' parking lot, Denise texted: *mt me H pking lot. 10 min.*

By the time she reached the hospital, the sun was going down. The long summer afternoons were golden, the light softening trees to a dark haze and turning the ocean to navy blue.

When she and her sister were ready, Denise decided, they would move somewhere there was no ocean, no winter, where the world wasn't made of rock and snow and ice water. Georgia maybe. Georgia in the pines, a little cabin. That would be perfect. Maybe a lake. Too dangerous, she decided as she parked the Miata in the darkest corner behind the building. Kids drowned in lakes all the time. In Georgia there might be alligators. Alligators liked children and little fluffy dogs. She'd read that somewhere.

Turning off the ignition, Denise lay back in her seat and waited. Paulette might not be able to get away instantly, but she'd come. Denise knew she would. They were twins. They had the exact same blood and bone and brain. They didn't have identical fingerprints. Had she ever Googled that in a hurry! What a drag it would have been if Paulette's fingerprints at the murder scene lit up Denise's own on IAFIS, the federal print identification base.

In everything that mattered, they were identical. Paulette would never let her down.

Ranger Pigeon and that damned picture. "Is this *you*? You remind me of *somebody*." The memory bit Denise in the butt again. In a fit of paranoia, she leapt from the car to put the top up. Nobody would be looking; still, it was best if she and Paulette were not seen together.

With the lowering of the sun, clouds came scudding from the southwest, and fog began to tease in from its hiding places out to sea. Good, Denise thought as she clipped the top securely down. Once she had hated the fog, hated the clammy dead touch of mist, and the confusion of veils across her eyes. Now it made her feel safer. To be hidden was calming, centering, like the world beneath the sea.

As she settled behind the wheel in the tiny car, a slash of light cut the deep shadow in the back of the building; the fire stairs, that was where the nurses left the building.

There were no reserved spaces; their cars had to be parked in the back lot, the dark lot, the lot where bad things could happen.

"Screw men," Denise whispered. "Screw them all. Bastards."

She thought to flash the headlights to identify herself, but there was no need. Paulette would know where she was. She would feel her in the gray cloak of encroaching fog the way one hand felt the other in a game of cat's cradle. Such an old game. Denise couldn't remember anyone teaching it to her. No cheery childhood memories of doting grandmamas or loving aunts.

Poor little Anna Pigeon and her poor little Elizabeth suffering from a surfeit of love. "Such a burden!" Denise mocked, her voice pitched low. "God, how does one bear it!" She should have gouged Pigeon's eye out with a spork.

Nope, nobody had bothered teaching poor little Denise a nice game like cat's cradle.

Maybe it was a memory of Paulette's that had traveled into her head.

God damn Anna Pigeon. God damn Denise Castle for letting her into her apartment, leaving her alone in the bedroom, for not hiding the photograph.

Now she and Paulette were going to have to speed things up. The luxury of time was gone. It had drained away like water down a gopher hole during the time Anna Pigeon was with her. Beady eyes licking over everything, foxy ears perked, the pigeon watched and thought while Denise did everything but spray-paint GUILTY on the clean white walls of her apartment.

Paulette had to move faster on the land sale, and Denise on tracking down the legacy advertised in the papers. If there was a legacy. She also had to give the NPS notice and get her pension papers filed. Everything had to be in place so they could tie up the loose ends and be gone before anybody knew there was any reason to think there were two of them, that they had anything to do with Duffy's demise.

"I don't have long," Paulette said as she slid in the passenger door. "I said I was going out for a cigarette. The head nurse is cool with that. She smokes a pack and a half a day."

"We'll have to quit when the family is complete," Denise said, though she'd never smoked a cigarette in her life.

"Complete?" Paulette questioned.

That Paulette didn't inherently understand annoyed Denise. She pressed the sensation down hard. Paulette was her sister, her other self; she could never be annoyed with her. Not ever. "We're going be a family," Denise explained patiently. "Like we wanted. Like we are supposed to be. It's the last thing we have to do before we go. We got rid of Kurt. Now, as soon as we are complete, we can go. Have to go, and sooner rather than later."

Paulette looked confused. Or maybe Denise just felt her confusion. The little shards of streetlights and security lights refracting in the rearview mirrors weren't sufficient to read a face.

"A family. More than just you and me?" Paulette asked.

Again the stab of irritation; again Denise shoved it down. "Families have children," Denise said too sharply.

"You said Peter had murdered your babies," Paulette said in a gentle voice. "Tell me how it was."

The irritation Denise was suffering wasn't for her sister, her twin. It was like the twitches, a case of nerves. She took hold of Paulette's hand and leaned back in the seat. The memory didn't come; it was always there, sharper and more detailed each time she revisited it.

"Four years ago I got pregnant," Denise said. "It was Peter's, of course. I loved my baby. I knew I wasn't getting any younger,

288

and I loved my baby so much."

"Did Peter beat you?" Paulette asked. That was how her babies had been murdered.

"He said he didn't want our baby. He said he never wanted children. He said he couldn't face it. He made me get an abortion." He'd said he'd leave her if she didn't get an abortion, that's what he had said, but it was the same thing.

"Something went wrong," Denise said. "Something got ripped. I was told I couldn't have any more children. Then Peter left."

"And married Lily and had a baby," Paulette finished softly.

"My baby," Denise said.

Paulette squeezed her hand. "Is that why you came? To tell me about the baby?"

Denise opened her eyes, suddenly back from the ugly trip down Memory Lane. Peter had turned what should have been a sentimental journey into a nightmare on Elm Street. "No. I came to tell you we have to move faster. It's that ranger, Anna Pigeon. I caught her looking at a photo of us. Then she peers into me. Icepick eyes. I got that shivery feeling you get when something bad is about to happen."

"Who took the photo of us?" Alarmed, Paulette jerked her hand out of Denise's.

Hot snaps of anger cracked up Denise's spine.

Not for Paulette. Nerves.

"It wasn't us exactly," Denise said. "It was me, before I got my teeth capped. My hair was blond then, and wild." For a moment she believed that, but it wasn't right. Her teeth hadn't been capped yet, true, but in the picture her hair wasn't like Paulette's. It was the same boring brown as it always was. For a moment, in her mind, she'd seen it blond and big like her sister's. Rubbing her face, she mumbled through her fingers, "Anna Pigeon knows. She stares at the picture, then gives me this smirky look and says, 'Is this *you*? You remind me of *somebody.*' She spent a lot of time with you at the house. She knows. Why would she say 'you remind me of somebody' unless she wanted me to know she knew I had a twin?"

There was a wrongness to her logic, Denise knew that; still and all, she felt it to be the truth. Knew it to be the truth. "Anna Pigeon will ruin everything."

Paulette sat quiet for a long time. Denise could feel twitches building in her hands, her feet. The sparks of anger flared in her esophagus until she thought she might breathe fire.

"Anna Pigeon, she's the ranger who came with you when the police were at my house?" Paulette asked, her words coming slowly, as if her mind were working hard between each utterance.

"That was her," Denise said. "Shit!" She slammed the heel of her hand against the steering wheel. "I never should have let the bitch out of the car. She's got a nose as long as a dachshund's, sticking it where it doesn't belong."

"I think maybe she knew I was me," Paulette admitted. "She looked at me like you said she looked at the picture, like she knew I was inside, there behind my eyes, and she was going to scrape me out like an oyster out of its shell."

Denise became still, no twitches, no angry motions. Staring at her sister, she let the awe that had been building since they'd found each other fill her whole being. Paulette knew everything that happened in Denise's head just as Denise knew everything that happened in Paulette's head. "Exactly like that. An oyster from its shell," Denise whispered.

"Oh God," Paulette moaned. "Maybe she looks at everybody like that. She's probably just the kind of person who really looks at things."

That wasn't it. Denise knew. Paulette knew, too; she just didn't want to admit it.

For a long time neither one of them spoke. Denise didn't feel alone in the silence. She felt *together* in the silence. Mostly.

"What do we do?" Paulette asked at last.

"I'll think of something. It's us against the world." Denise laughed because she knew it was true, the only truth.

TWENTY-THREE

The agony that stretched Heath's skin thin over the bones of her face fueled Anna's own fears. "Let's get started," she said, and turned away from her friend lest their terrors coalesce into panic. Eyes long since trained to look for spoor darted over the natural patio and the boulders surrounding it. A half-chewed bone — a project of Wily's, no doubt; flecks of brown tobacco, blowing in idle circles, eddying in the breeze where the walls formed a corner; faint tracks — the tread of Robo-butt's rubber wheels leaving bits of dried mud in the light burnishing of dust.

"It hasn't rained," Anna said.

"No. Why are we talking about the weather?" Heath was fighting tears. Anna could feel fear and shame and guilt boiling off of her like heat from pavement.

"Your wheelchair left tracks. See. Dry now, but you rolled through water. Why?"

Anna asked. In the zone where spoor and prey are all that matters, Anna barely heard Heath's sputtered curses as she backtracked to where the wheels had found enough water to make mud.

"The lobsters," Heath cried suddenly. "They were in a bucket there. Gwen put them down, and we forgot all about them."

"No lobsters, no bucket," Anna said. "Do you think John Whitman took them? Maybe when he came for Gwen, he took them home to eat them himself?"

Heath thought for a moment, then said, "No. I watched Gwen and John go down the lift. Gwen had her little book-pack full of things for Ms. Zuckerberg, and her purse. John wasn't carrying anything. Both hands were empty. I'm sure of it."

"Somebody took lobsters and bucket. E? Returning to the scene of the crime to rescue the lobsters from the pot?" Anna suggested.

"Yes!" Heath almost shouted. "Yes! She would have come back and gotten them. She would want to set them free. Save their creepy crustacean lives out of the goodness of her heart. Yes. Oh, God. How long does it take to let a couple lobsters go? Ten minutes? We're in the middle of the goddamn ocean. Not even five. She's been gone three hours and twenty-three minutes," Heath wailed. She looked at her wristwatch. "Twenty-six minutes," she amended.

Anna didn't bother to ask Heath if she'd called 911, the Coast Guard, or the army. She knew the drill: Nobody looked for adults — and for this, E counted as an adult — until they'd been missing for forty-eight hours. Nobody looked for an emotional teenager out of sight for a few hours.

Heath's eyes filled with tears. Anna turned her back lest the contagion spread.

Elizabeth, worrying her mother into a state of frenzy, and risking Anna's wrath, by vanishing; that wasn't the child Anna had godparented. E cared what people thought of her, especially the people she loved. Often Anna had wondered if she cared too much, spent too much of her childhood being a parent to those around her, taking care of everybody at the expense of taking care of herself.

It would take a momentous event to lift that burden from E, to make her as thoughtless as the average person. Unless Barnum & Bailey had pitched a tent on Boar Island, or Brad Pitt made an unscheduled stop, Anna couldn't think what might distract E from her customary responsibilities.

If Brad, Barnum, and Bailey were out of

the picture, the landscape became darker. Either E was not on the island or she was on the island but could not get back to the lighthouse. Anna tried to picture her curled up in the fetal position beneath the overhang of a boulder, Wily beside her. Asleep maybe.

Several hours was a long time to sleep on a rock.

A sixteen-year-old girl, possibly suicidal, definitely tormented, gone for hours on a rock not big enough to register on most charts.

That line of thought served no one.

"So, E came back and got the bucket with the lobsters," Anna said. "Describe it."

"It was a bucket. A regular bucket," Heath said. Then she threw her head back like a cat and yowled, "Elizabeth!"

Anna had seen Heath under pressure before. In life-and-death situations, physical stress and emotional pain, but she'd never seen her like this, losing control, becoming a victim herself.

"Think," she demanded. Then went on, "Bucket full of water and lobsters, the bucket would weigh close to thirty pounds. So E could lift it, but not carry it easily. Buckets are awkward. So she's got the lobsters, and she's planning on emancipating them. Elizabeth would know they'd die if she just turned them loose on a rock in the sun. Might as well go ahead and boil them, if she was going to do that. At least it would be faster." Anna followed a slopping trail where water had mixed with sand particles and dust, then been dragged through with a smooth shoe, probably Elizabeth's flip-flop. It led to the wall that protected the patio from the fifty-foot drop to the ocean. Anna leaned out and looked down the precipitous fall to the rocks below. "So she dragged the bucket to the cliff and looked over. That's a long way down. If she poured them over, the fall might kill them."

"The lift," Heath said.

"The bell ringing would bring you and Gwen running," Anna said.

"And she didn't want to see us. Didn't want to talk to us. Couldn't believe we would talk about boiling living things alive so we could watch them die." Heath's voice was climbing and diving as her mind drove it from self-hatred to despair.

"I need you to focus," Anna said. "Was the bucket metal or wood?"

"Metal," Heath managed, then pressed her lips together as if holding back a horde of wasps wanting to swarm out of her mouth.

"Five gallons or thereabout?" Anna asked.

Five was a standard bucket size.

"About." Heath let the word out before resealing her lips.

"Full of lobsters and water," Anna said. "Heavy." She studied the granite above where the water had spilled, then dried. "There."

"I don't see anything," Heath said, coming so close she rolled one wheel half over Anna's toes.

Anna ignored the pain. Heath had enough on her mind. "There," she pointed. "See where the metal bucket scraped the rock. E hauled it up here. Dragging." Following the marks, Anna climbed the sloping face of the boulder on hands and feet. Her left arm ached. Since she'd been wounded it had never recovered its full strength. Physical therapy had only gotten it so far. After that, Anna treated it with denial.

Eyes to the ground, she climbed and boulder-hopped past the ruined wings of the old house and around the broken upthrust of granite.

The north side of the island, scarcely as big as two football fields, was formed of enormous chunks of granite that had cracked and worn over the eons until it created steep rounded steps descending in giant leaps to the sea. Sunlight caught shining facets, making them sparkle. Scrubby mosses and lichens grew between the rocks as if they'd been there forever. Anna smiled at the thought. Of course they'd been there forever. They were rocks.

Fissures wide enough to accommodate the passage of a slender girl and a skinny dog made a grid pattern. The lines were not straight or square enough to look man-made, but nearly so. Varying heights of rocks blocked any view of the island's shoreline.

As she stared into the distance over the swells, it struck Anna how much bigger the Atlantic seemed than the Pacific. The Atlantic and Pacific would be the only two oceans Elizabeth had ever seen. Before Heath found E, she knew nothing about the world. She was homeschooled. Her reading skills were strong, as were her math skills. She scored high on the IQ test the therapist Heath had hired gave her. Elizabeth could cook and sew better than most grown women. She knew the names of the major stars and constellations. But about the world's geography and sociology she'd been taught very little.

A lot of nine-year-olds at least knew there were seven seas. Elizabeth hadn't. She hadn't even known there were fifty states. Heath said she hadn't been aware there were people of different colors or who spoke different languages. She hadn't known people were gay or monogamous.

No television. No movies. No radio.

The world of the cult compound had little variety; everybody was considered a brother or sister or cousin whether they were blood relations or not. Polygamous, white, religious, and completely contained between the dusty gold walls of a canyon west of Loveland, Colorado, was the only life Elizabeth knew until Heath had adopted her. For the seven years since, she'd been in Boulder learning to be a twenty-first-century little girl. Then a high school girl.

Then a shamed and shunned pariah.

Now she was suddenly half a continent from Colorado, from her friends, marooned on an island. A lot for a person to deal with, Anna thought.

There was little in the way of earth or plants to mark the passage of girl and dog, but Elizabeth had not been trying to cover her tracks, so Anna followed the trail easily. The heavy bucket had slopped, leaving traces of disturbance in the fine dust. Where Elizabeth slid off of one boulder and onto to a lower one, the bucket left scrapes on the stone when she'd dragged it after her. Wily, probably not with the intention of helping Anna, but one never knew when it came to Wily, had lifted his leg several times, leaving a faint darker stain on the sparse dusty grasses that clung in the wisps of blown earth.

Following the trail, Anna wended her way downward in zigzags between boulders until she reached a point where she could finally see the edge of the little island. Twenty feet directly below where she'd stopped, water lapped the rugged shore. Anna stared at waves beating themselves to a froth on ragged rocks.

E wouldn't have dumped the lobsters here; there were too many rocks to ensure they'd have a safe landing.

As Anna picked her way through the maze of giant granite blocks tumbled together around the base of the island, she lost sight of both sea and mainland. In a slot between two great chunks of rock no more than six feet apart, the maze ended abruptly in a three-foot drop to dark water. The slot between the boulders continued several yards farther, creating a narrow inlet protected from the wind and much of the power of the sea.

Anna squatted, studying the lip of the stone above the water. The edge was sharp, squared off at a neat ninety degrees, the face making a straight line down toward the water. Getting to her hands and knees to take advantage of the low-angled afternoon light, Anna could see where Elizabeth had smudged the dust as she sat on the edge of the rock, her feet dangling over.

A wave rushed up the narrow channel and exploded against the island, coating Anna's skin with chilling spray. Beyond the mouth of the slot was a thin feathery line: fog cat-footing in.

The wave was sucked back into the gullet of the ocean, baring the boulders walling the slot. Along the stones at the waterline were scrapes of brown and a single sketch of blue. A small boat had docked here more than once.

Any legitimate visitor would bring his boat to the jetty, ring the bell, and walk in the front door.

As Anna leaned forward to study the marks, a wavering fishy silver flashed beneath the water. Fourteen inches beneath the water, on a ledge, lying on its side, was a bucket. The bucket.

This was the end of the trail. This was where E had loosed Gwen's dinner guests.

Anna lay down on her belly and reached into the water, icy even in the heat of summer, and managed to snag the handle of the bucket and haul it out of the water. Setting it carefully aside, where it wouldn't drip on anything vital, she made a minute inspection of the place from which E had vanished.

Tiny grasses were uprooted from a crack near where Elizabeth's left hand must have rested. Sand had been swept away on one side of the rocks bordering where the boat came into the island's embrace.

Elizabeth had not jumped or swum.

She'd been dragged off of Boar.

TWENTY-FOUR

Again Heath looked at her watch. Less than two minutes had passed since last time. Finally she held it up to her ear. Ticking. Time and its petty pace were making her crazy. At minute twenty-four, Anna slid back down the same rock she'd climbed out over.

"Bucket track," she said succinctly as she dropped the lobster pail to the ground. "I found where Elizabeth dumped the lobsters. There were skid marks in the loose gravel on the rock. A handful of plants were ripped from a crack as if she'd grabbed them to keep from being pulled into the water."

Heath felt her heart stop. When it started again each beat struck a blow to her rib cage from the inside. "Slipped and fell?" she croaked. "Drowned?" This had to be what dying felt like. Everything was going black but for Anna's face. Maybe Heath was falling. She couldn't tell.

"I don't think so," Anna said as she trotted toward the lift. "Wily is gone as well, and there were scrape marks on either side of the rock crack where she set the lobsters loose. A small boat is my guess."

"She took a boat?" Heath said stupidly. Her ears were hearing words. She could see Anna's lips moving, but her brain was having a hard time making sense of things. "With Wily?"

"A boat took her, and I hope they took Wily and didn't just kill him and dump the body," Anna said as she opened the lift gate. "Coming?"

Leah said saltwater could damage Dem Bones's electronics. Leah said, "You break it, you buy it." She meant it. Leah was not a fanciful genius. To her a cliché was as good as a contract.

To hell with Leah. Heath couldn't take the time to get out of the thing and into Robo-butt.

"Of course I'm coming."

Anna turned and walked toward the lift.

Heath followed, the crutches giving her balance.

Anna was piloting the small NPS runabout, a single-engine boat with a canvas shelter over the steering wheel. Heath relinquished pride in favor of speed and let herself lean heavily on Anna's shoulder as the metal and electronics lifted her feet and legs from the dock and over the gunwale one at an excruciating time. With a push and a whirr, she was seated on the plastic bench that ran along the port side of the runabout. Anna held up an orange life jacket. Heath wanted to tell her to drop the thing, get a move on. Knowing it would take longer to argue, and she wouldn't win, she clenched her teeth and held her arms out so Anna could thread the PFD onto her shoulders.

"I'll get the straps," she insisted as Anna started to do up the front of the life preserver. Anna looked at her for a second.

"I will," Heath promised.

Evidently Anna believed her. She slipped into her own PFD, leapt out of the boat, untied the lines, leapt back in, and finally, finally, thankyoubabyjesus started the boat.

Breathe, Heath told herself. Breathe. Air came in through her nostrils. She seemed unable to force it down past the concrete closing off her throat.

"Where are we looking?" Heath asked. Her voice was nearly a whine. There was nowhere to look. Just ocean and drowned land.

"We'll start where the boat met up with Elizabeth and Wily. From there we will fan out in arcs. I will be looking for boats. You will be looking for anything, no matter how small, on the water. Every thirty seconds you will blow that whistle around your neck and shout Elizabeth's name and Wily's. When we lose the light, we assume they've made land somewhere — the boat was small, rowboat sized — and we stop. I call Peter, and the rangers start searching the park."

Heath nodded. Words were backed up behind her teeth, but not one of them meant a thing.

Evening, and the encroaching fog, rapidly cooled the air. As Anna pushed the throttle open, the rush of chill wind against Heath's overheated face felt like an acid wash until her skin became acclimated to the new element.

Darkness oozed in from all directions, the ocean, the edge of the sky, out from the islands, their skirts of rock turning black and ominous. Heath felt the world closing down, ending. "It's been hours, she's surely dead," she moaned. "I am such an idiot. I killed her."

Anna pulled the throttle to idle. Turning she stared down at Heath. "Do you want me to slap you?" she asked. "You know, the traditional cure for female hysterics?"

Heath blinked. Anna looked no softer than the granite, no warmer than the fog. Heath swallowed.

"Not necessary," she whispered.

"Good. Talk about something else. Tell me what Gwen's been up to. Anything. Watch and call and blow the whistle." Anna turned back to the control panel and pushed the throttle forward, not far enough to bring the boat up on plane, just above idle so voices could be heard over the engine noise and the wake wouldn't swamp anything that might be floating in the darkening waters.

Heath pulled the brass whistle Elizabeth had given her from under her shirt and life jacket. Sucking in as much air as her shriveled lungs would allow, she blew a long blast, then called weakly, "E! Elizabeth!"

"Good," Anna called over her shoulder. "Now talk to me for thirty seconds and do it again. Keep your eyes on the water."

Talk. About something else. Not the girl dying somewhere because Heath was a fool, a shit-for-brains fool. There was nothing else. Aunt Gwen, she thought, gone with John to Bangor. "Aunt Gwen delivered Ms. Zuckerberg's children." Heath said the words one by one like a not-so-bright schoolchild reciting a poem she didn't understand. When she'd done, she felt

308

herself sinking, her eyes unfocused on the endless deadly expanse of water turning the color of ink. Under all that icy black was a child of light.

"And," Anna prodded. "Talk to me."

Slowly, Heath rose out of the depths and forced herself to think of anything else. "Ms. Zuckerberg isn't doing well. Heart weak. Transient ischemic attacks. She's lost the ability to talk, Gwen said."

"Good," Anna replied, as deaf to the words as Heath was. "Blow, call."

Heath blew the whistle and called Elizabeth's name. Her voice was stronger. The talking was keeping her mind off the horror that wanted to suffocate her as surely as the water had suffocated —

"Ms. Zuckerberg can't talk," Anna said sharply. "When she gets out of the hospital, is she going to her kids?"

"No," Heath said. She knew what Anna was doing. She knew she needed it, but, at the moment, she resented Anna for it. Despair pulled at her with an almost pleasurable force, the way a steep canyon would if she stood — rolled — too close to the edge. Part of her wanted to fall into the nothing that was offered. *Coward,* she cursed herself. Sucking in a lungful of breath, she forced herself to speak. "No.

Her kids don't even —"

"Hush!" Anna said and cut the throttles to idle. "Listen."

Through the muffling of the coastal fog, now reaching halfway to Boar, Heath heard what sounded like a dog's yip. Then nothing. She blew a blast on the whistle. "E!" she screamed. "Elizabeth! Answer me!"

A thin, reedy bark pierced the fog.

"There," Anna pointed to where the mother-of-pearl of the sea met the pearl of the mists. A dark shape, trapezoidal, about the size of an old shipping trunk, touched the water. Then an orange smudge showed above it. The smudge moved suddenly. As they heard the splash of a body hitting the water, a girl screamed.

Anna shoved full throttle.

TWENTY-FIVE

Denise sat at her small neat table in a space between the living room and kitchen called "the dining room" on the lease. In front of her, on the shining black wood, was a spiral notebook of college ruled paper. The cover was bright red.

She laughed. The sound startled her. Covering the notebook with her forearm, she glanced around as if the laughter had emanated from another source.

She was alone.

No. That was the old Denise Castle. *She* had been creakingly, hauntingly alone. An open wound walking through a world of salt and thorns, she'd not dared let anyone close.

Being alone was not being lonely.

People liked to say that. People were full of shit. Alone echoed down hallways of the mind, shrieking with the shrill voice of icy wind through winter-bare branches. Denise had thought that she would be alone forever,

311

but that was just a lie the world told her. She wasn't even alone sitting by herself in her one-bedroom apartment in her single dining chair.

That was the first huge change. Massive. Making her not a ghost, but a guest, at the party. Better than a guest, family. For so many years she'd had to watch sisters and brothers, wives and husbands and children, being families while she was just herself, one hand clapping, a loose end, a fifth wheel. Families didn't even show her the courtesy of knowing they were the lucky ones. They fought and complained, disrespected each other, went years without speaking over a trifle, yelled at their children as if children were annoying pests they were forced to deal with.

Aborting babies.

Getting divorces.

Choosing not to be together on Christmas.

As if everybody had that choice, as if, for Denise, holidays hadn't been an inescapable nightmare, where, like a bird with no place to perch, she circled cold and alone high over lighted windows and laden tables, hoping that someone would invite her in, if even only for an evening. Then, if they did, it was worse because she knew she did not belong. They knew she did not belong. Once she was surrounded, all she wanted to do was get away, be by herself where the pain and shame wouldn't show.

Family cared enough to poke and nag, call too often and hug too tightly; they fell asleep with their head in another's lap, were carried to bed. They gossiped and worried and gave unwelcome advice. Family cared if you showed up for birthdays, chided if you forgot anniversaries, because your presence, mentally and physically, mattered. Family stimulated the psyche. Without it part of a person fell asleep, like a foot held in one position too long.

A part of Denise had gone to sleep like that. It was still alive, but didn't feel alive. It felt like concrete or asphalt. As time passed, the thought of trying to wake it, to suffer the miserable tingling of life returning, had become worse than knowing a portion of her being was as deadwood on a living tree.

Paulette had woken her without a twinge. Denise was fully alive for the first time in forever.

Then she'd killed a man.

Another huge new thing: life and death, both in her hands.

About life, she felt . . . That was it; that was the whole thing, she *felt*. Resentment, jealousy, spite: The stuff she'd been sustain-

ing herself with for so long was not *feeling.*
It was what replaced feeling, fake pain
directed outward so the real pain would not
eat the host alive. Becoming partially dead
to keep the other parts from being flayed.

Life *felt* good. What did adults say when
she was a kid? "You've got your whole life
ahead of you." She'd thought they were
idiots. Now she knew what it meant to have
her whole life ahead of her.

About killing Kurt, she should feel something. Like sex, or reading *Siddhartha,*
people were supposed to be changed by the
experience, somehow different afterward.
Killing another human being should be like
that. One day she was Denise Castle who
had never killed a person. The next she was
Denise Castle who had taken a human life
in sweat and blood and a plastic shower
curtain with yellow fishes on it. Those two
Denises should be different, but they
weren't. Sex and *Siddhartha* had been like
that for her as well. Not as big a deal as
advertised.

For a moment she marveled at the things
that had changed in the past week. Denise
Castle: alive, feeling, killer, family woman.

Almost a family woman. That would
come, she decided.

Alone and not alone, she returned to her

notebook and her list, items that had to be checked off before the whole life she had ahead of her could officially commence.

Kill Kurt (Denise)
Sell Land (Paulette)
Quit NPS (retirement pension) (D)
Find out about "Legacy" (if it exists) (P)
Car, car seat, etc.
Give landlord notice
Arrange for family — Mt. Desert Hospital (D&P)
Leave MA for GA or SC or NC (D&P&O)
Rent (D&P&O)
Buy (D&P&O)

"Kill Kurt" was checked off.

"Sell Land" had a tentative pencil mark next to it. Kurt's house was worthless, but the land was not. The land was paid off; Kurt's parents were dead. He had no brothers and sisters, and no children. Paulette said it was to pass to her on his death. Ownership wasn't an issue. Denise figured Paulette could get around four or five hundred thousand for the place. They should take less if it would move the property more quickly. Timing was important.

They would skip the balancing act of selling and moving. There was no way to know if it would sell in a week or six months. Banks had gotten paranoid after the big savings-and-loan scandals, but given location, location, location, Denise guessed it would move fast. They'd have to find a way to do the paperwork from out of state. By the time it was all settled, they had to be long gone.

The land sale would mean a big infusion of cash, which was good. Denise had about a hundred thousand of her own in investments, and her pension should come to around forty thousand a year, less everything. Maybe a net of thirty. They had enough.

Again she bent over the list.

Between "Sell Land" and "Quit NPS" she penciled in in tiny letters "Remove Obstacle." Not that she'd forget to take care of that particular problem. Denise had an excellent memory — or had until her nerves started going bad. Still, the lists weren't a memory aid; she made lists so she could check things off, have the satisfaction of seeing in black and white what she had accomplished.

"Obstacle" was the second most complex item on the list.

Changing from a pencil to a pen, she underlined it in ink. Denise had hoped she could erase it as unnecessary. That hope was growing slim to nonexistent. There was no doubt in Denise's mind that Anna Pigeon would remember who the Denise in the photograph reminded her of. Those kinds of things tickled at the brain until they were solved. Anna would remember it was Paulette. Given what a nuisance the pigeon was, she would put two and two together and get Murder. If they could move the project along quickly, Anna would only have to be put off for a couple of days, three at most.

Denise overwrote the underlined word in ink. To the side, in parentheses, she wrote "triazolam." Google said triazolam was common enough. As a nurse, Paulette would be able to lay her hands on a few tabs at the hospital. Needed or not, it was important to have the drug option.

For a moment Denise stared at the wall, eyes unfocused.

"Family" was next on her list, the most difficult of all the tasks. She and her sister would be getting a family. Denise smiled. When she was a kid, people would say of a pregnant woman, "She's in a family way." There was something lovely about that. Denise and Paulette were going to be in a family way.

It was poetic justice that lovely fertile Lily

was going to be their accomplice.

Lily took ergotamine for her migraines. Denise had Googled the side effects.

God, but Denise loved Google.

TWENTY-SIX

The surface of the sea had embraced the night. Foam and tendrils of mist sketched the waves with iridescence. There was no horizon; the line between water, earth, and air had been erased by the fog. As the boat leapt up onto plane, Heath, in her electronic bones, was thrown backward. Nothing looked real or solid, yet the hull of the boat slammed into the Atlantic as hard as if it traveled a surface of packed dirt. For a few heartbeats, half lying along the plastic bench, Heath thought she was falling, not just onto the bench but out of the boat, into the sky or the sea.

Since fate or bad luck had decreed Heath had to have one part of her body that refused to work and play well with the others, she was glad it was her legs. Losing her wits — even for a few moments — scared her a whole hell of a lot more than not being able to run and jump.

Sudden silence snatched her mind back into the boat. Anna had shut the engine down. Sucking the quiet into her lungs and mind, Heath struggled to right herself, ears tuned to the sound of the yip, Wily's yip. The happiest sound in the world. Second happiest.

"Blow your whistle," Anna said. Her voice was steady, familiar; it poured into Heath's ears like a homing signal.

The whistle was clutched so tightly in Heath's hand it felt hot when she put it between her mist-chilled lips. She blew two short sharp blasts.

"Elizabeth!" Anna yelled. "E!"

A litany of prayers babbled through Heath's brain: Please God let me find her, please God, let her be okay, please God, please, please, please.

The only sound was the lapping of the waves against the hull like a beast lapping at the blood of its prey. Again Heath had the sensation of falling, but this time it had nothing to do with vertigo. The place she was tumbling into was where the mothers of dead children fell. It had no bottom and no way out.

"Wily!" Anna called. She turned on a spotlight mounted on the gunwale next to the steering wheel. The beacon lanced out, an impotent light-sword. In the fog and dusk it hid as much as it illuminated, the light catching particles of water and refracting back.

A tiny scrap of orange flared for an instant between the glazed obsidian of the water and the gray blanket of fog. "There!" Heath cried, pointing. "Move the light back. There!" A bit of orange flickered in, then out, of vision as the swells moved up and down. "Keep the light on it!" Heath shouted.

Anna didn't reply. Leaving the light where it was, she pushed the throttle gently forward and nosed the boat in the direction Heath was pointing, following the long bobbing finger from the floodlight.

The ocean heaved another great sigh, and the scrap came into sight fifty yards ahead and to the right. "One o'clock," Heath shouted.

"I see it," Anna replied.

Unfortunately, Heath did, too. Every cell in her body was straining toward that orange scrap. The apparition stayed in view a moment longer this time. Not a lovely child in a life jacket. A monster. Short truncated arms poked through holes too big for them. A misshapen skull was sunk into the body of the flotation device. It looked as if the thing were covered in rotting seaweed.

Heath opened her mouth to scream.

Anna beat her to it. "Wily!" she shouted again.

"Over here," came a faint reply.

"What the . . ." Heath's mind cleared. Wily, the dog, was in the life jacket. For an LSD moment, Heath thought Wily had called out, "Over here." Elizabeth! E was invisible in the dark water, but she must be swimming next to him. Alive.

"Coming! Hang on," Heath yelled as she pushed the button to lift herself into a standing position. At the faint whirr of the machinery Anna shot her such a repressive look she immediately whirred her butt back down onto the bench.

Anna had the spotlight on the dog in the life jacket. Heath could see the sleek head of Elizabeth beside Wily, her face a pale oval against the black water. At idle, Anna eased the boat toward them.

Heath's mental litany turned from "Please, please, please" to "Thank you, thank you, thank you," the two fundamental prayers of mankind.

As they neared, Anna ordered Heath to throw Elizabeth a life jacket. Heath pulled off her own and threw it hard in her daughter's direction. Her arms were stronger than they'd ever been, and, thanks to wheelchair basketball, her aim was good.

Elizabeth clung to the life jacket with one hand and to Wily's scruff with the other, her head barely above water. Anna picked Wily out of the water first and deposited him at Heath's feet with a slosh of cold seawater. Never had he looked so much like Wile E. Coyote as he did at that moment, water running from his ears and muzzle, orange vest hanging on his bony shoulders.

E was next, fished out and dumped on the deck with little more ceremony than Wily had received. The light was going fast, and Heath could not tell if Elizabeth or the dog was bloody or bruised.

"What happened? Are you hurt? We've been looking for hours." Questions and comments poured out of Heath so rapidly there was no time for answers. She knew it but could not help herself. Connection to her child demanded it of her, and, denied the luxury of grabbing the girl and holding her so tightly she could never escape again, words had to suffice. "Why is Wily wearing the life preserver!" she demanded as she ran out of breath.

Into the silence that followed, E said calmly, "He can't swim, Mom."

"He can swim," Anna stated flatly.

"Oh, yeah, right, *dog-paddle,*" E retorted.

Wily shook, spattering them with water and making the orange vest flap around his skinny form.

Elizabeth laughed.

How could she be so goddamned calm! Heath was shaking so badly she could hear her legs rattling in their shells. Her chest muscles contracted until drawing breath was nearly impossible, and she could feel her heart pounding so hard it shook her clothes.

"How did you get out here?" Anna demanded.

"A boat took me," E said.

Heath could almost hear the "Duh!" in her voice.

"Kidnapping is a federal offense," Anna said as she snatched the radio mike from its metal holder.

"No!" E cried. "Don't go all law enforcement on me. A friend took me on a boat ride. A nice person."

Anna stopped and stared hard at Elizabeth in the growing gloom. "And you forgot you weren't Jesus Christ and decided to walk home?" she asked.

"My friend wanted to take me back, but I insisted. When we heard you calling and I realized how long we'd been gone, I was afraid you'd arrest . . ."

Silence followed that.

"Why would I arrest a nice friend?" Anna asked.

A person. A friend. Heath could guess why this mysterious individual was genderless. The friend was a boy. Heath had been asking herself what would make a wonderful, considerate child like Elizabeth so forgetful that she would terrify her mother. A boy. A nice boy. A boy/friend. God was good. She was going to shackle E to the iron stair railing in the tower and feed her nothing but bread and water until she was forty years old.

For another moment, Anna just looked at E and said nothing. Elizabeth was hugging her arms, shivering. Anna opened the tiny door under the hull, pulled out a blanket that looked as if it was made of tinfoil, then tossed it to E. "We'll sort this out later. Wrap up. Both you and Wily." She shot Wily a hard look. "You should have known better," she said to the dog.

With that, Anna pushed the throttle to full and turned the boat back toward Boar Island.

Both Wily and E had bathed and toweled off. Anna built a small fire in the great hearth in the outer room skirting the tower.

The evening was mild, but girl and dog had gotten thoroughly chilled. Anna also made tea. Elizabeth wrinkled her nose, then sighed. "Hot drinks, I know, the wilderness cure-all. Does Wily have to drink tea, too?"

Neither Heath nor Anna answered. Heath was seated in Robo-butt, her knees almost touching the overstuffed chair where her daughter was curled up. Elizabeth's feet peeked out from beneath a hand-knitted throw of purple and green. In T-shirt and sweatpants, her hair damp from the bath, and no makeup, she looked like a little girl. A delightful fact Heath knew better than to share aloud.

Sprawled in front of the hearth, Wily looked old and tired, his fur ragged and spiked with damp, his pointed ears at half-mast. Elizabeth might have deserved a ducking in icy water for being so thoughtless, but Wily didn't. The cold was hard on his old bones.

"Enough," she said to her daughter. "Tell us every single thing from the beginning of time."

"Billions and billions of years ago this was a vast inland sea," Elizabeth droned in a mockery of PBS specials.

"Don't," Heath warned. She wanted to be angry. It was spoiled by the fact that she

326

had not heard such sauciness from Elizabeth since before the razor-in-the-tub incident. That, and the fact her daughter was alive and in one piece.

"Just tell it," Anna said quietly.

"Aunt Gwen was going to boil some lobsters alive," E said. Heath saw the wince in Anna's gaze at the same moment it clutched her own chest.

"I freaked," E apologized.

Heath had come to the conclusion it was she and Aunt Gwen who needed to apologize.

"I mean boiling alive, how rotten is that? So Wily and I took the lobsters in the bucket and went over to the far side of the island to turn them loose. We'd got ourselves down to the water and were dumping the lobsters into the ocean when, whoosh! This little rowboat rushes in between the rocks and almost smacks my feet." She laughed, and then shared the memory that brought the laughter. "I dumped the lobsters right in the boat and they started sliding all around."

She sobered. "It wasn't funny then, really, only now. What with the cyber stuff and everything, I got scared. Anyway. We became friends and I went for a boat ride, me and Wily."

"That's it?" Heath asked carefully. "You

went for a ride with a friend?"

"I promised I wouldn't tell anybody," Elizabeth said.

Anna snorted.

Heath waited. E could occasionally keep secrets from her and Gwen, but never Anna.

"Wouldn't tell anybody what?" Anna asked innocently.

"You know, about him, and stuff." E had a pleading note in her voice. Anna ignored it.

"If there is something about him so dangerous that he made you promise not to divulge it to your mother, I think you'd better divulge it to your mother. And me," Anna said flatly.

"Not dangerous to me," E said. "Just him. He — oh God, I've told you he's a boy!" she almost wailed.

"Twice," Anna said. "Believe it or not, given we had a fifty-fifty chance of getting it right, we got that part right. We're betting a cute boy."

Elizabeth smiled and looked down.

"Now we know we got that part right," Anna said.

Heath said nothing. Anna was much better at this sort of thing than she was.

"So," Anna said. "You're on the back of Boar, down by the water, emancipating

328

crustaceans, and a cute boy in a rowboat floods in. Merriment ensues, and you and Wily go for a ride."

"Yes," Elizabeth admitted.

"Being as he was adorable, and you're adorable, and everything is adorable, you become 'friends' and lose track of time," Anna said.

"I guess," E said.

"Then, when he realizes grown-ups are about to ruin this idyll, he chucks you and your poor old dog into the freezing ocean so he can save his sorry ass," Anna said.

"It wasn't like that," E protested. "I was the one who wanted to do it. To help."

"And he needed help because . . ." Anna said.

E's face took on a mulish cast. She studied her fingers. Wily licked his paw. Anna stared at E. Heath tried to fit the information E had shared into a coherent picture.

"I didn't hear a boat engine," Anna said. "And I didn't hear oars in oarlocks or paddles on the gunwale. So your new pal — who cannot be named — muffles his oars? Fishy."

Studying fingers, licking paws, staring into flames, thinking.

"You know I'll find out who fishy boy is," Anna threatened.

E said nothing.

Gradually it became clear that the boy's identity was one secret E was going to keep. At least for now. Heath quashed the urge to bargain or plead. E's new "friend" had not killed or molested her, and when she asked, he'd let her go free. That, and the fact that Elizabeth was happy, allowed Heath to keep her peace. In a bizarre way she was pleased that Elizabeth refused to divulge the boy's — and of course it had to be a boy — name. It showed backbone, honor, a sense of being in control of her own world that the Internet creep had stolen from her.

Quiet ticked by to the comforting sound of Wily working the salt from between the toes of his right paw with his tongue.

"Hey," Anna said finally. "On a lighter note, your stalker is here in Maine and wants to meet you."

Elizabeth toppled over on her side and pulled the afghan over her head.

TWENTY-SEVEN

Denise sat cross-legged on her bed. In front of her was a silver laptop. On the screen was a full-color fish-eye view of the nursery in Peter Barnes's home. Baby Olivia slept upstairs across the hall from Peter's room. Peter and *Lily's* room, she reminded herself. Where they slept on the bed that Denise had bought secondhand and refinished with such care.

Lit by the light of a Blue Fairy lamp, Olivia slept in a pink bundle. They'd let the room get too warm, Denise noticed with irritation. The baby was kicking her tiny feet, trying to get free of the rose-colored burrito *Lily* had thought suitable for swaddling. Why didn't the woman just stick Olivia in a papoose pack and lace it up tight?

It had been a week or more since Denise had allowed herself this particular torture. Paulette had taken her mind in other, more satisfactory directions. Directions that didn't all lead to a dead end. She'd missed watching Olivia. In a way, she was more a mother to the baby than Lily was. A couple of days after the baby was born, Lily had one of her migraines and checked herself back into the hospital. When she got out, though, of course Lily didn't have to work for a living; she went back to her "activities."

Not Denise. Denise had always been there.

The day Olivia was brought home, Denise stuck a Nice Lady No Bad Feelings face on the front of her skull and trotted right over to her old home, where Peter kept his family. In a beautifully wrapped box was an expensive fragile figurine of a guardian angel.

A smile pasted so tightly to her face that her lips stuck to her teeth, Denise told Lily it was to watch over the baby.

Nice, good, little Lily had put it on a table overlooking the baby's crib, right where the tiny camera hidden in the angel's armload of brightly painted flowers would capture the entire room.

Denise had invested in several snazzy little wireless cameras. This was the only one she'd planted in Peter's house, but it wasn't the limit of her knowledge of the Barnes family.

Before Paulette, when Denise had been scarcely more than a festering sore, barely able to keep her mind from pouring out through her eyes like molten lava, she'd kept herself alive by spying on the happy couple, then, when baby made three, the happy family.

She knew Lily's routine better than Peter did. Maybe better than Lily herself did. She knew when the baby napped and how often she was changed, when she was fed and what. She knew dear Lily was dry as an Arizona gully in August and never produced a drop of milk from her pert little tits to feed her child. Denise knew what kind of formula she used and where she kept it.

After he'd summarily thrown Denise out into the cold, thinking himself oh so clever, Peter had changed all the locks. He was too stupid to remember the dog door. Denise had been in that house dozens of times over the past three years. She knew Lily preferred Tampax tampons, the kind that looked like pink bullets; she knew when Lily's period was and how many days it lasted. She knew Lily suffered from migraines and what she took for them. She'd discovered Peter took Cialis. That had been a good day when she'd found those in his medicine cabinet. He also suffered from periodic constipation and kept *Playboy* magazines in the back of his closet.

During those awful times, all Denise thought about was revenge, years fantasizing about how she would get justice. As an employee of the American justice system, she'd thought justice was catching and punishing the bad guys. She had been wrong. What American law enforcement did was not justice, it was revenge, and revenge was for people who were helpless to obtain justice.

Paulette had taught her that.

Paulette coming into her life was the first justice Denise had ever experienced. Justice wasn't about the bad guy. It was about the victim. Justice made what was wrong right again. Justice made the victim whole. Justice put the jewelry back in the jewelry box, the car back in the rightful owner's garage. Justice was restoration. When Paulette came, Denise's lost soul was restored to her. That was justice.

Understanding this changed Denise's worldview. Revenge was not necessary — not even desirable — if justice could be had.

However, her years spying on Peter Barnes's family weren't wasted. It was serendipity — or fate, kismet — that she'd done this groundwork. At the time, she'd spied and pried because she couldn't help herself. Or so she'd thought. Some part of her brain must have realized that this information would become important to the planning of the whole life she had ahead of her now.

Not revenge; justice.

"Good night, baby girl," Denise said, and closed the laptop's cover.

She checked her watch. It was nearly three A.M. Time to leave to meet with her sister. Given how fast things were moving, and how small Acadia National Park was, meeting in the flesh, even in the dark of night in the woods, was risky, but after Denise had gotten off work she found a note Paulette had left in her mailbox; their cell phones neither texted nor took voice messages.

The note read *I have to see you. Please come tonight. We have to . . .* The last words were scribbled out.

Clutching the note, Denise feared she would have a heart attack in the foyer. Paulette had waltzed right up to the boxes in Denise's apartment building, in broad daylight, and popped a motherloving note, with her handwriting on it and, undoubtedly, slathered with fingerprints matching those at the crime scene, into Denise Castle, Law Enforcement Ranger and Identical

Twin's mailbox.

Had Denise been a dog, she would have been mad enough to froth at the mouth. Thank God Paulette hadn't signed the thing. Might as well just add *P.S. We killed the prick. Love, the Bobbsey Twins.*

If anyone saw Paulette slip the note into her mailbox, Denise hoped they thought nothing of it. It had been with two bills and a flyer for used tires. Had Paulette come after the mailman, or had the mailman opened the box to put in the letters, seen the note, and read it?

"Doesn't matter," Denise said aloud. By the time the shit hit the fan, Paulette would be gone. One battered widow, no family, no friends, vanishes. A nonevent.

Denise changed out of her old pajamas. The new ones she'd ordered for her and her sister had arrived, but she didn't want to wear them until she and Paulette could wear them together.

Clad in dark clothes, she slipped quietly down the stairs and into her Miata. As on the night she'd disposed of Kurt, she would take the runabout to Otter Cove, then hike the short way overland. Covering the same ground more than once made her uneasy, but not as uneasy as taking the road. The inky shadow of the boathouse by the government dock on Somes was the only place she felt safe parking the Miata. Night diving was known to be her habit. If by chance the car was seen, no one would remark it there.

The NPS was understaffed and, at present, underfunded. Two weeks ago this would have pissed Denise off. Now park poverty was her friend. Acadia couldn't afford twenty-four-hour ranger coverage. On Friday and Saturday nights the last shift ended at midnight, on weeknights at ten P.M. Even Eager Artie would be abed by three A.M.

The Miata snugged into darkness by the boathouse, Denise rowed the runabout out a hundred yards. Probably an unnecessary precaution, but just because she was paranoid didn't mean somebody wasn't watching her. This was the downside of breaking the law — even when the law needed to be broken. Denise did not have a guilty conscience. In doing away with Duffy, she'd done the world a good turn, but it was like after she'd finished reading a mystery story. Once she knew exactly who, where, how, and when the crime was committed, it seemed it would be obvious to a two-year-old. To soothe her nerves she had to keep reminding herself that most people weren't all that bright. Better yet, most people didn't give a flying fuck unless it was a cop killed, or somebody they could use to make political hay.

Having shipped the oars, Denise fired up the engine and, at slightly better than idle, motored slowly down the sound. Air and water temperatures had reached sufficient equilibrium that the fog was shredding into thin feathers along the coast, eerie fingers given life by the light of a waning moon.

Boat firm beneath her, cool, fresh sea air in her lungs, Denise felt the iron band that Paulette's hand-delivered note had locked around her lungs loosen sufficiently to let her breathe deeply.

Please come tonight. We have to . . . Then the tangle of ink lines crossing out whatever it was Paulette decided they had to do. What could she have thought of that Denise hadn't? A few days before, Denise would have answered, "Nothing." The note and a few other things Paulette had done lately led her to believe identical twins weren't identical, as in *exactly* the same.

Denise shoved that thought aside. She and her twin were two sides of the same coin, peas in a pod, identical DNA. In everything that mattered there wasn't a particle of difference between them. She patted the front pocket of her black jeans where she had the list she'd made. Tonight they should be able to check off the meds and maybe the house. Paulette had had time to contact a Realtor, as well as two entire shifts to pinch the drugs.

Calmed by the eternal strength of the Atlantic surrounding her, Denise decided she wouldn't say anything about the hand-delivered note. Too many years in law enforcement had made her hypervigilant. That was all. Paulette, an infant-care nurse, couldn't be expected to see threats lurking behind every set of eyes. Denise loved that about her sister. Or she would, once there weren't threats lurking behind every set of eyes.

Denise expertly docked the runabout out of sight between two rocks, then followed the narrow beam of her tiny flashlight over the familiar ground between Otter and the old shed that Paulette had made into a nursery and was now their sanctuary from the world.

No light showed under the door. Clicking off her flashlight, Denise stepped beneath the roof overhang and put her ear against the wood of the door. Not a sound. Tapping softly, she whispered, "Paulette?" No answer.

Turning, Denise stared toward dead Kurt's shack. The back porch light was a blazing beacon through the trees. Paulette got off work at three A.M. She should have beat Denise to the nursery. Why was she in that rotting tomb of a house instead of in their secret place?

Paulette had been arrested for stealing drugs.

She'd collapsed of a heart attack.

Been run down by an SUV full of drunken tourists.

Panic drowning caution, Denise sprinted to where the porch hung precariously on the rear of the house. She leapt up the two steps, then stopped. The police might be inside, rangers, the sheriff, anybody. Denise stepped softly to the door. The knob turned easily. With three fingers, she pushed the door open a crack so she could see inside.

Paulette was sitting in a straight-backed chair at the small, beat-up kitchen table. Overprocessed blond hair was caught back in a purple scrunchie. She'd chewed off all of her lipstick. In pink scrubs, figured with Pooh-bears and daisies, she looked very young and helpless. A cup of coffee was between her hands. She was gazing into it as if the dregs would foretell her future.

"Hey," Denise said.

With a shriek, Paulette jumped to her feet. The mug toppled. Coffee poured over the edge of the table, dripping onto the dirty linoleum floor.

"God, but you scared me half to death," Paulette said with a shaky laugh. Before Denise had time to do more than blink, her sister had thrown herself into her arms and was hugging her with such force Denise could hardly move.

A rush of sensation overwhelmed her. Since Peter, three and more years ago, no one had touched her except strangers shaking her hand, or drunks bumping into her on their way to the men's room at the Acadian.

Babies needed to be touched. She'd read that. If they weren't touched they could fail to thrive, outright die.

Maybe adults were no different. Touch was life.

"Sorry I scared you," Denise apologized, all thought of the ill-considered note gone from her mind.

Paulette stepped away to grab a roll of paper towels off the counter. Ripping off half a dozen, she let them flutter to the floor, then used her foot to push them around, sopping up the coffee. The towels didn't get it all. What was left mingled with the yuck on the floor.

Perhaps not all the squalor had been

Kurt's doing, Denise thought uneasily.

Didn't matter. They weren't going to be here much longer.

"Why didn't you wait in the nursery?" Denise asked as Paulette dropped the towels on top of a bunch of other trash in an open-topped can near the refrigerator.

"Oh, I don't know," Paulette said vaguely. "I wanted a cup of coffee. I thought this would be more comfortable."

The sordid kitchen in the murder house more comfortable? More comfortable than the nursery, with its art and painted furniture and promise of things to come?

Denise let it go, just like she'd let the leaving of the note in her box go. "Why did you need to see me?" she asked.

Paulette pinched up a packet of Nescafé, shook it, ripped off the top, and dumped the contents into a plastic mug. Taking the kettle from the stove, she offered, "Coffee?"

Instant.

"I'm good," Denise said, and waited. Her nerves weren't in shape for waiting, not in the wee hours of the morning in a trailer-trash kitchen. Her knee began bouncing, her heel never quite hitting the floor.

Paulette sat down across from her and repeated her gazing-into-the-cup routine. The spill on the scarred vinyl tabletop

342

wasn't quite dry. Denise watched a tiny finger of it being absorbed into the cuff of the pink long-sleeved T-shirt Paulette wore under her scrubs.

"Did you have trouble getting the triazolam?" Denise asked, forcing an end to what was becoming an awkward silence.

Paulette hung her head. "I didn't get it," she murmured.

"Why the hell not?" Denise demanded, shocking herself with the outburst.

Paulette reached into the pocket of her scrubs and pulled out a handful of hypodermics with capped needles, each in its sanitary packet. "I got the needles," she offered pitifully.

Afraid to speak lest she batter her twin with abuse a second time, Denise stared at the empty hypodermic needles and nodded slowly. When she felt she could speak normally, she asked, more gently, "Did you put the house on the market?"

Paulette shook her head.

Gentleness vaporized.

Paulette hadn't done anything. Nothing. Anger geysered up Denise's throat, hot and sulfurous as the fumes of hell. Given that Denise had shot Paulette's husband up close and personal three times, pilfering a few pills didn't seem like a big deal. Denise tried to force the bile down, calm herself. Pilfering a few pills, no big deal; Paulette would see it that way after Denise explained it.

The problem was Denise shouldn't have to explain it.

How could Paulette be sitting like a lump of raw dough in this filthy kitchen and not see how important this stuff was? Crucial.

Paulette, Denise reminded herself, was the gentle aspect of them. Of course she wasn't as capable of stealing or killing as Denise was. But not to put the property on the market? How much nerve did it take to call a Realtor?

Probably Paulette was afraid it wouldn't sell, afraid of being disappointed. Denise understood that. Better to pretend you don't hope than be made to look a fool when you don't get.

Denise decided that was all there was to it. She knew Paulette's lack of faith in their *themness* would have annoyed her, had it been possible for her to be annoyed with Paulette, genuinely annoyed, not just bitchy because her nerves were bad.

"I started on our legacy thing," Paulette said with a brightness Denise knew was false, and a smile that had been perfected to ward off the blows of her ham-handed

344

hubby. Almost as if Paulette were afraid of Denise's displeasure.

Would that be bad? Denise wondered. Or good? Good, Denise decided. It showed Paulette cared, loved her.

"I used those old newspaper ads and sent postcards to the two PO boxes, the one listed in the original ad and the one listed four years later in that ad I showed you. Of course, even that was nearly a year old, but it could be something. It could be our mother," Paulette said, looking hopeful.

"Whoever put the ads in asking for twin girls separated at birth might have died or moved on," Denise said repressively. "More likely, good old Mom has decided nothing has changed, and she doesn't want us any more now than when she decided to chuck us out like so much garbage." Denise didn't think of the person who'd given them birth as "their" mother, just "the" mother.

Paulette twitched as if Denise had struck her. Unaccountably it made Denise angry. Guilt should have been what she felt, but she didn't. The cringing made her mad. "Please don't tell me you put this house as your return address," she growled.

"I put General Delivery like you told me," Paulette said softly, not looking up from her coffee. "Tomorrow I'll check. We could have got replies by then."

It was possible, Denise thought. Not probable, but possible. The legacy thing was just gravy, at any rate. They had enough. Counting on anybody or anything one couldn't control oneself was never a wise thing. Denise sighed, reined in her fraying nerves. Folding hands sticky with cold coffee from the tabletop one inside the other on her lap where they wouldn't betray her emotional turmoil, she said, "That's good. That's real good, Paulette. I'm sorry I got . . . Things are hard right now. Why did you drop the note by my apartment? What did you need to see me about?"

For a long moment Paulette said nothing. Denise could hear the wind soughing through the pines and imagined she could hear the surf breaking. Peaceful sounds, sounds she'd gone to sleep to for many years. This night they rasped over her eardrums like sandpaper over a sunburn.

"We have to stop," Paulette finally said, in such a tiny voice Denise had to lean halfway across the table to hear it, then couldn't believe it. A total non sequitur. Nausea washed through her. The overhead light, in its inverted bowl of dead flies, dimmed, then grew bright again.

Too weird.

Not a sudden onset of the flu or a brown-out. Nerves. Putting both palms on the table to steady herself, Denise managed to say, "Stop what?"

"Oh, honey, everything. Everything!" Tears welled up in Paulette's eyes and spilled over her lids, rolling fat and oily down her cheeks. In their wake were gray trails of mascara.

Desperately, Denise reached across the little table and took both her sister's hands. "No!" she cried, not knowing what she was saying no to precisely, but aware that she needed to stop whatever tide was washing her sister away from her. Though the tide was not of water, not of physical stuff, she held just as tightly as if Paulette were caught in an undertow. Almost, Denise could see her growing smaller and smaller as the distance swallowed her. "No!" Denise gasped.

"I love working with the babies. I can't do anything else," Paulette sobbed, her tears so copious they dripped from her jaw, plopping onto Denise's forearms. "If anybody at the hospital thought I was even thinking about stealing drugs I would lose my job."

"What difference does that make?" Denise nearly shouted. The room was spinning around them. She had to hold tight lest she and her sister be flung away from the table by the centrifugal force. "We're leaving. We're going to get another house in another town and you can get another job. We've been over it and over it, Paulette. We're going to have a life, be a family."

"If we leave Acadia — you quit your job and I quit mine — and we sell and we move, they will know!" Paulette said brokenly. "That woman, that ranger lady — I was out shopping this morning and I came home and she was here! Right here at this house. She was coming out from the back where the nursery is. First she sees that picture where you look like me, then she comes here and sees the nursery and God knows what else. Why would she be snooping around here unless she thinks I killed Kurt or she thinks we are related? This isn't even her job. She's a park ranger. She knows we are doing things. We have to stop, just stop everything, don't do anything, just be quiet and normal and do our work and not be noticed. Maybe later . . ."

"Maybe the pigeon knows something, but that doesn't mean we stop. We stop her. That's all. I have a plan. We just distract her for a couple of days. No big deal. We just give her something else to think about, then we get our ducks in a row quick as anything, and we're done. No muss, no fuss," Denise pleaded.

Denise wanted to shake Paulette until her teeth rattled. How could she not realize there wouldn't be a later? They couldn't afford a maybe. This was their one shot; this was the brass ring, the lottery, the planets in alignment. It was a once-in-a-lifetime thing. And it had to be accomplished before Anna Pigeon could put two and two together and get twins.

How could Paulette be so stupid that she didn't get that?

All at once Denise understood why Kurt Duffy slapped his wife around.

TWENTY-EIGHT

Anna sat with Wily, Gwen, and Heath on the stone apron overlooking the sea. The sky was scattered with a herd of ephemeral sheep, as small and puffy and regular as if a child had drawn them. The sea was impossibly blue, navy in the shallow troughs and teal where the water thinned at the crests of the waves. This far north, the afternoons slipped into evening with exquisite slowness, the sunlight, rich as wild honey, striking diamonds from both the ocean and the granite.

Anna found it hard to believe that people bothered to torment and injure one another when there were so many better ways of spending one's time. Given the choice of a moment such as this or trolling the Internet, or shooting a hairy naked man, why would anyone choose the troll or the hairy man?

"Have you recovered from E's going

AWOL?" Anna asked.

Heath sipped her bourbon. "Like it never happened," she said.

"She's lying," Gwen said mildly. Gwen was fortified with a glass of white wine, her feet resting on the rounded footrest of a classic Adirondack deck chair. "After much consultation, she has decided to pretend it is okay. I have not. In my day — and I very much think today is still my day, thank you very much — boys come to the door and meet the family."

"The boy remains a state secret?" Anna asked. "Do we even know for sure it is a boy?"

"Of course it's a boy," Gwen said. "Don't be ridiculous."

Anna smiled. Of course it was a boy.

"I wanted to forbid E ever to see the little bastard again," Heath said. "But I actually think she would have disobeyed. Yesterday E asked to 'go out' for a while. Like there was a mall nearby. Jesus. I managed to say yes without spitting."

"You get points for that," Anna said.

"Fortunately I was gone," Gwen said. "I think I should have spit."

"You were in Bangor with the owner of the island?" Anna asked to be polite.

"Yes. Christine has had several heart attacks. This last was accompanied by another stroke. She can't speak, and her left side is completely paralyzed. It's hard to see her so agitated. She fell trying to get out of bed. Dez said she had scribbled something about wanting to see her children."

"Elizabeth came back from her second 'date,' " Gwen said. "You were probably right to let her go."

"Right. Because she came back when she said she would, I should get Mother of the Year," Heath said. "If she hadn't . . ."

Heath didn't finish that thought. She didn't need to.

Maternal fear, so palpable Anna could almost see it, curled like fog around the wheels of Heath's wheelchair. "E didn't let any interesting information slip?" Anna asked, hoping to distract her friend from the nightmare possibilities.

"Nope. If she wasn't happier than I've seen her for a long time, I might consider thumbscrews," Heath said. "E is sticking with the basic 'nice friend' description of Boat Boy."

Anna would have liked to see Boat Boy behind bars, if for no other reason than that he took her goddaughter out in a boat that had but a single personal flotation device, muffled his oars, and refused to meet the parents for fear of being arrested.

"If I was trawling for a sixteen-year-old girl, a cute boy would be my bait of choice," Anna said.

"Don't think I haven't obsessed on that. And mentioned it to E about six hundred times. She insists that's not it. The child smirks and hums to herself," Heath said sourly. "If he's a pervert I will skin him with a dull Boy Scout knife, one square inch at a time, drench him with gasoline, and set him on fire." Abruptly Heath went silent.

"You two are scaring me," Gwen said mildly. "Talk about something joyful."

"Murder, then. Murder is always entertaining," Anna suggested.

"The murdered lobsterman — the second lobsterman killed recently, right? The first was shot with a rifle for stealing . . . poaching?" Heath asked.

"There's nothing to indicate the two killings are related —" Anna began.

"Smells fishy to me," Heath said.

"John says the two incidents have nothing to do with each other," Gwen said. Both Heath and Anna looked at her.

"And John knows this why?" Anna asked.

"It turns out — and this just breaks my heart — that the first lobsterman, the one shot because he and his son were suspected of robbing traps, was Will Whitman, John's son," Gwen said.

"God," Heath groaned. Her compassion ground deep. Anna knew she was thinking of losing Elizabeth. Anna could imagine, if only intellectually, what it must be like to lose a child, like losing a particularly magical cat or a dog one had bonded with. Maybe worse.

"John says his son is innocent, for what it's worth," Gwen added. "His grandson is still missing, trying to clear his father's name and keep himself out of the line of fire, I guess."

"John is probably right about Will Whitman's and Kurt Duffy's deaths being unrelated. Whoever killed this guy Duffy appeared to be a little more personally involved than a man gunning down a poacher. Duffy was shot three times — twice through the shower curtain —"

"And, one assumes, other parts of his anatomy," Gwen said.

"With a small-caliber weapon," Anna finished. "Then apparently smothered with the shower curtain. Since us 'acting' chiefs haven't much to keep us occupied, I cruised by the widow's house. It's not exactly park jurisdiction, but I thought I'd interview her just for the hell of it. Nobody answered the door. I walked around to see if Ms. Duffy was hanging out clothes or sunbathing.

"Talk about depressing. The yard is packed dirt with a broken swing set. The chain on one of the swings was banging against the metal pole in the wind. It was like a scene from Edgar Allan Poe, if Poe had been born in a trailer park in 1967."

"For whom the bell tolls," Heath said amiably. "Isn't the spouse the first suspect? An abused spouse in this case, wasn't she?"

"When all else fails, it's the wife," Anna said. "But I doubt that was the case this time. From the state the bedroom and the deceased were in, there was an all-out battle. Ms. Duffy doesn't seem to be the kind who could fight a sick puppy and win. What possesses a woman to marry a Kurt Duffy?" she wondered aloud. "Move into his hovel, cook his dinners, launder his sweaty fish-smelling undershorts?"

"As my father used to say, 'Perhaps Mr. Duffy has talents we are not privy to,' " Aunt Gwen said.

Anna grunted.

Heath struck a match to light her cigarette.

Elizabeth emerged from the house, "He's back," she announced.

From the sound of her voice, Anna knew it wasn't the boy with the boat.

"Read it out loud," Heath said to her daughter.

Elizabeth held the phone in front of her at eye level. " 'You didn't show up you lousy pig-faced C asterisk asterisk T,' " she articulated carefully.

"You're kidding!" Heath exclaimed. "A filthy cyberstalker who balks at the C-word?"

"He also misspelled 'lousy.' L-O-W-Z-Y. Loh-zeee," she said in the tones of a demented Hollywood Chinaman. "Sheesh! Even in text-speak we have our pride."

Then she laughed.

Anna sighed. No matter how old a woman grew, there wasn't much a cute boy couldn't cure.

At least for a while.

Anna hoped Boat Boy wouldn't break E's heart. At sixteen heartbreak was a miserable thing. Age did nothing but make it worse. Hearts that didn't grow harder as the years passed acquired an ability to love that young people could only imagine.

The text didn't prove the boy with the muffled oars, and the fear of law enforcement, wasn't a monster. It did suggest that he was not the cybercreep. Unfortunately there was more than one kind of monster in the world.

Heath lit the cigarette before the match burned her fingers, breathed in a lungful of smoke, blew it out. "Our Fox River thug ruined the F-word forever. Now this toad is going to ruin all the other bad words."

"Pig-faced asterisk asterisk is my favorite so far," Elizabeth said.

Heath shot her a sideways look, squinting through the smoke from her cigarette. "I think you're beginning to enjoy this," she said.

Anna heard the joy beneath the pretense. No one could miss how much happier Elizabeth was since her ersatz abduction, and E's happiness was Heath's happiness. "Anything else in the text?" Anna asked.

E's eyes tracked back to the cell phone. " 'Same place, same time, day after tomorrow or else.' 'Or else' is in all caps."

"Are you being stalked by a ten-year-old?" Heath growled. "What does 'else' mean?"

"I don't think I want to find out," Elizabeth said, her good humor gone, anxiety dragging down her cheeks.

Anna thought for a moment, her fingers absently ruffling the feathers of Wily's tail; he'd flopped down between Robo-butt and Anna's chair. Threats were tricky things. Most went unfulfilled. Most. However, if the stalker wanted to meet with E, it was not to do her a kindness. "Or else" could be nothing. It could also be an ugly bit of business.

It was tempting to think the stalker would be mollified by contacting his victim in the flesh. He would say what he needed to say, be heard if he needed to be heard. Anna suspected that more than one person who climbed into a clock tower with a repeating rifle did so because they felt they could not be seen, could not be heard, could not break through the indifference of the world — or the bureaucracy — any other way.

One might be tempted to believe that a meeting would cancel out the "or else." Not Anna. To stalk and bully with the intensity this creep had shown was to prove oneself beyond the pale of society. Now that he was demanding to move from the ether into the corporeal world, he went from a psychological threat to a physical threat.

Resources were limited. Jurisdictions, considering the crime was instigated in Colorado and conducted from the cloud, were a mess. Stalking was illegal, but cyberstalking? That had yet to be dealt with in any definitive way.

Information was limited. None of them had a clue as to who this was. It could be someone connected to E's past in the compound, someone connected with the kidnapper who had taken her and the other girls, an enemy of Heath's — or even Anna's — or a random psychopath. He might recognize them or not. They might recognize him or not.

"We need to set a trap," Anna said.

"Anything to end the suspense," Heath said.

"What can I do?" E asked.

"Nothing," Anna told her. "You're the bait."

TWENTY-NINE

Until Peter, the parks had been Denise's salvation. At thirteen she'd gotten drawn out of the bleak misery that was her life to become a junior ranger and never gone back. During college she worked as a summer seasonal. After graduation she got her permanent status as a GS-3 taking fees at the entrance booth. From there she'd moved on and up. Until Peter Barnes had stopped time.

Ranger Castle, that's who she'd been, who she'd respected, who she showed the world. Ranger Castle was the only persona available to her that she'd ever been able to stomach. Now she was Denise Castle, civilian: no green and gray, no flat-brimmed hat, no badge, no cordovan-colored leather belt or boots.

Denise had quit the NPS, stepped out of her life, away from the things that had once defined her, and it had been easy. So very,

very, insultingly easy. It pissed Denise off just remembering it. During the drive to headquarters to start the paperwork for her retirement, she'd wasted brain energy trying to think of plausible answers to the inevitable "Why so sudden? Why now? We'll need at least two months' notice. Who can take your place? We'll need time to hire a replacement. We have to plan a retirement party! You'll need to stay to train your replacement. If you stay another three years you'll get blah, blah, blah."

Nope.

Basically it was "Don't let the screen door slap your ass on the way out."

Her whole life, and no gold watch, nothing but a bunch of forms to sign, a couple of brochures, and a teensy wad of cash every month. She'd cleaned out her office in a matter of minutes. The only thing she'd left behind was an oversized model of an outrigger canoe Peter had bought her on a trip to Hawaii. She hated the thing. She'd only taken it because he wanted it. Well, he could have it.

Shitheads. Let them rot. The NPS, potlucks on the lawn, campfire talks, scraping tourists' automobiles off rocks was not her whole life anymore. Her whole life was ahead of her. Her real life.

Bastards. Pricks. The lot of them.

At least the fact that the NPS was no longer her good buddy lessened the guilt she felt at raiding the evidence room for a couple of rufies — Rohypnol, the date rape drug. They had been taken off, of all people, a gynecologist — Denise would have thought he'd have had his fill of women's parts — up from Boston, who'd gotten himself arrested in the park a few years back. It had yet to go to trial. Probably never would. The guy was a rich doctor.

Rohypnol, added to a dash of Valium she'd had in the bottom of her medicine cabinet, should work as well as or better than the triazolam. Paulette hadn't been able to lay her hands on any at Mount Desert Hospital. At least she said she hadn't. Denise suspected her sister lacked the gumption to steal it.

Or maybe the motivation.

No, Paulette wanted this new life as much as Denise. Maybe she didn't know it quite yet, but she would. Until then, Denise could do the heavy lifting. She was used to that. Once they had a home, were a family, Paulette would come into her own. Denise was sure of it.

For the second time in as many days, Denise crept up to the shed-become-nursery

362

behind her sister's house. Her brain fizzed with the plan she'd come up with, loose ends popping like bubbles in a Scotch and soda. Rushing these things was never good. That was when mistakes were made.

No choice, she told herself.

Denise had insisted they meet in the nursery this time. Tapping on the door, she called Paulette's name softly.

"Come in," Paulette answered. Denise slipped through the door. Paulette had a single kerosene lamp lit. She was sitting in the low rocking chair. Her clothes were all in dark colors, and she wore lace-up sneakers. Good. Denise had been afraid she'd get here and Paulette would have disobeyed her. Paulette had asked why Denise wanted her to dress all in black, and Denise hadn't answered. Her plan wasn't something to be dealt with over the phone.

Denise dumped the heavy sack she was carrying as she folded down onto the hand-hooked rug at her sister's feet.

The sense that time was running out for them was driving Denise too hard for her to put off what she had to say. "I have been thinking about what you said, Paulette, about Ranger Pigeon being on to the fact we're twins, and then you finding her snooping around the nursery," she said without preamble.

"Not exactly around the nursery," Paulette said. "Just behind the house, really."

"Oyster out of a shell, that's how she looked at you. That's what you said."

"I guess," Paulette admitted.

Denise stared at her.

"Yes," Paulette said in a firmer voice. "I think she's been around the nursery. I felt it."

"Right," Denise approved. "You can see how that makes the death of good old Kurt not as simple as we thought. What had been a perfect murder now has a big fat hairy flaw in the ointment."

"Fly," Paulette said.

"Whatever. Anna Pigeon is that fly, that big hairy flaw. She's an obstacle," Denise insisted. "A serious stumbling block on the road to our new life."

"Oh." Paulette looked away. She stood, crossed to the crib, and picked up the little bear, her back to Denise. "If she's been back here, I haven't seen her. She hasn't tried to talk to me or anything. Maybe she was just, you know, poking around like rangers like to do." She set the bear down carefully in precisely the same place it had been before.

Why was Paulette being obstinate? "She might not have come back; more likely she did and you didn't see. The pigeon has all the pieces to you and me and Kurt dead and you at the Acadian. She's not stupid. She's an obstacle, and the obstacle has to be removed," Denise insisted.

Paulette spun around, her hands to her cheeks like a cartoon of "noooooo." "Do you mean kill her?" Paulette exclaimed. "Miss Pigeon is a ranger, law enforcement, like you. I've seen it in every movie. If a cop is killed — probably even a tree cop — the CIA and FBI and everybody start a huge manhunt!"

Denise stifled a sigh. "It's not like that. I know you're scared. I'd be, too. But we're not going to do anything drastic," she said, forcing a smile and a soothing timbre to her voice. "What I've got planned is more like a prank. It'll be seen like a prank. Ha ha, no big deal. You'll see. Rangers play pranks on each other all the time. Nobody gets their panties in a wad. We'll snatch the pigeon — like frat boys snatch each other for a joke. We'll keep her in here for a couple of days, then, when we've finished, we'll call somebody to let her out. Nobody gets hurt. We get what we deserve."

"You're sure?" Paulette asked. Denise's twin appeared to be growing younger and younger as Denise watched. Years dropping from her voice and face. Denise was growing older. At present she felt they weren't identical twins at all, that she was the much older sister and had to take care of Paulette.

"I'm sure," she said warmly. "We need more time, just a few days more to get everything we need. If we can . . . pull our prank on Anna Pigeon, it will buy us that time. We'll finish everything on our list, then we'll buy a nice big car and we'll go south until it's spring all year around, and we'll buy a nice house."

Paulette smiled wistfully. "It would be wonderful to have a nice new house," she said. "One that was clean and pretty, where nothing was broken or patched."

"That's what we're going to have," Denise promised. "Tonight we'll remove the obstacle. Over the next few days we'll tidy up, then off we'll go. An adventure."

Paulette's smile firmed up, her age steadied at about fourteen, or so it seemed to Denise. Fourteen would have to do.

"I got water for her," Denise said, pulling three liter bottles from her canvas sack. Without a word, Paulette gathered them up and carried them to a shelf next to the crib, where she arranged them in a neat row. "I brought these." Denise dug in her bag. "MREs from the fire cache. The park will never miss them. And these." She pulled two pairs of handcuffs from her belt. "Anna Pigeon will be fine. Just for a couple of days. I hoped you had an old bucket around somewhere."

"A bucket? What for?" Paulette asked as she piled the MREs in a tidy stack beside the water bottles.

"No bathroom," Denise explained.

"Yuck!" Paulette made a face. "Wait." Dropping to her hands and knees, she felt around under the crib. "If it's only for a couple days . . ." She dragged out a pink potty-training toilet. "It's nicer than a bucket." For a moment she studied it, then turned to Denise. "It's awfully small."

Paulette was so naïve, so sweet, like a little kid untouched by the whole real, nasty, shitty world. At times Denise thought maybe Paulette wasn't all there, wasn't quite right in the head. That would mean Denise wasn't right in the head either. They were identical twins. Being crazy wasn't a new thought. Things had gotten blurry and odd in the last while, maybe a year, maybe more. Nerves.

"Anna Pigeon has a skinny butt," Denise said. "The potty is perfect. We do it tonight."

"I didn't get the triazolam," Paulette confessed. "I can look again tomorrow. We could do it tomorrow, couldn't we?"

Denise knew Paulette wouldn't have gotten the drug. Of course she knew. There wasn't anything she didn't know about her identical twin. To Paulette this was just talk, just a game. Paulette didn't think this was going to happen; she didn't think they deserved a life together. Kurt had beat that out of her.

Denise knew better. This had to happen.

"Not a problem," Denise assured her. "I got it all worked out. You don't have to worry about a thing."

"I did get this," Paulette said, brightening. "It's about the legacy. It came to General Delivery this morning." She held an envelope out to Denise. It had been opened. That irked Denise. The legacy was something they shared — or should share. Paulette should have waited until they could open it together.

Having unfolded the single slip of paper from the envelope, Denise turned it to the lamp so she could read the letters. *The woman who put the ad in the paper regarding the twins is very ill at present. I would not want to see her hurt or disappointed. To that end, I would like to meet with you before I share your card with her. There is a legacy, two to be accurate. We can talk about that when we meet.*

The number of a cell phone followed.

"Sounds like a con," Denise said. "People run all kinds of con games. This sounds like one of them. Did you call her?" she demanded. Her tone was too rough. Paulette aged a little more, and her mouth turned harder. Ugly, Denise thought.

"I didn't," Paulette said. "But I want to. I think it's real."

Paulette wanted to get back with their biological mommy, Denise thought bitterly. No matter that Mommy was obviously a heartless tramp. Paulette would probably want to hang around and nurse Mommy back to health, and to hell with her sister, her identical twin sister.

Denise rode a wave of anger until it subsided, leaving her tired and determined. "We'll do whatever you want," she said. "First let's get tonight out of the way, okay? Please?"

"Tonight?"

Denise said nothing, just kept a half smile pasted on her face. Paulette looked at her for long enough that Denise thought she was going to come up with another argument, distraction, or reason to postpone what they had to do.

"Just for a couple days, then we let her go," Paulette said.

Denise felt a rush of relief as great as the anger had been. "I love having a sister," she said.

"Me, too," Paulette said.

THIRTY

Paulette was in the boat; she had the needle with the mixture. Denise had explained what needed to be done, and Paulette had understood and seemed confident she could do her part. The sea was flat, and there was a gentle onshore breeze. Everything was as it should be, Denise told herself for the hundredth time. Once, like the whine of a mosquito near her ear, the thought surfaced that this part of the plan, disabling Anna Pigeon, wasn't crucial. A flash of the pigeon's eyes over the picture frame, or the tilt of her head as she'd interrogated Paulette, pulled the thought back into the depths. This was not a time to take even the slightest risk. If they failed, there would be no time to recover.

Since Kurt had died and Ranger Pigeon started poking her nose in, Denise had had that awful feeling she got as a child when she tried to balance a broom on her nose.

Never could she run fast enough to keep it from falling down.

This was the second-to-last major step; then they were home free, free to have a home. She concentrated on that to keep the noise of the boat engine from bouncing off her sensitized eardrums with the force of a cataclysm.

Denise had coddled and pampered the little runabout's motor until it was as quiet as a fifteen-horsepower Evinrude could get. Unfortunately, on a still night, its high-pitched growl carried across the water like the wailing of an infant.

Before she could clearly see Schoodic's rocky point in the ambient light of a moonless sea, Denise cut the engine. For a minute she breathed, letting the magnificent silence erase their trespass.

The water was flat — or as flat as the restless Atlantic ever was. This was good. High seas would have postponed this adventure. Time had become a creature of three dimensions, slippery and short and sliding fast through Denise's fingers.

Having pried off the lens covers, she lifted the binoculars to her eyes.

Schoodic Point, as advertised, was pointed. It was a peninsula on the end of a peninsula that ended in a spade-shaped stone skirt digging into the ocean at the mainland's southernmost shore. Schoodic was a bleak beauty of rock, stone, sea, and sky. Fashion shoots favored it for high-end clothes, the emaciated models teetering over the round rocks in high heels, believing that people were staring because they were pretty and not because they looked like idiots. Weddings were often booked at Schoodic Point.

A hard, uncompromising beginning to married life, Denise thought as she swept the shore with the binoculars. An ugly parking lot scraped a flat place above the beach and nearly ruined the aesthetics. This night Denise forgave its existence because it had the decency to be empty. It was after three in the morning, and RVs weren't allowed to park overnight, but they often tried to get away with it.

No RVs. No sedans with thrashing bodies in the backseat.

"We're clear," she whispered to Paulette. "We paddle from here."

Frizzled blond hair tucked under a black watch cap, small body hidden under a black long-sleeved T-shirt, black sweatpants, and black running shoes, Paulette was merely a shadow in the bow. Denise thought of herself as a strong, strapping woman. She saw Paulette as fine-boned and delicate. Odd that she and her sister were the same height and weight, same shoe, glove, and bra size. Paulette's shoulders were hunched, and her chin was down, as if she tried to disappear into her own skeleton. Black ops were not her forte. Well, Denise thought, they weren't hers either. She just did what she had to do. Paulette would see that. After the fact, when done was done, she would understand.

Both women had blackened their faces with makeup. Denise didn't know what the Delta Force guys or the Navy SEALs used, or what football players put under their eyes, but she and her sister had made do with a mix of Paulette's black, gray, and dark blue eye shadows. The effect was all she could have wished for. But for her hands, Paulette looked to be little more than a texture on the night seascape.

As did Denise. Invisible twins. Could invisible people still be identical? Sort of the visual equivalent of the tree falling in the forest: Could one no-thing be exactly the same as another no-thing? Denise wondered as she watched Paulette's white hands float up like the ghosts of long-dead starfish and close around the handle of a paddle.

In an inexpert attempt to get the paddle in position she struck the blade against the gunwale. The clunk was loud enough to wake sleepers in Nova Scotia.

Maybe Denise suffered from nervous twitches, but she was beginning to think her sister was just clumsy. She swallowed an oath.

"I'll paddle," she whispered, making her voice extra kind to stifle the traitorous thoughts about her twin.

The runabout was a bitch to paddle. Denise had done it enough that she could make it work. Work was the key word. Outboards weren't meant to run on manpower. Or, in her case, womanpower. By the time she managed to catch the crest of a good wave, and ride the surf into the rocky beach on the point below the parking lot, sweat was pouring down from her temples and between her breasts.

As the swell that beached them retreated, it dragged small stones along with it, clattering back toward the ocean floor. If she timed it right, the racket of the stony surf would cover the racket of beaching the boat.

Denise was over the side in a second. Even in midsummer the water off the coast of Maine was cold. She was used to wearing a wet suit complete with booties. Cold feet were the least of the dangers, she reminded herself as she shoved hard on the stern to move the boat out of the reach of the surf before the Atlantic could turn it into flotsam. Paulette sat like a statue in the bow, making the going that much tougher. Again Denise felt irritation rise up her spine to scratch like a metal rasp on the back of her brain.

Lot of stress, she reminded herself. Lot on our plates. "Us against the world" was not as romantic as fiction writers would have it. "Us" could get real bitchy. Things would be better — like they used to be those first few times they were together — once they got straightened away, got the legacy, the pension, the money from the sale of the house . . .

Denise slammed her mind shut against the list. It grew longer every minute she dwelt on it, longer and heavier, each chore another lead weight on her metaphorical dive belt threatening to drag her down, drown her.

Paulette jumped from the boat, grabbed the bow with both hands, and began to help drag it up on shore.

See, Denise told herself. Not irritating. Good and right.

The previous day Denise had driven to

the peninsula on reconnaissance to find a secluded spot to cache the boat. It didn't need to be totally hidden, just out of casual sight should a ranger be on patrol — not likely; there weren't enough green-and-gray bodies for round-the-clock coverage on Schoodic either. More likely would be a nosy insomniac out for a ride.

She'd found a shallow dry creek to the side of the point not too long a walk from the employee housing area and the old US Navy base — now a rotting hulk of dorm rooms and hallways — but far enough so that the sounds of their arrival wouldn't wake any of the summer seasonals, or the sculptors on Schoodic for an artists' retreat.

Psychically speaking, killing Kurt had been no big deal. He was a lout and a bastard, and even his best friend was over it in a beer or two. Even without killing, this would be different. Paulette was right. There would be cops all over a federal law enforcement officer going missing. Since Pigeon was "acting" chief, Denise hoped there'd be a time lag before the NPS declared her disappearance officially suspicious. Then Denise wasn't sure who-all would descend, but she was sure it was going to be a big deal. Hence: black clothes, black face, surgical gloves for the event, and a getaway boat hidden in the scrub.

Leave No Trace.

That was a Park Service motto. Good old NPS, Denise thought with a smile. Good old Superintendent Peter, moldy green and moth-eaten gray down to his grubby little soul. This was going to look bad on Happy Daddy's résumé. A perk she'd not considered before.

Paulette was making a lot of racket puffing and grunting as they dragged the boat into the wash. After they'd settled the runabout, Denise could still hear her breathing. Paulette hadn't kept herself in shape. Denise stared over the dark shape of the hull between them. Despite the black makeup and the brim of the ball cap, she could see that Paulette's face was crumpled like a little kid's before it starts to shriek.

"Are you okay?" she asked softly.

"I have to pee," Paulette said. A nervous titter escaped her lips.

"Because you're scared?" Denise asked.

"I guess." To Denise's surprise, tears started cutting white stripes through the powder on Paulette's face. All her irritation was blown away on a gust of pity. Paulette was the softer Denise, the gentle Denise she could have been if not for the foster homes and other bullshit. Tonight was going to be hard on Paulette because of her tender heart. As soon as she could afford the luxury, Denise decided, she would have the compassion Paulette had. For now, she was grateful that her heart was hard as flint, that it had been pounded and tormented until it barely beat. Right now, tonight, that hardening was going to pay off. Paulette would understand how it had to be, if not right away, then when they were in their new house and their new lives.

Sitting on the keel of the boat, Denise patted the wet fiberglass beside her. Obediently, Paulette came around the stern to sit next to her. Denise took her sister's hand between both of her own.

"This isn't like it was with Kurt," Paulette snuffled. "It's hard to take someone when you don't want to hurt them, when they're not bad, just too smart and in the way."

"It is," Denise admitted. "I can do it without you if you like," she offered, though, in truth, she didn't think she could. "We're not doing alibis or anything."

"No alibis because we both live alone, it's the middle of the night, and no one will suspect us anyway," Paulette said, repeating exactly the words and intonations Denise had used when they discussed the venture in the boat. Denise looked at her hard, trying to figure out if she was being mocked.

No, of course she wasn't. Paulette would never do that. Twin souls would sound the same, would speak as one. Of course. Same DNA.

"Can't we just not do it? Turn around and go home?" Paulette pleaded, glancing up at Denise from under the ball cap.

Denise felt as if she towered over her sister, like a Goliath, a monster. This was as much for Paulette as it was for her. More. Compassion burned out on sudden unexpected anger. Jolted by the intensity of the fury, Denise's tongue clove to the roof of her mouth.

They had been through this. "It's just for a couple of days." Denise forced herself to go through it again. "She'll sleep through most of it. Then we tell somebody where to find her. No harm, no foul."

"Sorry, sorry," Paulette said before Denise could say any wrong words and ruin everything forever. "Of course we can't just not do it. Let's do it. Let's go. Right now."

"Don't have to pee anymore?" Denise asked as Paulette rose.

"I couldn't if I wanted to. All my sphincters are slammed shut," Paulette said, and produced a wan smile.

Denise smiled back. Paulette was trying.

Paulette was a trouper.

"We'll be fine," Denise promised. "Do you have the stuff?"

Paulette unzipped her waist pack and checked the contents as Denise had seen her do half a dozen times since the boat left Somes Sound.

Paulette lifted out a syringe with a plastic safety cap over the needle. Holding it near her ear, she shook it. Paulette had crushed the rufies to powder using the bowl of a teaspoon to mash the tablets against the bowl of a soup spoon. Denise had thrown in a Valium for good measure. When the powder was as fine as they could make it, they mixed it with tap water and drew the resulting liquid into a syringe.

Denise remembered how Paulette's hands shook, setting up a tiny tempest in the spoon, how her own had shaken so much they lost some of the precious stuff.

Two street-made rufies, 1.0 mg of Valium. There wasn't anything on the Internet about the mix, but enough Rohypnol could cause unconsciousness and even coma. Coma would be good, Denise thought, startling herself. She didn't want to kill the pigeon any more than Paulette did. Still, a coma would be a whole lot easier for everybody concerned.

"Two rufies and a Valium is a lot," Paulette said. "Maybe too much."

"You should know. You're the RN," Denise said. She'd meant to sound complimentary. It came out waspish.

"LPN," Paulette said in a barely audible voice.

For a moment the letters made no sense to Denise. Paulette was a nurse. Nurses were RNs, registered nurses. Then she remembered. LPN meant licensed practical nurse. No better than an EMT.

"A Candy Striper?" Denise demanded, aghast.

"It takes a year to get accredited. RNs take four or five years." Paulette hung her head so low her forehead nearly touched her knees. "Some of us do injections, but there's always a doctor's okay, or an RN to help. I don't know whether injecting Rohypnol instead of swallowing it will make a difference. What if she ODs?"

"Shit." Denise forced herself not to roll her eyes. What if she did OD? Would it be worse than if she didn't? Worse, of course, in the sense of murder, but worse all around? For her and Paulette?

"It can't kill her," Denise said firmly. "I Googled it."

THIRTY-ONE

Anna's sleeping mind conjured up a wasp. The insect was stinging her bicep. Instantly she was awake, but, for a moment, she couldn't remember where she was. Not Rocky. Acadia. No Paul, no roommates, yet a shadow, as wide as it was tall, clotted the vague light between her eyes and the ceiling.

"Hey!" Anna barked. Squeaking like a colony of bats, the shadow changed shape and squeezed toward the door. Not a shadow — this invader was corporeal in nature. Shadows were the stuff of silence. This apparition was making a hell of a racket.

"Who are you?" Anna yelled as she threw off her covers. There was a brief scuffle as the night creature tried to shove itself through an opening half its size.

Leaping free of the bedclothes, Anna yelled: "Stop!"

The black shape wrestled with itself for a moment, then popped through the bedroom door into the living room. Anna scrambled for the light switch. In the unfamiliar room, she was slow. By the time she'd flicked the light on, she could hear the sound of feet pounding down wooden stairs. More than one person, two, maybe three. A wave of dizziness overtook her; sound was behaving oddly; the light seemed to shimmer. She brushed her wrist over her eyes.

Hers was one of four apartments in the building used for employee housing on Schoodic Peninsula. The structure was divided in half, two floors on each side, an apartment on each floor, the two halves connected by an open-air breezeway and stairs. Though it often happened in cookie-cutter dwellings, these weren't drunken neighbors wandering in the wrong door. Drunken neighbors wouldn't run; besides, at present, Anna's was the only apartment occupied.

It could be park visitors. As far as vacationers were concerned, rangers were always on duty, always there to stanch the bleeding or lend a cup of sugar. Since Anna — like a lot of the old guard — still refused to lock her doors, a couple might have wandered in and been scared into running when she awakened.

"Hey!" she shouted again. "Hold up."

In three strides she'd crossed the small living room. As she reached the head of the stairs, two humanoid shapes careened through the downstairs breezeway, running out into the parking lot with more speed than grace.

Not tourists with bad manners. Sinister miscreants. "Damn!" Anna muttered. She staggered, caught herself on the railing, then turned and ran back into her apartment. For an instant, she stood beside her bed, trying to remember why she'd come back. "Intruders," she said, and she pulled on her cordovan boots, grabbed her SIG Sauer from the drawer in the nightstand, and, stark naked but for boots and gun, hurtled out of the apartment, down the stairs, and into the night.

In the middle of the employee-housing parking lot, she stopped, eyes wide, ears open. Without warning a blackness as heavy and dark as igneous rock rolled over her brain, crushed her vision, and clogged her ears. Anna's joints turned to water. She fell hard on her knees.

Pain cleared her mind. She could hear sneakered feet scratching on pavement; the intruders were headed across the access road toward the renovated Rockefeller building used as the Schoodic Education and Research Center. Beyond the Rockefeller building were the crumbling ruins of an old navy base's housing wings.

Currently the research center was home to granite sculptors doing a summer workshop. Possibly her wee-hours visitation was from feral artists, but Anna was more worried about the artists as victims or hostages than as perpetrators. Though one or two of the huge, labor-intensive granite monoliths did look like the work of troubled minds.

As her vision cleared, she saw the two figures running hard toward the plaza where the sculptures were being carved. She heaved herself to her feet and, boots ringing on the asphalt, sprinted after them.

"Stop or I'll shoot!" she yelled. She wouldn't shoot. Rangers didn't shoot fleeing suspects even if they had slithered up to one's bedside in the dead of night.

The dreamlike sensation of running ever slower through air viscous as mud dragged at her legs. Distance — or her perception of it — underwent a sea change. The ruined barracks wavered, retreating in an undulating wreck of roof lines. The Rockefeller building, no more than two hundred yards from her apartment, refused to move closer as she ran; then, suddenly, the immense granite sculptures were looming over her.

Anna didn't so much stop with intent as simply cease to move because her body chose stagnation regardless of what her mind ordered it to do. The retreating human-shaped fragments of darkness had run past the sculptures. Immobile, she watched as they reached the barracks where the wings of the ruined building came together. Her eyes told her they vanished like smoke; her mind suggested they'd probably run down one of the stairwells that let into the basement level.

Even if her legs had not ceased to function properly, and the night had not broken all the laws of physics to become a nauseating, undulating mess, Anna would not have given chase. Nothing short of a shrieking child or a mewling kitten could induce her to pursue bad guys into that haunted hulk in the dark.

The abandoned barracks was two stories of smashed desks, shattered walls, mirror shards, falling staircases, and other sharp-edged detritus. In that place, if fleeing felons didn't kill you, tumbling down stairs or broken glass would.

Broken glass would what?

With sudden alarm, Anna wondered why

she was naked, why she was standing in the shadow of lowering chunks of granite with her gun in her hand. She had no recollection of kneeling, yet she was on her knees on the stone.

Stinging in her upper arm claimed her attention.

Clumsily, she brushed at it. Something clinked to the paving stones of the sculpture yard. Stupidly, Anna stared down at it, eyes and mind disconnected. Part of her brain knew she should recognize the shape. Most of her brain was atomized, loose dust blowing in a windy night.

A syringe. The item that fell from her arm was a syringe. There was quarter of an inch of liquid in it.

Evidence of something.

She picked it up, holding it like a dagger. Forget evidence. Two weapons were better than one. Weapons against what?

People were hiding in the old barracks; she'd been chasing them. They had stuck the needle in her arm while she was sleeping.

Light. She needed light if she was going to go into the garbage- and rat-infested derelict building. Light and backup; she had to get a flashlight and a radio and a pair of underpants.

First she had to get up off of her knees. At one time she knew how human legs bent and flexed to execute this intricate maneuver. No more. She wasn't even sure where her feet were. She could neither see nor feel them.

A clunk startled her in a vague way. Rolling her head carefully to the side, she looked down. Somebody had dropped a gun — a SIG Sauer — beside her right knee. Careless bastard. What kind of idiot dropped a gun?

Me, she thought. My gun. Bending at the waist to pick it up, she fell face-first onto the granite paving. A cracking jarred the interior of her skull. Nothing hurt. Her skull felt as if it had been hurled against a wall, but nothing hurt. Or if it did, she couldn't feel it.

Straightening her arms, she forced her head and shoulders up from the ground. Sculpted works in progress, high as houses and cut into fantastic shapes, moved slowly around her, waving and leaning like grasses in a breeze. The brick and stone facade of the beautiful old building beyond rose as high as Half Dome, its many windows blank and lifeless.

"Help," she creaked. The noise she made was so thin and tiny she thought of the

Woozy in *The Patchwork Girl of Oz,* the creature whose roar was supposed to bring down mountains but in reality was a teeny squeak. It didn't matter. Sculptors were artists. Artists didn't go around rescuing people. When the shit hit the proverbial, nobody ever yelled, "Is there an artist in the house!"

Anna pulled her knees under her to sit on her heels. In an attempt to scrape off the toxic fog devouring her brain, she scrubbed at her face. Pain that should have come when she fell blindsided her. She cried out feebly. One hand came away black and wet. Blood was pouring down over her left eye, blinding her.

Paul will still love me, even if the corner of my head is smashed, she thought. The image of her husband, Paul, in all his strength and calm, centered her. She was able to find her feet and push to a standing position. Her pistol was still on the ground, an infinite distance from her eyes. Teetering sickeningly back and forth in her boots, she tried to decide if it would be worse to leave her gun and go find a radio or stay with her gun and . . . what?

Just stay with her gun.

Besides, she was naked. She'd been reminded of that when she looked way, way down at the gun. No clothes. Naked outside in the weird with no clothes. This had to be a dream. That was a relief. Peculiar dreams were not strangers to Anna. There was a foolproof test to see whether one was dreaming or not. It wasn't pinching. That was silly. It was flying. If she could fly, that was proof positive she was dreaming.

Anna tried to lift her arms. They did not reach Superman-in-flight position, only zombie-seeking-edible-brain position.

No flying.

Not a dream.

Again she looked toward the ruins. The stairwell was disgorging its recent meal, bipedal shapes bulging forth to be delineated by the faint light of the stars. The creatures who'd put a wasp in her dream, a drug in her veins.

Anna raised her gun hand. "No further," she said. "Move and I soowt." She'd meant to say "shoot." The bonk on the head, or the chemical they'd injected, turned her lips to rubber. The figures halted, murmured, then came toward her.

Anna pulled the trigger. Nothing. Her hand was empty, the gun ever so far away on the ground by her foot.

The figures separated, moving slowly in her direction. Ninjas, black clothes and hoods and faces, with four white hands, fake as plastic mannequins' hands, floating along beside them. They were wearing surgical gloves.

Coming to butcher the kill, Anna thought as she tipped into nothingness.

Thirty-Two

Denise couldn't take her eyes off the fallen woman. In the starlight, Anna Pigeon was faintly luminescent, as if she'd been swimming in phosphorescent plankton. The boots, incongruously dark, made it appear as if her legs had been lopped off just below the knee, leaving white stumps. Anna's hair, always in a single fat braid, was spread out around her in a dark fan shot with silver, a protective cape that reached to her waist.

Denise didn't know what she had expected to happen when they'd set out on this venture, but this wasn't it. Despite the fact that three of her bullets were in him, Kurt Duffy had roared and fought. That made it self-defense in a way. Killing should be a positive or negative choice, not made in hot blood, necessarily — cold blood was fine — but with a real sense of commitment. One *committed* murder; murder didn't just happen. The gun didn't just go off; the victim

393

didn't just run into the knife seven times.

Since she wasn't murdering Anna Pigeon, just removing an obstacle for a while, she'd pictured it happening in a prosaic, workaday kind of way. Or peacefully, like taking out the garbage on a Sunday afternoon. The unconscious body would lie in its own snug little bed, drifting quietly into deeper and deeper sleep. Then Denise and Paulette would wrap her tidily in one of her blankets and haul her to the runabout.

Not this blood-and-snot-filled gun-toting drama.

Also, in her mental picture, Anna Pigeon would wear a pair of pajamas, for Christ's sake, or a T-shirt and panties. What kind of lunatic leaps up and gives chase wearing nothing but a pair of cordovan NPS boots, even if she is drugged?

Naked was bad in an unsettling way. Naked was vulnerable and very female. Naked gave a body a gender and an age. "She should wear fucking pajamas," Denise hissed. "Rangers get called out at night."

Paulette said nothing.

The shushing sibilance of the sea washed between Denise and her sister. Usually the sounds of the ocean soothed Denise. These rasped. The clacking of rocks as they were rolled by the receding waves clattered like a plague of demented cicadas.

Anna Pigeon's hand twitched. Passed out on major drugs, the woman seemed to still be reaching for her gun.

"Oh God," Paulette whispered. "What do we do now?"

Trained to the call of "Gun!" Denise ran forward quickly and kicked the SIG out of the reach of the weak and groping hand. At a safe distance from the moribund ranger, she retrieved the weapon and shoved it into the waistband of her pants at the small of her back. Unlike Paulette, Denise had opted for black Levi's instead of sweatpants. The denim waistband held the gun firmly.

"We get her to the boat," Denise said.

"Shouldn't we get her some clothes first?" Paulette asked plaintively.

The toe of Denise's sneaker twitched out and struck the downed woman in the shoulder.

"Don't kick her!" Paulette exclaimed.

Like that was worse than drugging and snatching her.

Denise made no reply. She hadn't meant to kick her. Her foot had jerked out of its own accord. Nerves.

"We can lend her some of our clothes," Denise said. "She won't need much. She won't be there for long. Help me pick her up."

Paulette didn't move. She was looking past the naked ranger toward the housing area. "Maybe we should go back to her room. She's going to need some things. Maybe she takes medication . . . and tooth-paste . . . that kind of thing," Paulette said.

Denise thought about that for an instant — not the meds or the toiletries, a blanket to cover her up. Anna had made it fifty or sixty yards from her apartment. There was nothing but open road and parking lot between where she lay and her bed. A sculptor up late smoking dope, or doing whatever sculptors did in the dead of night, might see them. "Too risky," she decided. "I'll take her arms, you take her legs. Put a hand under each knee; it'll be easier that way."

Paulette tiptoed gingerly around the crumpled form on the paving stones. Leaning down, she lifted one of the booted feet and pulled the leg. With the leverage, the senseless woman rolled to lie upon her back, hair veiling her breasts. Half of her face was covered in a black mask. Denise stared until she realized that it was not a mask; it was blood.

"She's bleeding!" Paulette exclaimed. "Why is she bleeding?"

To Denise, it sounded as if her sister blamed her, suggested she'd kicked Anna Pigeon in the face. Her toe had only just tapped the woman's shoulder. "She must have cut her head when she fell," Denise said curtly. "Get her legs." Moving briskly to give herself more courage and authority than she felt, Denise grabbed a limp wrist in each hand and lifted the upper body.

The used syringe fell from Anna's lax fingers. Denise dropped the hands. Flesh thudded against the ground.

"Careful," Paulette whispered. "We don't want to hurt her."

Denise grunted. Stepping on the needle, she pried the plastic up until the needle snapped off. She put the syringe in the front pocket of her jacket. Both she and Paulette had worn surgical gloves when they filled it; still, forensics would be able to tell what drugs were used, maybe match them to the rufies missing from the park's evidence locker. If anybody even thought to check there. The syringe itself might be a special kind Mount Desert used exclusively. One never knew what mattered and what didn't until it was too late.

The bit of evidence secured, Denise grabbed Anna's wrists again and whispered, "Grab her legs."

Paulette grabbed the top of the boots and pulled Anna's naked legs up and apart. A whimper escaped her as she slowly lowered them again, boot heels carefully together. "I can't!" she wailed softly. "It's like rape. Please, let's get her some clothes. Or put her back in her bed and leave. She won't remember us. You said she won't remember anything."

Denise wanted to lash out at Paulette, but a part of her felt as her sister did. Not about putting Ranger Pigeon back and pretending it never happened, but about one woman prying apart another woman's legs and stepping between them when that woman was naked. It was icky. The worst kind of icky, the kind that stuck to the inside of your skull for years.

"Right," she said to herself; then, to her sister, "But we can't go back. We're way beyond that. We can't leave her. Let's do this. Come take an arm. We'll drag her so her feet stay together and we're not . . . you know, looking at her that way. We don't have to drag her far. Jumping out of bed and chasing us, she did half our work for us. Another couple hundred yards and we're good to go. All the hard part over."

Paulette came up beside Denise but made no move to help. Denise shoved one of

Pigeon's arms into her hands.

"Ranger Pigeon was nice to me the morning Kurt was found," Paulette said, looking into the bloody mask of a face.

Denise heard faint accusation in her sister's tone and bit back a harsh response. Paulette was her gentler self; she had to respect the Paulette half of her personality even when it was a huge pain in the butt. "Everything is going to be fine," she said calmly. "We've come so far. We do this and we're almost free. Think of our house in the pines somewhere warm. Think of being a family and never being cold or alone again."

Paulette took in a deep breath. "Okay," she said. "You're right."

Denise exhaled in relief. "Here we go," she whispered.

Both of them pulling moved the body at a snail's pace. Anna Pigeon couldn't have weighed more than a hundred and ten pounds, a hundred and fifteen at most, yet she apparently had made a deal with gravity; the earth seemed to hold her fast. Agonizing minutes passed as they dragged her from the granite apron in front of the Education Center onto the road to Schoodic Point, where the boat was stashed.

"Shit," Denise muttered as one of Anna's boots came off. Half a yard more and her heel was red with blood. Or, in the moonlight, black with blood. Denise was imagining the red color.

"We have to stop," Paulette said. "We're scratching her bottom and her legs all up."

"We're making a ton of noise," Denise said. Dumb and Dumber move a body, she thought. Murder wasn't glamorous; she knew that from killing Kurt. Neither was kidnapping, but it shouldn't be stupid. This was stupid, like a bad movie.

For an awful moment, Denise flew free of her body. From twenty feet up in the air she looked down at herself and her sister dragging the drugged ranger. They were ludicrous, absurd. Minuscule black ants, intent on abduction, hauling along a naked human. Insane. The picture whirled, and Denise crashed back into her own skull.

Not absurd, necessary.

Okay, absurd, but necessary, Denise admitted to herself. They had to do this to get what was owed them. She was sorry about Anna Pigeon, but Anna would have sided with the Peter Barneses and the Kurt Duffys and stripped Denise and her twin of everything. Again. Thrown them out to rot with the garbage. Again.

On second thought, she wasn't that sorry about Anna Pigeon. She should have kept her nosy little pigeon beak out of things that were none of her business, kept her beady little birdy eyes off of other people's things.

"Let's get her up," Denise said as she dragged the ranger's limp arm around her neck, hoisting her half of the inert form. "Like this, like we're walking a drunk. Then we won't be scratching her. It'll be okay. Put her arm around your neck." After more fumbling clown antics, they had the unconscious woman between them and were moving forward. Denise cursed herself. Anybody with half a brain would have worked all this bullshit out before doing the deed. The pigeon was to blame. If she hadn't nosed around they wouldn't be in such a rush, moving too fast to think things through properly.

With Anna draped around their necks, they traveled at a fairly good pace. Pigeon's toes dragged, but there was nothing Denise could do about that.

Within minutes they had trundled their catch over the rough cobble-sized stones of the point to the wash where they'd hidden the runabout. Unseen. Unheard. Like they'd never been to Schoodic. Like none of it had ever happened.

"We're good, we're good," Denise gasped, breathing in gusts as much from fear as exercise. Together they lowered the body, laying it out on the stones. "Catch your breath," Denise told her sister. "Almost done." Leaving Paulette standing over their captive, Denise went to turn the runabout right side up. The boat and outboard motor were heavy, but, unlike handling dead humans, Denise was accustomed to handling the runabout. She pried it up onto her knees, then flipped it easily over onto its keel.

Looking back over the gunwales, she expected to see Paulette getting the pigeon ready to drag over the side and into the boat. Instead, Paulette was sitting on the ground, in the rocks, her palms held to her cheeks and her feet in front of her like a little kid.

"We can't do it," Paulette said, eyes fixed on the prone naked ranger. "The shed won't be a good prison. She'll get out. Everybody will be swarming the island looking for her. Kidnapping is a serious crime. We could get the death sentence."

Like murder wasn't a serious crime — but then, Paulette hadn't murdered anybody. Denise had.

"How can we keep her quiet, even for a day or two?" Paulette wailed, her voice rising too high, too loud. "Hikers and tourists go in the woods, they could hear. Hand-cuffed, how can she get to the toilet? Feed herself? If we do it, she'll see us. Or hear us. We should have thought this through. Keeping her drugged all that time could hurt her. She could OD or dehydrate or something. I won't."

Paulette sounded mulish. More than that. She sounded firm.

What a miserable time for my sister to develop a spine, Denise thought. What a miserable time to get a conscience. Rage of the kind she thought she only held for Peter and his ilk rose up in her gorge hot as lava.

Paulette was staring up at her beseechingly, the ruined blond hair wisping out from beneath the black ball cap. Though they had been born only minutes, maybe seconds, apart, Denise realized Paulette was much younger than she was. Denise had to take care of her. You didn't rage at a child. Especially not if that child was you when you were little, back before they ruined you. Besides, Paulette was right. A nutcase who would run after you naked with a gun wasn't a person who would be easy to keep as a pet for an hour, let alone a couple of days.

Swallowing the molten anger, Denise walked around to where her sister sat beside

Anna Pigeon. Crouching, she lifted one of Pigeon's arms, then laid two fingers over the pulse point at her wrist. For thirty seconds she concentrated. Having laid the hand back on the stones, she shifted, put her first and second finger on the ranger's trachea, and let them slide down into the hollow where the jugular vein was closest to the skin. Again she concentrated on feeling for a pulse.

It was there, thready and faint.

Making an executive decision, Denise removed her hand.

"Too late, Paulette," she said. "She's dead. You killed her."

"Oh God," Paulette murmured, and began to rock back and forth.

Denise sat next to her and put her arms around her. "Shh, shh," she whispered. "It's all good. This is how it was meant to be. I killed Kurt; you injected the pigeon and it killed her. That's how it had to be. We did nothing that wasn't supposed to happen. Things are just happening to help us now instead of hurt us. I'm going to take care of everything. No need to worry. Shh." She laid her cheek against her sister's. Paulette was calming at her touch. Denise savored the sensation of being of use, of value, to another human being.

"Are we done?" Paulette sniffed.

"Almost," Denise said. "I just need to find a garbage bag."

THIRTY-THREE

There was sensation of a sort. Anna didn't know if it was life, death, dreams, or something altogether different. As in a dream, occurrences that would have been staggeringly bizarre to the waking mind, felt ordinary.

Zen.

That thought wafted through the utter darkness inside Anna's skull. In dreams one was truly in the moment: no worries for the future, no regrets from the past, no expectations, therefore no surprises. The entire universe created in the mind, and the mind created in that universe.

A sliding sensation followed by a hard whack to the small of her back startled Anna free of philosophy. Pain was real and actual. Pain made a person care, and damn quick, what was going to happen next, and what had happened a second ago. Pain meant she wasn't dead and she wasn't dreaming. Life was happening.

Further than that, she couldn't fathom. "Breathe," she told herself.

ABCs: airway, blood, circulation. Breathing was first. Of course she was breathing. Alive, one did that sort of thing. But it wasn't easy. Almost, she had to tell her diaphragm to drop, her lungs to expand. Not an out-of-body experience; more a trapped-in-a-worthless-body experience.

As consciousness and breath fluttered in and out, pictures came back fleetingly: the jab, the wasp, the chase. Like old Polaroids, colors were muted and images fading like ghosts at sunrise.

Shadows had come to her room and pricked her arm. She had chased the shadows. Now she was blind and couldn't move. By the slick fabric clinging to her face, and the faint rubbery smell, she guessed she was in a big plastic sack. So, perhaps not blind, merely temporarily unable to see.

Drugged. Paralyzed. In a sack.

But not scared or unhappy. To the contrary, Anna felt fairly chipper. The drug, though powerful and paralyzing, had potential as a recreational drug. Nice of her kidnappers to think of her feelings. For a moment, Anna felt warm and fuzzy toward her shadows.

Then one of them stomped on her ankle. Roaring filled her ears. The two happenings were unrelated. The roar was an engine. Her sack and she were in a boat, or had been dumped in the backseat of a car. Boat. No car had that high whiny sound. A go-cart maybe.

Who kidnapped anybody with a go-cart?

For a while Anna faded. She knew she existed, she knew she was cold, but she had little opinion regarding these things. On some level she knew she was in deep trouble. People were not drugged and bagged and carted out to sea in a go-cart unless they were going to be disposed of.

Oddly, she didn't care overmuch.

Then the whining growl of the engine was gone. Anna's mind rose from the depths as if the harsh noise had been holding it under. Silence was a balm. Opening her mouth, she tried to breathe it in. Plastic stuck to her lips and tongue. Hands grabbed at her, latex screeching on plastic as fingers plucked and slipped on her shroud, then pinched and clutched, trying for better purchase. Heavy breathing and grunts filtered through the bag, but no voices. Not that it mattered. There would be no harm in her identifying the voices. The dead tell no tales and all that.

Dead. That sounded so melodramatic.

Anna would have liked to fight, just to say she had, that she'd gone down swinging and taken a few of the bastards with her, but she was unable to lift a hand or make her lips form a word.

As she was manhandled up to where her belly pressed hard against the gunwale, the boat rocked dangerously. Just as she was thinking how grand it would be if it cap-sized, and her shadows had to escort her to Davy Jones's locker, her head plunged into the cold. Plastic form-fitted itself around her mouth and nose, and she couldn't breathe.

Another heave and the rest of her followed out of the boat. Every inch of Anna was pressed with cold plastic. The ocean was too cold. Anna didn't want to die in the cold. Maybe she'd suffocate or die of hypo-thermia before she drowned.

"It's not sinking," came a shrill voice.

Well, that was good news.

In the fetal position inside the garbage bag, Anna felt the sea roll her onto her back; then she spun weightless into the sucking cold.

"There she goes," a calmer voice said.

Not much of an epitaph, Anna thought.

THIRTY-FOUR

They motored back to Somes Sound, Paulette as uncommunicative and dark as a lump of coal in the bow of the boat, Denise's mind fixated on Ranger Pigeon's demise. Not her drowning or suffocating or ODing or whatever finally took her out, but how weighty deadweight was. Manhandling the body was much harder than she would have believed. In the gym, Denise could bench press her own weight, one hundred twenty-five pounds — or could when she was in her early thirties. Yet moving a soon-to-be-dead body that weighed a bit less than that had been backbreaking, even though there were two of them doing the manhandling. Dead — or deadish — people were denser than living people, physically speaking, and just as uncooperative.

Denise was glad that the killing portion of her new life was at an end — maybe at an end. One thing did tend to lead to another.

Obstacles would always pop up when one least expected it. Kurt had been a given, but the Pigeon thing, that was extemporaneous. Either way, Denise had reached the conclusion that killing people was more work than it was worth in a lot of ways. Hitler probably would have won World War II if he hadn't wasted so much time and energy killing people who didn't need killing.

Kurt had needed it. That hadn't made it any easier. Anna Pigeon hadn't needed it; things just got away from them, choices lopped off, until killing her was the only good one left. That didn't make it any easier.

Paulette, too, wasn't making things any easier. Denise watched her sitting in a heap as the boat cut neatly through the gentle swells. Paulette was more delicate than Denise had thought anyone who shared her DNA could be. It must be that nature made them both the same, but nurture had toughened Denise up. Nurture for Denise had been a brutal series of beatings and betrayals. Of course Paulette had been abused by her husband. Probably she was too old by then for the abuse to have any effect other than beating her down, Denise thought, whereas she — what? Had been beaten up?

However it worked, it was obvious that

the removal of Anna Pigeon, though it had given them more time — a day, maybe a day and a half — had been harder on Paulette than it had been on her. Maybe it had broken some bit of her sister that could compromise the plan. Denise sensed that waiting while feds, rangers, and whoever else swarmed around looking for the missing Pigeon would be a bad idea. Paulette would fold under the pressure. Denise didn't like to think it, but she herself might have issues. Her nerves, once as strong as steel cables, had begun to fray. Age might account for it. Or Peter Barnes. Everything. Not that she'd fold under pressure, but she might explode. Either would mean disaster.

Time, in this case, would not heal all. It was a bomb. Denise could feel it ticking. Paulette or Fate or dumb luck was going to trigger the explosion soon. That this was so was felt in her viscera, as palpable as an electric current. Even with Pigeon out of the picture, things would have to be moved up. Way up. The sale of the Duffy shack, the so-called legacy, and family.

Tomorrow night they would tick "family" off the list, then get the hell out of Dodge. Do the rest long distance. Denise had no doubt that once they were out of sight, they'd be out of mind. A has-been ranger retires and moves. A bleached-blond house-wife, with an iron-clad alibi for her husband's murder, sells the house where he was killed and leaves town. Nobody would connect those nonevents to a missing acting chief ranger from Rocky Mountain National Park. No connection between Denise and Anna, Anna and Paulette, Denise and Kurt, or Paulette and Denise.

All that could screw the pooch now was Paulette babbling or Denise going postal. So: tick, tick, tick.

For Denise that meant the night, though nearly spent, was not yet over.

By the time she got the runabout moored, and Paulette headed for her bed in the shack, only fifty-six minutes remained before dawn. Sunrise would be at 5:03 A.M. At five Peter would get out of bed and go to the bathroom to pee. At 5:04 he would be pulling on his running clothes; 5:10 and he'd be out the front door swinging his hands side to side and jogging in place. He would run 4.5 miles. Depending on how he was feeling, he would be gone thirty to thirty-six minutes, getting back to the house around quarter to six.

Rather than sleeping in like a sane woman, little Lily flower got her lovely little ass out of bed at 5:15 every morning, checked on the baby — didn't pee, she did that between midnight and three — and went down to make her darling hubby coffee.

Like Peter couldn't poke the button on the coffee machine before he left.

She'd poke the button, then, while she waited for it to brew, prepare Olivia's first bottle of the day, setting it in a pan of water to heat. Microwaving wasn't good enough for Lily's baby. No nuked fake milk for Olivia.

After the burner was on low, Lily would go upstairs and brush her teeth and comb her hair so she'd be all nice and minty fresh for that big sweaty kiss Peter would plant on her when he came huffing back for his coffee.

That gave Denise a four-minute window when nobody would be in the kitchen.

Years of covert surveillance were paying off big-time, Denise thought with satisfaction. Those long nights with binoculars, the skulking in the woods, following in rental cars, hadn't been insanity, it had been foresight. A lot of what she'd seen as problems were turning out to be plusses.

She'd been going to tell Paulette about this step in the plan. Then she learned her twin wasn't a real nurse, just a nursemaid. If she'd been a real RN it would have been good because Denise would have been more confident about the dosage. Since she wasn't, Denise hadn't said anything out of spite. Now she was glad. Given how shaken the Pigeon thing had left Paulette, the less she knew of the sordid details, the better.

Originally, Denise had planned to do this when she could take her time and make sure she got everything just right, not have to rush things to get it all done in a four-minute time slot. Most days, at two fifteen, Lily put the baby's food on to warm, then went upstairs to make the bed. Picturing it, Denise shook her head in the dark as she climbed into her Miata. What kind of a nitwit makes the bed at two in the afternoon?

Still, that left a seven-minute window. Tons of time. Denise should wait until two fifteen, but she wouldn't. Couldn't.

Tick, tick, tick.

Four minutes would have to do.

Five A.M. sharp, Denise pulled the Miata into its customary space, the place she parked for her breaking-and-entering activities. A dirt road, a quarter of a mile down from Peter and Lily's house, led to a construction boneyard no more than a hundred yards behind their property. One day a home would be built there. For the past several years it had been from whence Denise's forays into the Barnes family homestead had been staged. Car tracks could link her to the place if anybody got that far into the investigation, but she wasn't too worried. Big machinery was in and out during working hours: trucks, bulldozers, frontloaders. By noon the tracks of the Miata would be well and thoroughly squashed.

She popped the trunk, walked around to the back of the car, and unerringly laid her hands on the crumpled McDonald's bag half wedged beneath the first aid kit. Inside, wadded in a used napkin, were three white pills, crushed to a powder. Having retrieved one of the unused Mount Desert syringes, Denise filled it half full from her water bottle, poured the powder in, shook it a few times for good measure, then stowed it carefully in her jacket pocket.

"What the hell," she whispered, and threw the bag onto the ground. Maybe she'd get lucky and the litter would blow into Peter's backyard.

THIRTY-FIVE

Heath's eyes opened to unremitting black. Where in hell was she? Clearly not in her bed in Boulder. Momentary panic from watching *Premature Burial* too many times as a kid engulfed her. The adrenaline rush brought her to full alert.

This wasn't the first time she'd woken up and not known where she was. After the accident, when she was on medications and changed hospital rooms or therapy venues, it often happened. The amnesia seldom lasted more than a second or two. A calming thought.

Ah, lucidity!

She lay in her little bed on Boar Island, and the black was not unremitting. At ground level, the tower had little in the way of natural light, but halfway up the winding stairs was a bar of living dark, dark like the midnight sky or the surface of a lake on a moonless night. There was a difference between living dark and the dark, she presumed, of a coffin six feet under.

What had wakened her?

In a second, it came to her. The lift bell had rung. Or a bell on a buoy in the ocean. Heath had seen those but never knew what they were for. To let fish know the wind was blowing? As far as she knew, both Elizabeth and Gwen were asleep in the rooms above. It was possible they could have descended the iron stairs and slipped through her room undetected. Possible but unlikely; the old stairs complained bitterly when they were used.

Heath switched on the bedside lamp, found her phone, and pinched it on. Dawn had not yet creaked. Surely John Whitman had more sense than to come calling on his lady love at this hour. She smiled, imagining the crusty old seaman serenading Gwen as she leaned over the rail around the top of the lighthouse.

Wily opened his eyes from his chosen spot at the foot of the stairs, where his charges would trip over him should they try to elude his vigilance.

"I've got ringing in my ears," Heath said to the dog.

Wily thumped his tail.

The ring must have been from a buoy, or

a ship's bell. Ships did have bells, Heath remembered from old books. They told time by them. Probably they now set all the sailors' cell phones to ring at the appropriate hours. Heath turned off the light and settled down to go back to sleep.

Again the bell rang.

Definitely the lift bell.

The lift bell rang when it was called down to the jetty, and it rang when it was sent — or called — to the top of the cliff. When they'd retired for the night, it had been at the top of the cliff. Two bells; somebody had called the lift down, gotten on, then sent it up. That somebody was now on the island.

In the wee hours.

"Damn," Heath muttered. Wake E? Call Gwen? Flash an SOS to the mainland? "Why aren't you barking?" she suddenly demanded of Wily. He swept his tail over the wide boards of the floor.

Since Wily wasn't alarmed, Heath felt safe enough to see what was happening before she roused the house. The last thing she wanted was to make this ivory tower — such as it was — feel unsafe when Elizabeth was experiencing just how unsafe most of the world was.

A metal bar on legs, like a spare clothing

rack, but narrower and much stronger, stood over the head of the bed. One of Leah's designs, it was lightweight, stable, and easily broken down into a civilized-sized carrying package. It was a great help when Heath overnighted away from home.

Using the bar, she hoisted herself upright, then pushed her legs free of the covers and the mattress. From there it was a fairly easy swing into Robo-butt, parked next to the bed. In one of Robo-butt's saddlebags, among other things, was a small Maglight. Heath took it out, clicked the switch a couple of times. Satisfied the batteries hadn't gone dead, she dropped it into her lap.

Rolling toward the long tunnel through the tower wall of the lighthouse, she asked, "Coming, Wily?"

The steady pad-pad of his paws on the flooring behind her was reassuring.

Though there was no moon, the arc-shaped main room of the tower, with its floor-to-ceiling windows, was surprisingly light. The sea seemed to maximize ambient light, catching the stars on the whitecaps. The granite Maine was built on had that same reflective quality, thousands of tiny facets polished by the centuries until they shone like mirrors.

Heath twisted the dead bolt, then shoved open the door with the foot of her wheelchair. Still showing no signs of alarm, Wily trotted out in front of her onto the apron of granite. Warily, she rolled after him. Halfway across the natural patio the lift platform came into view. A pile of pale stuff lay on it.

Wily trotted toward it.

"Wait," Heath called, afraid whatever had been sent up at this ungodly hour was dangerous, poisonous, or vile in some other way.

Wily ignored her, stepped delicately from the landing onto the platform, sniffed the pile, and whined. Heath clicked on the tiny flashlight, shoved the butt end into her mouth, and rolled slowly toward the dog and his catch.

It looked like a mess of fish caught in a net. Another gift from the sea provided by Gwen's beau? Wouldn't fish be nasty after even a few hours lying about? Heath rolled nearer. Saliva drooled down her chin. Since she needed both hands to roll in a straight line, she ignored it. Wily wouldn't mind. He'd been known to drool a time or two in his life.

The dog turned in a tight circle, sat down, threw his head back, and howled.

It wasn't a net of dead fish. It was a dead

421

woman. She lay on one shoulder. Both arms were stretched above her head, the wrists tied to one of the rings used to secure cargo to the lift floor. She was naked but for one boot and the wild netting of red and silver hair.

Anna.

For a heartbeat, Heath denied it was she. Anna didn't lose, didn't die, didn't quit. Anna wasn't beaten and trussed and delivered like the morning paper. If Anna wasn't invincible, what chance did ordinary people have?

Reality snapped back.

"Gwen! Elizabeth!" Heath shouted, the Maglight falling from her jaws to her lap. She jerked the brass whistle free of the neck of her pajama top, put it to her lips, and blew for all she was worth, three piercing blasts.

"Oh my God, Anna!" She rolled until one of Robo-butt's wheels was on the lift. Having put the brakes on, she levered herself out and slid down next to the body of her friend. The Maglight rolled onto the lift platform to lodge against Anna's naked breast, the light shining ghoulishly up beneath her chin.

Heath laid a hand on Anna's bare shoulder. The skin was ice cold and felt firmer than it should. "No, no, no," Heath was whispering. "Gwen!" she shouted again. Gwen was a doctor. Gwen would make it okay.

"Anna," Heath said. "Can you hear me? You're going to be just fine. Fine and dandy, damn you." As Heath murmured in a kind, reassuring voice, a voice designed to bring kittens out from under houses and rangers back from the dead, she lifted the hair from Anna's face and neck. A mass of it was pasted to her back with blood. Blood showed dark on her butt and the heel of her left foot.

"What have you been up to?" Heath asked as she felt for the carotid pulse. "You're alive," she said, more for Anna than because she was positive the weak flutter against the pads of her index and middle fingers was blood being pumped through veins.

"What is it?"

Heath turned to see Gwen, tying a robe around her, trotting toward where she sat with Anna. E, in tank top and pajama bottoms, followed close behind, her small narrow feet silent against the rock.

"Move aside," Gwen said the moment she identified the incident as medical. "Elizabeth, run for blankets."

As Gwen fell to her knees beside Anna,

Heath wormed herself into a position where she could attend to the binding around Anna's wrists. The ties were cut lengths of yellow line, the kind used in boats. They weren't tied tightly. Circulation wasn't compromised, and had Anna been conscious, she could easily have escaped the bonds. Balancing as best she could on her hind end, Heath untied Anna's wrists and began massaging her cold limp hands.

"She has a pulse," Gwen said, "but it is weak and too slow." Heath said nothing. Elizabeth was sprinting from the house with an armload of blankets. Gwen was running her hands over Anna's body, palpating for injuries, breaks, and bruises.

Elizabeth dumped three down comforters onto the ground. Heath pulled one over and began covering Anna.

Gwen sat back on her knees. "Nothing I can find. Hypothermic probably. Contusions on back, buttocks, and right heel. One lump above her left temple. That might account for the unconsciousness, but it could be any number of things. We have to get her inside and get her warmed up, then get her to a hospital as soon as possible."

"She's awake," Elizabeth whispered.

Heath leaned down so she could see Anna's eyes. They were half open.

"Hi," Anna said in a voice as creaky as a rusted gate hinge.

The eyes drifted closed again.

"That was informative," Heath growled. Seeing Anna helpless frightened her. Heath had always been a person who turned fear into anger. At the moment, she was furious and terrified. Laserlike heat burned inside her skull. Heath half believed that if she ever saw whoever did this to Anna, she could flay him using just her eyes.

For a quarter of an hour there was no talking. A comforter was ruined as the three of them dragged Anna in from the lift. Gently, they hoisted her up onto the couch, then packed down quilts around her naked body. Without being told to, Elizabeth found heating pads in one of the closets.

With a last look at Anna, she slipped into the kitchen, to microwave the pads and boil water for hot drinks, Heath assumed. While Gwen was Velcroing a blood pressure cuff around Anna's upper arm, Heath was searching the contacts list on her phone for Peter Barnes's home number.

The silence was broken by Anna.

"Stop," she croaked.

"Hey!" Heath said with relief as she put the phone to her ear.

"No calls. Not yet," Anna managed, and,

"Help me up."

Sitting up was perhaps not the best of ideas, but both Gwen and Heath had known Anna too long to think telling her to stay still would be efficacious. Gwen left the pump bulb on the cuff dangling to put an arm around Anna's shoulders, helping her into a semisitting position against the pillows piled on the arm of the sofa.

"You need to go to the hospital," Gwen said as Heath was asking, "What happened?"

Anna clutched the sides of her head as if the two soft voices were a cacophony. "What happened," she echoed. "Before you . . . Tell me what happened. I'm so cold."

With use, her voice was normalizing, but the words were slightly blurred — not the slur of a drunk so much as the drawl of a person from a very, very deep South.

"A man said he thought I was a lobster," Anna mumbled, shaking her head. "No. That can't be right. Yes. He thought I was a lobster. Said he thought I was . . . And now I'm here." She dropped her hands to her lap and looked hard first at Gwen, then at Heath.

"What are you guys doing here?" she asked with a certain petulance.

"We heard the lift bell," Heath told her.

"Wily and I found you on the platform."

Heath watched, letting the information sink in through whatever was clouding Anna's perception. Anna's eyes roved the room as if to see where she'd washed up. "Boar," she said finally. Heath, Gwen, and Elizabeth, drawn in from the kitchen by Anna's voice, nodded like bobblehead dolls. Gwen took two heating pads from E. Having peeled back the blankets, she began arranging them along Anna's ribs.

Anna watched her for a long moment. "I'm naked," she observed.

"That's how we found you. Wearing only one boot. That one." Heath pointed to the sodden cordovan-colored boot standing solitary watch on the cold hearth.

"E, would you please make Anna a cup of tea, real warm but not hot, lots of sugar," Gwen said.

"No sugar," Anna said as E turned to go.

Gwen tilted her chin at her great-niece. Anna would be getting sugar.

"Do you remember anything?" Heath asked.

Anna thought. Heath waited, her fingers drumming lightly against the face of her phone, itching to call for help. "May I call Superintendent Barnes now?" Heath asked.

"Not yet. I . . ." Anna's voice faded out.

Her train of thought had evidently derailed. "Let me figure out what happed first," she said, finding her way back.

Had Anna not been showing signs of returning life — if not sanity — and Gwen not been a doctor, Heath would have made the call regardless of Anna's protestations. As it was, Anna seemed to be out of danger.

Danger of what, evidently not even Anna knew.

THIRTY-SIX

Anna was awake. A dozen times before, she'd thought she was awake, only to slip back into nightmares until she could no longer tell what was real, what had happened, and what was only a dream.

Only a dream.

There was no "only" about the dreams that pulled her down. They were a force as powerful as any she had encountered. They followed her into the waking world and threatened to drag her back.

"I am awake," she said. Her voice creaked. Her tongue was as stiff and dry as weathered wood. If taste was any indication, weathered wood from the bottom rail of an old pigsty.

"You're awake," a kind voice agreed. "And alive."

Anna rolled her eyes, eyeballs scratching against lids that felt packed with sand. "We'll see," she rasped. Heath was bent over her, a huge annoying smile on her face. "I feel like shit. My face hurts."

"You're hungover," Heath said, still grinning like a fool. "Your head got a hard whack, but it isn't broken, according to Aunt Gwen."

Anna reached up with shaking fingers and felt above her eye. There was a lump the size of a walnut, and tender to the touch. Not broken; that was good news. At least not broken on the outside. The gray matter inside of her skull felt as if it had been scrambled like eggs. Lying down was disorienting, and she struggled to sit up. The room spun. Her stomach lurched into her throat. A hammer wielded by an invisible hand slammed into her left temple.

"Do you want to sit up?" Heath asked.

"Of course I want to sit up!" Anna grumbled. "Do you think I'm flopping around because I like looking like a landed fish?"

"Somebody got up on the wrong side of the ocean today."

Elizabeth was perched on the end of the couch where Anna lay. Anna tried to glare at her, as Heath, more trouble than help, worked to get her into a seated position without falling out of her wheelchair.

"E!" Heath said. Rising smoothly, Elizabeth trotted around the back of the sofa. Between the two of them, Anna was shoved and shored up into a sitting position.

"Damn, but I feel like shit," Anna said as bile rose up her gorge. "I'm going to be sick." Heath bobbed out of her line of sight, then bobbed back up again, a bowl in her hand.

"Gwen said you might be," she said, putting the bowl between Anna's hands.

Anna retched into the bowl, spewing up thin acid and stinking chunks.

"Done?" Heath asked gently.

"Don't be so nice," Anna said. Nice made tears threaten, and Anna was too sick to cry.

Heath smiled. "Take this, would you, E?"

"Eeeeew," Elizabeth grimaced as she removed the mess from Anna's lap.

"How long was I asleep?" Anna asked.

"Half the day," Heath said. "Gwen thought rest was the best thing for you. She gave you an antibiotic, but we didn't try and clean or dress your wounds."

"I have wounds?" Anna asked, surprised. When every inch of one's body hurt, it was hard to tell.

Elizabeth was back on her perch. "One of your heels is all scraped up, and your bottom has major road rash."

An image of her booted toes, seen down the length of her naked body, bouncing along black asphalt flashed through Anna's mind.

"I was dragged," she said, more to herself than them.

A cackle of questions battered in stereo. "By who? Where? Why? Do you remember? Dragged?"

Anna ignored them. Her skin was too tight, her hair stiff and matted; thinking was difficult. Poison pervaded her being. She was sick unto her bones.

"I need a shower," she said softly. Then, raising her head, she looked into Heath's concerned face. "A shower."

Heath and Elizabeth exchanged glances. Anna glowered. "Help her with a shower, E," Heath said finally.

"I don't need any help." Anna stood up, tottered, then fell back on the couch. For a moment she sat blinking stupidly as resistance drained away. "That would be good, E," she said with moderate civility. "Thank you."

Leaning against the tile wall for support, hot water pouring through her salt-encrusted hair, Anna began to feel slightly more human. Most of the night and the day before were a blur. She remembered going to bed. She remembered seeing the toes of her boots. She remembered plastic sticking to her face. She remembered someone saying she was a lobster.

Four memories that didn't add up to anything. Caked in salt, contusions on her butt and heel, a knot on her forehead, a small hole that ached in her left arm, up by the shoulder, probably a needle stick: drugged, dragged, and dumped into saltwater. Without the aid of memory, logic dictated that much. Since she was not dead, one could assume she had subsequently been fished out of the saltwater. Heath and Wily had found her naked, tied to the cargo ring on the lift, shortly before sunrise.

Again, since she wasn't dead, logic suggested she was put there by the fisher-of-out, either so she would receive help or as a warning to the island's residents. E, as a stalkee, being the most obvious.

Both theories were absurd.

That didn't make them untrue.

"Are you still alive?" Elizabeth asked from the other side of the shower curtain.

"Getting there," Anna said. She could see the girl's shadow where she sat on the commode, standing by in case Anna fell or drowned.

"Let me know when you're ready to do your back," E said.

Elizabeth's comfort with her own and

other people's bodies was a wonder to Anna. Nudity, injury, snot, puke, washing hair, clipping toenails — E did these things for other people as casually as she did them for herself. Maybe loving someone who occasionally required personal assistance had given her these skills. More likely she was born with them, and loving Heath had brought them to flower.

John Donne said no man was an island. He didn't say anything about women. Anna keenly felt her physical isolation from the rest of the human race, with the exception of her husband, Paul, an isolation she preferred. Every woman in her own skin, every mind in its own cranium.

Until she couldn't take care of her own skin or trust her own mind.

"I'm ready," Anna said.

"Incoming," Elizabeth replied cheerfully as she opened the shower curtain. Anna braced both hands against the opposite wall, holding herself up, while Elizabeth carefully washed the scrapes on her buttocks.

"Not as bad as we thought," E said. "Sort of like a skinned knee, but all over. Not so much bleeding as oozing. Some bleeding on your bottom, but nothing as bad as your heel. Aunt Gwen did that up while you were out cold. Now that the bandage is wet, she'll have to redress it. She said your heel is pretty much like hamburger. Nothing broken, though. She didn't want to mess with your back until you'd slept. We took a look at it. Heath and I thought we should put you out of your misery, but Aunt Gwen said it wasn't too bad, and it isn't."

Whoever had dragged her across the pavement must not have dragged her far, Anna decided. A protracted trip would have left her skinned alive.

"Where is Gwen?" Anna asked, mostly to keep Elizabeth chattering. Unlike the prattle of other people, the prattle of her goddaughter was soothing, like rain on a tin roof. Usually Anna listened for clues of what was happening in E's world, and heart, and mind. Sometimes, like now, she just rode the flow of words, enjoying the murmur of a happy life burbling past her ears, a sweet cacophony more soothing to the soul than silence.

"Aunt Gwen is in Bar Harbor meeting Dez Hammond — one of the old ladies who lived here — for coffee. Aunt Gwen felt guilty about abandoning you, but she said it was very important. An errand for Chris Zuckerberg, the other lady, the one that's sick. Some sort of meeting Ms. Zuckerberg was too sick to go to.

"Aunt Gwen took her medical bag. She said she was going to get a DNA sample or something. She had a glass tube and Q-tips and everything. Very *CSI*. Of course she wouldn't tell us what it's about since it's a doctor thing."

Anna's knees were growing weak. Her arms, bracing her against the shower wall, were tiring. "Are you about done?" she asked.

"Done," E said. Anna felt a towel being draped over her shoulders. Pulling her aching arms away from the wall, she noticed a red mark on the inside of her arm at the elbow. "Another needle stick," she said, turning to show Elizabeth the way a little girl might show her mother a splinter.

"That was Aunt Gwen. She took blood while you slept. You didn't even move an eyelid," Elizabeth said with obvious pride in her aunt's needlework.

"Took blood?" Anna echoed stupidly.

"*CSI* on every channel today. She's getting it tested for drugs," E said matter-of-factly.

"She's not in law enforcement," Anna said.

"She's a doctor. They do all that blood stuff."

Of course. "I'm not thinking straight,"

Anna admitted.

"Duh," E said, holding out a second towel for Anna's hair. "Sit."

Obediently, Anna sat on the lid of the commode and let Elizabeth towel-dry her hair. Gray splotches floated in the corners of her eyes, as amorphous and will-o'-the-wisp as her recollections of the previous night. The shower had washed away the salt, the blood, and the last of the anger she'd brought with her from the other side. Without the anger, her brain was a cold and sluggish thing, thoughts being forced out like the last of the toothpaste from the tube.

"Was I raped?" she asked, before her brain had time to mention that might not be an appropriate question to ask a sixteen-year-old girl, and one's goddaughter at that.

"Nope," E said as if it were the most obvious question in the world — and it was. "Aunt Gwen said there was no evidence to indicate any kind of sexual trauma. She did a rape kit anyway. Don't worry. The rest of us, even Wily, were banished from the entire house while she did her exam."

Anna was absurdly relieved. Bad enough if E and Heath had seen that sort of thing, but if Wily had, she'd have had to resign from the pack in shame.

Three taps sounded on the door. "Are you

guys about done?" Heath asked. "E, your visitor has finally seen fit to come, so make sure Anna has something decent on."

Both caught the sour emphasis Heath put on the word "visitor." Anna raised an eyebrow.

Turning to take a terrycloth robe from a hook on the back of the bathroom door, Elizabeth said, "It's my friend."

"The one with the boat," Anna said.

"Yes."

"What made you decide to blow Boat Boy's cover?" Anna asked.

"Before, he needed you not to know more than you needed to know. It's the other way around now," Elizabeth said as she held out a thick yellow chenille bathrobe.

Anna snorted. Now she was on a need-to-know basis with her goddaughter. Elizabeth had grown from a skinny little kid into an entire human being, and Anna had seen every bit of it, a terrifying miracle.

"Are you going to arrest him?" Elizabeth asked.

Anna stood and let her goddaughter help her into the robe.

"I sure as hell feel like arresting somebody," she said.

THIRTY-SEVEN

The shower worked wonders. Anna was fairly steady on her feet. Her mind was clear enough for minor calculations. The mirror proved unkind. There was a nasty bruise on her forehead, her skin was pasty, and her eyes had dark circles beneath and red rims around. No beauty contests would be won today.

As she walked from the bath into the room around the tower, the lift bell rang.

"That will be Aunt Gwen," E said, hovering behind Anna's right shoulder. "She wanted to be in on this, and her meeting with Mrs. Hammond was over."

Elizabeth settled Anna on the sofa with so little fuss, Anna didn't even mind. Heath rolled in from the kitchen to hand Anna a mug of steaming cream of tomato soup. Tears stung the corners of Anna's eyes. Tomato soup was just the thing, the only thing, her stomach wanted. When she was growing up it was the food for ailing children. Dotted with chicken pox, she and Molly had sat across from each other at the scarred old kitchen table spooning soup with oyster crackers. Later it had been mumps and tomato soup and ginger ale. Then measles. Because of tomato soup, she and her sister had lived to adulthood.

She sipped, sighed, and silently blessed Heath with a smile. "Where's Boat Boy?" she asked.

"He went to meet the lift," Heath said, rolling over to one of the wide windows. "Seems Gwen decided John Whitman should be here."

Despite the healing magic of soup, Anna wasn't up for a party. "Why?"

"Boat Boy is named Walter. Walter is John's grandson," Elizabeth said.

"Curiouser and curiouser," Anna said. Then, "Walter Whitman? As in *Leaves of Grass*? A poet, no less?"

Evidently E hadn't heard of Walt Whitman. Anna would fix that another day. She took another fortifying slurp of soup.

Gwen, John, and Walter Whitman came in from the patio.

Boat Boy was so handsome Anna scowled. Light brown hair waved back off a square brow in what had been called a surfer cut when she was in college. Shoulders were broad and arms muscled — from rowing boats with muffled oars, no doubt. Lips were chiseled, eyes wide set and a deep rich hazel. The plaid shirt straining across his chest was almost a cliché in its woodsy perfection.

Unless John had more than one son, Boat Boy Walter was the son of the lobsterman shot for poaching, the boy accused of being an accomplice.

Gorgeous, an orphan, and a fugitive.

Anna had to admit, had she been sixteen and marooned on an island with annoying adults, she would have jumped ship with this boy in a heartbeat.

"This is my grandson Walter," John said.

Anna opened her mouth to introduce herself. What came out was "I'm not a lobster." Clapping her mouth shut, she frowned. Kaleidoscope fashion, parts of her lost night were spinning through her gray matter.

"A lobster trap," Walter said apologetically. "I thought you were a lobster trap. It was wicked hard gettin' you out of the drink."

"Lobster" was pronounced *lobstah;* "hard" was *hahd.* Coming from the Apollo-meets-Ralph-Lauren vision, the hard New England accent sounded out of place, yet it, too, was charming. Anna reminded herself that often as not, Prince Charming turned out to be just another clown.

"Let's all sit," Gwen said sensibly. "This may take a while."

Walter and his grandfather sat on the outer edge of the chairs, elbows on knees, hands clasped, the way Anna remembered the hired hands sitting when she was a kid. Comfortable, assured, but not wanting to be seen to be taking the boss's hospitality for granted.

"You saved my life," Anna said to Walter. "Let's start there and work our way back. That way I'll be in a more forgiving mood when we get to the kidnapping of my god-daughter."

Anna had been shooting for a spot of humor, a little levity to ease the proceedings. Through a furry brain and a swollen lip, the words came out more like a threat. John started a low grumble in his throat. Wily echoed it from the cold hearth, where he lay watching the proceedings with interest.

"Her bark is worse than her bite," she heard E whisper.

"She bites?" Walter whispered back, then caught Anna's eye and grinned sheepishly. "No disrespect meant," he apologized.

"I do bite," Anna admitted with a sigh. "But I'm not rabid, so, if it happens, you'll survive."

"Tell the woman your story," John said, jutting his chin in Anna's direction.

"You'll know by now, it was my dad was shot by Billy Gomer. Killed for poaching," Walter began uncertainly.

"I didn't know the shooter's name, but I'd heard," Anna said. It had been two, maybe three weeks since this boy's father was murdered. Walter's words — and, to give him credit, tone of voice — were matter-of-fact. The eyes and the small muscles around his mouth told Anna of the grief and strain. "You were accused of doing the same," she said before sympathy could get the better of her.

"That's right. But we were no poachers. Neither my dad nor me. It was about a patch of good fishing that was being fought over and we won. We were taking forty to fifty percent more lobsters out than Gomer ever did, so he starts saying we were taking from his line. He and my dad got into it, and Gomer shot Dad. Killed him right there." Walter clamped his lips together and stared at the floor. These were not men who wore their hearts on their sleeves. Pain was not for public consumption.

"Is this Gomer fellow in jail?" Anna asked.

Walter's grandfather barked a bitter laugh. "Billy is goin' on eighty. Twelve kids, nine of them boys, and all got a patch and a vote. There won't be any goin' to jail for Billy Gomer."

"Mr. Gomer is mean to the soles of his boots," Walter said, shaking his head. "But he's known to be honest. I think he believed me and Dad were poaching because he couldn't believe the truth, which is we're better fisherman than he ever was."

"I'd say that's about right," John added. "I'd say old Gomer believes himself. Since he's sworn he'll shoot Walter if he gets a chance, I don't much care what he believes or doesn't believe." The older man's jaw set in a concrete square. Anna would not want John Whitman as an enemy.

"I don't think he will," Walter said. "The fight was always between him and Dad. Much as I'd like to see it, I don't think there's any good to be had by lockin' Mr. Gomer up. He's sure to die in a few years anyway."

Another day Anna might have been fascinated with the ins and outs of lobster fishing in Maine. At present her head was heavy and her face hurt her, and undoubtedly hurt them to look at. "I'm sorry about your dad," she said as kindly as she could manage. The soup had helped. She almost liked herself.

Her well-meant words started to eat away at Walter's stoicism, so she went on. "But how does this relate to saving my life and kidnapping my goddaughter?"

John Whitman stood abruptly. "There was no kidnapping." His scarred hands were balled into fists. Suddenly he wasn't quaint or colorful.

"It's okay, John," Gwen said quickly. "Ranger humor."

"I don't have much use for park rangers," John grumbled.

"They grow on you eventually," Heath said dryly.

Slowly, John lowered himself back onto the edge of the chair, his hands again folded between his knees.

Walter took his time, looking first to his grandfather, then to Elizabeth. He must have found what he was searching for, because he went on. "Mr. Gomer's talk got my fishing license suspended, pending investigation."

"An investigation that isn't going to happen," John said grimly.

"Probably not," Walter agreed. "People forget others' troubles pretty quick. The lines Mr. Gomer shot Dad over are right here off the island, between Boar and Mount Desert. Rich beds. I figured if I could find out who was stealing from the traps, I could clear Dad's name and get my license back."

"So you went into hiding, and have been watching the area?" Anna asked.

"That I have. I'd been camping out in the old wing of the house, the one seaside."

"Walter was our ghost, remember, Mom?" Elizabeth asked.

Heath nodded. A story Anna would have to hear later. Clearing his father's name, and his own, to get his fishing license back might have struck Anna as a silly piece of teenage posturing in another place. In Maine, once the Whitmans' licenses were suspended, their trap line would have been farmed out to another fisherman.

Chances were good Walter had worked with his dad and granddad since he was old enough to mend traps. He'd probably apprenticed for two years under his father to get a license. Lobster fishing might very well be all he knew and all he wanted to know.

"You've been living on Boar and watching the water at night?" Anna clarified.

"That's about it," Walter said.

"You were watching last night," Anna said.

"I was. I saw a boat I've seen before. A

small dark-colored outboard. Both times before, I lost it. Weather once, and once it was just plain too dark to see where it went. It has no running lights. There are three green LED lights near the bow, but they're no bigger than that." With his thumb, Walter indicated the tip of his little finger. "And they aren't bright. Decoration maybe. Whoever owns the boat dives at night. Robbing traps is my guess. Last night, there was some light and the seas were calm. I saw that same boat coming onto the line of traps, so I rowed out as close as I could without them noticing me."

"Muffled oars," Anna said.

"That's right, and their engine noise to cover for me."

"More than one?" Anna asked.

"This time there were two in the boat. Last two times just the one. I saw them throw something over the side. I figured they were up to something, so I pulled out what they'd tossed in."

"My exceeding good luck," Anna said. "Which way did they go?"

"They came from the north up by Schoodic, and headed down toward Somes Sound when they left."

"And you were stuck with a very strange catch," Gwen said.

"Odd things get thrown in the ocean," John said.

"Anna is an odd thing," E said.

"You put me on the lift?" Anna asked.

"I knew the bell would wake up Elizabeth, and I knew her great-aunt was a doctor," Walter said. "I suppose I could have stayed, but I couldn't see what use it would be to anybody."

Anna thought about that for a moment. There was really no point in his staying. Her desire to dislike young Walter was slowly being overwhelmed by warm cozy feelings.

"Why did you tie me down to the cargo ring?" she asked in a last attempt to find fault with the boy who stole Elizabeth's heart — and kidnapped Wily.

"So you wouldn't fall off," he said simply.

The tail end of Anna's dislike vanished like a snake down a hole. All in all, she was glad to see it go. Disliking people was labor intensive at the best of times, and today wasn't the best of times.

THIRTY-EIGHT

There had been little more either John or his grandson could tell them. Anna had been wrapped in black plastic — either a bag or a sheet. Walter had torn it open. The plastic had been lost at sea. If there was anything in the bag with her, he hadn't noticed. Nor could he tell them any more about the mystery boat than he already had.

The Whitmans left for Bar Harbor, promising to look for the dark boat on their way into town. Walter promised he'd call E in the morning.

Elizabeth was positively wriggling with delight at having her beau outed and approved. Walter seemed as pleased as she to be out of the shadows. Another point for him.

Anna held out no hope the Whitmans would find the runabout that had nearly served as her hearse. Not only had it been headed in the opposite direction — Somes instead of Bar Harbor — but there were coves and jetties, private boats and commercial, in a thousand places in the waters around Acadia. Small, dark-colored, outboard — didn't narrow it down much.

The lift bell had barely rung, lowering the Whitmans to the jetty, when Gwen had a blood pressure cuff around Anna's upper arm. "A friend of a friend, a doctor at Mount Desert Hospital, was more than kind. She ran the tox screen on your blood. A heavy dose of Rohypnol and a muscle relaxant. You should be feeling better by tomorrow, almost your old self," she told Anna.

That was good news. Anna had been doped once, and once slipped LSD. By good fortune she'd never been given anything highly addictive or — so far — fatal.

"I wish rufies were harder to come by," Heath said. "If you pay attention to the news, it seems there are more date rape drugs than sex ed classes in most school districts."

"I'd hate to have a daughter in this day and age," Anna said.

"Ah, but you do," Gwen murmured.

That was another drawback when it came to children. One got fond of them, and then they went speeding away in a convertible with a bottle of Jack Daniel's and no seat belt.

"Have you yet seen fit to share with Heath why you didn't want the medical establishment or law enforcement called?" Gwen asked as she pumped the rubber bulb tightening the cuff.

"She did," Heath said. Heath was sitting in Robo-butt near the cold hearth, one hand idly playing with Wily's right ear, the other holding a glass half full of bourbon-and-water.

"Murdering me doesn't make sense," Anna said, feeling the slight claustrophobia the tightening of a blood pressure cuff always gave her. "I've been trying to work it in with the cyberstalker and/or the Duffy murder — not because either makes sense, but because they are the only items of interest I've been involved in since coming to Maine. I think I might have a better shot at getting to the bottom of it if I remain dead for a while."

"A hundred twenty over seventy. Better than most twenty-year-olds," Gwen said, deflating the blood pressure cuff. "I can see wanting to stay dead — no one pesters the dead. But won't the Acadia people wonder where you are? Aren't you acting chief ranger?"

"I called in sick, told Peter what I was up to. We argued. I won," Anna explained succinctly.

A cell phone played a few bars of "Yankee Doodle Dandy." "That's mine," Gwen said. "Would you get it, E?"

Elizabeth picked up the phone. "It's Mrs. Hammond," she said, passing the phone to Gwen, who sat on a stool at Anna's side.

"Dez," Gwen said into the phone. Her face went tight and tired. Without the burning energy within, her flesh pulled down. Pouches showed beneath her eyes. Shadows hollowed her cheeks.

Shangri-La, Anna thought as she watched her friend aging in front of her.

"Okay," Gwen said. "Okay. Let me know if I can do anything. Soon as it comes in, I promise. No, I don't doubt it either. It's a crying shame, that's what it is. Call me tomorrow?" Gwen pushed the off button but continued to stare down at the phone.

"What is it?" E asked.

Anna knew it was death. Death masks weren't just for the dead. Many times she'd seen them slipped onto the faces of survivors. Gwen wore one now.

"Chris died today, while Dez and I were in Bar Harbor," Gwen said.

Heath rolled over and put her arm around

her aunt. E knelt on Gwen's other side and laid her head in her lap. Gathering of warmth and strength, being enfolded in the arms of loved ones, Anna knew, was beneficial for most people, so she watched in respectful silence. Wily, probably feeling sorry for her because she was not exactly of the human race, jumped up beside her on the sofa. A pain-filled whine let her know what the thoughtful gesture had cost his old injuries.

Gwen sniffed and rubbed her eyes. "It's not as if Chris and I were close. For the past twenty years it's been mostly Christmas and birthday cards, maybe a call now and then," she said after blowing her nose. "It's not a surprise. Chris — and Dez and I — knew she wasn't going to live to a ripe old age. It's just that the timing couldn't be more tragic."

"Because she was so young?" Heath asked. To Anna she said, "She wasn't even sixty."

"Fifty-seven," Gwen said. "Had her first heart attack at fifty-four."

"Is that usual?" Anna asked.

"More so now than it used to be, what with obesity, blood pressure drugs, and so on. Chris wasn't obese. She had a weakening of the vessel walls in her heart muscles. Every doctor has a theory, but none of us agree — not that I know much about hearts over the age of ten."

"Is that what you and Dez met about? Ms. Zuckerberg's health?" E asked. As for Anna, Chris was just a name to Elizabeth.

"No. Worse in a way. Because we were out, Dez wasn't with Chris when she died. That will be hard on her. They've been together over fifteen years," Gwen said. Sighing, she moved from the stool to a comfortable armchair. "I could do with what you're having, Heath."

"Anna?" Heath asked as she rolled toward the kitchen where the bourbon bottle lived.

"No more drugs for me in this lifetime," Anna said.

"Lesbians?" E asked.

"Why does everybody have to be a lesbian!" Gwen snapped. "They became friends when they were girls. Dez was the maid here when the babies were born. After Dez's husband died, and Chris's health started to go, she came to live here with Chris. Lesbians! For heaven's sake. Can't anybody just be friends with anybody anymore?" Gwen grumbled.

Heath rolled back in with an obviously much-needed bourbon. Anna had never seen Gwen irritable. The pediatrician's mood was always so bubbly Anna occasionally wondered if she prescribed a little something for herself.

"This baby thing is new," Heath said. "Until we got to Boar, I didn't know Chris had children. I didn't know she'd ever been married."

"You said she didn't have kids," E said accusingly.

"So I did," Gwen admitted. "That was an attempt to keep you out of more misery and keep Chris's secret. I failed at both. It's been a long day. Now that Chris is gone, I guess her old secrets can't hurt her. Chris never married, but she did have children. Forty years ago — forty-two now, I guess — when Chris was fourteen, she gave birth to twin girls. Here on Boar Island. I was the doctor. It was my first paying job out of medical school. Her mother — a witch spelled with a *b* — didn't want anyone to know her daughter had gotten pregnant. Because Chris was a minor, the witch didn't need her consent to give the babies up for adoption — or so she said. There was enough family money to make her right, no doubt.

"A few years ago a couple of things happened. First, Chris's mother finally had the decency to kick the bucket — Chris had never gotten free of her, not really — and

Chris had her first heart attack. That was when she decided to find her daughters if she could."

"Nearly sixty and still afraid to admit she'd had twins when she was fourteen?" Elizabeth asked. "People now would be going on talk shows and writing books about it."

"Not Chris. From age eleven to age thirteen, Chris was molested by their rabbi. When she became pregnant, she told her mother. Her father tried to beat the truth of who the real father was out of her. Her mother packed her off to Boar Island with only herself and a maid — Dez, all of twelve years old — for company," Gwen explained.

"Her own mother didn't believe about the rabbi?" Elizabeth asked. "What a rat."

"Worse," Gwen said. "Her father didn't believe her, but her mother knew she was telling the truth. The rabbi was beloved and rich and the witch didn't want to damage her own social standing by crying 'Pervert!' "

"Did she find her daughters?" Heath asked.

"Three or so years ago she put an ad in the papers, you know the sort of thing — seeking identical twins separated at birth, would now be thirty-something, legacy involved," Gwen said. She took a swig of bourbon and held it in her mouth for a moment before she swallowed. Anna took over the task of fiddling with Wily's ears.

"She didn't get an answer to that ad, or the next one, or the one after that. Assuming the girls would have been adopted out locally, and quietly, and without any paper trail, Chris only put ads in papers around this area," Gwen told them. "All of a sudden, last week, somebody answered an ad from a while ago. Chris was so excited. Not a good thing when your blood vessel walls are disintegrating. She insisted that Dez and I go meet with the woman — Dez to question her, me to get a DNA sample if the woman was willing."

"You'd have to," Anna said. "The word 'legacy' should have brought out every greedy woman for miles. I'm surprised there were no responses to the first ads."

"Mainers are a decent people," Gwen said.

"When they're not shooting each other for poaching," Anna whispered to E, who'd joined her and Wily on the sofa.

"I took the sample, a cheek swab, but Dez and I think she's legitimate —"

"Not literally," Heath said.

Gwen frowned at her, then went on. "Other than the bleached-out hair, she is the spitting image of Chris when she was in her early forties: same color eyes, same overlapping front incisors, same oval face and straight eyebrows."

The description tugged at Anna, but she let it pass. After being drugged, bagged, and dumped, a little paranoia was surely normal.

"How did she know she was a twin?" E asked. "I mean if they were separated at birth and all that, you wouldn't know, would you?"

"That was the only fishy part," Gwen said. "We asked her that same question — though believe it or not, neither one of us thought of it at first. She said she had recently found her sister, but she wouldn't tell us who it was, or if the sister knew about our meeting — nothing. Though she seemed like a good woman, if on the naïve side, I couldn't help but wonder if she planned on sharing the legacy with her twin, and of course she has to. Chris needs to give them both the news. Needed to."

The sun was low over Mount Desert, knifing into the room in a wedge of rich coppery light. Gwen squinted into the shaft of dancing motes for a moment. "Chris died. Damn. She will never get to see her daughters — not even one of them. It just makes my heart ache."

"What's the legacy?" E asked. Anna had been wondering the same thing but had become too civilized to blurt it out at the graveside, so to speak.

"Boar Island, this house," Gwen said. "There isn't much left in investments, but I imagine one could get a pretty penny for a private island off the coast of Acadia National Park. The historic value of the lighthouse would be worth something, I would think."

"Jeeze, yuh think?" Heath mocked gently. "I bet this rock would be worth millions of dollars to some rich New Yorker who wants a six-thousand-square-foot summer cottage to use for a couple of weeks each year. Not a bad legacy. Juicy enough to want to steal it from your sister."

"That's the good news part of the legacy," Gwen said, then sighed again, more deeply this time. "The bad news is that their biological father —"

"The child molester the witch was so into protecting," Heath butted in.

"Died of Huntington's disease," Gwen finished.

"Shit," Heath breathed. Gwen shot her a reproachful glance.

Elizabeth stared at her mother, then turned to Anna. "What's the big deal? He was a pervert. Who cares if he died? It's not like they'd want to look up dear old Dad for the holidays. I sure wouldn't."

"Huntington's is hereditary," Anna said. "There's a fifty-fifty chance the child will have the disease if one parent carries it."

"It is a terrible disease," Gwen said. "Pitiless. It's a neurodegenerative genetic disorder, which means the nerve cells in the brain break down. There's a whole host of symptoms ranging from loss of motor control to severe psychiatric disorders and dementia."

"Gosh," Elizabeth said. "You'd think they'd know they had it already."

"Most people start showing symptoms in their late thirties and early forties. Sometimes it manifests earlier or later, but if you didn't know your family history, you might not know what was happening to you," Gwen told E. "That's what Chris was worried about, that they wouldn't get medical care if they had it, or that, without the money from the sale of Boar, they couldn't afford it. A person with Huntington's can live twenty or more years after the first onset of symptoms, getting progressively worse and worse."

"Is there anything you can do about it?" Heath asked.

"Not much," Gwen said.

"Then who'd want to know they had it till they had it?" E asked.

Anna suspected she wasn't so much asking anybody in particular as demanding answers of the universe. Why would anyone want to get tested? A fifty percent chance of no longer worrying about it. Why would anyone who wasn't worrying about it want to know?

Gwen answered E's question. "There are some drugs that show promise. There's also the issue of safety to self and others."

"Driving," E said.

"Gas stoves, matches, babysitting, getting lost, knocking over hot coffee, the whole gamut of dangers, and we haven't even gotten to psychiatric issues," Gwen said. "At some point it becomes unsafe not to seek medical care."

"My biological father is dead and I don't know his medical history," E said. "Could I have it?"

"You could," Gwen answered slowly. "But you're more likely to get cancer or pneumonia or hydrophobia. Huntington's is rare. If you're going to dwell on it, I'll get you tested."

"You don't have the gene," Heath said. "Your father died in a motorcycle accident when he was fifty-five, remember?"

"Right," E said, sounding relieved rather than sad. Anna was unsurprised. E's father had been absent since she was eighteen months old. "Did you tell her — the daughter?"

"We didn't. Chris wanted to do that," Gwen said. "Now Chris is gone. I'm afraid the twins do have the gene. This poor woman seemed to have some cognitive dysfunction. We had to repeat ourselves. Sometimes she appeared confused, unnaturally docile."

"Maybe she just isn't very bright," Heath offered.

"She also showed chorea. Involuntary movement in her hands." Gwen flicked her wrist.

Suddenly, what had niggled in Anna's brain snapped into place: bleached blonde, overlapping front teeth, cigarettes being flipped out on the ground.

"Paulette Duffy?" she asked.

THIRTY-NINE

Once again Anna was sitting at Peter Barnes's kitchen table. As superintendent, he could keep a nine-to-five, Monday-through-Friday schedule if he wanted. Since the baby had been born, he did. Lily was watching television in the front room; Olivia, in a soft pink Onesie, was curled up on the couch beside her, making tiny grunting sounds like a piglet.

Anna set her teacup down and gazed past Peter at the charming picture on the couch. Mother and daughter, happy, safe, beautiful. Would that it would always be so.

"Elizabeth's cyberstalker has sent an ultimatum," she said more abruptly than she'd intended. "E's supposed to show up alone, in person, at a time and place to be determined. Or else."

"Preying on children! God, but it makes my stomach turn! Throw in sexual perversion and I'm ready to change my stance on

463

the death penalty," Peter said. He didn't glance at his baby girl, but Anna noticed his head jerk as if he'd been going to and stopped himself. Attitudes changed when one had skin in the game. Taking a hit while fighting for the principle of a thing was fine, but when the good fight began to cause collateral damage to innocents, how to be a hero became more complex.

"Heath would be too conspicuous in her wheelchair, and logically, the stalker is someone who knows Elizabeth; ergo, he might know Heath or me or even Gwen. I was hoping to borrow an unknown face so it won't be only me and Gwen. Though smart and fierce, Gwen is small and somewhere north of seventy-five."

"There's always the Bar Harbor police, the Maine State Troopers, the sheriff's department," Peter said dryly. "All perfectly legitimate and, from what I've experienced, competent options. Not as reassuring as an elderly pediatrician, I'm sure, but they do their best."

"I have great respect for small-town police and sheriff's departments," Anna said. "They see a little of everything and have to deal with it by themselves. They tend to be generalists, the way rangers were in the good old days, before we carried guns. It's the

464

time frame and subject matter that make me want to keep it personal."

"How so?" Peter asked.

"With cyberbullying, police don't yet know what to do, where they stand, what the procedure is; nobody really does. The police back home more or less blew Elizabeth off. Not out of malice, more out of this-isn't-my-jurisdiction.

"The or-else meeting is tomorrow. That's not much time to coordinate with officers who may not deal well with a girl from Boulder, Colorado, hiding out in Maine, who says she's meeting a stalker who posts dirty things about her on the Internet. I doubt we'd get things sorted out in less than the twenty-odd hours we've got."

"Put the guy off. Tell him you'll meet day after tomorrow, or next week," Peter suggested. "That might give you time to get things set up with local law enforcement."

"It might. It also might scare him back into the cyber woods. Then E will have to live not knowing when the bastard is going to pop out again."

"I wouldn't wish that on anybody, especially not a teenaged girl," Peter said.

"Marriage and fatherhood have made you downright sensitive," Anna joked.

"Estrogen seems to have a civilizing effect

on me," he admitted. "I can't give you anybody. I shouldn't have let you and Denise go on NPS time. Bad judgment on my part, and let's hope it stays our little secret, at least until I'm retired. What I can do is give Artie the day off — you're on sick leave — and if you and Artie choose to spend the day hanging out with septuagenarian aunts and underage girls, that's your business."

Anna's eyes were blurring. Drug residue. She blinked rapidly to clear them.

"You look like shit," Peter told her kindly. "You should have let me come out to Boar."

"I had cabin fever," Anna said. Talking hurt — her upper lip was bruised — but nothing like the pain in her left heel or her butt. Gwen had bandaged her various scrapes. Anna felt like she was wearing diapers under her jeans. "I needed to get off the island. I'll be back in Schoodic tonight."

"Hoping for another attack?" Peter asked. He took a sip of hot tea, raising his eyebrows over the rim of the cup at her.

"No. I'm dead, don't forget," she said.

"Right. How's that supposed to work for us?" he asked.

Anna rubbed her face. "I must admit I wasn't thinking too clearly when I wanted to stay dead. I had a sort of half-baked notion that I could appear like the ghost of

Hamlet's father, and the guilty parties would fall down and confess, or at least look much amazed. Trouble is, this ghost doesn't know to whom it would be profitable to appear. Now I think I'd like to stay dead until we get this business with the stalker over with. If I'm dead, nobody will be taking potshots at me."

"Artie and I made a quiet visit to Schoodic today and had a look around," Peter said. "We found a broken needle — the kind that fits in a plastic syringe — in front of the Rockefeller building. It's been bagged and will be tested."

"Gwen went through the Mount Desert lab," Anna told him. "Rohypnol and muscle relaxants were in my blood."

"Good to have friends in high places," Peter said. Being superintendent of a major national park couldn't get evidence tested in a four-hour time frame: lack of funds and facilities, the need to stand in line behind other law enforcement organization at shared labs. "We found your other boot," he went on. "Once it's been through the system, you can have it back. It was about halfway between the Rockefeller building and Schoodic Point. Schoodic was probably where the boat was beached. Nothing interesting in your apartment or on the stairs."

"No *CSI Acadia*?" Anna asked with a smile. "No tiny thread or droplet to lead us to the bad guys?"

"Sorry," Peter said. "Have you remembered anything new?"

"I don't know," Anna said honestly. "The Rohypnol has an amnesiac built in. It's not total, but everything is stretched and warped, like the memory of a dream. Walter said there were two people in the boat, and I sort of remember two people in my apartment — or the parking lot or somewhere. I haven't any idea whether I really remember two or, because I was told there were two, I think I remember. Most of the day I've been poking at my poor raddled brain. I think I might think the two were small. I think I might think they were dressed like ninjas, all in black. I think I might think they wore white gloves like Mickey Mouse. I don't trust my own memories. Before I can believe myself I need corroboration from people that weren't stoned out of their minds."

"We talked to the sculptors," Peter said. "Nobody saw anything or heard anything. We talked to your boyfriend — Walter Whitman —"

"Don't speak ill of my savior," Anna said. She sipped her tea. Earl Grey. Right up there with tomato soup for curing what ails.

"Seems like a good kid. A little monomaniacal about clearing his dad's name, but I can understand that."

"Good thing he is, or I'd be sleeping with the fishes," Anna said.

"He gave us a statement about the boat that dumped you, and precisely when and where that dumping occurred. We put out an APB to the Coast Guard and local marinas. Today I'd hoped to get a diver down where you went in. Something might have fallen from the bag you were in, or their boat. Problem is, Denise Castle, the ranger who drove you around, is our only certified diver, and she just retired."

"She went through with it?" Anna was surprised at that. Denise didn't strike her as a woman who had anyplace else to go. It wasn't anything the woman had said or done, it was the starkness of her apartment: nothing personal, no pictures with people in them, family, friends, or even co-workers. Just that one bedside photo from which Peter Barnes had been amputated.

"She did. I think she was as shocked as everybody else."

"Struck me that way, too. She'd not talked about it before?" Anna asked.

Peter looked into the other room, where his wife and child nestled in the flickering

469

light from the television. "Why do you ask?"

"Not sure," Anna said.

Peter sighed and rubbed his jaw like a bad actor trying to indicate he's thinking. "Yes and no," he said finally. "She seemed to be happy here, but — you know Denise and I lived together for eleven years?"

"I remember, vaguely," Anna said.

"After the first shit was done hitting the fan, Denise seemed okay. Then Lily came and the baby. Denise seemed fine with that, seemed totally over the split. She brought Olivia a really beautiful coming-home gift — an angel figurine from Lenox, not cheap — and has been nice to Lily. I happen to know Denise has no family and no real friends, so on the one hand, I was surprised she just up and retired without any notice. On the other hand, there have been a few times I've caught her looking at Lily or me, or seen her face go kind of odd when somebody mentions our house, that makes me think she might not be as much over the split as she acts. So I wasn't surprised she up and retired. Does that make sense?"

"Why now?" Anna asked. The timing of an incident could tell one a great deal. That was the moment when something changed. "After hanging on through the split, the marriage to Lily, the birth of Olivia, why did Denise choose now to retire?"

"Who knows," Peter said wearily. "I haven't a clue as to why Denise does anything. We got Walter Whitman squared away with the local police," he said, changing the subject. "There wasn't an arrest warrant out for him. Town police try and stay out of lobster wars. If there's any danger to Walt, it'll come from other lobstermen. John Whitman thinks blood has cooled enough the kid could come out of hiding, but that won't get him his line back. Without fishing rights, he hasn't got a future. At least not around here. I told him to talk with Gwen. If he's going to be squatting on Boar to do his spying, it should be with the owner's permission."

"The owner is dead," Anna said. "Chris Zuckerberg bought the farm this afternoon."

Peter sat back in his chair. Inwardly, Anna flinched. Wrapped up in her own troubles, she'd forgotten that Peter probably knew Ms. Zuckerberg. Not only was Acadia a small world during the winters, and people got to know one another, but any self-respecting superintendent would want to have some kind of relationship with his rich, private-land-owning neighbors.

"Sorry," Anna murmured as she hid her nose in her teacup. "Did you know Chris had kids?"

"I didn't," Peter said.

"Twins, girls, adopted out at birth. Chris was trying to find them when she died. Actually had found one — or thought she had. Paulette Duffy."

"Mrs. Kurt Duffy?" Peter asked.

"That's the one," Anna said. "Odd, isn't it, how one day you've never heard of Paulette Duffy, then she's popping up everywhere?"

"Not so odd. Every time I learn a word I've never heard before, guaranteed I'll hear it three times before the week is out."

"There was a legacy, enough to make murdering a husband worthwhile if one didn't wish to share. Though, from what I hear, most women would have murdered Kurt Duffy for free," Anna said.

"Iron-clad alibi," Peter said. "Half a dozen acquaintances and strangers can attest that she was in the Acadian at the time of the murder."

"But if Paulette is Chris Zuckerberg's long-lost child, she has an identical twin sister," Anna said.

Peter digested that for a minute. "Damn," he said finally. "So mysterious twin sits at the Acadian while Paulette kills her husband?"

"Maybe," Anna said. "Or maybe the other way around. Or maybe they're both innocent."

"Speaking of innocents."

Lily was standing in the kitchen door, Olivia in her arms. "It's Livvy's bedtime."

Peter leapt up like a terrier offered a treat. "Come on," he said to Anna. "You can be an aunt."

Because they clearly thought she would like nothing better than to watch them tucking their baby into its bed for the night, Anna obligingly rose and followed the familial parade up the stairs.

As she would have expected, the nursery was a froth of girly pink, but well done and spotlessly clean. An old-fashioned white antiqued-wood dressing table, with a large looking glass in a matching frame, mirrored the bassinette with its rows of white lace, a mobile of pink and blue and yellow ducklings hanging from the hood.

Peter and Lily cooed and prattled. Anna looked at the guardian angel. It was a lovely thing, not the usual flowing skirts and tiny feet, but a bell-shaped dress with many colors and sturdy handsome wings. On its arm was a basket of flowers.

Anna picked it up.

"Denise gave Livvy that," Lily said.

"Wasn't that sweet of her?"

Anna turned it over.

"Sweet," she said, but either it wasn't a Lenox or it had been broken and repaired. The bottom was patched with plaster of paris.

FORTY

It was late when Denise finally staggered into the foyer of her apartment building. Her mailbox was empty. She'd half expected a note from Paulette reporting on her latest betrayal.

There was nothing. Good, she guessed. Maybe.

Using the handrail as if she were a woman twice her age, Denise dragged herself up the stairs to her apartment, fumbled the key into the lock, and nearly fell into the front room.

This had been one of the longest days of her life, and it had come at the end of one of the longest nights. Exhaustion swelled like a balloon in her chest. Her head throbbed. Her hands jumped with nerves. Exhausted, but not sleepy, not the least little bit. High-pitched, sharp-edged nervous energy sang through her veins, sawed through her bones, and squirted acid into her belly until her throat burned nearly to her back teeth.

The Miata, her pathetic attempt at joie de vivre after Peter had summarily tossed her out, was gone. She wouldn't miss it. In its place, paid for in cash — it took as long to pay the idiot salesman in cash as it would have to get a loan and buy it on time — was a midsized Volvo XC90. Safe. That was what she wanted in a car now, safe and family-friendly. The car had cost a good chunk of her savings, but there was no choice. A family couldn't drive around in an accident waiting to happen.

For color, she'd chosen white. There were a zillion white sort-of SUVs with mommies and kiddies in them on every road in America. The Volvo would blend in.

Dropping keys and purse onto the coffee table, Denise let gravity suck her butt down onto the sofa. Her apartment. Sterile and neat and utterly hers. Nothing where it shouldn't be. Everything where it should. This was gone, too. Or as good as. She'd turned in her two-week notice to the land-lord. In winter, she would have been stuck with six weeks' rent money. In summer, apartments were at a premium, so she'd only had to flush two weeks' worth of rent down the rat hole.

Rat.

Paulette.

"No, no, no," Denise muttered, banging her head against the soft back of the couch with each word.

Denise had quit her job, bought the most expensive car she'd probably ever own, given up her apartment, and killed two people, for Paulette. Not to mention the hundreds of dollars she'd dumped at Walmart that afternoon. All the while she was hacking off chunks of her life so that their new life together might have a chance at success, Paulette was betraying her.

It was because of the Walmart shopping spree that Denise knew this. Thinking it would look odd for a retired ranger, who had given two weeks' notice to her landlord and was supposed to be moving out, to be carting armloads of goods upstairs to her apartment, Denise had taken the risk of driving the lot of it to Paulette's house in broad daylight. In a new Volvo, she figured if any rangers saw her, they'd never think it was her. Fancy Volvos and GS-9s didn't exactly go together.

Paulette hadn't been home. At first, Denise was relieved. This wasn't the time to be arguing about what she'd bought and why and where it should be kept.

Denise had driven behind the house to unload her purchases into the nursery. Paulette wasn't in the nursery. Where was Paulette if she wasn't at work and she wasn't at home?

Denise trotted through the trees to the house. Forcing the kitchen door didn't take much brute strength. A firm shove of her shoulder overwhelmed Paulette's flimsy attempt at security. Since they were family, Denise didn't consider it breaking and entering, more like she'd forgotten her key. Paulette should have been home. Denise needed to reassure herself that nothing had happened to her sister; that she hadn't panicked or gotten sick.

Denise needed to know where Paulette was.

The old ads for twins separated at birth, along with the postcard with the cell number on it, were on the kitchen table amid the coffee rings. That was all Denise had to see. She knew what Paulette had done. She'd called the person to ask about the legacy. While Denise was buying and selling and giving notice, Paulette was meeting with their *mother,* or some lawyer or con woman. Undoubtedly Paulette was drinking up whatever bullshit this individual was pouring out. Undoubtedly Paulette was babbling out their secrets with girlish gusto, hoping for a big fat legacy or, worse, the loving arms of the bitch that had whelped them.

Denise groaned. Sitting forward, she held her head between her hands, pushing hard on her temples with her palms. Her disposable cell phone had fallen from her bag and lay on the coffee table. She could call Paulette, let her know this shit wasn't going to fly.

A hand detached itself from Denise's head, floating into her field of vision. Not like it was her hand reaching for her phone, more like it was a detached hand, like a balloon-hand in the Macy's Thanksgiving Day parade, floating on wires high above the crowd, then settling down toward the tiny phone on the table.

Denise reached out with her other hand, caught the one floating, and shoved both of them between her knees. "Poison thoughts," Denise whispered. "If you think poison thoughts you'll die."

Instead of taking up the phone, she opened her laptop. A glance at the time told her Olivia would be in her crib. If she was lucky, Peter and Lily would have finished their bullshit cooing and baby-talking, and cleared out of the room. Seeing a baby, a new life, free of the crap that was dripped into every human's veins over time until the whole person was a toxic waste dump, would settle her, calm her mind. Keep the poison thoughts from killing her. At least for a while.

She tapped on the mouse pad, opening the live feed to the camera in Olivia's nursery. Peter and lovely little Lily bent over the bassinette making faces they thought were amusing but, in truth, were scary and ugly. Then the world spun, the camera showed the wall, the ceiling, then . . .

"Shit!" Denise screamed, throwing herself back against the couch cushions, covering her eyes. When she uncovered them, all was as it had been, Peter and Lily cooing, the world right way up, Olivia in her bed.

For an instant Denise could have sworn she had seen a face. The face of a dead woman. Anna Pigeon's face. The video wasn't recorded; she couldn't go back. Had she been able to, there would have been no point. She had seen Anna Pigeon's body in a black plastic sack sinking beneath the waves of the Atlantic.

The fear and paranoia burning like acid in her gut were from fatigue, not because of anything real. She'd not slept for over forty hours. Too tired and thoughts got crazy. Way too tired and one could even hallucinate.

Anna Pigeon was dead.

Paulette was her soul, her gentle self, her family.

Obstacle removed; identical twin good and right and safe.

There was no Anna.

Paulette might have gone to meet somebody, but she wouldn't break trust with her sister, her identical twin sister. The legacy was for them, for their family. Denise herself had told Paulette to pursue it. Paulette might even be meeting with a Realtor. Could be Denise was wrong about the meeting with the legacy person.

But Denise wasn't wrong. She could hear how right she was barking down among the chunks of disappointment and misery in her brain's junkyard.

"Doesn't matter," she said aloud.

The day — and the night before — had been good, she told herself. Better than good. Denise took out the slip of paper she'd been carrying in her front pants pocket so long it was growing soft. From her bag she got a pen, one with red ink.

Kill Kurt (Denise)

"Check," Denise said, and put a neat red check mark next to it.

Sell Land (Paulette)

"Better be soon," she muttered as she

passed that one over.

Remove Obstacle (D&P)

Denise paused. The dead pigeon's upside-down face blinked like a strobe light, setting parts of her mind afire. "Check," she hissed, and scribbled out the words with such force that the pen tore through the paper.

"Stop it," Denise said aloud. Her hand flicked. The pen flew from her fingers, fell to the white sofa, and rolled, leaving a thin red trail. Denise forced herself to look away from the bloody little snake-track on the perfect white of the fabric. "Calm. Slow and steady wins the race. Nerves. Fatigue. Finish and rest. That's a girl," she crooned to herself. When she felt the spate of rage diminish, she went back to the list, carefully avoiding glancing at the ink stain.

Quit NPS (retirement pension) (D)

"Check!" Denise said as she marked it.

Find out about "Legacy" (if it exists) (P)

Denise was sorely tempted to check that off, as a sign that she believed in her sister. That her sister believed in them. If she didn't know for sure, though, she couldn't do it. She never broke her own rules. Well, hardly ever.

In a spirit of compromise, she set aside the pen, fished a pencil from her purse, and put a pencil mark next to that item on the list, a faint gray check mark. For now that would have to do.

Car, shopping, etc.

"Check!" and check.

Give landlord notice

"Check!" and check.

Family — Mt. Desert Hospital (D&P)

The injection into the four-ounce, hermetically sealed waxy box, the seventh of those in Lily's cupboard, would be used by lovely little Lily late in the afternoon tomorrow. Lily used sixteen ounces each day.

That wasn't enough to check it off the list.

After nearly two days without rest, the pen that had so recently flown from her hand of its own accord became too heavy to lift. The list blurred. Denise leaned back on the couch cushion and rubbed her burning eyes, wishing she hadn't sacrificed the last of her Valium to the obstacle issue. Tomorrow *Family* would get checked off, then, one by one, the rest of the list. She would do it tomorrow. After all, tomorrow was another day.

Scarlett O'Hara had said that.

But then, Scarlett O'Hara was one crazy bitch.

FORTY-ONE

Denise's scalp stung, her eyes stung, her nose stung. In law enforcement training at FLETC, the students had been pepper-sprayed — "to know what it feels like." Sadistic bastards; they just liked tormenting the new kids. Right now, right here in Paulette's kitchen, she felt the same sensations. Besides that, her neck was going to snap.

"What's next? Waterboarding? Do you do this once a month?" she asked.

"Every six weeks. You get used to it," Paulette said as she finished rinsing the bleach from Denise's hair. "Done. You can get your head out of the sink."

Lifting her head with the care she'd use lifting a bowling ball with a soda straw, Denise straightened in the chair while Paulette wrapped a towel around her head.

"You're going to be beautiful as a blonde," she said, disappearing into the bedroom.

Denise wasn't sure about that. There were other reasons she'd decided to bleach her hair tonight, reasons she chose not to share with Paulette — at least not yet.

Paulette reappeared brandishing a blow-dryer.

"As beautiful as you?" Denise teased.

"Just exactly as beautiful," Paulette said with a laugh.

"Identical," Denise said with an answering smile. She was teasing her twin sister, in fun. If the painful process of stripping the color from her hair had no other use, Denise still would have done it. Playing beautician, Paulette was relaxed, smiled more, even laughed. For a while she seemed to have forgotten the dark web they were weaving, some strands already destroyed forever, some yet to be spun. Denise felt the glow of awe she had experienced that first night as they sat in front of the mirror in the bedroom looking at themselves, at each other, at *theirself*.

This was what it would be like all the time. Once they had a place of their own, safe in a warm part of the world, every night they would laugh and tease, watch movies and eat popcorn. That wasn't part of Denise's childhood, yet she'd done that sort of thing with Peter. At the time it must have been nice, but that recollection had been rotted and discolored by the times between then and now. As a memory, it was a corpse, and that corpse stank like carrion.

Paulette plugged the blow-dryer into an outlet on the counter. Hot air blew over Denise's neck, breathed past her right cheek and ear. She closed her eyes. Her sister was fixing her hair. Right out of one of those books she used to vandalize at the library when she was a kid. The happy family bullshit that infuriated her. Maybe it wasn't fiction after all. Maybe all those Dick-and-Jane children's authors weren't lying through their teeth.

The new Volvo was parked behind the shack. The back porch light was off. Still, it was a risk for Denise and Paulette to be together. The closer they got to endgame, the more dangerous it was to be seen in one another's proximity. People didn't remember much about random days. They remembered where they were when Kennedy was shot, what they were wearing when the World Trade Center towers came down, what they had for dinner before they'd gone to see *The Dark Knight Rises* in a movie theater in Aurora, Colorado. Denise didn't want anyone popping out of the woodwork and saying, "Yeah. I saw Denise Castle and

Paulette Duffy together right before the shit hit the fan. You know, they were real chummy. They even kind of looked alike."

Denise wanted to leave Maine unremarked and unremembered. She wanted Paulette to drift out of the minds of the people who knew her the way perfume drifts out of a bottle. The best way to get away with murder is never to be suspected in the first place. Once law enforcement decides on a person of interest, they keep sticking their noses up that person's ass if for no other reason than it makes it look like they're doing something when they don't know what the hell to do.

Unfortunately, they had to be in the house; the bleach job required running water. That turned out to be a perk. Denise didn't want Paulette going out past the Volvo and seeing all the things she had bought. Later, Paulette would be glad, grateful even, but it might be hard for her to understand at the moment. Besides, they were having fun! Good, clean family fun. Like a couple of Mormons, Denise thought, and was taken aback at her sourness.

Having fun must be like a lot of things in life. To do it right required practice and training.

Denise's hair was dried. Paulette had set

the electric rollers next to the sink and plugged them in. She insisted Denise wasn't to look in a mirror until the process — she called it a "transformation" — was complete. After the transformation would be the "reveal."

Though she'd lost the thread of why they were happy, while the curlers heated, Denise went on pretending she was. Paulette rolled her hair as the television played a reality show where people made assholes of themselves and a laugh track, like Denise, pretended it was funny.

Paulette combed out her hair and insisted on putting makeup on her. Feeling like a clown, Denise went on pretending. Maybe fun was like faith for alcoholics, fake it till you make it.

Eyes closed, promising not to peek, she let Paulette lead her through the bedroom and into the bathroom.

"The mirror's smaller than the one on the bureau, but the light's better," Paulette said, excitement bubbling in her voice. "You can look now."

Denise opened her eyes, expecting to see hair like Paulette had, broken and dried out like an overused broom. Regardless of her decaying attitude, Denise was impressed by the reveal. In the mirror was a beautiful woman. Smooth, blond, gleaming hair waved down past her chin. Soft rose colored her cheeks. A darker hue made her lips look fuller, younger. Mascara rimmed her eyes, turning the muddy hazel to dark green.

For a long, long moment Denise didn't know who she was looking at. She knew she was in the body of the person reflected in the mirror, but that face, that hair, those lips had no connection whatsoever with Denise Castle, dour and green and gray to the shattered remnants of her soul.

"Do you like it?" Paulette asked anxiously.

Denise nodded. The beautiful blonde in the mirror nodded.

If she'd had Paulette five years ago, if she'd gone blond, curled her hair, worn makeup, would Peter have needed space? Would he have chucked her out? Fallen in love with Lily?

"Doesn't matter," Denise snarled, and the plump pink lips in the mirror snarled with her.

"You hate it!" Paulette cried. Over her shoulder, reflected in the glass, Denise saw her sister's eyes fill with tears, her open happy-face curl into a pained wad.

"No. I love it. I was thinking of something else." Denise tried to undo the damage, but the moment had gone.

Though she primped and complimented her own reflection over and over, Paulette wouldn't cheer up. Denise was never so glad to see the back of anyone as she was to see the last of the pink scrubs disappear out the front door when Paulette left for work at seven forty-five.

"I'll lock up," Denise promised from where she sat on the sagging dirty couch. "I just want to finish this episode of . . ." Denise had no idea which show was on. Assholes. That was what was on. Fortunately, Paulette was more intent on leaving the dudgeon than she was on what Denise was saying.

The moment Denise could no longer hear the burr of the Duffys' pickup truck on the asphalt, she leapt to her feet.

She worked quickly, not because she was afraid Paulette might come back for some reason but because she wanted to get out of that house, out of the room where she'd killed Kurt, and away from the ammonia fumes of her new persona.

Under the bed, she found a suitcase. Rummaging through drawers with the insensitivity of a hardened burglar, she grabbed what she thought Paulette would need. One suitcase would have to be enough. What Paulette had was cheap and tired. They would both buy new wardrobes once they were settled. Cosmetics, shampoo — all the gooey stuff — they could pick up on the road.

Suitcase slammed shut and zipped, Denise snatched a set of scrubs and a pair of Crocs out of the closet. Stopping, she looked around the room. This was the last time she would see it. If things went as planned, Paulette would never see it again.

On the back porch, suitcase in hand, scrubs over her shoulder, Denise stopped again. Turning back, she stared at the weathered wood on the side of the house, the torn screen door, the peeling paint of the trim. Too bad a fire would call attention to the place. But for that, she might have thrown a match into the tinderbox.

Given her mood, if she could have, she might have burned down the world.

FORTY-TWO

Cybercreep had mandated a night meeting. Because it was the height of the season, bars, cafés, and many shops were open until eight or later. Cecelia's Coffee Shop was open until nine thirty. The cybercreep said they needed to be there at nine.

Everything about the time bothered Heath.

Poor little creep probably was hoping for darkness, she thought. Too bad the sun wouldn't set until nearly ten o'clock. That failed to comfort her. Dusk was probably worse. Often it was harder to see at dusk than it was in the middle of the night. Dusk was like a gray fog; normal shapes fooled the eye, strange shapes appeared familiar.

Of course, Bar Harbor would be lit up for the tourists.

Light was probably worse than dusk. Light meant shadows. Black shadows under docks, between boats floating in black water.

Everything about the place bothered Heath.

Why not midnight in a haunted house, or in the deep dark of the forests? Anna said the lonelier the place, the easier it was to spot the bad guy coming, to see where he parked, to hide in place until the appointed hour. In towns there were crowds; plenty of people that wouldn't be him, and only one son of a bitch who would. Hard to tell the good guys from the bad guy.

Meeting in town probably meant that he wasn't planning on kidnapping E. That, too, bothered Heath. Since it was almost a guarantee he meant Elizabeth no good, if he didn't intend to take her, then he must intend to harm her. An attack in town would be sudden, like a lightning bolt from a cloud of tourists, all but one of whom were innocent. A gunshot? A head shot? Heath shuddered at the image and gasped.

"You okay, Mom?" E asked. They were just rounding Bald Porcupine Island. E was seated beside Heath in the stern of John's boat as it turned toward the dock at Bar Harbor. They were holding each other's hands, leaning close to be heard over the noise of the engine. Gwen was at the console with John.

"Never better," Heath muttered. "Never better."

"Would it cheer you up if I told you that you look like a whale that got spray-painted at a 'Back to the Sixties' party?" Elizabeth asked.

Heath stared down at her lap. She was wearing Dem Bones beneath a riotously colored maxiskirt. Over that was a long fuchsia tunic with turquoise embroidery down the front that Anna had picked up at the thrift store where she bought the skirt. Heath's punishment for insisting on being part of the festivities. Sunglasses were out since Cybercreep had opted for night ops, but she wore a moderately battered purple sun hat with a wide brim. All in all she was, if not a perfect picture, at least a pretty good likeness of an overweight tourist with a good heart and bad taste.

If the pervert did recognize her, she would never forgive him.

He won't, she told herself, as she had insisted to Anna. For the past seven years — all of her life with Elizabeth — anyone who knew her knew her in a wheelchair. Many never saw past the wheelchair. Upright, walking, even with canes, was the ultimate disguise. Heath Jarrod was "the lady in the wheelchair," not "the fat lady hobbling down the sidewalk."

"And you look like a fourteen-year-old boy," Heath teased her daughter.

Elizabeth smoothed her palm down the flat front of her shirt, her breasts squashed beneath the Kevlar. "This thing is more uncomfortable than a bra. I'm surprised Anna wears one."

"I don't think Anna's worn a bra since she burned her last one in 1971," Heath said.

"The bulletproof vest," E said with exaggerated patience. Heath had known what she meant; she'd just wanted to make herself think things were a joking matter when they weren't.

"Regulations," Heath said. "Otherwise, I expect she wouldn't."

"Will she have somebody else's tonight?" E asked. "I hadn't thought about that. If I have hers, will she be, like, vulnerable and stuff?"

"Anna can take care of herself," Heath said. As the words came out of her mouth she remembered Anna tied to the lift, naked, unconscious, and covered in blood.

As if her mind were running along the same channels, Elizabeth said, "Anna isn't getting any younger."

"Older is tougher, like beef and redwoods," Heath said.

"Do you know where she'll be?"

"No. Not exactly. She's sort of wandering the general area. But she'll be close."

Cybercreep had insisted Elizabeth come alone. Unless he was a total idiot, he had to know that there would be watchers, that this was a trap as much for him as for E. He must be gambling that no one would dare be too close, that he would have space to do whatever it was he wanted to do, then get away before they could catch him.

"Maybe he just wants to talk," Elizabeth said.

"Let's hope so," Heath replied grimly. "We're here."

John had cut power. Under his experienced hands the boat was gliding effortlessly alongside a dock below a large parking lot that served the picturesque downtown area of Bar Harbor. Nimble as his own grandson, John Whitman leapt over the gunwale to snick two yellow lines fast, one at the bow and one near the stern.

Walt had wanted to be a member of the party. Anna had nixed that. Heath had no doubt the nixing was a waste of breath. What red-blooded young hero wouldn't want to save the damsel if he got the chance? Walt would be lurking somewhere around

the town square. Since he had been unknown — even to her — until the previous
day, Heath wasn't worried his appearance
would scare the cybercreep into hiding or
precipitous action. In fact, Heath hoped he
would disobey Anna. If Heath had her way,
the town would be full of young, strong,
kind, brave boys in love with her daughter.

Young, strong, kind, brave, *sane* boys.

Were boys who bullied, took sexual advantage, loved pornography, and the shame and
subjugation of women, technically insane?
Given that society at large behaved in much
the same manner, didn't that make the
nasty boys the norm? Was virtue, once its
own reward, now a symptom of a mental
disease?

Physical demands chased away the bitter
thoughts as, with the help of John and Elizabeth, Heath disembarked and got herself
squared away on the pier: hat firmly on
head, crutches in hand, tunic over thick
waist and legs, feet pointed toward the landing ramp.

From the low dock, Heath could see that
the town was lit up and the parking lot was
full, but little else. It wasn't more than a
couple hundred yards — and two ramps —
to where she had chosen to plant herself for
the duration. Over the past couple of weeks,

she'd gotten good with Dem Bones. Two canes were still needed for balance, but her gait was relatively smooth and her endurance far greater than it had been at the start. Still, she didn't want to use up her strength getting up to city level and through the parking lot, so she waited while John unloaded Robo-butt and Gwen unfolded it.

Gwen stayed with the boat while John rolled Heath up to the pavement, then halfway down the long parking area. There, he took the wheelchair and left her and Elizabeth standing in the shadow of a Chevy Suburban. He and Gwen would wait with the boat, ready to leave if leaving suddenly became necessary.

The time was eight fifteen; the sun was low in the west, veiled with clouds, the sky a deep lavender. Heath's eyes took a moment to adjust to the bright lights and big city. They had expected some foot traffic at this hour, but the square was packed with bodies. "What in hell . . ."

"People are wearing their pajamas!" Elizabeth exclaimed.

"And bathrobes and slippers," Heath said. "And I thought I looked silly."

For a minute or more they stared at what looked like a combination sleepover and shop-a-thon. "Lookie," Elizabeth said, pointing east of the parking lot where a lush lawn stretched in a smooth green apron down to the Atlantic. A vinyl sign, hung between two poles, read SEASIDE CINEMA! TONIGHT SHOWING *THE PAJAMA GAME.* Though it was not yet dark enough to start the movie, blankets were already spread, and pajama- and nightgown-clad moviegoers were lined up buying popcorn and sodas at a snack bar made to look like an old horse-drawn wagon.

Around the grassy area, the shops had doors open and lights on. Handwritten signs advertising Night Owl Specials, Midnight Snacks, and Pajama Party Sales were stuck on sandwich boards on the sidewalks and taped in windows.

"Holy shit," Heath breathed. "Talk about the unexpected."

"I bet this is why Creep-O wanted to meet 'day after tomorrow.' I wondered about that, but just thought he had a dentist appointment, or date, and wasn't free to torture people yesterday. I bet he was waiting because there'd be this big crowd today."

Heath bet her daughter was right. She bet she wanted to call this whole thing off, run — or walk mechanically — back to the boat, escape to Boar Island, disable the lift so nobody could call it down, and barricade her daughter in the tower.

Anna was here, she reminded herself, and a beefy ranger named Artie. Walter was surely here somewhere. Elizabeth was wearing a bulletproof vest. She knew not to eat or drink anything given to her by anybody, including waitstaff. She would never be out of Heath's sight or Anna's.

Damn, but Heath wished she knew where Anna was. It took an effort of will not to try to find her in the flannel-and-fleece crowd.

"Are we ready?" Elizabeth asked. "I feel overdressed."

To Heath's eyes Elizabeth looked beautiful, and as fragile as a butterfly fresh from the cocoon. She wore skinny jeans, tennis shoes — for running, Anna had insisted — and a loose boy's plaid shirt Walter lent her to disguise the thickening of the vest. Heath gazed at her daughter so long that Elizabeth started to roll her eyes. "Sorry," Heath said. "You look fine."

"Fat," E said. "Somebody should tell Anna that Kevlar makes you look fat."

"Go," Heath made herself say.

E walked farther down the parking lot. A few rows before the street, she stopped and hid in the shadow of a pickup truck, the kind that look like they're on steroids and have never hauled anything heavier than the ego of their owner. Both E and Heath would stay out of sight until twenty minutes of nine. At that time, Heath would make her way across the grassy square and pretend to window-shop in the stores to either side of Cecelia's Coffee Shop. At ten minutes of nine, Elizabeth would enter the square from the parking lot, walk straight across the center of the lawn where the most light and people were, and take a seat at one of Cecelia's outdoor tables. If no tables were free, she would stand with her back against the wall of the coffee shop, watching the square, until she was contacted. Artie, the only person other than Walt that they were sure would be a stranger to the cybercreep, would already be in place, seated at an outdoor table absorbed in the American obsession of drinking caffeinated beverages while staring at electronic devices.

If the creep did contact Elizabeth, and did not attempt anything hostile, both Heath and Artie would photograph him with their devices. Artie and Anna would tail him when he left. No attempt to capture him would be made near Elizabeth. Less dangerous that way.

If the creep made hostile motions, Artie would take him down.

Heath ran through this in her mind as her

legs were propelled off of the concrete and, with scarcely a hitch, onto the lawn. Canes were a great help. People tended to make way for a wheelchair, not so much for canes, but some. When they didn't, she batted them gently with the end of the cane, and apologized. Dem Bones was miraculous, but running obstacle courses and doing ballet had yet to be programmed into it.

Crowds. Dense crowds.

This bothered Heath more than the time and the place.

Artie was armed, and licensed to carry concealed weapons when off duty, as was Anna. The density of the crowd made that problematic. A bullet could easily pass through the villain and into two or three innocents before it came to a stop. At the moment, Heath didn't care if it mowed down all of Pajama Land, as long as E was safe.

Anna would care, as, Heath presumed, might Artie. Better no guns, she told herself as she maneuvered around a big man with a bushy beard wearing blue footy pajamas and a Red Sox baseball cap. E would be too close to the action; it would be too easy for a bullet to go astray. If the cybercreep had a gun —

No, Heath told herself firmly. That was not a thought she had allowed herself to entertain for the past forty-eight hours, and she wasn't going to entertain it now. If the bastard had a gun he wouldn't need all this meeting business. He could wait outside their house, or E's school in Boulder, and just blow her away at his convenience: no waiting, no air travel, no coffee date.

Sweating so profusely her hands were slick on the rubberized handles of the canes, Heath reached the far side of the square where Cecelia's was located. Twelve o'clock — that was what had been decided so they could tell one another where to look: The green was a clock face, Cecelia's was twelve o'clock, the grassy point — now the cinema — was at nine o'clock, the parking lot where she and E entered six o'clock, and the west part of town three o'clock.

Heath was across the narrow street from the coffee shop at twelve o'clock, the outdoor movie theater at nine o'clock on her left. For a minute or two she stood still, breathing, trying not to sweat, to fit in as a general-issue tourist at a pajamarama. If such a thing existed.

After a moment she spotted Anna. Had she not seen her in costume before she left Boar, she wouldn't have recognized her. Munching popcorn, Anna was leaning against a tree at about ten o'clock, ankles crossed. Her long braid was concealed beneath a loose flowing shirt over wide-legged soft palazzo pants. A Greek fisherman's cap, the cheap kind available in most of the souvenir shops, was pulled low on her forehead. The greatest disguise was the makeup. Anna Pigeon wore red lipstick, smoky eye shadow, and mascara. Beautiful and urban on someone else, it was oddly disturbing on the ranger, rather like seeing false eyelashes on a young Clint Eastwood.

Anna had to have seen her; Heath looked like the *Mayflower,* as envisioned by Peter Max, under full sail, but her gaze wandered past and through without a flicker of recognition.

Encouraged by the sight of her friend, Heath managed the step off the curb and crossed the street to the shops. Artie looked up as she passed. He didn't recognize her. Heath felt a mild lift of her spirits.

Facing a children's bookstore as if she were shopping, she watched the reflection of the front row of cars in the big parking lot at six o'clock appear and disappear as waves of people ebbed and flowed over the green space. She didn't see Elizabeth until she was halfway across the square, seeming very small in the big shirt and dark, tight jeans. Shoulders slightly hunched, she looked around as she walked, peering into the faces of the people she passed.

That was okay. Cybercreep would expect Elizabeth to appear frightened. After all, he'd spent weeks carefully fraying every single one of the girl's nerves. One of these happy people in bunny slippers was feeding on E's fear at that very moment. Anger, so intense it dimmed her vision, flooded Heath's entire being.

Her vision didn't clear. The world was viewed through a glass dimly. Heath's head swam; her balance faltered.

Lights had gone from the windows. Gone from the square.

Her tenuous vision of her daughter's reflection had vanished.

FORTY-THREE

First the streetlights around the green went dark, then the lights on the storefronts. The sky had faded from lavender to deep blue. The pajama-clad throng melted into amorphous shuffling grays and blacks, an occasional spark of red or green as beams of flashlights startled color from a sleeve or back.

Sharp pieces of the previous night flickered through Anna's brain: shadows shifting into ninjas, gun falling from her hand, darkness sucking her down. Dizziness overtook her. Blindly, she reached out for the tree trunk. Coarse bark brought her back to her body; the ancient strength of the tree steadied her.

Slowly, Anna squatted, carefully set her box of popcorn on the ground, then rose, stepping away from the tree.

Music began, a loudspeaker playing the Broadway overture to *The Pajama Game*.

Specters that had been born on the residue of Rohypnol faded. This was not a flashback, not a vast conspiracy to throw Elizabeth into the dark. The movie was about to start. Simple, prosaic, *Pajama Game* in pajamas, quaint, colorful, charming, and a huge pain in the ass.

Irritation burned in the pit of Anna's stomach. She had not foreseen this. A blind woman should have known that when the movie started the lights would go down. Cybercreep had known it. The people in the square had known it. Anna was the fool. Had she time, she would have cursed herself. Taken by surprise, none of them might have time, especially Elizabeth.

A chill of hypervigilance shivered through Anna. Cold tingled in her feet and hands and the top of her scalp. Whatever was going to happen would happen now, while people were on the move, while the lights were down and the area still crowded.

Counting on the invisibility cloak created by her shade tree and the lowered lights, Anna leapt onto a park bench. Her skinned left heel cursed her with a stab of pain. She ignored it. From the higher vantage point, she could see over the milling crowd. Most were drifting toward the lawn in front of the movie screen. A few continued to shop, eat, and talk in the shadows beneath awnings of stores and branches of the maples in the park. Blankets were being shaken and spread. Last purchases were being made at the snack bar.

Soft, fleecy, plaid stuffed animals in the arms of children and some adults, pillows and blankets in baskets: This was not the stuff of creepiness. Who looked like a sexually perverted bully in footy pajamas? Fuzzy slippers and terry robes could disguise a lot of sinister intent.

Despite the sudden change in atmosphere, Elizabeth was staying on track, walking a little slower than before but still heading straight — or as straight as she could through the pajama swamp — for Cecelia's.

Good girl, Anna thought.

Keeping E in her peripheral vision, she began searching in ever wider concentric circles out from her goddaughter, automatically discarding the very young, the very old, and families holding hands as parents walked children toward the cinema. A young man, rising and walking in the opposite direction of the crowd, his stride that of a man on a mission, caught her attention. Walter Whitman. He had been sitting on a low stone wall between the grassy movie space and the sea. As she could have predicted, he was making a beeline for Elizabeth. Clearly he, too, had been watching her.

Heath was in front of the children's book store beside the coffee shop, her back to the windows. By the panicked way her head bobbed and craned, she had lost sight of her daughter.

On the west side of the grass, at about two o'clock on their imaginary clock face, a single man wearing khakis, a short-sleeved blue shirt, and sandals with socks stood on the sidewalk. In the dim light, age was hard to guess, but he had a full head of dark hair and stood, hands in pockets, with the slouch of a man in his twenties or thirties.

Anna punched *WM2* into the text line on her cell phone, then hit send. Artie, attention torn from his laptop by the change in illumination, turned back to it. Heath took her cell phone from a pocket in her smock and looked down into the pale blue square of light. Then both looked for the white male at two o'clock.

A shake of the head let Anna know Heath didn't recognize him, but then she wouldn't necessarily.

Artie stayed with WM2. Anna continued her scan. Elizabeth was nearly across the grassy area, about fifty feet from the coffee shop. Two of the tables had been vacated by moviegoers. Once E was seated, she could take out her cell phone, put it on the table, and see the texts. Anna had wanted her to keep her hands free at all times and, when approaching the meeting place, to do nothing that might scare Cybercreep away.

Three doors down from Cecelia's, a dumpy woman emerged from an ice cream shop, her head a puff of pink lace in a many-tiered curler cap, her robe a tatty old blue-and-white-striped cotton. Plump doughy hands clutched a large satchel to her chest. By the contours of her figure, Anna guessed it must be filled with Red Hots, Jujubes, Goobers, and other treats one only ate at the movies.

A stride or two behind Elizabeth, and five yards to her right, a man paralleled E's path. Paunchy, hair thinning, stoop-shouldered: Anna put him in his early forties. He wore red-and-blue plaid flannel pajama bottoms and a pale blue, zip-front, lightweight jacket. On his feet were hiking boots. His face was unremarkable except for a simian brow that didn't match the ordinariness of his other features.

WM//E3, Anna texted. She knew they would understand the white male at three o'clock and hoped they would understand

510

the parallel mark.

Artie glanced in WM3's general direction. Sitting, he wouldn't be able to see the man. Heath was having trouble spotting the guy as well, her head moving back and forth and looking suspicious as hell.

BCOOL, Anna typed. Shrinking in on herself, Heath settled. Then the shrinking ceased. Heath regained her stature the way a resurrection fern will after a good rain. Heath had seen Elizabeth.

E had reached the road that separated the shops from the grassy space. Walter, Anna noted, was making his way toward Cecelia's using the sidewalk. A clever boy. Anna was sorry she'd nixed his coming.

No one else stood out from the thinning crowd. No beady-eyed perverts slinking around in their pj's. Had the cybercreep seen Heath or Anna and disappeared back into whatever hole he lived in? Was he standing them up to throw them off guard the next time he called for E to meet with him, or the time after that, so he could strike when they were no longer alert?

The crowd on the green had thinned to twenty or so stragglers. Stores were still doing a desultory business. The man in sandals went into the ice cream shop. Paunchy ceased to parallel E's path and veered onto an intersecting course. The woman in the curler cap stumped stolidly down the sidewalk, evidently bent on getting a Frappuccino to wash down the candy.

Elizabeth reached the coffee shop. She slid into a chair at one of the abandoned tables, took out her cell phone, and began fiddling with it.

The man with the paunch stopped fifteen feet shy of Cecelia's. Standing on the curb before the narrow street, he squinted as he stared across the road to where E was sitting. Artie moved his laptop so he could watch him without seeming to take his eyes off the screen.

Paunchy shoved both hands into the pockets of his windbreaker, his protruding brow shadowing his face.

Anna's brain, still tainted with the Rohypnol, reeled: the doughy hands, the oversized bag clutched to the woman's breast. This was important, this was trying to take her mind from its set track.

The man on the curb pulled a black rod from his pocket. Anna couldn't make out what it was, but it wasn't flat; it wasn't a cell phone. Pink Curler Cap was almost to Heath, her small sneakered feet marching determinedly along the dull gray concrete of the sidewalk.

Anna's brain locked between the dumpy little woman in the old housecoat and the man with the black rod. Walter bolted through the fog swaddling her mind to smash into the man on the curb. The boy didn't hit him with a football tackle or a fist; he plowed into him like a ship at ramming speed, the entirety of his strong young body smashing into the smaller man, knocking him ten feet onto the green.

"Get off me! Get off me!" the man screamed as Walter followed him down and pinned him to the turf with his weight. "Help! Help!" the man cried. No one moved to help. Anna had worked in tourist destinations most of her life. Tourists had no connection to other tourists, no knowledge of who was who, no faith in their instincts. They seldom sprang into action. There were too many unknowns in an alien environment.

The rod had flown from the downed man's hand. Rolling across the asphalt of the road, it flashed a bluish beam of light. A flashlight; the man had taken a flashlight from his pocket to fight the gloom.

Artie was on his feet and running toward where Walter held the shrieking little man down.

Doughy hands. White. Plump. Dimples for

knuckles.

Anna had seen her before, at the first coffee shop meeting. She'd had curly red hair then, but the same hands, the same bag. Whirling, she saw the woman in the pink curler cap drawing on a welding glove, the glove she'd seen peeking from the bag the last time.

One hand gloved, the other dipped into the capacious bag and came out with a can, the flat, squareish, metal kind that holds lighter fluid. She was passing Heath, whose attention was fixed on the tangle of men yelling and wrestling on the green.

"Run, E!" Anna shouted. "Run!" Galvanized by decision, Anna shot across the lawn, legs pumping, lungs filling to bellow again: "Run!"

Heath's head jerked in her direction. "The woman!" Anna screamed.

Ten yards separated her from her goddaughter.

The woman with the lighter fluid dropped her bag. Pinching the can in both hands, she aimed a stream of fluid at Elizabeth's face.

FORTY-FOUR

From out of a swirling mist of blind panic, Elizabeth emerged into focus. Heath felt her blood pressure drop twenty points. Without a glance at her mother, E slid into a chair at a table near Artie. She took her cell phone from her pocket and laid it on the small round tabletop. Heath's fingers closed around her own phone in the pocket of her brightly embroidered tunic. It took all of her self-control not to snatch it out and text E just to feel some small line of connection.

Tearing her eyes from her daughter, Heath forced herself to continue her search of the people straggling from shops or toward the cinema. Anna's WM3 was stopped at the curb. This man had pervert written all over him, from his baggy-butt pajama bottoms to his beetling brow.

Seemingly from nowhere a dark shape, like that of a black bird of prey stooping on an unwary rabbit, crashed into the man so hard his feet left the ground and he flew sideways several yards. Elizabeth squeaked. Heath might have squeaked herself. It was Walter. God bless him, Heath thought. God bless the boy.

Abandoning his laptop, Artie leapt from his table and went to help E's boyfriend. Elizabeth, per Anna's orders, was remaining seated until the all-clear was sounded, but her eyes were as round as a startled child's as she watched her tormentor exposed and laid out by two men.

Heath hadn't recognized the man. He didn't even look familiar. Such was the virulence of the attacks he'd mounted, so imbued with specific hatred, she'd expected Elizabeth's stalker to have a personal agenda. How could a total stranger develop such an oozing rotten loathing of a lovely young woman he'd never even met?

Then again, they might have met. Perhaps a fleeting exchange in a Best Buy or at a Walgreens. Twisting it in his mind, the man had imagined a relationship. Elizabeth failed to play her part, so he imagined betrayal. Then he plotted revenge.

Relief washed through Heath, weakening her, floating her physical fatigue to the surface. Fortunately, they would soon know why and who. Knowing would lay a lot of ghosts to rest. Knowing would keep Heath, and more importantly E, from wondering if black slime underlay the warm smiles and kind words of friends and acquaintances. Heath doubted knowing would promote understanding. Perverts had a perverted way of looking at the world. In their heart of hearts, they believed everyone would behave as badly as they did if they got the chance. Virtue was only a mask. Reality, the pervert believed, was what he lived.

Before Heath could finish drawing in her sigh of relief, she heard a scream.

"Run!"

Anna was pelting across the green, sprinting toward the coffee shop.

Elizabeth looked up from her cell phone.

"Run!" Anna screamed a second time.

Elizabeth half stood, then sat down again, evidently remembering her orders to stay put.

A short woman in a pink curler cap passed Heath, blocking her view of the men struggling on the lawn.

"The woman!" Anna cried.

Confused, Heath turned toward Elizabeth. The stumpy little figure was stopped at Elizabeth's table, standing so close, E couldn't get up without overturning her chair. A large, shiny, purple tote bag slid from the woman's arm, exposing an enormous paw.

It was a hand in a welding glove. In that hand was a can of what looked like lighter fluid.

Heath was easily ten feet from her daughter. Without thought, she dropped her canes and lunged. The legs Leah had crafted from electronics and metal responded to the sudden weight of her upper body moving forward. Dem Bones propelled her at nearly a run. Torso foremost, metal and hinges activated to their utmost, Heath was hurtling toward Elizabeth's attacker, utterly out of control.

The woman raised the can, pointed the nozzle at Elizabeth, and started to squeeze. E shoved her chair back and tried to rise. Heath slammed past the frumpy woman and careened into Elizabeth. Both of them went down in a tangle of arms, legs, and chairs.

"Whore, Jezebel!" a woman's voice drilled into Heath's back. Sizzling and popping like a firecracker booth going up in flames seared the air. The small of Heath's back began to burn.

A loud thud and the crashing of more chairs cut off the shrieked epithets. "Stay down!" she heard Anna yell. "Stay down,

God damn you."

"It's on me!" A high-pitched scream. "It's on me."

"Artie!" Anna again. And, "Keep her down."

A gasp came from nearby, and then Heath heard a small voice in her ear. "Mom, you're squishing me."

All of her weight and all of her electronics were pinning Elizabeth to the pavement. Heath tried to lever her upper body off, but her arms were shaking, muscles as weak as overcooked pasta. "I can't move," Heath panted. "Push me."

Small strong hands shoved against her shoulders. Heath was raised far enough that she could see her daughter's face. So beautiful. "Are you all right, E?" Heath's voice quavered with tears. Some good she was in a crisis. Dead wailing weight.

"I think so," Elizabeth said uncertainly.

"Help me! It's on my face!" the obscene woman screamed.

Elizabeth pushed Heath until she could roll off. There she lay on her back, helpless as a stranded beetle, the electronic legs still twisted.

Anna moved into the airspace above. "You okay?" she demanded.

"Yes," Heath managed.

"You?"

Heath heard Elizabeth repeat, "I think so."

"What's that smell? What's making that noise?" Anna asked. Elizabeth was sitting up now; Heath could see her if she craned her neck sideways.

"I don't know," E said.

Heath drew in a breath, tasting the air: singed fabric, burning plastic, a biting acridity. She listened to the sizzling crackling noise coming from beneath her. The small of her back burned like fire. Though there was no flame and no smoke, the woman must have managed to ignite the lighter fluid before Anna tackled her. Some of it must have struck Dem Bones' power pack, where it sat across Heath's hips.

Heath sighed. "I think the smell is me on fire. I'm afraid the racket is the sound of a couple hundred thousand dollars' worth of electronics being destroyed."

Anna had her rolled over and her shirt ripped up the back before Heath could say anything else.

"Artie, call an ambulance," Anna said.

"What's burning? Where is it burning?" Elizabeth was asking.

"No fire," Anna said. "Acid. Battery acid is my guess. E, go into the coffee shop and bring as much clean water as you can and scissors or a sharp knife. Do it now, and do it quickly." Heath felt her hips being jerked sideways and heard what sounded like fabric ripping. Facedown, a view of nothing but table legs and an overturned chair, Heath felt helpless.

Nothing made her angrier than feeling helpless.

"Talk to me!" she said through clenched teeth.

Instead of a reply she felt a cold wet cloth drop onto the small of her back. "Dab gently. As much water as you can without dripping. We don't want to spread the stuff," Anna said.

"Got it," E said.

"Artie, see if you can get Cybercreep to shut the hell up and get some water on her face to dilute the acid," Anna said.

"Talk to me or I'm going to bite you!" Heath said.

"Sorry, Mom." E's voice was shaking as bad as Heath's. "The can had battery acid in it. A little got on your skin above Dem Bones. Anna has cut away the shirt and the straps so we can get anything that has acid on it away from your skin. It ate right through your skirt. It's like horror movie special effects. Dem Bones is practically melting. Most of it got on the power pack."

Heath groaned. "There goes your college education."

A wet sobbing litany of "My face, my face, oh no, my face, she wouldn't be pretty without her face, little baby-faced whore, he wouldn't look at her with no face, not my face, no, no . . ." burbled in a monologue from the other side of the table.

"Are the cuffs on?" Anna asked.

"In front, so she can wash her face," Artie said.

"Help me sit up," Heath told Elizabeth. Before E could start to argue, Heath said, "Please," in a tone that was so pathetic she was almost embarrassed to use it to manipulate her only child.

As they'd done a thousand times before, Elizabeth braced her knees to either side of Heath's and, locking wrists, pulled her to a seated position. Once Heath was stable, E moved behind her and knelt, making herself into a living backrest.

Not more than a couple of yards away the woman in the pink curler cap was sitting on the ground, dribbling words and snot as she dabbed at her face with fat little white hands forced closed with silver handcuffs. Acid had splashed onto one of her cheeks and the side of her mouth. The flesh was red and beginning to blister.

522

This mewling miserable creature was the person who had filled E's life with threat and filth, then tried to burn her face off with battery acid.

"Who in the hell is this?" Heath asked.

Anna, who was standing slightly behind the woman talking on her cell phone, reached down without interrupting her conversation and pulled off the curler cap and, with it, a red curly wig.

Blond hair tumbled out. Blue-framed glasses fell from her nose. Heath didn't recognize her, although, through the snot, the blistering, and the smeared, mud-colored lipstick, she did seem familiar.

"Mrs. Edleson?" Elizabeth gasped.

FORTY-FIVE

The adrenaline dumped into Anna's system during the excitement of capturing Elizabeth's cybercreep had drained away. Despite the fact that she had slept a good portion of the day, Anna was so tired she could scarcely breathe. Drugged sleep did not refresh the way natural sleep did. Rather than resting, she felt as if she'd spent those hours in a morass of thick oily dreams and mind-numbing traps from which she could not escape into consciousness.

Hunched over the steering wheel of the patrol car used by erstwhile ranger Denise Castle, Anna was aware of her vision tunneling until all she could see was the red taillights in the lane ahead as she followed the second of two ambulances to Mount Desert Hospital.

In the first, with two female officers from the Bar Harbor Police Department, was Mrs. Sam Edleson, the flesh of half her jaw and lower lip eaten away by the acid she'd intended to use to disfigure Elizabeth. Often the why of a crime remained unknown long after the who, what, when, where, and how had been solved. Not so this time. Regardless of the pain talking must have caused with her ruined lip, Terry Edleson wouldn't shut up about why.

According to her, E had lured poor chinless Sam to the dark side with her wanton ways. So bewitched was Sam that he talked of Elizabeth, raved about her firm young flesh, and spied on her through the hedge between the houses.

Abused himself.

First, goodwife Terry had tried to warn E of the dangers of harlotry by destroying her reputation on the Internet, using pornographic images to shock her into good behavior, as well as to make it clear to Sam just what sort of girl he was obsessed with.

Such was the power Elizabeth held over Sam that he actually liked the pornographic images.

Go figure.

Then came the night when Elizabeth was at the Edleson house, when Tiffany had been sent out with her little brother, the night when Elizabeth had all but forced darling Sam to sexually assault her. That was when Terry realized she had to take it to the next level.

She began making threats.

Even then Elizabeth failed to loose her hold on Sam's libido. A couple of off-duty cops roughed Sam up. A rude "uniformed female" visited Terry in her home. That was the handwriting on the wall, Terry told Anna and the Bar Harbor policewomen, and in big black letters it said ELIZABETH WOULD NEVER LEAVE SAM ALONE.

Unless she was made hideous with acid burns to her face.

When her smooth soft flesh was furrowed and scarred, her gentle mouth melted, her brown fawn eyes white with blindness, then and only then would Sam be free.

At that moment, except for the fact that it was illegal to execute an insane individual, Anna could have wrung Terry's fat little neck with as little remorse as a turkey farmer on Thanksgiving eve.

Breathing deeply, Anna banished the wretched Mrs. Edleson from her mental jurisdiction. If the woman died in the ambulance, her face rotted off, if she went to hell, to prison, or back to Boulder — it was all the same to Anna.

Rohypnol hangover and fatigue ruined her powers of concentration. Fantasies of a long sauna to sweat out the toxins, a massage to unknot the muscles, and a husband's shoulder to lay her head on were about all she was willing to hold in her tattered cerebrum for more than a second or two.

That and the taillights.

The second ambulance, the one Anna followed with such dogged determination, carried Heath, E, and Gwen. The area of Heath's back affected by acid burns was small. Most of the acid had struck Dem Bones' power pack, only a small amount hitting bare skin. Cool water, quickly applied, kept the burns superficial, probably second degree at worst. Anna had no way of knowing what Heath's leaping, lunging, falling, and floundering with chairs and girls and electronic exoskeletons had done to the unfeeling half of her friend's body.

The dual red eyes of the taillights wavered as Anna's eyes watered and strained. Blinking, she pushed her face closer to the windshield. The movement set off the scrapes on her butt and heel, scabs cracking, blood oozing. Considering the possibilities, she'd gotten off lightly. Yesterday's contusions, and the shoulder she'd used to take down Terry Edleson, were the worst of it.

After a miserable eternity, the ambulances

turned off the winding road out of the town of Bar Harbor and into the front lot of Mount Desert Hospital. As hospitals went, Mount Desert was small. Its age and the warm brick facade robbed it of the sterile futility the sight of most hospitals stirred in Anna's breast.

The ambulances pulled up beneath a bright sign reading EMERGENCY. In a fog, Anna nearly rear-ended the vehicle carrying Heath before she realized the flare of tail-lights meant it had stopped. Cursing softly, she backed out, drove around the corner into the dimly lit lot, and parked the borrowed Crown Vic.

Levering herself out of the driver's seat, Anna grunted. Gone were the days she could tackle someone and wrestle them to the ground without paying for it. Tomorrow, no doubt, she would discover a medley of bruises where Terry had managed to get in a few licks before she was subdued.

As she walked back to the emergency room entrance, she nearly bumped into Peter Barnes. Staring up at the towering form blocking out the light, she was momentarily disoriented. "Did I call you?" she asked stupidly.

"No," Peter said, taking her arm as if she needed steadying. "Are you okay?"

"Fine," Anna said. "Who called you?"

"Nobody. Anna, let's go in and sit down, maybe get somebody to look at you." He began steering her into the harsh lights of the ER waiting room. "Lily will be here in a sec. Why don't you tell me how it went tonight with your stalker, why you're here."

Peter was talking in the gentle tones used to calm crazy people, or people too sick to stand any kind of shock.

"It went fairly well," Anna said. His assumption of her frailty annoyed her, but since she couldn't think of anything she'd rather do than sit down for a minute, she let him lead her to a chair.

"Who got hurt?" Peter asked.

"Heath, but not badly, I don't think. The perp has facial burns, fairly severe I hope. The stalker was Elizabeth's best friend's mother. A woman who baked the girls cookies. Her husband had a hard-on for Elizabeth, so his wife trashed her on the Internet. A couple of weeks ago, he tried to molest Elizabeth, and the woman went psycho. Blamed E. Tried to squirt acid in Elizabeth's face."

Anna let her head drop back and closed her eyes against the fluorescent lights.

"But you're not hurt?" Peter insisted.

"You mean in addition to being dead?"

Anna asked.

"Yes, in addition to that." Peter's chuckle, low and throaty, almost like the purr of a cat, washed reassuringly over her.

"Bumps and bruises," she said. "Other than that, nary a scratch."

"Oh my God! What happened to you!" came an exclamation.

She opened her eyes. Lily Barnes.

It finally occurred to her to wonder why, if she hadn't called him, Peter was here, and why Lily was here at all.

"What happened to you?" Anna countered, wincing as she dragged her butt over the plastic, pulling herself up straight in the chair

"Olivia got real sick," Lily said. "Vomiting, diarrhea, then a seizure. God, it was terrifying. The doctor thinks she may have an allergy or ingested something toxic. We've been wracking our brains. Paint on the bassinet? Dog fur? I'm going to have to go over the whole house with a Q-tip."

"Is she okay?" Anna asked, rubbing her eyes. Fine grit scraped across the sclera as if she'd spent the day at a windy beach.

"Yes. She's sleeping. The doctor thinks she'll be fine. They just want to keep her overnight for observation because of the seizure," Lily said. The young woman's brave smile looked ragged around the edges. Sinking down, she settled on the edge of the chair next to Anna. Lily laid her hand gently on Anna's arm and, with seemingly genuine concern, asked, "What happened to you?"

A nurse pushed through the glass double doors on the far side of the waiting room. One of the doors flashed Anna's reflection at her. The mystery of why people kept asking what happened to her was solved. In the fracas, her braid had come undone; her hair was hanging witchlike around a face drawn and white with fatigue. Unused to wearing makeup, she'd rubbed her eyes until they were ringed with black mascara. What lipstick remained on her lips was only in the crevices, like red stitches.

Anna laughed abruptly. "I'm better than I look." She laughed again. A worried frown formed two lines between Peter's dark eyebrows. "No. I'm good," Anna said to put him out of his misery. "Just tired and, obviously, frighteningly disheveled. No new wounds. I'm sorry about poor little Olivia."

"Why don't you stay at our house?" Lily offered. "It's nearly an hour's drive to Schoodic. We have plenty of room."

Anna accepted gratefully. "I'll be over after I check on Heath," Anna said. "I'll try and be quiet."

"Don't worry," Peter said. "I doubt we'll be getting a whole lot of sleep until we have Olivia home safe and sound." A pained expression crossed his face. "I hate to ask . . ." he began.

"Ask," Anna said.

"Denise forgot a model in her office. She bought it when we went to Hawaii once. I was going to drop it by her apartment as a sort of good-bye peace offering. Given the situation, would you mind?"

Anna would, but she didn't have a baby in seizures, and a checkered past with the model's recipient.

"Not a problem."

"You go ahead and find your friend. I'll stick it in your car." Peter took her keys. "I'll leave these at the front desk."

Anna nodded her thanks and went to find Heath.

FORTY-SIX

Denise watched Peter and Lily leaving the hospital. Hand in hand. Enough to make a person want to puke. When Denise and Peter had been together, Peter wouldn't hold hands in public. Too much like a Hallmark card, he said. Big ranger man was self-conscious showing his softer side, he joked. What a load of crap.

Didn't matter. Tonight he was going to lose that softer side. She wasn't after revenge, Denise told herself. The fact that Peter would suffer was just a perk. Denise was all about justice.

The radio she'd conveniently forgotten to return to the NPS when she retired lay on the passenger seat. She looked from Peter Barnes to the radio. All day she'd had the thing on, waiting for the shit storm about the missing Anna Pigeon to hit the airwaves. Nothing. Either nobody noticed the pigeon's comings and goings or they weren't talking about it. Maybe they booted it upstairs and were quietly waiting for the FBI to come and save their collective ass. Denise didn't believe that. The NPS considered itself the search-and-rescue experts. They would have mounted a search. Everybody would have been on the radio all day to show how important they were.

Never mind, Denise told herself. Not her problem. Silence was golden.

After the adorable Mr. and Mrs. Barnes had driven out of the parking lot, Denise punched a number into her disposable cell phone and waited. Three rings. Four. What was Paulette doing that was so important she couldn't answer the goddam phone?

"Hello," came a whisper in Denise's ear.

"Time to take a smoke break," Denise said. "Bring a face mask, hairnet, and one of those sterile coat thingies." She punched the END CALL button without waiting for her sister's response.

From various trips to Mount Desert Hospital on EMT business, and, once, to have her tonsils out — a thing like mumps or measles, a real bitch when you were an adult — Denise had a fairly good idea of the layout. What she needed from Paulette was specific locations of patients, things that were fluid and couldn't be easily predicted.

That, and where there were cameras, if there were any.

Ten minutes later by the dashboard clock in the new SUV, Paulette finally saw fit to emerge from the rear door of the hospital beside the Dumpster. In the wan light of the single security bulb, she looked around furtively, the items Denise had asked for clutched to her breast. Even in pink teddy-bear scrubs she managed to look as guilty as hell.

"Holy shit," Denise breathed. Paulette had to be kept out of any kind of heat that might be generated by this night. She probably lacked the capacity to lie about her age or weight, let alone a felony murder and all the rest.

Denise tried to tell herself that this was good, this was the honest half of herself, this was her innocence lost, but she wasn't buying it. Paulette needed to grow a back-bone if they were going to have a good life together. At least for the first couple of years. After that they could let down a little, relax, and enjoy themselves.

Finally deciding the coast was clear, Paulette trotted toward the Volvo.

Denise leaned across the console and pushed the passenger door open. Paulette climbed in. "What are we doing? Oh my gosh! Look at you! In scrubs and the new hair color you could be me." She laughed.

Paulette had a lovely childlike laugh. Denise smiled, feeling better for the moment. They looked more alike. That meant they were more alike. It was the ravages of the world that had driven them apart, even in Denise's mind. This felt better. Them laughing. Or at least, Paulette laughing.

"Did you come to show me the new outfit?" Paulette asked.

Annoyance returned.

Like she'd call her out of the hospital in the middle of the night when the world was about to stop spinning to show off her new hair and matching scrubs. The ignorance wasn't Paulette's fault. Denise's decision not to share tonight's activities with her sister had been a hard but necessary one. She wouldn't change her mind now.

"No," Denise answered, and was proud at how upbeat and normal she sounded. "There's one last thing I have to do before we can —" She started to say, "Leave this shithole," but that, too, was not something Paulette needed to know at this point. "Get on with things," she finished.

This next part was key to her plan working well. Without it, the plan would still work, but it would be a good deal riskier.

536

"Are there any women in the maternity ward who have babies, born babies, I mean, not fetuses?" she asked, trying for nonchalance and managing only monotone.

"There's Mrs. Frazier in 307," Paulette said. Then, "Oh no! You don't mean to take that poor woman's baby! She was in labor for twenty-two hours. The baby is only a day old. Not that it matters how old she is. Honey, I love you for thinking how much I wanted a baby, and I did, but you can't take her baby."

"No, no, nothing like that," Denise lied. "I just wanted to know if you had extra duties or anything that would keep you away from the infant care ward."

"No. Mother and baby are resting comfortably," Paulette said, parroting a phrase she'd heard the real nurses use, Denise assumed.

"There's a camera at the ER doors and one on the nurses' station on the second floor that I know about," Denise said. "Are there any others?"

Paulette thought about that for a moment, then ticked a list off on her fingers. "There is one at the main entrance. One in ICU. One in the infant care observation room. I don't know about the adult rooms on the first or third floor. There aren't any in the patient rooms — patients don't like that. None in the operating rooms or halls — the doctors don't like that. I think that's all. Maybe one in the pharmacy, but I don't know for sure. I've never seen it. Why? Denise, what are you going to do?"

"Where is the infant care observation room?" Denise asked.

"Second floor, between the nurses' station and the stairs. Why? Denise, tell me what you're going to do." Paulette was demanding. That was new. Though she'd wanted her sister to show a little spunk, Denise didn't like it.

"Nothing scary," Denise said. "Tying off a few loose ends."

"Do I have to do anything?" Paulette asked. "I wouldn't like to do anything that would be against doctors' orders or hospital policy."

Denise stifled a sigh of exasperation. This part would soon be over. From then on it would be smooth sailing. "Not a thing," she assured her sister. "All you have to do is stay near the nurses' station where you will be on camera for an hour or so."

"I can't just hang around. People will wonder. I have work to do," Paulette whined.

Whined.

Denise couldn't believe it. They were on the cusp of their new life, with all the things they'd always wanted, and her twin — her twin, for Christ's sake — was whining about what people might think.

"Just stay there, or go to the ER, or find an excuse to go to the main entrance foyer. All that matters is that you stay on camera so you can prove where you were."

"What are you going to do?" Paulette asked again. Tears welled up in her eyes, green and glowing in the light of the dashboard, lending them the sinister effect of eyeballs floating in a poison soup.

"I'm going to save a life," Denise said. "Don't forget to wedge open the door." She handed Paulette an old flip-flop she'd purloined from Paulette's closet. Planning was everything. Rushing was an invitation to disaster. Too bad one seldom got a choice.

She waited until Paulette was back inside the building, then waited five more minutes to give her time to reach the nurses' station. Having squirmed into the sterile yellow paper jacket, Denise used the lighted mirror on the back of the sun visor to tuck all of her hair beneath the hairnet — a white paper cap — then put the face mask on, securing the straps firmly behind her ears and pulling the cap down until not so much as a lobe showed.

She'd overthought this portion of the plan. Cameras wouldn't matter. The fact that she was identical to Candy Striper Paulette Duffy wouldn't matter. The sterile gear hid her identity far better than the Lone Ranger's mask hid his. Surgical gloves finished her preparations. She let herself out of the Volvo, beeped it locked, and walked toward the back door of the hospital.

Denise retrieved the flip-flop Paulette had used to keep the door from closing, tossed it into the Dumpster, and slipped inside. The fire escape stairs were as expected: metal treads, pipe hand-railing, concrete floor and walls and ceiling, no windows, dim lighting, and devoid of human life. Like most people, nurses avoided physical effort in even its most modest guises. Moving quietly, she climbed to the second floor. Opening the heavy metal door an inch, Denise peeked out.

Nothing but a long hallway with doors to either side. Some were open, the light from televisions and reading lamps spilling out along with the desultory murmur of TV shows. A nurse carrying a tray with half a dozen miniature paper cups, the kind hospitals put meds in, walked past the semicircular desk where two other nurses sat, eyes on computer monitors. As far as Denise could see, Paulette had been telling the truth. There were no cameras at either end of the hallway, just a single round black eye pointing at the space in front of the desk. Halfway between the fire stairs and the nurses' station, just as Paulette had said, was a large window beside a glass door.

The observation room.

For no apparent reason, Denise's foot shot out, smacking into the door with a hollow thud. The nurse with the tray of pills stopped. She looked back over her shoulder as if she'd heard. Holding her breath, Denise waited, afraid to move the door even the half inch it would take to close it. Finally the woman shrugged and went about her business.

No worry, no worry, Denise chanted silently. Hospitals had to be full of things that went bump in the night. Bedpans falling, patients banging on their bed rails, doctors dropping wads of cash on the polished floors, interns fornicating in broom closets. Maybe that was only on television; still, hospitals had to have noises.

No worry.

Denise stood stock-still until her breathing slowed, then silently closed the door and began to ascend the steps. Between the second and the third floors was a smell of cigarette smoke. Midstride, she halted. A nurse or doctor too lazy to walk down to the parking lot might have stepped into the fire stairs for a quick puff. Denise waited for the sound of an inhalation, a butt hitting the floor, a door opening or closing. Nothing.

The smoke smelled stale. Maybe it was from earlier, even a day or more earlier. Cat piss had nothing on cigarette smoke when it came to the staying power of the odor. That was a habit Paulette was going to have to break.

Denise did a quick peek around the bend in the stair. No smoking gun. She crept up to the third floor and opened the door a crack for surveillance.

The door closest to the fire escape, from where Denise watched, had a square metal plate with the number 311 on it in black numerals. If the numbers followed the rule of even on one side and odd on the other, 307 would be four doors down and to the right.

The hallway was empty. Denise's fingers scampered over her face and head, reassuring her that the mask and hairnet were in place. They were. Forcing herself not to walk too fast or too slow, Denise went down the hall, noting the numbers on the doors. Room 307 was where it was supposed to be. No light showed from the little rectangular window in the door. Peeking in, Denise could see it was a private room. This was good. Retirement was making her stupid; she hadn't thought what she'd do if it was a double. It wasn't. This was a sign this was meant to happen.

In the single bed was a woman-sized lump limned by the pink of a nightlight. Between the woman and the door was a low crib bed. In it was an infant lying on its belly, a hand no bigger than a quarter spread like a starfish on its cheek. Denise took a deep breath, stepped briskly in, gathered up the infant, turned, and stepped briskly out.

"Point of no return," she whispered as she carried the baby toward the stairs.

The new mom hadn't woken. The child didn't scream.

All good. All signs this was meant to happen.

FORTY-SEVEN

Heath's burns had been dressed, and, as Anna had surmised, they weren't severe. There was bruising of her lower limbs, and a hairline fracture of her left shin. Both her palms were skinned and one finger broken. Given the night's events, all of them had gotten off lightly.

Anna should have taken her leave after the reassuring results of Heath's exam were delivered, but she'd stayed on, feeling a sense of comfort in the company of Heath, Elizabeth, and Gwen. When she'd been younger — like last week — she'd craved solitude and silence, the peace of wide open spaces and infinite sky. Now the small room, crowded with people she cared about, all alive, all warm, fed, and sheltered, wrapped comfortingly around her like a soft blanket.

A loud click announcing the opening of the door startled Anna's eyes open. She had dozed off in the chair beside Heath's bed. A nurse in pale green scrubs stuck her head in. Maybe a hospital shift change; Anna hadn't seen this woman before. She was in her fifties with small, brown, very bright eyes in a narrow lined face. Frowning, she glanced around the room.

"What is it?" Gwen asked.

"Nothing, not a thing," the nurse said. "Sorry to bother you." She pulled her head back and closed the door softly.

"Odd," Gwen said.

"She probably can't remember where she left her last patient," Elizabeth said. "That or visiting hours are over."

"Visiting hours have been over for a while," Heath said.

"Then why —" E began. Heath raised her eyebrows and tilted her head toward Gwen. "Right," E said. "It's who you know."

"I've been thinking, it's going to be weird seeing Tiff," E said after a moment. "After us getting her mom arrested and what not, I don't think we can really be friends anymore. I mean, how would that work?"

"It probably wouldn't," Anna said. "Too much blood under the bridge."

"Too bad," Heath said. "Tiffany is a nice girl. None of this is her fault or," she said, looking pointedly at her daughter, "yours."

"I know," E said. "Even though I know it,

it feels like I could have done *something.*"

No one argued with her. Anna felt as if there must have been something she could have done or seen or sensed that would have kept things from going as far as they had. Only the fact that Elizabeth wasn't in ICU, blinded with severe acid burns to her face, kept her from dwelling on what might have been.

"What will happen to Mrs. Edleson?" Elizabeth asked Anna.

"She'll be charged with assault — not just attempted; the acid got on Heath. That's a charge she'll have to face here in Maine, I expect. It was Maine law she broke. As for the cyberbullying, I'm not sure if there are statutes in place for that in Colorado or Maine state law. It's my guess she'll get a slap on the wrist. Community service. I doubt she'll do any jail time. If she does, I expect it will only be sixty days or so. If she gets a halfway decent lawyer, he will plead her out with time served and probation. Maybe an order not to go within X number of feet of you or your home."

"Not fair!" E cried.

"Life is not fair," Heath said. "Who knew?"

Gwen laughed.

Again the door to the room was opened.

In hospitals no one knocks. This time it was a security guard, easily over sixty and overweight. Anna hadn't seen any security around the building or the ER when she'd arrived. Maybe he came on for the night shift.

" 'Scuse me, ladies," he said, smiling an apology for the interruption. "I hate busting in on you like this. I just need to take a look in your bathroom."

"Sure," Heath said. In silence they watched him waddle to the bathroom, open the door, and look in. He did the same with the tiny closet.

"What's going on?" Gwen asked.

"Nothing for you to worry about," he said. "Good night." And he was gone.

Gwen got up and smoothed down the front of her blouse. "I'm going to find out what the fuss is about. Anybody want me to bring them back anything? Coffee? Coke?"

Nobody wanted any more caffeine.

"It is getting late," Heath said to Anna. "I think you've saved the world enough times today. Why don't you go home? You look worse than I feel."

"I'm good," Anna said automatically.

"I'm staying," Elizabeth said.

Anna managed a smile. Elizabeth had been attacked by the neighbor lady, shamed before her entire high school, and probably lost her best friend in the bargain, but she was happy. Her joy showed through the layers of concern she had for her mother and for Anna. By E's lights, Walter was the handsome prince on the white horse who had slain her personal dragon. Never mind that Walter had mowed down an innocent man, and managed to lure Artie away from his post, or that her mother had taken a splash of acid meant for Elizabeth, or that Anna had smashed her shoulder and elbow all to hell taking down Terry Edleson.

The cybercreep was out of Elizabeth's life, and a beautiful boy was in it. God was in his heaven and all was right with her world.

Anna wouldn't have had it any other way.

Gwen popped back into the room. "Nothing to be alarmed about," she said. "A baby has been misplaced. It will turn up. They always do." Stifling a yawn, the older woman sank down on the foot of Heath's bed.

"None of you need to stay any longer," Heath said firmly. "We're all worn out. You were snoring, Anna."

"I don't snore," Anna said.

"Hah!" E snorted.

Heath rolled her eyes. "You have taught my child to snort," she accused Anna.

"I taught myself to snort! Anyway, I don't

snort," E insisted.

"I'm staying," Gwen said. "Hospitals aren't much about caring for patients anymore. They are about following doctors' orders and medical protocols. Without an advocate, a patient gets about as much TLC as you might expect if we abandoned you under an overpass."

"I'm staying, too," E said.

Anna rubbed her eyes with her fists, smearing more mascara around. Nothing remained for her to do but sleep. "Okay, I'm for bed. If you need me, I'll be at Peter and Lily's."

As she tried to shove herself up from the plastic chair, the shoulder of the arm that had taken a bullet during the Fox River misadventure, the one she'd used to slam Terry Edleson to the ground, locked up. Squeaking, she held herself halfway out of the chair, unable to get up, unable to lower herself back down. "Damn," she said as Elizabeth and Gwen leapt up to help her.

Standing, she shook out her arms. "Good as new," she said, balling her hand into a fist to prove everything was working.

"Get that shoulder X-rayed," Gwen said.

"It's not broken," Anna insisted. "Just banged up."

She had no intention of spending the rest

of the night being alternately pestered and ignored by a bunch of people in scrubs. Straightening her back, she walked to the door without limping, wincing, or whimpering. Success beyond her wildest expectations. Fortunately they were on the first floor and not far from the main doors. Anna picked up her keys at the registration desk, then made it to the parking lot without scaring any children with her likeness to a zombie, or attracting unwanted attention from medical personnel.

Having unlocked the Crown Vic, she crawled into the darkness of the rear seat and closed the door. In the privacy of the cramped chamber she managed to escape from the long-tailed shirt. The Velcro straps of her borrowed Kevlar vest — E had worn hers — released with a satisfying ripping sound. Sighing, she let the thing fall to the seat beside her. Beneath the vest, her tank top was soaked with sweat.

For several minutes she sat reveling in freedom from the Kevlar and the grating fluorescent lights of the hospital. Fluorescent lights made Anna feel brittle and tired. Someday scientists would undoubtedly discover the light penetrated flesh and corroded bone matter. Rubbing the ache in her shoulder, she tried to remember whether or not she'd seen a bathtub at Peter and Lily's. A long hot bath would be a passable stand-in for the sauna, the massage, and the husband.

Once she felt sufficiently recovered to drive the six miles to the Barneses' house, she gathered her courage.

For decency's sake, she put on the shirt and fastened a few buttons. Traversing from the rear seat to the front to climb behind the wheel wasn't as easy as she'd pictured it. Finally in place, she closed her eyes and leaned her head back against the headrest for a moment.

"I'm getting too old for this shit," she whispered. Opening her eyes, she saw the item she was to deliver before she could go to bed. A two-foot-long model of a Hawaiian outrigger canoe was sitting on the passenger seat. "And miles to go before I sleep." She groaned and turned on the ignition.

The way to the Barneses' home led back through Bar Harbor, then to the east a quarter of a mile before the road forked, the western fork crossing the narrow land bridge connecting Mount Desert Island to the mainland. Denise's apartment complex was on the way. Anna slowed as she drove by. A light showed in the upstairs apartment where she'd changed into Denise's clothes for the first fruitless attempt at the cyber-creep.

Denise's little green Miata wasn't in evidence in the parking spaces beneath the complex. A white Volvo had taken its place. Anna snugged the Crown Vic neatly, and illegally, behind the Volvo. Her errand would only take a second. Even if the car didn't belong to Denise, she should be back to move the Crown Vic before anyone needed to leave the complex.

On her first two visits the stairs had made no impression on Anna: short, one level, a romp in the park. This trip she felt all thirteen. Good deeds were never a good idea. Leaning against the doorframe of Denise's apartment, she knocked, then rang the doorbell. A long silence followed. Relief crept in. Anna wasn't up for even the short exchange of "This is yours" and "You're welcome."

"Who is it?" Denise's voice came from behind the door.

"It's me," Anna said.

There was no peephole.

Feeling foolish, Anna opened her mouth to announce herself properly, but "me" must have been sufficient. Anna heard the slide of bolts and the rattle of a door chain.

The knob turned, and the door swung open.

Paulette Duffy stood in the spill of light, her blond hair falling around her face, her pink scrubs rumpled, the front stained, a silver laptop computer held at her side. Anna stared stupidly. Paulette gaped at Anna in absolute shock, mouth open, lips pulled back showing nice, neat front teeth.

Pieces fell like bricks through Anna's mind and into place: the photo by the bed of a younger Denise before she'd gotten the overlapping front teeth fixed, Mrs. Duffy's blond hair, identical twins, Huntington's disease, the uncontrolled movements of chorea, short-term memory loss. Mood swings.

This was Denise. Denise was the other twin.

In the instant it took for this to flash through Anna's mind, she realized that Denise might have murdered Kurt Duffy while Paulette was establishing her alibi in the Acadian Lounge, and here Anna had come gimping up the stairs in the middle of the night with no weapon, no backup, no vest, and no radio.

"Hey, Denise," Anna said. "Love the hair. Peter said you'd left this in your office." She held up the canoe in both hands.

"Thank you," Denise said. She didn't

reach out for the canoe.

Anna took a step back.

From within the apartment came the high gasping wail of a baby crying.

Denise swung the laptop at Anna's head. Reflexively, Anna threw up her arms, using the canoe to deflect the blow. Her shoulder locked. The laptop smashed through the thin balsa wood, shattering the model, to strike her above her eye where the knot from her last head trauma had yet to begin to heal.

"You're dead" was the last thing Anna heard.

When she regained consciousness, or what she assumed might be consciousness, she was blind. She tried to open her mouth to scream, but it was sealed shut. Struggling, she tried to figure out where one arm started and the other left off. A soft smelly pillow was hot against her chest. Her legs had been welded into a single unit, like the tail of a mermaid.

"Stay still or you'll kill her."

The whisper was close. Without eyes, Anna couldn't tell if the whisperer was in front of her or behind her. "Denise?" she said. What came to her ears was a muffled "Hunhh?" Duct tape, or something very like, had been put over her mouth. Probably her eyes as well. She could feel the pull on her eyelids when she tried to open them.

"In your arms is a baby. If you fall down, or fight, or do anything except exactly what I tell you to, you might crush her. You might asphyxiate her. You might snap her little neck." As directionless as fog, as sibilant as wind in the eaves, the whisper rasped around Anna. "You might jam your chin through the soft spot in her skull and get baby brains in your mouth."

Words hissing in her ears, Anna became aware of the life she held in her arms. The smell was a dirty diaper, the heat a tiny body, the softness the rounded contours of an infant. Lowering her head, she felt downy hair tickle the underside of her chin. This had to be the baby Gwen had so airily assured them would turn up. Denise had taken it.

Ransom? Anna wondered. Was the child the child of a rich person? Auction the little creature off to a barren couple, or sex traffickers? It seemed a bit ambitious for a retired park ranger. Kidnapping was America's least favorite sport. Hard to pull off, severe penalties, and a live product: Anna doubted law enforcement officers would risk it. At least not sane law enforcement officers.

Denise Castle might not be entirely sane. Huntington's could cause mental disorders; Gwen had said that. If Huntington's mixed with regular craziness, the results might be bizarre.

Peter Barnes had spoken of how Denise looked at Lily, how she looked at Olivia, how she reacted to the mention of her previous home. Was the baby some kind of compensation for losing her relationship?

Did it matter?

Not much, Anna thought. What mattered was the life duct-taped in her arms. If there was life.

There was no movement. If the baby breathed, she couldn't hear it. Had she crushed it already? Squeezed the little rib cage until the baby couldn't draw breath? While unconscious, had she folded over and smothered the child? Darkness greater than blindness gripped Anna. Her heart grew cold and still. Her hands, each taped tightly to the opposite elbow to provide a cradle for the infant, were useless but for the little finger on her left hand. She could bend that one. Denise had missed it in her wrapping. Gingerly, Anna poked the baby. It didn't move or cry. She poked it again harder.

Feeble squirming, then tiny baby feet kicked into her damaged joint, making it throb. "Thankyoubabyjesus," she meant to say. "Mmmghhh" was what reached the air. Anna allowed her heart to recommence beating.

Craning her neck until her shoulder knifed her in the back in self-defense, Anna managed to nuzzle the infant's face. The baby's mouth was not duct-taped shut. Anna allowed herself a meager trickle of relief. At least the child would be able to breathe as long as Anna could keep her exhausted muscles from collapsing and squashing the poor thing.

"I'm going to cut the tape on your ankles," the whisper said. "You're going to get up and walk quietly where I tell you to." The tip of a sharp object poked into Anna's cheek under her right eye. "If you are not absolutely compliant, I will poke out this eye, then the other, and so on. Nothing I do can be bad because you are a dead pigeon, and dead pigeons have no rights. If you understand, nod your head."

The prick of flesh beneath her eye receded. Anna nodded. Strands of hair were plucked from her head. Her hair had been taped down along with her eyelids and arms, effectively pinioning her head in one place. An image of Gulliver, surrounded by mallet-wielding Lilliputians, his head staked to the ground by his hair, flashed through her mind. The benefits of a reading life, she thought absurdly.

Again she nodded, more firmly this time. Maybe there was some slippage. Maybe she could trade hanks of hair for greater movement. Something to keep in mind.

A hand insinuated itself beneath her left elbow, where it was taped tightly to her ribs. "Up," the voice breathed. The hand pulled. Anna floundered to her knees, mindful of not crushing the baby, of not losing her balance and falling on it, while the voice — Denise Castle's, she assumed — continued popping, "Up, up, you. Get up. Up."

Without sight, the Rohypnol remaining in her system, combined with fatigue and shock, compromised Anna's balance, making her unsteady on her feet, unsure where this "up" was. Her inner ear insisted she was listing to starboard, but when she tried to compensate, she was jerked the other direction by the hand beneath her elbow.

"You hurt that baby and you're dead meat," Denise said, full voice this time.

Anna shuffled her feet further apart, centering her weight carefully around her spine. The sense of toppling to one side diminished. Palpable mist slid over her skin. Anna staggered back.

"It's just a shawl, you stupid bitch. Stand still," Denise ordered. The shawl was arranged around Anna's face. A few more hairs were plucked from her head as Denise tucked the fabric around her arms and the child held in them.

"You are going to be a good little pigeon. Don't even think of trying to fly the coop or make any kind of noise. If you do, you could fall down the stairs and kill the baby," Denise said.

Hands landed hard on Anna's shoulders, sending a crippling wave of agony down her side. The hands propelled her forward. The baby began a thin wail.

"Then your eyes would be gouged out and there'd be no more of your peeking and pecking," Denise said as she turned Anna to the left. They stopped. There was the sound of a door shutting. "Keep that baby quiet."

Again Denise was muttering. They must be out of the apartment, in the hall.

"Stairs," Denise said.

With Denise muttering, "Step, step, step," Anna felt her way down, relying on the hand under her elbow for balance.

Thirteen, Anna counted in her head. They

were down in the parking area.

"You can't make anything easy, can you?" Denise growled.

Hands fumbled at Anna's crotch, and she wondered if she was being sexually assaulted, but Denise was only digging the keys to the Crown Vic out of her pocket.

A beep, then Denise poked, prodded, and cursed Anna and her burden into the seat of a car. By the height of it, Anna guessed it was the white SUV parked where the Miata had been on her first visit.

"Stay," Denise ordered. "Or you're dead."
You're dead.

Denise had said that the instant before Anna lost consciousness from the blow to her head with the laptop. It hadn't been a threat; it had been a statement. When Denise first opened the door, her face had gone slack with shock at the sight of Anna.

That was when the scene with the ghost of Hamlet's father should have played out. Anna's one shot at acting in a Shakespeare play and she'd blown it.

No one but Heath's family and Peter knew Anna had been "killed." Denise had gone pale because she believed Anna was dead. Ergo Denise had been the one to dump her body into the sea. Denise and

Paulette. Walter had seen two people in the boat.

Anna felt the shoulder strap slide across her arms, pushing the baby more tightly against her chest. A click let her know her seat belt was fastened. Since Denise had killed her once, thrown her into the ocean, then knocked her unconscious and taped her up like a mummy, this nod to safety had to be about the baby. Denise wanted the baby safe, her talk of Anna killing it notwithstanding. The baby was what was important.

Anna was just being moved from point A to point B. Never a good thing for a victim. Point B was always nastier than point A. Once they were there, Anna could be disposed of without interference. That was the reason point B held such an attraction for kidnappers, rapists, and murderers.

The baby continued to whine.

Anna wished she'd called Paul before she'd left the island, wished she had taken the first plane home, never stopped to do her good deed for the day, wished the child would stop crying, while at the same time taking comfort in the fact that it had sufficient air with which to cry.

"Hmm, hmm," she crooned, and brushed the infant's head with her duct-taped lips. The baby wailed louder, its fragile skin abraded by the rough tape.

The driver's door opened. "All set?" Denise asked as if she and Anna were going on a routine campground patrol.

Not knowing what else to do, Anna nodded as much as her netting of hair would allow, then a bit more, hoping to loosen the tape.

"Good," Denise said. Denise had been gone less than two minutes; she had to have put the NPS patrol car in another of the parking spaces beneath the rental units. If the apartment the slot was assigned to was occupied, it would be found as soon as the renter came home and wanted to park. If the apartment was vacant, it could be days. Still, Peter and Lily were expecting Anna. Peter knew where she'd been going. When she didn't show in an hour or two, he'd come looking. He'd find the car.

That was something.

Being on the move seemed to soothe Denise. Gone were the hissing and the hurrying. Anna heard mirrors being adjusted, a seat belt fastened, the engine coming to life. The SUV backed out of the narrow space. Off to point B.

Had Anna decided to set a trap to catch herself, she couldn't have done it more thoroughly. She was alone, unarmed, injured, fog-brained, and had delivered herself into the hands of a deranged kidnapper. The proverbial handwriting had not merely been on the wall, it had been all but tattooed across Anna's forehead. Denise liked to dive at night. Denise had a boat at her disposal. Denise had refused to be seen near Paulette the morning after the murder, was paranoid about Anna being in her apartment, reacted bizarrely when Anna had asked about the photograph where her teeth were identical to Paulette's, showed the same chorea as Paulette Duffy.

Shaking her head, Anna groaned.

"Okay?" Denise asked.

Anna nodded.

The distraction of the cybercreep had kept her from paying attention to what was going on in the park, the park she'd been brought in to help protect and preserve. Instead, she'd played hooky, worked on personal issues, and one of the rangers nominally under her supervision had gotten away with the attempted murder of Anna and, probably, the actual murder of Paulette's husband.

Almost, Anna felt she deserved what she was getting, what she was going to get when Denise reached point B.

Almost.

FORTY-EIGHT

"We're here," Denise announced.

Here, Anna knew, was between fifteen and thirty minutes by car from Denise's apartment. First, Anna guessed, they were headed to Paulette's house, but they didn't go into a house. They went into the woods. Pine needles slithered underfoot as they walked the last hundred yards or so, and the smell of sap was strong in the night air. They were in a shed or garage, Anna surmised. She'd heard the unmistakable sound of a padlock being unlocked.

"Sit," Denise ordered.

Blind, a baby bound to her chest, the best Anna could do was get to her knees and sit back on her heels. Duct tape made for secure bondage. Little of Anna remained mobile.

"God," Denise fumed. "You're such a pain in the ass."

A hand pushed hard on Anna's shoulder,

toppling her onto her side. To keep the child from harm, Anna took the full weight of the fall on the point of her left shoulder. Her face was ground into rough carpet as her legs were pulled out of their bend. The baby began to cry, a few decibels higher and angrier than its ongoing pitiful mewling.

Ripping sounds filled Anna's ears; then she felt her legs being taped together again, once at the ankles and once at the knees. Clearly, Denise had a higher opinion of Anna's threat level than Anna did. She doubted she could best a fly even if she had a swatter and a head start.

"There," Denise declared, when Anna was trussed up again. "Sit up."

Struggling like a landed fish, Anna tried to bring her torso up to right angles with her legs. She failed.

An exaggerated sigh heralded the coming assistance. Hands slid under her shoulders and pushed her up.

"This will hurt," Denise said.

Since a significant portion of Anna hurt, she hardly winced as Denise carefully pulled the tape off of her eyes.

"Won't have to get those brows waxed for a couple years," Denise said.

Her face was so close it was all Anna could see, and it was out of focus.

"No reason you can't talk," Denise said. "You can even scream if you want. Nobody will hear you." Crouching in front of Anna, Denise gently worked the duct tape free of Anna's mouth.

Drool ran from her newly freed lips and dripped on the baby's head. Air, constrained by fear and pinched nostrils, rushed in through Anna's mouth. She felt her chest expand against the tight wrapping of tape and the soft bundle of life she held in her arms.

"Better?" Denise asked, her head cocked to one side like that of an alert Chihuahua.

"Yes," Anna said. "Thanks." Absurd as it was, Anna was genuinely grateful for these small kindnesses. Beggars couldn't be choosers, but they could show gratitude for the scraps given them.

As Anna's eyes cleared of tears from the stinging removal of the tape, the room that coalesced around her was not what she had expected from her garage or shed theory. Lit only by the light of a single kerosene lantern was a room built of rough wood. The curtains on the windows were open, showing a warm sunny forest outside. They weren't windows, she realized dazedly, but mullions and frames over a painting of a summer forest scene. A crib with a stuffed bear in it sat in the corner. Beside it were a child's tiny chair and a potty-training toilet

Denise had brought her — and the baby — to a nursery.

"Nice, isn't it?" Denise sat down in a rocking chair with low arms and looked around the small space with obvious pride. "It's a shame we won't get to use it. We'll have to build another just like it at our new place. It could be like a playhouse."

Despite the kindly light of the kerosene lamp, Anna's captor's face looked drawn and pale. The youthful glow the blond hair lent her had faded.

"Tired," Denise said, as if affirming Anna's thought. Dragging her hand down over her face, fingers pressing gently on her eyelids, she mimicked a gesture that Anna equated with the living closing the eyes of the dead.

A thousand questions boiled in Anna's mind with such fury that she couldn't get any to separate themselves from the maelstrom to form words. Her palms, each fastened tightly to the opposite forearm to make a basket for the infant, were growing numb. She could no longer feel the child breathing, but, with her eyes uncovered, she could see the tiny baby she held. Snot bubbled out of a nose as small and soft as a peony petal. The crying had stopped. Now the child looked up into Anna's face with vaguely trusting gray-blue eyes.

"You took the baby from the woman in the hospital," Anna said to Denise. Her voice cracked from a throat so dry Anna could barely swallow. Without being asked, Denise got up, crossed to a shelf, and took out a bottle of water from half a dozen stored there. There were also several army surplus MREs, the kind Anna hadn't seen for years, and two pairs of handcuffs. Anna looked longingly at the cuffs. After her time in duct tape, they looked positively humane.

"Sort of took the woman's baby, but not exactly," Denise said, unscrewing the cap on the water bottle. She held it while Anna drank. Water was a fluid of many magical properties. Anna's throat opened; her mind perked up; hope flickered where the water left its trail of strength.

"What do you mean sort of?" Anna asked. "How do you sort of take a baby?"

Denise smirked as she regained her seat in the rocker. "That isn't the baby you think it is. Guess who you're holding?"

Anna stared down into the baby's face. To her, all babies looked pretty much alike. This one was pink and round with a blank little face and wide open eyes. Why would she be expected to know this baby?

Disparate facts, stored in unrelated places in her cerebrum, began to flock together like blackbirds into a pine tree: Paulette Duffy, an infant care LPN, Peter and Denise together, Peter and Denise apart, Lily and Olivia, Denise's sudden retirement, Olivia mysteriously ill and transported to the hospital where Duffy worked.

"Peter Barnes's baby," Anna said.

"My baby," Denise flared. "Olivia. What a stupid name. We'll give her a better one."

"Olivia wasn't the baby that went missing," Anna said.

"Hah!" Denise leaned forward, her elbows on her knees so her face was on a level with Anna's. "The camera over the door in the infant care observation room is pointed at the crib. I walked in, back to the camera, carrying one baby, backed out, still not facing the camera, with another baby. Peter doesn't even know his child has gone missing. That's how much he cares about her. Do you think the baby should have water?" Denise asked, her face suddenly worried.

"Probably, but done up like she is, I'm afraid she would choke. Don't you want to hold her?" That was a question new mothers and grandmothers asked Anna. For some reason, women were supposed to want to hold infants. If Denise was among them, maybe Anna would be given an opportunity to do . . . well, some damn thing.

For a long moment, Denise sat, chin in hands, elbows on knees, studying Anna and the baby. "I don't want to hold it," she admitted at last. Anna didn't think Denise was talking to her so much as thinking out loud. "I thought I would. I really thought it would be like when my sister and I realized we were two parts of a whole. But when I carried the baby out of the hospital and didn't feel much, I figured it was because things were so, you know, tense. Then back at my apartment all she did was cry. I tried holding her, doing the rocking thing. She kept on crying. She didn't feel like a part of me, not like Paulette, more like a fish trying to flop its way out of a soggy newspaper."

"Babies aren't for everybody," Anna said sympathetically. "No big deal. I never went much for babies. Tell you what, nobody knows she's gone. We could take her back and nobody would be the wiser."

Denise straightened up. She actually appeared to be considering the suggestion, and Anna felt a tiny spark of hope.

Then Denise shook her head. "No," she said firmly. "The closeness will come. It will just take a while."

"Why don't you cut the tape so we can let her out of my arms? Then at least she can have water," Anna said.

"Soon," Denise promised. "If Paulette comes back from work and everything is hunky-dory, we won't need you for a hostage. Then we'll leave, and in a few hours, I'll send an anonymous message saying where you are and that will be that. No muss, no fuss."

Anna doubted she would be left alive. In their previous encounter, Denise had proved to be an individual who chose not to strain the quality of mercy in any meaningful way. A bullet to the back of the head or a one-way night dive was more likely.

Again Denise wiped her face, fingertips pressing on her eyelids. Anna took the opportunity to see if she could bite the duct tape closest to her chin. She couldn't, not without crushing the baby.

"I know Paulette is your sister," Anna said.

Denise laughed. "My identical twin sister." Shaking her head, she smiled to herself. "I'm still having trouble believing it's true. Too good to be true usually isn't."

"Oh, it's true," Anna said. "I know a lot about your family."

Denise had lifted the water bottle she'd used to give Anna a drink partway to her mouth. Her arm froze, suspending it midway between the chair's arm and her face. Her eyes narrowed. It didn't take a psychic to see the aura of paranoia and suspicion that darkened her visage. Paranoia: That was one of the symptoms Gwen had mentioned for Huntington's. Committing murder could make a person a tad jumpy as well. Kidnapping, Anna suspected, was hell on the nerves. Denise would have to be crazy not to be paranoid.

Since Anna had nothing to lose, she chose to feed it.

"I know she's your identical twin," Anna said, shooting for the tone of someone starting on a long list of sins. "I know the woman who delivered you as babies. I know the legacy that your biological mother wanted to share with you."

The water bottle flew from Denise's hand. Rolling, it left a dark wet trail across the rag rug where Anna sat. Denise hadn't thrown the water intentionally. Her hand had spasmed.

"Now look what you've done," Denise cried. Rising from the chair, she retrieved the bottle and set it on a small table beneath the pretend window. Hair whipping wildly, Denise looked around the room. "There's nothing to wipe it up with."

"It's only water. It will dry," Anna said calmly. "I know about your dropping things, too. You didn't used to be clumsy; now you drop things. Same with Paulette." Anna wasn't quite sure where she was going with this, just hoping that things would shake loose in a way that was more conducive to her surviving the night.

Denise growled, or grunted — a sound associated with animals, not humans. Reaching behind her back, she drew something from her waistband.

No surprise, a SIG Sauer 9 mm. Most likely the one Anna lost that night on Schoodic. The gun had never looked as big in Anna's hand as it did in Denise's. Viewed from the wrong end, the gun barrel seemed to take up half the room.

"Stop playing games with me," Denise said coldly. "If you know something, tell me. Otherwise, I'll blow your head off. I might do it anyway. You are supposed to be dead already, so what difference would it make?"

The thin yellow flame from the lantern reflected in Denise's eyes. There wasn't much else there that Anna could see. Not the panic at the spilled water, the confusion at not wanting to hold "her" child, the warmth when she spoke of her sister: Her face reminded Anna of a patient her sister, a psychiatrist, treated. Molly had taken Anna along on a visit to the mental health facility to see a woman who suffered from severe autism. A screaming fight between three other patients had overloaded the woman's senses and she'd shut down.

Denise had that same look, as if the soul had moved a very long way from the windows, so far it almost couldn't be seen. Denise didn't look insane. In fact, she looked saner than anyone Anna had ever seen, if sanity could be measured by control. She exuded the vibe of an individual totally detached and completely dedicated to the task at hand.

A few times in her life Anna had thought she might be going to die. She thought that now. No one knew anything about death. No one came back to report on how it went down, what followed. Dead people gave no interviews, wrote no books.

Perhaps that was the reason that, though afraid, Anna wasn't nearly as afraid as she would have been if she'd been asked to speak in front of a crowd, or crawl down a skinny cave passage. Those things were real and scary. Death wasn't real. It was the last page, the fade to black. It was hard to be truly terrified of an event that wasn't quantifiable, that wasn't quite real.

"No games," Anna said evenly. The baby quieted. Glancing down, she checked to see if it had expired. Olivia's eyelashes were unbelievably long. They quivered on her round cheeks as her eyes moved beneath the closed lids. Still alive.

"No games," Anna repeated. "A woman I know, Dr. Gwen Littleton, delivered twin girls forty-some years ago. The babies were given up for adoption. Gwen and the mother became friends. The mother's health was failing, and she decided to try and find her daughters."

"Makes sense," Denise said. "She's about to kick the bucket. Don't want to die with abandoning two little girls on your conscience. Might go to hell. Tidy up with a quick 'so sorry I fucked up your lives,' and off to heaven goes Mommy."

Denise's voice, hands, and trigger finger were rock steady. If she'd gone over the edge in the past few minutes, she hadn't landed on Anna's side. "Is there anything you want to get off your chest?" Denise asked in a flat voice. "I'm the closest thing you're going to get to final absolution."

"You'll lose your hostage," Anna said. She'd wanted to sound reasonable, but her voice cracked, and she had to swallow to clear her throat.

"We can work around it," Denise said, and her finger tightened on the trigger.

"If you shoot me, you could hit your baby daughter," Anna said.

"I'm a crack shot," Denise said.

"No. You used to be a crack shot. The legacy is you have Huntington's disease; you can't control your hands," Anna said. "You put three bullets in Kurt Duffy from no more than ten feet away and none of them were anywhere near fatal."

"Bullshit." Denise pressed the muzzle of the gun hard against Anna's forehead. "Now I can't miss."

"Wait," Anna begged desperately. "You pull the trigger, this close, and the report will deafen Olivia. Rupture her eardrums. She'll be deaf as a post her whole life, and it will be all your fault."

"Put your fingers in her ears," Denise snarled.

"I can't," Anna said.

Denise glared at her. Turning suddenly, she yanked open the door and stormed out of the room. Through the open doorway all was in darkness until, about forty yards away, the overhead light in the SUV came on. Denise dove into the vehicle, only her legs sticking out.

Anna took the time to look around the room. The place was childproofed. Nothing that could be used as a weapon, even if she had use of her arms and hands, came to her attention.

A squawk made Anna's heart lurch; then a voice called her number, then Artie's. An NPS radio lay on the low table under the fake windows.

The caller was the superintendent. They'd discovered Olivia was missing. Panic vibrated in his voice. Anna had to stop herself from shouting that Olivia was okay, that she had her. Not only would Peter not hear, but Denise would be interrupted in whatever she was doing in the Volvo and hurry back to the shed.

Without fingers or even toes, pushing the TALK button on the side of the radio to reply would be an interesting exercise in ingenuity. Since that was Anna's only option, she wriggled around until her back was to the radio and, shoving with her heels, began pushing herself along the rag rug an inch at a time toward the low table. "Sorry, Olivia," Anna said as she managed to lever herself to her knees by bracing one elbow on the tiny chair by the crib. If she'd already killed Peter's child, it wouldn't matter. If she hadn't, this wouldn't be the fatal move.

Anna nosed the unit over to the wall, then pressed her chin as hard as she could into the TALK button. Maybe she depressed it a hair, maybe not; still she said, "Anna Pigeon, maybe near the Duffy house. Help!"

Denise banged back into the shed, slamming the door behind her. "Stupid bitch," she hissed. In two strides she'd crossed the room. The radio was slapped onto the floor. "Sit." Denise shoved Anna until she fell back against the wall and her rump slid down to the floor.

A pair of Bose earphones was in Denise's free hand. She squatted beside Anna, then carefully settled the phones over the baby's ears.

"There!" she said, standing. Snatching the gun out of the waistband of her pants, she pressed the muzzle to Anna's temple. "This time, promise me you'll die."

Anna closed her eyes and wondered what a person was supposed to think at a time like this.

"Denise? Honey?" The door was pushed open. Paulette stood in the faint spill of lamplight, her pink scrubs as rumpled as pajamas in the morning. "My God!" She stepped in and closed the door behind her. "Denise, what are you doing? Put that gun down." Her eyes on the baby, she stepped onto the rug in front of Anna. Dropping to her knees, she wailed, "No! You promised you wouldn't take the baby." She reached out as if she'd scoop it out of Anna's tape-and-bone bassinet, then froze. "This isn't the Frazier baby. Denise! What have you done?"

"She's kidnapped Peter Barnes's daughter, Olivia," Anna said. "The baby is sick. It was in the hospital for observation."

"Shut up!" Denise snarled.

"You're dead!" Paulette exclaimed, noticing Anna for the first time.

"Yes I am," Anna replied, wondering if it was true. "I've come back to save this child. If we don't get her back to the hospital, she'll die."

"Olivia Barnes? The three-month-old admitted for a seizure? Denise, you said you were going to save a life!" She looked up at her twin accusingly.

"I did, Paulette," Denise said, the gun lowered to her side. "I did. It was the only way. Lily, her mom, has Munchausen-by-proxy syndrome. She poisoned Olivia with ergotamine so she could go to the hospital and be the big hero. If we don't get the baby away, eventually Lily will kill her."

Paulette rocked back on her heels. "How could any mother . . . Oh, Denise! This is so awful. What can we do?"

"We have to get the baby and ourselves away from here, leave no hint to where we've gone, or that it was us who saved the baby," Denise said.

Mood swings was an understatement; she sounded so rational, so believable, that for a second Anna wondered if it could be true. "Ergotamine," Anna said suddenly. "How do you know the baby was poisoned with ergotamine?"

Paulette looked from her sister to Anna, then back to her sister. "The doctors didn't know what made the baby sick," Paulette said. Tears flooded her eyes. "Oh, Denise! You did it! You poisoned one of my babies. You . . ."

"Help!" she screamed, scrambling to her feet. "Help! Somebody help me!" She reached the door and pulled it open.

The gun rose from Denise's side, leveled on Paulette's back.

"Gun!" Anna yelled because that's what she'd been trained to do.

A flash of muzzle fire and a blast, so loud in the small room that it numbed Anna's eardrums, shook the shed. Denise was turning, gun in hand. Before she could aim a second shot, Anna fell to her side, the baby affixed to her chest toppling with her, and whipped her legs out, knocking Denise's feet from under her. The gun hit the floor and skittered to the center of the round rug.

Cursing, Denise crawled for it. Whiplashing her feet, Anna managed to kick the SIG Sauer. The pistol slid over and stopped against Paulette's thigh. Paulette Duffy lay facedown, halfway in and halfway out of the nursery, a stain of blood blooming across the pink teddy bears on the back of her scrubs. There might have been life left in the woman, but Anna doubted it. The bullet had entered the left side of Paulette Duffy's back below the shoulder blade near the spine. The heart had probably been next on its trajectory.

Denise followed the gun. Trying to beat her to it, though the gun was out of her reach now and, she expected, forever, Anna flipped open and shut like a broken jackknife, getting nowhere. No crying from the baby. She hoped she hadn't smashed it.

Denise didn't grab up the SIG Sauer. Coming to her knees beside her sister's bleeding body, she covered her mouth with both hands. Moving in slow motion, she turned her head toward Anna. The hands floated down.

"What have I done?" she asked in a bewildered tone.

"You've killed your identical twin sister," Anna said. "Shot her in the back."

With a keening wail, Denise dragged Paulette up from the floor, cradling her in her lap. Denise's newly blond hair fell over Paulette's face, mingling with Paulette's bleached mess until no difference could be seen between them. Identical noses close, one face in repose, the other in a rictus of grief, Denise's tears dripped onto Paulette's cheeks.

From somewhere in the room the radio crackled. "Anna . . . Duffy house . . . Roadblocks . . ." Anna's message had gotten through.

Arms wrapped around her sister, Denise began to rock. As if an invisible hand arrested her movement, she stopped suddenly. Misery blinked out, cheeks still awash with tears, Denise looked almost happy. Anna watched as her hand dipped into the pocket of Paulette's smock. Pulling out an empty unused syringe, she held it up to the lantern light and smiled.

Using her teeth, Denise uncapped the needle. Thumb on the plunger, she jammed the needle into her carotid artery and ripped downward. Blood sprayed out in a crimson wave, then pulsed ever smaller fountains of red. The sisters' blood mixed until both were dyed red with it and Anna couldn't tell where Denise began and Paulette left off.

Sirens sounded in the distance. "Your daddy is coming," Anna whispered to Olivia.

Expelling a sigh, Anna looked away from the tragedy clogging the door, her eyes moving to the painted sunlight through the fake windows.

There had been an instant, a moment in time, when Anna might have been able to say or do something that would have stopped Denise, saved her life.

But it would not have been a kindness.

ABOUT THE AUTHOR

Nevada Barr is a novelist, actor, and artist best known for her *New York Times* bestselling, award-winning mystery series featuring Anna Pigeon. A former National Park Service Ranger, she currently lives with her husband in New Orleans, LA.